The Danger Within

E. L. Pini

Producer & International Distributor
eBookPro Publishing
www.ebook-pro.com

The Danger Within
E. L. Pini

Translation from the Hebrew by Tal Keren

Contact: pini@pini.co.il
ISBN 9798704137290

THE DANGER WITHIN

E. L. PINI

Time to go home & cook supper & listen to
the romantic war news on the radio

My Sad Self
by ALLEN GINSBERG

PROLOGUE

"Amsterdam! Brussels! Paris! Frankfurt!" Imad fired off the names of the cities with contagious enthusiasm. "And finally, Rome! You'll finish your journey in Rome, and go on vacation, back home, to... the kid's name is Mohsan, right?"

"Mohsan." The passenger nodded, and his face lit in a soft glow. The fact that Imad had bothered to remember the boy's name moved him, and he hurried to wipe a tear away from his eye. "Mohsan," he mumbled. "My Mohsan."

Imad smiled understandingly and handed over a colorful cardboard box with a photograph of a toy tank covered in colorful LEDs. "It drives around, flips over, fires just like the real thing. Solid engine, wireless remote... this is for him, and this is for you." He handed over a small, fancy wooden box. "Open it."

In the box lay a golden Rolex, set with small diamonds. Dumbfounded, the passenger opened his mouth, but Imad spoke over him: "This is the gift that God gives us. Time! And you, try to enjoy it." He squeezed the passenger's shoulder.

"Good luck! *Allah Ma'ak...*" God be with you.

Imad's driver helped the passenger climb into the Range Rover that drove off to Port Sudan, where he would embark on his perilous journey.

Imad watched, thoughtful, as the cloud of dust grew distant and eventually disappeared into the yellow desert of Hadhramaut.

"To see Rome and die." Imad smirked with some bitterness and returned to the operations board in his office, pushing the troublesome thoughts out of his mind.

BOOK 1

1.

The passenger held a Lebanese passport rife with stamps. He carried little cargo, no laptop and no cell phone. In his suitcase, the screening equipment in Schiphol Airport registered only neatly pressed clothes. Procedures demanded no additional checks for passengers without phones or laptops, even in the case of keffiyeh-wearing Arabs whose foreheads gleamed with sweat.

"*Allah hu akbar*; in him we shall trust and fulfill our destiny," the passenger muttered, attempting to raise his spirits. He tossed a glance at the wristwatch, which filled him with pride.

The diamond-studded Rolex drew the airport security guard's attention.

"Nice watch," he said, nodding appreciatively.

"Time. That is all God gives us, time. And I try to enjoy it," said the passenger, staring at his feet.

The screener saw nothing but a man of faith and sent him on his way.

The passenger raised his head, buckled his belt, and wiped the cold sweat from his forehead and the back of his neck before hurrying over to the gate. He then boarded the flight to Brussels.

The watcher, who'd been observing all this from the upper balcony, left his vantage point and rushed to the restrooms. He locked the door of the stall behind him and sent the video via Telegram. His hand shook as he struggled to break the SIM card, and eventually he had to crack it with his teeth before managing to tear it and flush it, along with the small burner phone, down the toilet.

The new Saudi passport hastily handed to him in the airport in Brussels, the red keffiyeh with the golden *agal* he wore—as Imad had ordered him to—all screamed for extra attention. Belgian airport security were exceedingly polite, but similarly inquisitive, asking him to pass again through the screening device. They'd taken no chances since the suicide bombings that had killed thirty-two Belgian citizens.

"Once you've passed one screening, you've passed them all," Imad had told him before the flight, and he clung to those words now like a lifeline.

Just three more flights, and he could go home, to his Mohsan.

"*Inshallah*," he muttered fervently. "*Inshallah!*"

The local watcher left his post and entered the restroom. Another broken SIM went down the drain, and another box was checked on the operations board in Shabwah, under similar ones denoting airports in Paris, Frankfurt and Amsterdam.

Passport control in Rome was the passenger's final stop before his flight back home. By this point, he was exhausted and impatient, and he was beginning to notice a wetness spreading around his lower abdomen. After passing the passport control booth, he hurried into the restroom, crouching and ashamed, and discovered the wetness had come from the recently sutured surgical incision, which had been weeping pus down his stomach and onto his clothes. He patted it down with paper towels and covered it as much as he could.

A driver wearing a baseball cap and holding a cardboard sign reading "Dr. Mahmoud Rantisi" picked him up from the airport. Only now, behind the dark-tinted windows of the taxi, did he allow himself to break into tears.

"You okay?" asked the driver, glancing at him in the rearview mirror.

The passenger wiped his nose and nodded. "Where are we headed now?"

"Restaurant, get something to eat," replied the driver, turning his gaze back to the road.

Only when the taxi arrived at Via Pietro Tacchini did the passenger finally manage to choke down his tears, even managing to laugh slightly in embarrassment. The driver pulled up in front of number 13, at Ambasciata d'Umbria. A long line had formed on the sidewalk, and some Hebrew could clearly be heard in the crowd. The Israelis, true to their reputation, had probably flocked there after hearing of the charcuterie platters provided on the house to make the wait more bearable.

"So, want to talk to your son?"

The passenger wiped his face and blew his nose, nodding excitedly.

The driver turned to him, and his eyes rested momentarily on the Rolex.

"Nice watch," said the driver. "Trade?"

The passenger stared at him, bewildered.

"I'm kidding. I just want to see how it looks on me," said the driver, holding out his hand.

"Could I have the phone now?" asked the passenger.

"Certainty."

Smiling shyly, the passenger removed the wristwatch from his wrist and gave it to the driver, who handed over the phone. "I'm going to take a piss," said the driver. "Give you some privacy."

As the driver climbed out of the taxi, the passenger dialed, hands shaking. He tried to guess which of his children would answer the phone. He loved them all, but his favorite had always been Mohsan, his eldest, despite—or perhaps because of—his mild mental disability.

"Babaaaaa!" Mohsan whispered. "Baba…!"

The driver, standing with his back to the car, clicked the remote. The locks on the doors clicked shut. The passenger gave a puzzled look but shrugged and went on talking to his son. His lips stretched in a wide smile, finally showing some relief from the tension of the past day.

The driver slipped into a nearby alley, pulled a cell phone out of his pocket, punched in some numbers and sprawled down on the black cobblestones for good measure.

A deafening explosion tore through the air.

Twenty-two people waiting in line outside the restaurant were killed instantly. Others had been wounded and were trampled by the panicked tide of patrons rushing outside. The taxi had been doused in highly flammable chemicals and soon burned to a crisp, leaving the security forces who arrived at the scene with no remains from the body, and no forensic evidence whatsoever.

2.

During those weeks, I hadn't managed to speak to Eran even once. I took a day off, planning a few errands and a lot of Eran. Before I went to bed, I planned tomorrow's agenda and laid out a schedule in my Google calendar.

06:00-07:00 Go for swim (look into new Ironman training plan).

07:15-08:00 Paleolithic breakfast.

08:30-09:30 Dr. Rafi Shahaf, get Garibaldi's teeth cleaned.

10:00-18:00 Eran. +weeding +pruning his grapevine.

From 18:00-12:00, I wrote, "only God knows." And I had planned on reading *The Dramatist* by Ken Bruen—an eternally drunk, mad and beloved Irishman—and maybe swim for another hour. On the days I can't find the time for a swim (namely, most days), the four slipped discs in my spine give me all kinds of hell.

As it turns out, I really shouldn't have left things up to God. I woke up around 7:30 and had to skip my swim. Realizing this would take its toll later that day, I started on breakfast. I warmed the espresso mug on the fumes rising from the machine, browned the bacon strips and laid them aside on a paper towel. In the remaining grease, I fried four eggs, brown-shelled and orange-yolked, from the copious chickens pecking around in Shuki's vineyard. They used to tell us to carbo-load before heading into action. Now they say we should load up on protein, plenty of vegetables and fatty meats.

Another espresso, and I surrendered myself for a moment to the gentle April breeze and the scent of citrus blossoms that it carried.

"Well, isn't your life just peaches," said Eran, and his tall form draped in a pressed dress uniform turned its back to me, walked to the grave and faded away. I wanted to tell him how wrong he was, but I knew I'd get the chance eventually.

I live in Agur, a settlement on the Judaean Mountains, located on the highest peak in the region. The massive kitchen carries into a west-facing grapevine pergola. Plot A, measuring a bit over an acre, ends in a fault that creates a small cliff. Underneath lie around six acres of vines, Petite Sirah and Cabernet Franc.

Looking west on a clear day, you can see Ashkelon's power plants to the south and the massive chimneys of Reading to the north, and even the deep blue of the sea. Shuki, who owns the neighboring vineyard, works and harvests our vineyard, and in return I get as many bottles as I like. This naïve arrangement suits us both.

On the edge of the cliff, facing the view, I raised Eran's headstone. It's where we sit together and talk, and occasionally share a bottle of Shuki's excellent wine.

I stood up. The next item on the agenda was considerably more difficult: to somehow transport Garibaldi—a magnificent Neapolitan mastiff weighing as much as I do, around two hundred and forty pounds—to Dr. Shahaf, our veterinarian, and get his teeth cleaned. Garibaldi, on his part, was perfectly aware that loading him onto the jeep has only one possible outcome and was determined to avoid said outcome. He rubbed his massive head against mine, and each time I reached for his collar, he turned to present me with his ass and wagging tail.

I decided to play this smart and took a strip of bacon out of the fridge, waving it in front of his face. As he sat there planning his next move, I spotted Adolf, Garibaldi's colleague—a large Malinois, previously from Oketz, the IDF's counterterrorist canine unit. He approached from my flank and nonchalantly snatched the bacon. I pulled a leash on him and tied him to the ancient fig tree. First object—neutralized. I opened the car door, clinched Garibaldi in a double nelson and pulled him back into the jeep along with me, walking backwards with my arms hooked under his front legs and my face smooshed against his.

The odors that surrounded me as he incessantly licked my face made it clear that I was taking him to the vet come hell or high water. I fell back on the car seat, pulling the great beast on top of me. The double nelson had been his downfall. Finally, he was inside. I scrambled out the other door and went around to the driver's seat, victorious and covered in drool.

And then the phone rang.

"Get down here ASAP. Froyke needs you."

"But I—"

"*Bubinke*," scolded Bella, principal staff officer for the DM—the director of the Mossad—"get down here now. You're flying today."

3.

"Six dead Israelis," said Froyke. "This is no coincidence, and even if it is, I don't give a rat's ass. Find them and destroy them. A personal favor, do this as a personal favor to me!" he concluded with his usual reiteration.

I was stunned. Froyke was difficult to provoke and had never been an advocate of retaliation and bloody vengeance. And what was I supposed to do about Shabwah? My missile convoy project. And what about Anna? She had volunteered back in January to run the Shabwah hospital, and only recently, her obsessive flings with Imad had developed into something resembling a steady relationship. It wasn't until earlier this spring that she'd even attempted her first transmissions.

It had taken three weeks of constant, gut-wrenching tension, ending only recently, until the people around her stopped paying attention to her daily running habit. Until her first transmissions were finally received, loud and clear. A customized Bluetooth transmitter was implanted into the state-of-the-art running computer on Anna's armband, programmed to relay her messages to the transmitters concealed in the photovoltaic cells of the solar farm. From there the transmissions were picked up by the assigned satellite and bounced straight into the facilities of military intelligence Unit 8200, in the no-man's-land between Ramat HaSharon's organic strawberry farms and Herzliya. If everything went off without a hitch, we should receive an early warning whenever Imad and his buddies planned to dispatch an Iranian missile convoy to south Lebanon or the Gaza Strip. That early warning would then enable the preparation required to terminally neutralize the convoy.

Due to the unfortunate absence of digital mind readers, this kind of warning can only be achieved through the human element. Like many handlers, I'd developed a sort of fatherly protectiveness toward my asset—and, in blatant disregard of protocol, much more than that. Anna was the most extraordinary woman I'd ever met. A sharp, bright intellect, a wild personality, and sex appeal to rival Marilyn Monroe's.

Froyke was saying: "The ones sending the missiles and the ones who sent the suicide bomber to Rome, they share a goal, and a background. Maybe even..."

He fell silent and placed a hand on my shoulder. "Don't worry. One single peep from Anna and you're back on your project. But in the meanwhile, I want you on this."

I held out a hand. Froyke ignored it and hugged me instead.

"You okay, Froyke?"

"Five-by-five," he replied.

"Five-by-five or five-by-ten?"

"Ehrlich... just get on the damn plane."

"You're supposed to say it's peaches, Froyke, everything's just peaches."

Froyke shrugged in response, and I could tell that no peaches would come of this. Something was troubling my old man.

4.

Bruno Garibaldi arranged for my swift VIP route through the airport and picked me up. Bruno is more or less my counterpart in the AISI, the Italian foreign intelligence service. My glorious mastiff, Garibaldi, is named after him—if I'm its father, Bruno is its grandfather.

We drove straight from the airport to see the Ambasciata d'Umbria. Roberto, the owner, was a close friend of Bruno's. He ran an excellent place, one in which we'd consumed a great quantity of wine and meaty protein over the years. Now it looked like post-Vesuvius Pompeii. This sort of soot-coated destruction made sense in the Dahieh suburb in Beirut, where it was a natural staple of the local lifestyle. But here, in the heart of colorful, lighthearted elegance, it became distressing, disturbing.

The Gendarmes securing the perimeter solemnly let us through. Large, dark bloodstains spotted the sidewalk. The Italians, unfortunately, have no ZAKA[1]. Roberto wandered the ruins, stunned, bruised and covered in black soot. Bruno ran toward him and they hugged. I hurried to reach out my hand before he got around to hugging me as well. I measured the distance from the remains of the entrance to the charred skeleton of the taxi with my steps. Twenty feet. The blast radius had left nothing to chance. I asked Roberto how many of the

---

1 Voluntary emergency response teams in Israel who aid in the identification of the victims of terrorism, road accidents and other disasters, and where necessary gather body parts and spilled blood for proper burial. -TK

customers preferred cash to credit. Roberto glanced at Bruno, who nodded. "Over ninety percent of the patrons pay with credit cards."

I snapped a picture of the restaurant's sign, which had oddly survived the blast and now appeared to float in midair. I sent the photo to Nora, with instructions: Digital Albert would get into the restaurant's accounts and pull out the percentage of Israeli credit cards.

The Israeli victims had been three couples, Cohen, Ziv and Perlman—the families of military industry workers, celebrating their retirement together. Tragic, really. *At least they didn't bring the grandkids*, I thought, feeling a sudden rage. Like Froyke, I was never an advocate of reprisals and blood vengeance. An organization like ours should operate according to established goals and strategies, not vendettas. It's the politicians, on both sides, who divert us into those esoteric, nonstrategic, excessively bloody news items. And still, I was infuriated by the six dismembered bodies of those pensioners, hardworking welders and smiths, workers for the military industry. I promised myself, and Froyke, that I wouldn't stray from my goals. But before all that, I intended to find the fucker responsible and beat him into a bloody pulp.

We left Roberto and drove to Harry's bar on Via Veneto, the location of Bruno's "private office"—a dimly lit booth, furnished in heavy wood and leather.

"Two Macallan, *piatto di salumi* and some peace and quiet," Bruno tossed at the waitress as we entered. Once she had delivered our provisions and left, he drew his head closer to mine, stared at me pointedly, and whispered, "You ever heard about something called pentaerythritol tetranitrate?" He raised his eyebrows, waiting.

"PETN," I replied with a calm that I knew he'd find maddening.

"CH2ONO2, detonation velocity eight thousand, four hundred meters per second. It hasn't been used since World War I due to oversensitivity to heat and friction."

"Why do you ask?"

"Please, make yourself comfortable. Take your shoes off," said Bruno, unable to mask his frustration. I shoved off my $890 Guccis, which were supposed to fit "like a glove" and instead fit like my ass. Bruno went on, "Only ashes left from the taxi and its passengers. We have nothing… the remains of one body and the doors locked. The driver probably locked it from the outside, put some distance between them and activated. The taxi's stolen, and no one saw the bastard's face. Your people probably think it was aimed at the Israelis. I don't. You guys always think everything is about you."

"Could it be business-related?"

"No," said Bruno. "I checked. Roberto pays very generous protection, directly to the local boss."

"If it isn't business, the only reasonable alternative is Islamic terrorism. And if so, why has no organization taken responsibility for this boast-worthy feat?"

"You're right," he said. "That is unusual."

Nora got back to me, informing me that the amount of Israeli credit cards didn't even reach 0.005 percent of the restaurant's annual revenue. I let Bruno know. He raised his eyebrow and swallowed the insult.

"Zero point zero zero five percent of revenue, and ninety percent of the trouble. Always the same with you guys. This is not an anti-Israeli attack, Mr. Ehrlich. These Islamists want to conquer us. Us!" He struck his chest with his palm. "Toss all of them back into the fucking desert."

We concluded the meeting with homework—Bruno would check his European colleagues for other uses of PETN as a primary explosive, and I'd try to track its supply routes. The driver and the bomber operated within Italian borders, so I was expected to leave their identification to the local authorities. We both knew this wouldn't happen, and neither of us brought it up.

Bruno dropped me off at the Hotel Excelsior and got out of the car to hug me. A motorcycle sped by us, nearly taking the door of Bruno's Maserati with it. I had to apply friendly force to stop him from running after it. Bruno settled for three full minutes of continuous swearing, never repeating the same word twice. It reminded me of another motorbike that had passed us by five years ago, when Bruno and I had met. It was our first collaboration. A jihad network was planning a series of bombings at the embassy, the Great Synagogue and the Jewish school in Rome. We eliminated them all, though there were a few we could have arrested. Bruno preferred to save the taxpayers some money and avoid blackmail kidnappings. The only one who managed to escape was the commander—an exceptionally bright young man by the name of Imad. The same Imad Akbariyeh now commands the Shabwah camp, the last real foothold of jihad in crumbling Yemen, from which he sends his convoys to both the Sunni Hamas in Gaza and The Shiite Hezbollah in Lebanon. This previously unheard-of combination between Sunni and Shiite terrorism was probably what had allowed the camp to survive the chaos.

This same Imad, of course, abuses Anna on a daily basis. I'm still convinced, to this day, that he was that biker who flew past Bruno and me five years ago. And for a brief moment, I wondered if he could be the one who'd passed us just now. Bruno had finally exhausted his arsenal of profanities and was asking when to pick me up tomorrow.

"Pick me up? Where are we going?" I asked.

"To the airport. Time to show you the door."

5.

East of Shabwah camp, on the hills looking over Hadhramaut, stand a dozen whitewashed prefab buildings. The UNICEF Child Hospital. The medical staff consists of seven volunteer doctors and one dental hygienist. The hospital is run by Dr. Anna von Stroop, who specializes in pediatrics and ultrasound. Her second-in-command is Dr. Patrice, a Jewish pediatrician from Paris. To the east of the hospital, behind a massive bulge in the earth—nearly a hill—lies the solar farm. Two and a half acres packed with hundreds of photovoltaic cells, converters and generators. The farm—capable of producing up to 1,650,000 kilowatts—was planned and installed by an Italian company, Green Systems Energy (GES). The company won the bid by the World Bank after it offered three years of quarterly service and maintenance, free of charge.

Dr. von Stroop sat in her office, downed the remaining cognac in her glass, grew angry at herself, and immediately brushed her teeth. Her classic beauty was accompanied by a veneer of hard resilience, further emphasized by the short, boyish cut of her full blond hair.

She breathed on her palm to check that the smell of the toothpaste overcame the cognac, hung the stethoscope on her neck, and left, heading toward the patients' rooms. The white prefabs shone like suns, forcing her to shade her eyes. If it weren't for the solar farm reinforcing the meager trickle of electricity provided by the Yemenites, this place would be uninhabitable, she thought.

She began her rounds with the children. The lines of her face, usually angular and symmetrical enough to have been drawn by a computer, softened instantly when she approached the beds. The children trusted her completely, surrendering to her compassionate hands. For tough, hardened desert children, this is no small matter. Hamid, the "nurse" appointed by the fighters, lumbered behind her, his green scrubs occasionally flashing a glimpse of his camouflage combat uniform. Hamid was posted by Imad "to help translate," and mostly to guarantee that the medical staff, and the equipment, was devoted to his fighters. Hamid maintained a reasonable distance from her, paying close attention to the doctor's pear-shaped ass and perky breasts. Anna arrived at Abdu's bed—a sweet Sudanese child with jet-black skin, whose leg had been amputated. She stroked his hair.

"Hey, *Schatzi*, remember what we learned yesterday?" Abdu and Anna bumped fists.

"Yeah," said Abdu, "but I don't know how to say it..."

Anna smiled. "*Messer, Gabel, Schere, Licht, sind für kleine Kinder nicht.* Knife, fork, scissors, flames, have no place in children's games."

An electronic whine suddenly erupted from Hamid's walkie-talkie, followed by a stream of instruction in Arabic. "The commander requests you come to his office, immediately!" he relayed to Anna.

"Whose commander?" challenged Anna, her eyes never leaving Abdu's medical chart.

When she was finished, she met Hamid's discomfited gaze. "I'm busy right now. Tell him to call me when my shift's over."

She kissed Abdu on the forehead and left to wash her hands with disinfectant in the small restroom near the staff room. She took off her scrubs and pulled a striped Valentino blouse over her head, draping it over the tailored jeans. She closed her eyes and smoothed her hands over the fabric. She liked this shirt. She then took off her black horn-rimmed glasses and examined the minuscule beginnings of a line near her eye. A flash of concern momentarily clouded her bright features. The pressure was still there, whenever Imad summoned her.

Three months ago, when she'd met Avner at a hotel in Rome and tried on the hand-sewn Valentino blouse, she'd realized that when the fear would appear—along with the weakness that followed—she would wear this, and overcome them. It was clear, when she looked into Avner's loving eyes, that he would always be there for her when she needed him. When she asked him whether a white-and-blue striped blouse wasn't a bit on the nose, he smiled and pulled out another wrapped box. Inside was Steven Harper's *Dreamer*, and he opened and flipped through it to point to the sentence, "The best spy hides in open day, where everyone can see."

Occasionally, in moments of weakness and regret, Anna returned to that book, that sentence. She derived a great deal of satisfaction from the ability to be someone else. To be on the outside, looking in on that new someone, being able to decide how she behaved, how she interacted with the people around her. With courage? Indifference? Contempt? Compassion? Would she choose an immediate, or delayed response? Her control of the character was perfect. Unlike her control of herself.

At times, when the weakness appeared, she felt as if she were dreaming; the ground dropped away from under her, plunging her into a deep, black void. Without end, without gravity. The dive was curious and not necessarily unpleasant, languid somersaults and delicate, gentle drifts, like a space capsule ballet. No end existed to this void, nor, apparently, a way out. Terminally adrift, Anna thought, and wished for a final, powerful blow to end it all. It was truly addictive.

She shivered at the sound of the metal hinges. Imad walked in, wearing his camouflage uniform, hugged her from behind and kissed her neck. Anna tried to turn around, but he held her there.

"Look into the mirror," he said, pressing his forehead to the back of her head. She fiddled with the sophisticated armband computer in her hands and looked into his burning black eyes, framed in long, thick eyelashes.

"What do you see?"

"A horny, exotic Arabian prince that I'd very much like to fuck."

She reached behind her to hug his neck before glancing at the armband. "Later, though. I have to go on my run. Join me this time?"

"Running! In this heat?"

"I have surgery today. If I don't go now, I won't go at all." Inwardly she added that forgoing the run would mean failing to report to Avner, and she attempted unsuccessfully to calm the slight twitch in her eyelids.

Imad was about to reply but stopped short when his walkie-talkie sounded an irritating buzz.

He awarded it a glance and his face grew solemn. "I have to go now. You are absolutely insane. Take a water bottle with you. And when you get back, I'll show you who gets to fuck whom." He kissed her neck and left.

Anna smoothed her fingers over the striped shirt one last time before changing to her running clothes and beginning a slow jog toward the solar farm. The sun beat down on her, and the heat of the golden desert sand penetrated the rubber soles of her running shoes and burned her feet. Annoyed, she wondered why the hell Avner had positioned the farm so far from the hospital, though she quickly realized that the distance and the small hill were reason enough.

She fondly recalled Avner, wearing the green technician coveralls, accompanied by Albert the tech genius, Luigi and several other Italian technicians—innocent and perpetually cheerful—as they'd installed these panels while playing Puccini arias on the mobile karaoke machine.

Anna stretched her neck, using the stretch as an excuse to raise her eyes and scan the sky. She activated the satellite location app on her running computer to find that her satellite was, indeed, approaching—she imagined that she could almost see it, a dim, sort of pale star, progressing with infuriating slowness. It would take forever for the satellite to reach its optimal reception point.

As the satellite approached, she aimed her armband at the nearest row of solar panels and pushed the "reset" button twice, just like Albert had shown her. She counted three seconds and typed in distance and heart rate data that granted her a "Boston Qualified" status for the Boston marathon. If the computer says you can run the Boston marathon, you're in good shape.

When Avner received the BQ result, he'd realize that a substantial missile convoy was preparing in Shabwah. The number of the first decimal place in the heart rate denoted the number of days remaining until the convoy headed out. If the date of departure was unknown but could be estimated, the heart rate would exceed ninety, so the number of days would be counted without the zeroes and divided by two—meaning a pulse between ninety and one hundred read as four to five days until the convoy's departure. An unusual pulse of over one twenty denoted a late warning, under three hours until the departure of a previously unknown convoy. If everything went smoothly, the transmission would be received in the encrypted transmitter in one of the solar panels, and from these it would be continuously transmitted to the satellite, over and over again for five minutes. When the five minutes had elapsed, any record of the transmission would be purged from the solar panel transmitter. Another push of the "reset" button would erase any evidence from the running computer.

At times, Anna wondered why Avner had enabled such limited communication: the dates of the convoys, a call for extraction, and that was it. Anything more complex, she had no way of reporting—but he always told her, "KISS," and kissed her before adding, "Keep it simple, stupid. The convoys are what matters. The rest isn't worth risking you."

Anna punched in the appropriate code—a missile convoy would leave Shabwah in four to five days—and began jogging back to her room. On the way she passed Hamid and flashed him a smile. He didn't return it, only stared at her. A small shiver went down her spine as she ran past him to her room to shower before her surgery.

6.

Anna's transmission called for an immediate assembly of all members of the "Forum," or as Froyke referred to it, "the national steering committee for Yemenite affairs." The usual members of this committee, apart from Froyke and yours truly, were Ami Kahanov from the Service[2], and Tamir, a young major from the operating division of the intelligence corps, a good kid whose tall figure and confident posture reminded me of Eran. Representatives of the relevant intelligence-gathering units as well as representatives from the operational end units, the air force operational division, the Matkal special reconnaissance unit and marine commando Flotilla 13. Apart from the usual forum, representatives from Unit 8200, from the satellite division of Visual Intelligence Unit 9900, and of course G, the new commander of air force operations.

"Froyke won't make it," Bella informed me and suggested that I take Nora with me to avoid "embarrassing the organization."

Nora, my intelligence officer, laid out the decrypted data that signal intelligence had gotten off the satellite, as well as an up-to-date review of the Iranian missile arsenal, and our preventive action aimed at "Quds Force," which had forced them to seek out new smuggling routes.

She added that according to our most recent intel, the missile con-

---

2 The Shabak or Shin Bet (usually referred to by the rest of the intelligence community as "The Service") is Israel's internal security service. -TK

voy could leave Shabwah on its way to the Gaza Hamas at any point over the next twenty-four hours. As for the exact contents of said convoy, she assured us that "you'll know as soon as we do," adding that "an update could arrive at any time." I gave her a surreptitious thumbs-up—she had done an excellent job—and she replied with an undecipherable look that could've meant anything from false modesty to *who did you think you were dealing with here?*

Colonel G, who'd been one of the air force's finest combat pilots, was only recently promoted to command the air force operational division. This was his baptism by fire. Perhaps for this reason, he left his dark Ray-Bans on throughout the entire meeting. After taking his seat at the head of the table, he signaled with his laser pointer to one of the technicians. A large plasma screen rose up from the conference table.

Colonel G drew a red laser circle around the Shabwah camp.

"We're prohibited from operating within Yemen. Too much politics," he said and shifted the laser toward the Sinai desert. "We can't operate in Egypt for similar reasons. This is what's left." He lasered a small circle around Port Sudan, near the Sinai border.

"This is our hunting ground," he concluded, suppressing a slight smile. "Unfortunately, not far enough from here to get the Iranians jumping to conclusions."

A loud beep nipped G's rookie philosophical bullshit in the bud. It was Ami's pager. He apologized and got up to make the call, only to speak a single "okay" into the phone on his way out of the room before spinning around to face the rest of us like a magician waiting for applause.

"If you ask me"—he pulled out the rabbit— "we have confirmation that our Gaza Hamas buddies are waiting on an SA300 missile battery."

G whistled, a low, appreciative sound. "The SA300 is classified as a tie-breaker. It's the most effective operative antiaircraft system the Russians have. We should attack immediately, before it's operational."

He presented a mobile missile system on the screen and added,

"You're already familiar with our OB[3]. Four F-16Is to bomb the convoy, four more for cover, one with electronic countermeasures—and just in case, there'll be two fuel tankers and two 669[4] rescue choppers in the vicinity." He glanced at his wristwatch. "If there are no questions, I really need to fly. Thank you."

"Good luck, if we don't see you before then," I added, attempting to fill the void of Froyke's absence. G smiled, gave me a two-finger salute, and left.

I really would've liked to know how Ami, that sly fox, had managed to confirm the Gaza shipment at precisely the right moment. I caught his attention and signaled him to meet me outside so we could talk, but then I got bogged down by the group of joking young intelligence and air force officers, and Tamir, whose every glance made me think of Eran. I remembered how pleased I had been when he was summoned to interview for Unit 8200 before he was drafted, and how he'd instead forced Ya'ara and me to sign the form permitting him to join a combat unit despite being an only child. Ya'ara wouldn't hear of it, at first—eventually, she'd conceded. "He's a big boy," I'd told her. "Practically a man. He knows what he wants." *Today he's a big dead boy.* My thoughts spun to Anna. *Another big girl, who is still alive. What'll happen to her after the convoy is destroyed and they get around to damage control? I have to extract her, as soon as possible.* This despite the fact that my paranoia had no actual, concrete justification. No problems had arisen thus far. On the contrary—her relationship with Imad seemed to grow closer by the day. Anna, sexy and uninhibited, with the beauty of a Greek goddess, mostly preferred women, but left a sliver of hope for the occasional male. Her innate madness only made me want her

---

3 Order of Battle. The hierarchical organization, command structure, strength, disposition of personnel, and equipment of units and formations of an armed force. -TK

4 The heliborne Combat Search & rescue extraction Unit of the IDF Air Force. -TK

more. On top of all that, she came from the perfect family. Her grandfather was the SS Colonel von Stroop. Her aunt, "Tante Hannah," had been known to crush the occasional head of a Jewish baby against the wall. Her father was a multimillionaire who mostly funded anarchist organizations. Her mother was killed in a Baader-Meinhof street fight, after firing at two policemen while attempting to escape a robbery of a Deutsche Bank in a town near Bremen.

Anna, who wanted more than anything to atone for her insane legacy, had volunteered with Doctors Without Borders and, out of all of the possible godforsaken shitholes, landed in the Balata refugee camp near Nablus. The same refugee camp where her mother and her buddies from the Baader-Meinhof Group had gone to study the art of intelligence gathering, urban warfare and sabotage. Her presence in Balata was the only reason we'd met, and I sometimes wondered how coincidental that encounter had actually been.

"The usual?" Ami asked with a sort of fatherly patience, pulling me out of the fog of self-doubt and into an equally cloudy reality.

"Affirmative," I replied. "But to sum up, Froyke is convinced that the Rome bombing was aimed at us."

Ami started the jeep. "What about you?"

"Nope. Seemed more like a pilot to me. It started in Rome, but it won't end there."

"He usually listens to you."

I nodded, adding, "He said it doesn't matter, they killed three good Jewish families and that pisses him off."

"Understandable," said Ami. "Where was he today? Leg thing again?"

"Tests. He's at Hadassah Hospital. Bella says it doesn't look good. And it ain't just his leg."

"Kishon cancer[5]?"

---

5 The Kishon is a highly polluted river which the IDF used extensively for diving and swimming training. Many ex-Flotilla 13 (Navy special forces) soldiers later blamed this training for their being diagnosed with cancer.

"I really hope not," I said, thinking someone should really some up with a combat doctrine for the war on cancer.

Eran, Ya'ara, and now Froyke? Am I on some heavenly shit list?

7.

Babai greeted us with a flurry of *ahlan*s and pats on the back. I secretly hoped that this genial Palestinian had no idea what Ami and I did for a living. Ami assured me that we were good.

We were seated at our usual table, a fair distance from the rest, with a full view to the tall, noisily crashing waves of the Mediterranean. I've always loved the smell of the sea, and I closed my eyes, indulging in it. I felt it widening my nostrils, letting more oxygen into my system.

A young waiter, just barely a teenager, set the table with thirteen small appetizer plates, a bottle of El Namroud arak, two glasses and ice. We both ordered deep-fried red mullets. I squeezed half a lemon over the fish and sprinkled the chopped parsley, and then Ami switched our plates.

"Freeloader," I grumbled at him and squeezed the second half of the lemon.

"Really squeezing that lemon for all it's got," he answered with a mouthful of fish. "A lot of that going around."

We clinked our first glasses of arak.

"Now talk," I said.

Ami glanced around and pulled his chair closer to the table.

"My guy from Gaza, the one who confirmed the intel on the SA300s? He has a cousin, abu Seif, lives up in Ghajar. Works for me too. He sells drugs to a Hezbollah gang. I turn a blind eye, which really pisses the blues off—not that there's much they can do about it—and get pretty decent coverage, sometimes more than decent. What you might actually give a shit about, if you ask me, is the word I just got from two different sources, the Gaza guy and his cousin up north. According to them, this old fuck called Qawasameh, a clan elder who lives in Balata, recently received a grant of… wait for it… thirty thousand dollars from the Iranians."

Ami refilled our glasses and downed his immediately, apparently waiting for my applause. But I was battling an internal nightmare scenario, one in which Ami's snitch reports back to the bad guys that the Israelis had intel on a convoy about to leave Shabwah, and their source… was Anna.

I refused to imagine the rest. The arak bottle had been completely neutralized by this point. Ami flipped it over and tapped the bottom. No arak came, but the boy came running with a new bottle and a plate of fish, which he placed at the center of the table.

"Sargo, red mullet, White Steenbras, baby mackerel. On the house. *T'fadalu*, enjoy."

"*Shukran*, thank you."

"*Afwan*."

The arak draped over my senses like a soft blanket. Thirty thousand dollars from the Iranians could mean only one thing. The recipient had a son who had become a shahid—a martyr. The Iranians nurture the shahids, compensate them for the property destroyed by the IDF, and pay around twenty grand to the family of any shahid who accomplishes a quality bombing. Thirty grand, that's about the highest they'll go—reserved only for the truly spectacular.

"Have you seen any serious shahid action lately?" I inquired.

Ami shook his head. "Nope. Which is why I'm telling you."

We each retreated into ourselves. This was how our meetings usually ended. Both Ami and I carried our fair share of baggage.

"Uncle Ami" was a substitute father to Eran whenever I was away on some bullshit mission that took longer than expected. And I'd played guardian angel to Tikva, Ami's old lady, making sure that she had a steady supply of her fabled Keytruda—impossible to get in Israel—until it was no longer needed. The Big C had defeated her eventually, and in many ways him as well.

"And if you ask me," he said, "this Qawasameh might be linked to your thing. But I'm just guessing here. Anyway, I'll look into the Iranian grant, and if it's what I think it is, we'll have to look into accounts in Italy, Saudi Arabia, France… fuck me, everywhere."

We kept drinking, and afterwards Ami offered in utter seriousness to drop me off at Agur, but, due to the arak and the time, he was forced to leave me at the government central facility in Tel Aviv, where I'd left the jeep earlier.

"Sure you're okay to drive?"

"If you are, so am I," I replied, but I didn't feel as confident as I knew I sounded. Still, I climbed into the jeep and headed home.

8.

The second bottle of arak was precisely one bottle too many. I reluctantly abstained from the enjoyable twists and calm agricultural landscape of Route 383, instead choosing the dull efficiency of Highway 1. I was blinded by the headlights of approaching vehicles, forced to shield my eyes and thus block a significant portion of the road. I'm not entirely certain, but I believe my eyes closed at least once, and by the time I'd opened them, I had to break left in a panic to return to the road.

I got home just in time for the final newscast of the day, which mostly involved the Rome bombing and interviews with the victims' families, neighbors and colleagues. The three pensioners worked eight-hour shifts, sometimes nights, crouching over their lathes and drills and white-hot welding machines, and when they'd finally taken the single holiday they could afford, some fuck-hole went and murdered them. It's different when the victims have names and faces, children and grandchildren. I promised them, and myself, and mostly Froyke, that I would find said fuck-hole and personally destroy him. Hebrew labor, locally sourced.

I turned the TV off and tried to focus. *The convoy*, I thought, *when does the convoy leave?* According to Anna's latest estimate, the threatening procession of "tie-breaker" antiair missiles that G had been so worried about left in twenty-four hours. The photos from the NSA satellite also pointed to unusual activity in the camp. Our satellite was apparently in the satellite garage for some periodic maintenance.

How would I extract Anna without raising Imad's suspicions, and without exposing her to our American comrades? And what about Froyke, who was still in the hospital? "It ain't just his leg this time," Bella had said. Then what the hell was it? And how would I locate and capture the Rome bombers, who hadn't bothered to leave as much as a crumb of forensic evidence?

It was as though an electron gun was implanted in my brain, accelerating thought particles to bounce around and crash into my skull. I got up from the couch, placed my head under the faucet in the shower, let the water run over my face and neck. When I took my head out of the water, I realized I had forgotten to bring a towel, and instead shook my head to spray off the droplets like a dog drying off from sea. Garibaldi stared at me curiously, and I thought I noticed a forgiving smile on his large face. Adolf was his usual apathetic self.

Nir, who used to serve under me back in The Unit before becoming chief dog handler in the Oketz canine unit, had given me Adolf after his handler had been killed at the Nablus Kasbah. Adolf had refused any attempt to assign him a new handler and had eventually ended up with me.

"He can be catatonic, sometimes. A perfect match," said Nir.

"Why Adolf?" I inquired. "After the late Mister H?"

Nir softly patted the dog's head, but Adolf froze in response, standing at stiff attention.

"There you have it. He's exceptionally obedient, but extremely ruthless when attacking. So, yeah, we named him after Herr H."

Suddenly I remembered that I hadn't weeded around Eran's grave yet. My flight was scheduled to leave tomorrow afternoon, and it wasn't like I was getting any sleep tonight anyway—I'd sleep on the flight. In that case, I had time. Just needed to clear my head a bit. I arranged my tasks in my Google calendar, in order of urgency:

1. Weed and clean around the tombstone.

2. Check on Froyke.

3. Talk to Nora and Albert. I need them to plot the course of the suicide bomber, and that of the explosives. Who is the supplier?

4. Plan Anna's extraction. This would require the director's approval. This could probably wait because it wasn't that urgent—unless… I tried to put the thought away, but it bounced back with a vengeance. What if it became necessary to extract her immediately? Froyke… Froyke had to get better.

5. Be patient. At least until Ami found out why the old man from Balata had gotten his Iranian grant. Like Ami, I also had the vague feeling that this was somehow related to the Rome bombing.

I went to the shed and took out a large green garbage can, gardening tools and powerful quartz lighting. I pulled out the nut grass that had taken root around the grave—you have to take out the tuber, or it grows back. I pruned Eran's grapevine and drastically reduced the number of grape clusters, to deepen the flavor. That was how Eran and I liked our wine. I washed the grave and the black basalt headstone, which Froyke and Ami had transported from Ramat Hagolan in The Unit's REO truck. I embraced the cold stone.

Time doesn't heal. It's really quite the opposite. The pain of the grief, of missing him, grew sharper and cut deeper with every passing day. I hugged the rock as hard as I could, but the pain wouldn't stop. Eran's face was lost in a haze, like the pixelated blurs that hide the faces of anonymous sources on TV, and I couldn't reach him—sometimes it felt like the pain just grew sharper with time while the image of Eran faded.

I'd recently read, in Haruki Murakami's *Norwegian Wood*, the following sentence: "Death in that place was not a decisive element that brought life to an end… but one of many elements comprising life." To me, it seemed to be the other way around—Eran's life had been a brief segment, lost and forgotten within a long death. I loved him so much. My baby… those chubby legs and the sweet, soft baby smell that I'd inhaled obsessively, that intoxicating scent that clung to him, or to me at least, until he'd left me. These days, I can no longer recall the smell. Garibaldi, who'd sat in silent observation up until this point, got up and licked my face, attempting to comfort me.

"Come," I said, and the two beasts escorted me to the bedroom. I collapsed on the bed and fell asleep fully clothed.

9.

At 6 a.m., I dove into the pool and swam two miles in sixty minutes, as per the Ironman training regimen recommended by the Mossad trainer.

After that I drove to Hadassah Hospital. I blatantly ignored the protesting security guard at the entrance to the oncology department and entered the room. The sharp smell of acetone hung in the air, one I'd recognized by this point as the stench of chemo, mixing with the smell of piss and sweat and whatever they put in the air to mask the disinfectants and the other medicinal smells. They combined to create a silent, powerful despair. The smell of surrender.

I noticed Froyke's prosthesis tossed on the floor by the bed when I entered the room. I picked it up and leaned it against the wall. As slowly as humanly possible, I raised my eyes and looked at him. Froyke was hooked up to a terrifying assortment of equipment, tubes and electrodes, which gave him a vaguely Transformer-like quality. I wasn't sure if he was breathing on his own spontaneously or on a respirator, if his condition was stable or steady or whatever goddamn expression they use, which all mean the same thing—my friend is fucked. Another one bites the dust.

My father was killed in '73, the Yom Kippur War, at the battle of the Chinese Farm. I was born after he died, knowing him only as a gravestone. Mom would visit him every Friday and return crying and muttering, introducing me for the first time to that odd phrase—"what I feared has come upon me." Job had managed to fuck with my head twice already with this bleak decree and seemed to be building toward a third.

I leaned down, bringing my head near Froyke's nose. He was breathing. When I placed a hand on his damp forehead, a pleasant voice from somewhere behind me exclaimed, "Excuse me!"

I turned to face a smiling, visibly amiable young woman, quite pretty, in a white lab coat. As I attempted to guess if she was a student or a girl scout volunteer, she held out her hand. "Verbin."

"And how is this information relevant to me?" I replied, fully intending to get out of there as soon as possible. But something about her kept me there.

"Are you his son?" she asked, with a glint of hope.

"Negative," I said. "A friend. I'll be on my way. Good morning, Miss..." I read the name tag on her chest. "Doctor Verbin? Really? A doctor already?"

"Negative." She smiled. "Spare costume left over from Purim[6]."

She radiated warmth like sunlight on a cold day. I was fascinated.

"Ehrlich!" A hoarse whisper rose from Froyke's bed. His lids rose heavily, and he nodded me over, a slight, nearly imperceptible motion. I poured water into a cup, but he shook his head. I lowered my ear to his lips.

"You catch those schmucks yet?"

I stroked his forehead and politely signaled for the pretty doctor to piss off. She whispered something in the security guard's ear and they both left the room. I have those rude moments sometimes.

"Not yet," I whispered. I found a handkerchief and gently wiped the sweat from his brow. I told him about the imminent departure of the convoy and my fears regarding Anna. He waved them away and sank back into his pillow. I realized it was time for me to go. I considered finding the pretty doctor and apologizing—she didn't deserve my attitude.

I went out into the hall. She was nowhere to be seen. I sent myself a reminder—"Verbin. Froyke's doctor"—and lumbered away from there.

---

6 Purim is the Jewish holiday on which costumes are customarily worn.—T.K.

I hate hospitals, and I especially loathe the idea of a cancerized Froyke, plugged into tubes and respirators and smelling of acetone and despair. Eran, Ya'ara and Froyke were the people I'd loved most in this world. After Eran was killed, Ya'ara had disappeared, evaporated into thin air. I'd tried to hold on to her as best I could, tried to convince her to make a brother for Eran. She'd just smiled her sad smile, and after that it was only a hologram of her floating around the house, tall and barefooted as I loved her most, in a thin floral Bavarian summer dress, a thick blond braid and a rectangular men's watch on her thin, sculpted wrist. Until the day I brought Eran back, with his slab of black basalt. Bella had told me then that Ya'ara stayed only to look after me until Eran got there, and only then allowed herself to return to the Bavarian skies. I wondered if the Bavarian angels called her Ya'ara or Forest[7].

I sat in the jeep and lit a cigar. The smoke swirled up into my nasal cavity, around my brain. I needed some shielding before coming back down to earth. I wrote myself another reminder, the second one in an hour, to contact this Doctor Verbin once the project was over. I tried to understand what had compelled me to be so unpleasant toward the attractive, mesmerizing physician, with her striking smile and impressive self-confidence. Interpersonal communication had never been my specialty, and interacting with someone unfamiliar always seemed exhausting, and rarely worthwhile. I hadn't been in a serious relationship since Ya'ara—apart from a brief, surprisingly cheerful fling with Nora, my intelligence officer, which we'd mutually agreed to end so it wouldn't get in the way of work. And of course, the forbidden—yet entirely unavoidable—affair with Anna.

The cigar went out. Time to go. The GPS app informed me that Highway 1 was clogged—an excellent reason to take the picturesque Route 383 to the facility. I shoved in the USB drive, and it was Otis Redding, of all people, crooning through "Sittin' on the Dock of the Bay." It wasn't Pavarotti, but it somehow perfectly matched the landscape.

---

7 *Ya'ara* is the feminine form of *Ya'ar* (Hebrew: forest).—T.K

10.

Nora, Albert and I were cramped into the small alcove in Digital Albert's "office." Albert, so named after Albert Einstein, was in fact Guy, a Unit 8200 alum—a short, bespectacled geek, who had accrued an impressive number of location successes over the years. Prominent among these was the location of General Muhammad Suleiman, special presidential adviser to Bashar Al-Assad, at Tartus near Lattakia. There we'd introduced him to his maker, with the assistance of three Flotilla 13 snipers who had risen from the sea to place three bullets into his skull. One for each sniper.

Albert and Nora tore like barracudas through the croissants I'd bought and started on the coffee I'd made them.

"No idea," said Nora, sounding as desperate as every intelligence officer sounds at the beginning of a project. She made a point of clarifying that we had, in fact, no legs to stand on. Even our primary assumption—that this attack had been initiated by a jihadist organization—was based on nothing more substantial than a hunch.

I tried to construct some kind of organized work plan. In cases like these, the first goal is always to define the "target bank"—the other potential targets—and defend it. If we'd known who had carried out the initial attack, we could at least guess, with a reasonable degree of confidence, the contents of this target bank. If we'd known where the explosives had been made, or bought, we could eliminate that channel, delay the next attacks, and get some breathing room for intelligence gathering. Most Western intelligence organizations were currently tied up with this thing, and right now, they were all in the dark.

"What about you? Found anything?"

"Affirmative," replied Albert, adding, "The coffee is very bitter. Very, very bitter." He made a face and went back to typing with finger-numbing speed, never glancing at the keyboard. He looked like Arthur Rubinstein, playing Chopin on some Friday afternoon at a kosher Catskills hotel, surrounded by purple-haired Polish ladies.

"Bingo," Albert suddenly piped up, looking up from his screen, which currently exhibited the security camera system in the airport in Rome.

Nora informed me that she thought my coffee was excellent, apart from the lack of milk and sugar and the possibly irreparable damage to her taste buds. She added that as far as she knew, when they were going over the videos in search of suspects, "they'd only focused on men..."

Albert cut her off with some sexist nonsense, but I wasn't paying attention—something had suddenly fallen into place.

"PETN is extremely dangerous, first and foremost to the person building the bomb. Extremely sensitive to heat and friction. Today it's only used in tiny quantities in compounds like Semtex. If a professional—which is definitely what we're dealing with here—chooses to build a bomb entirely out of PETN, it might mean that it served another function, apart from the actual explosion," I said, sloshing around the remains of the coffee in my cup.

They didn't seem to follow.

"Nora, if you wanted to initiate a series of bombings in Italy, Germany, anywhere else in Europe—which central property would you look for in your explosive of choice?"

Instead of replying, Nora collected the coffee cups and went into the kitchenette. She made some milky coffee-like concoction for Albert and herself and handed me an espresso.

"Drink your gross poison," she said. "And I'd like my explosives to be undetectable, either by security scanners or personnel."

"Amazingly, you're right. Don't let this become a habit," I said. "At least, that's the same conclusion I came to. And I'm guessing that if that's the case, the first shahid wouldn't have tried to hide the fact that he was an Arab from airport security. Maybe just the opposite… and maybe, just maybe, it turns out that his name is Qawasameh…"

Nora raised her head and widened her doe eyes at me. I shoved the lascivious thoughts aside and added, "But this is just a shot in the dark at this point. No actual evidence. Ami's working on it… meanwhile, proceed as usual. And stay in touch with Ami."

Nora nodded and sipped her coffee-flavored milk.

Two seconds later, an urgent notice came down from operations—a new transmission from Anna. The convoy was leaving early, which means D-Day got pushed up. The convoy was expected to reach the hunting ground at 0300.

"I gotta go." I got up and headed for the office. Nora came after me, stopped me, and handed me a large yellow envelope.

"Your tickets and documents." I was momentarily stunned. Bella never let anyone else handle my flight arrangements. "The evil hag—I'm sorry, I mean your BFF," Nora corrected, "is on a flight to New York. Her daughter's having a baby."

"Look, my flight to Vienna was postponed. I need to get to Cyprus, to Larnaca. Let's get to operations. You're coming with me."

"What, you mean just the two of us? But—"

"Don't worry, we'll leave now, fly back tonight. We have until three a.m."

Nora flashed me a skeptical glace.

"Nora, I need you there."

She kissed me on the cheek, appeased. "Now you're talkin'."

11.

The upside-down pyramid that housed the Royal Ministry of the Interior in Riyadh, Saudi Arabia, exuded the same condescending foreignness that characterized most public buildings in this part of town. The hundreds of local palm trees, which seemed to bow down to the glass-and-steel monstrosities, emphasized its foreignness even more.

The passenger, about seventeen or eighteen years old, ordered the limo driver to pull up by the sidewalk and aimed the telescopic lens toward the ministry's entrance hall. The entrance area and screening equipment were manned by bored-looking security personnel.

"Let's go around again," he ordered the driver, who dutifully drove back down King Fahad Road all the way to Airport Road and back up again. A thin trickle of ministry workers was beginning to spill from the large elevators into the entrance hall, and the security personnel had taken their posts in preparation for the first end-of-the-workday wave. Due to some odd planning mistake, the growing torrent of people leaving the building made it nearly impossible for the guards to properly screen everyone coming inside—thankfully, at the end of the workday, there weren't many arrivals.

The passenger reminded the driver that he was to remain there and ostensibly talk on his cell phone, which would in fact be used to document and record the incident. The videos would be sent to Imad, as well as to one of the activist groups in Riyadh, and from there sent in real time to news agencies everywhere.

When the young man walked down the palm tree boulevard leading to the main gate, he couldn't help but wish it were possible to simply blow up the needle-thin base of the upside-down pyramid, watch it topple over like the World Trade Center.

The passenger reached the main gate, where he was ushered by a security guard toward the screening machine. He placed his wristwatch and his keys in the small tray but kept the constantly recording phone up in his hand, raising his hand. Another wave of impatient ministry workers pushed him back, and he waved questioningly at the security guard. The guard signaled him to just go around the security screening.

The entrance hall wasn't full yet. The passenger signaled back that he would wait patiently until the passageway cleared. The guard, apparently approving of this attitude, smiled back. The passenger stroked his large belly, remembering how astounded Dr. Taissiri had been when, before the surgery, he'd asked him to put as much of the stuff inside of his stomach as possible. A huge flood of workers spilled out of the elevators, filling the hall on its way to the exit. The passenger hurried toward the screening machines, grinning at the security guard, who returned a somewhat forced smile.

"Smile!" he ordered the security guard.

"I'm sorry, sir?"

"Smile, please. For the camera." The passenger pointed at his cell phone.

The guard smiled at the camera, and the passenger activated the charge.

Jay Heller, a political and military correspondent for BBC News, was visiting Riyadh as a guest of the crown prince. In an interview for local news, he noted that, while the deadly attacks in the European capitals and here in Riyadh had most likely been carried out by the same group—the Al-Qaeda branch in Yemen—the goals of this latest attack appeared to be different. The strikes to the heart of Europe had been a demonstration, meant to show the Western world that 9/11 had been just the beginning, that the bin Laden assassination had done nothing to stop the Islamic revolution. The bombing at the core of the world's most powerful Sunni nation, however, delivered a different message—the prince's liberalization and Westernization efforts were unwelcome, unwanted, and doomed to failure. This was an assault on the very heart of Saudi national security, which utilized the ultimate weapon of global jihad: humiliation. The crown prince, Prince bin Nayef, and the entire Saudi kingdom had been deeply, inconsolably humiliated.

12.

"If anyone can lead us to the explosives supplier, it's Abrasha," I was telling Nora, who paled at every hint of turbulence. Abrasha, who ran his weapons and security business from his office in Larnaca, was not just a major general (res.), but a major player. This was, granted, back in the days before every toilet stall featured the sexual harassment bulletin. I warned Nora, but she just laughed me off. She was captivating when she laughed. A long and slender body, topped by large, round breasts, like I'd once assumed only Hollywood could provide. Her mouth featured a slight overbite of white, dangerous teeth. More than once, I'd imagined her picture inside the frame of a "Wanted" poster, the kind you see in westerns, covered with a black stamp reading: "PUBLIC MENACE: SEEKING HUSBAND."

"If I managed with you," she replied, "I can handle any asshole."

Weizmann, who'd been Abrasha's driver since he was a paratrooper battalion CO, picked us up at the airport in a gleaming black Range Rover that made me wonder if perhaps, in my old age, it might be wise to find a more comfortable job.

Larnaca looked like a blend of 1950s Tel Aviv, Jaffa and Gaza. We felt right at home. Abrasha was waiting for us in a private room at the back of "the best Turkish restaurant on the island." Apart from a small gut and grayer hair, he looked exactly the same as he had in the Service. After he and I hugged and kissed at great length, he stared deeply into Nora's eyes, kissed her hand like a Polish nobleman, and broke into praise of the restaurant and the local sheep. We mixed the ice in our glasses of Turkish rakı, while Nora mixed sweet orgeat in hers.

"Do you know," Abrasha asked Nora, "what gave birth to the Rebetiko?" He didn't wait for a reply. "It is, in fact, a protest song, over the fact that from the same exact products used by the Turks to create one of the best cuisines in the world, the Greeks can't seem to cook a single proper meal."

Nora smiled, and I asked him if he could get me some PETN.

Abrasha understood why I was asking and grew serious. "They make the stuff in small quantities in any large explosive factory," he said. "But these factories mostly sell to armies. Hard to believe that's where your explosives came from."

He then told us about a Soviet explosives factory near Chernobyl that was currently controlled by a local oligarch who'd bought it for practically nothing. This guy was apparently the main provider for private parties. The product was distributed by three sellers, all of them former KGB and Spetsnaz.

The sound of a siren suddenly wailed from the nearby room. Abrasha turned up the volume on the ancient TV set in the corner of the room. An Al Jazeera broadcast, live from Riyadh, routed through CNN. A Red Crescent ambulance, covered in Arabic, entered the frame. The camera panned to a reporter describing a mass-casualty bombing in Riyadh. Cut to the studio, where some political analyst was saying that "at this point, no Saudi official is able to explain how an explosive was carried into their Ministry of the Interior, the entrance to which is as heavily monitored and screened as any airport." This was accompanied by old stock footage of the entrance gate, the screening equipment and its small conveyor belt. The analyst went on to say that, unlike at airports, all visitors to the ministry were subject to frisking. This bombing defied explanation, he concluded—barring some sort of ministry collaborator—and so far, no terrorist organization had claimed responsibility, just like in Rome.

"Shit," Abrasha said, still chewing, and hurried to knock back the remainder of his rakı.

"Rome two days ago, and now Riyadh… it's like a serial killer," he said, thoughtful. "No way of knowing when and where he'll strike next."

"A serial killer murders one victim each time," Nora blurted out. "This one doesn't settle for less than twenty."

At least this time, I thought, trying to find some small comfort, there were probably no Israelis around.

"The Saudis are pissed as hell right now. If they could, they'd crush Al-Qaeda like flies," said Abrasha, adding, "Let's see what the darknet has to offer. Lay some bait around, see if anyone come nibbling."

He shot me a glance to make sure I knew what he was talking about—darknet, the internet's underworld—then slipped into a Tor browser and surfed to a network named Unfriendly Solutions.

"Saudis are pissed as hell," he muttered again. This could have potential, I mused. Serious potential. A common enemy can easily mark the beginning of a beautiful friendship.

Abrasha pulled out a ridiculously thin Sony tablet, and his sausage fingers began moving with surprising speed. "I tossed out there that I'm looking for a large quantity of that stuff of yours, from a Syrian IP."

"Why Syria?" Nora inquired. I wanted to reply, but instead let the old geezer do the honors—if only because of his typing prowess on the small, smooth touchscreen, which I found quite impressive. He had just opened his mouth when Nora clarified, "Obviously, you wouldn't use your own IP—but why Syria?"

After several seconds, she figured it out; Syria was swarming with arms and ammunition dealers at the moment. Exact identification would be impossible in this climate.

We quickly downed our little coffee cups. Abrasha once again kissed the back of Nora's hand. "I need a moment alone with the kid."

Nora shot a glance at me. I nodded, and she left the room along with Weizmann.

Abrasha, to my absolute lack of surprise, asked what was in it for him if he embarked on this momentous endeavor with us. I asked what he wanted, and he requested my help to win some Ministry of Defense auction. I promised I'd get Froyke to try, and that was good enough for him.

"So, you fucking that beautiful creature?" he asked, nodding toward Nora's presumed location outside the room.

"Are you insane?!"

"Mind if I give it a shot, then?"

"Sure," I said, "if you've got a spare set of balls. Listen, Abrasha, I need a chopper for an extraction in Hadhramaut. You got anything?"

"Hadhramaut? One of our guys?" he asked, genuine worry coloring his voice.

"One of our girls," I replied. "And a bombshell at that."

Abrasha rubbed his chin. "Look, your CIA buddies have a secret base in Djibouti, right on the Yemenite border. No one knows it's there."

"Yeah," I replied, "no one apart from the Senate committee of inquiry and the reporters covering it. The Predator compound."

Abrasha nodded. "The compound and its logistics are run and maintained by a private company, which happens to be a large client of mine." He shot me a look, and I responded with the appropriate respect.

"The company's air fleet is led by a close friend, Crazy Jule. He ran extractions back in 'Naaam." Abrasha attempted a Southern drawl. "The best chopper pilot in the Night Stalkers. Ten in advance, another ten when the job's done, cash—don't expect a receipt, either—and he'll get anyone out of anywhere. If I tell him there's gonna be action, he'll fly it himself—and that's the best you could possibly want. Who's running the mission? A team of yours?"

"Negative. Just me and a friend."

Abrasha raked his hand through his thick salt-and-pepper mane. "How about I join you?" He sucked in his gut, looking about as comfortable as a stuffed turkey. "Free of charge," he added hurriedly.

"Next time," I said. "When we organize a pensioner tour."

"Still the same little prick, I see."

When we entered Abrasha's wood-paneled office, we found that Nora had made herself at home and taken over the computer, hooked up to a large monitor on the wall. "We've already received two responses to Abrasha's request. One of them goes by Schwadron, the other's named Tupolev."

"Interesting," said Abrasha. "The market must be on fire. Those are actually two of the three distributors—I'd expected replies from a bunch of small fry, to be honest."

"We'll look into them," I said, "but my guess is that we want the third guy—that one who didn't reply, and probably won't anytime soon."

Abrasha nodded appreciatively. "Your friend here," he told Nora, "is too smart to be an Arab hunter, certainly for the ridiculous salary he makes."

"Get to it," I snapped, rejecting the momentary impulse to feel sorry for myself.

"Distributor number three, since you asked nicely, is a monumental asshole by the name of Victor Zhdaniev. An ex-major in the GRU, ex-Spetsnaz, responsible for a small genocide in Grozny. They call him 'the Chechen.' He works with a bunch of old Spetsnaz buddies, his personal-security-slash-operations team."

"Huh," I said, interested.

"If you decide to make contact, tread with caution. Build a rapport. Buy some conventional weapons first—pay in full. Buy more. As for your stuff—approach the topic carefully. Look out for his buddies. They're not a bunch of children, or, like Raful would say, 'drugged bugs in a bottle'[8]..."

At 23:00 we landed on a small runway in Herzliya. I somehow managed

---

8 Rafael "Raful" Eitan was an extremely quotable (among other things) Israeli general and former Chief of Staff in the 70s and 80s, known for his anti-Arab views. He famously referred to Arabs as "crazed (lit. "drugged") bugs in a bottle."—T.K

to retrieve Dr. Verbin's number from my brain, but as I was dialing, I realized this thing was doomed from the get-go, and I should really just forget about her. She was charming, true—captivating, even—but I was fairly certain she wasn't looking for something casual, and I wasn't looking for commitment. Besides, if she were interested, she would've called.

I hung up before she could answer. I had about two and a half hours before the meeting in the Pit. I hoped to sleep for at least two.

13.

Air force operations at the Pit, thirty minutes to H. The technical team was going over the lists of contacts and passwords one last time before H-Hour. Froyke made it, but he looked like death. I hugged him gently and updated him on the meeting at Larnaca, including Abrasha's bid at the upcoming MOD auction. "He deserves it this time."

Froyke promised to speak to the DM later that day and handle the auction thing as well as my new "Pissed-Off Saudis" project. G walked over and patted me on the shoulder. I wished him luck. The commander of the air force walked in with his staff officer. Someone passed a piece of paper along, divided in four columns: Black coffee. Instant. Black with milk. Tea.

02:45—The satellite images lit up the plasma screen. G ran radio checks with the airborne pilots. Everyone was ready. The squadron commander led the formation.

02:55—Another radio check.

02:58—"Auntie has entered the party zone," informed the squad ron leader.

03:00—The satellite was tracking the convoy, fifteen trucks—fifteen missile batteries.

"Closer," requested the commander of the air force. The camera zoomed and focused on the covered trucks. It was impossible to make out the missiles.

"SA300, silhouette's a perfect match," the air force intelligence officer asserted, and a satisfied smile pulled at the air force commander's lips.

03:05—G flashed a nervous glance at the commander, who approvingly nodded his head.

03:06—"Engage!" G croaked. Craft one and two fired on the first truck, while three and four fired on the last one—four trucks exploded and burned, blocking the escape route for the others. Two trucks desperately broke off, driving off the road and into the desert. They didn't get far. The rest of the trucks were abandoned by tiny, frantic figures, like so many field mice.

Must be nice, I thought, considering the pilots. Sterile, bloodless war, no mud, no sand in your eyes, never seeing blood or hearing screams. Like a game.

"Engage! Engage!" G rushed them unnecessarily, and the air force commander glanced at him, seeming amused.

03:07—The airplane quartet stabilized, formed into a new attack formation, destroyed the remaining trucks. It looked like a movie scene, like slow motion. Each plane took a truck. Another pass, four more trucks went down. Hellfire and secondary explosions on the ground. The squadron leader and his lieutenant helped themselves to the final two.

03:09—"Executed!" the squadron leader informed us, adding, "Executed successfully. Roger, out."

The younger members of the staff broke into a round of applause, which slowly died when they realized none of the veterans had joined in. My eyes searched the room for Tamir, the young major from the operating division who reminded me so much of Eran. But he was no longer there.

"Good work," said the air force commander. He waved his hand and left the room. G approached me, looking like he might attempt a hug. I hurried to shake his hand before he got around to it. The technicians drifted around, patiently waiting for us to leave so they could start prepping the Pit for the next shift. Froyke seemed ashen and exhausted. I extended my arm, but he insisted on standing up on his own. We left for the parking lot. His limp seemed worse, much worse.

"You must know, they'll grow up," Froyke said, apparently feeling my apprehension at the young officers' applause. "They'll grow up."

I couldn't wrap my head around it. Could it simply be the difference in age and experience that created such different responses to this professional, successful attack? I felt no joy of victory at the sight of those dozens of burning, fleeing grasshoppers, running from their trucks to be shot down from above. If anything, a degree of empathy for the grasshoppers. And mostly, there was a sort of emptiness.

"Let's discuss your Pissed-Off Saudis," he said.

"Sausage."

"What?"

"There's a Russian at the old central bus station, mostly serves breakfast to construction workers. Herring, dried *vobla*, soft-boiled eggs with sausage and bacon, teacup full of vodka. Good for the thinking process."

"Not a bad idea."

"Vodka and sausage?"

"That, too," said Froyke. "But I'm talking about your Pissed-Off Saudis." He added air quotes. He paused for a moment, thinking, and eventually said, "If any of this leaks, we're eating crow."

We got in the car and headed to the old central station, and I asked Froyke what was with all the smiling. He explained he was thinking of his father. "They had a kind of ritual, every morning for thirty, maybe forty years. Dad would eat the herring with the buttered rye and then drink his vodka teacup—more of a mug than a cup, really. When he'd finish the cup, he'd reach for the bottle, as if to fill it again. Mom would yell and scold, and he would tell her, 'Yudit, after I drink a cup of vodka, I am a new man. And this new man—does he not deserve a cup of vodka?'"

14.

The rising dawn swallowed up the lights that illuminated the office of Imad Akbariyeh. Imad's adversary was on his last legs—another joyless victory in Mortal Kombat X. Time moved slowly, annoyingly so. Outside the door stood Husam, Imad's driver and bodyguard, trying to find the words to relay the dire news. Najib, their man in Sudan, had reported that the convoy was completely destroyed, most fighters dead. The body of Nasser, Imad's younger brother who had driven the first truck, has been positively identified.

"Perfect kill," Imad listlessly declared his victory, just as Husam entered. One look at him was all it took. "Talk!" Imad ordered, slamming down his laptop screen.

"Four F-16s. They took down the first and last trucks, then went after the rest, one by one."

"Nasser?" he asked, already knowing.

"At the head of the convoy. First to go. I'm sorry, boss. Nasser was a man of—"

"Yeah," said Imad, deep in thought. "My brother was a man. And now he's a dead shahid."

He suddenly burst out laughing, wildly, stopping only when he was forced to suck air into his lungs. "He recently asked me, my little brother, if each shahid gets his own seventy-two virgins, or if they're supposed to share." His face grew solemn and he mumbled, "Baba. Baba's gonna kill me."

"What's that, boss?"

Imad didn't reply. He stood by the table with his back to Husam, taking deep, heavy breaths.

"I think," he said eventually, "that some fucker around here lets them know whenever we send a convoy."

"It's their satellites, and the American satellites. They see everything," said Husam. Imad ripped the cables out of their sockets and smashed the laptop on the floor. It shattered loudly. "I don't think it's just the satellites. There had to be another source that alerts them before the satellites can pick up the convoy."

Imad leaned against the edge of his desk, looking at the broken black line that Nasser drew, marking the convoy's route. *This is all that's left of the boy*, he thought; *a broken black line*. And then Baba's face appeared before him, his eyes red and accusing. From now on he would dedicate his life to avenging Nasser and Baba, and to banishing the Jews from Palestine. Cure this guilt.

He stormed out of his office, passing the hospital's small, flag-ornamented plaza, eventually stopping in front of Dr. Patrice's office. The pediatrician, the Jewish volunteer, Anna's second-in-command. Husam came running. "*El-dam ma bisir maye*," he muttered, cocking his pistol. *Blood is thicker than water*. He reached for the door handle… and stopped. No. A Jewish doctor from Paris? Too predictable. The Jews were bastards, but they weren't idiots. If they even had anything to do with his position here, they'd pulled those strings without his knowledge, just to create bait obvious enough to remove suspicion from the actual mole.

He passed the door and walked to the next. The office of Dr. Anna von Stroop. He waved Husam away and delivered an accurate kick, smashing the lock but leaving the door intact.

15.

"You only had to knock," said Anna, downing the remaining cognac in her glass.

"You haven't been sleeping properly," he said.

Cold sweat beaded on Anna's back. She poured herself another drink.

"Bad dreams. It happens some nights… and you? What are you doing breaking doors at four in the morning?" She smiled at him, picking up the Valentino blouse from where it was draped on the chair and slipping it on.

"Nasser was killed."

"Your brother Nasser? Oh, I'm sorry. I'm so sorry."

She held him softly, bringing the glass to his lips and tilting it into his mouth, as if she were giving medicine to a petulant toddler. She pressed her lips to his forehead and cheeks and eyes, covering his face with a flurry of kisses. Her tears flowed down his cheeks. She moved to kiss his ear, which she knew to be one of his erogenous zones. She wanted him inside her now, more than anything.

The tension he had brought into the room began to dissolve. Imad pressed against her body as if trying to disappear within. She herded him toward the bed, looking deep into his dark eyes, trying to work out what he knew.

"Too many cameras in the sky. American satellites. Israeli satellites. They know exactly when a convoy leaves. They crush it and murder everyone inside."

"I… I prefer not to know about these things."

His hand rose to her throat suddenly, closing firmly around it. "Are you sure you don't want to know?" he roared, squeezing.

The cold sweat on her back and the twitch in her right eyelid were symptoms she knew all too well. Unless she pulled herself together and showed some resistance—right now—she would crack. Imad squeezed tighter, and she began to wheeze. He loosened his grip a bit and stared into her eyes, into a cool blue that revealed not a drop of weakness.

Anna wouldn't betray him, he thought, releasing her neck. He stroked her hair, saying, "Someone in this camp is giving them information about the convoys. The satellites are just a last-minute warning."

Anna wet her lips, her nostrils flaring slightly. A terrified doe, staring into the shotgun's barrel. Imad felt his anger dissolve at the sight. This was a crucial phase of the game—now the frightened animal must resist the hunter. A final struggle, to assuage any suspicion. She slipped her hand between his legs, cupped his testicles and squeezed—apparently tighter than she should have, because Imad leapt to his feet in alarm and slapped her, hard.

"Bring the cuffs." His voice was stiff.

Anna cradled her burning cheek. "I… you like it when I grab you there."

"Only when I tell you to! You see that?" He pointed at the ornamented copper handcuffs that hung at the side of her desk.

"I thought we were over this game."

Imad wiped the sweat from his brow. "It isn't a game. And nothing is over."

He grabbed her by the neck and forced her flat against the table. Time to surrender. Anna parted her lips slightly and licked them. Imad pressed his lips to hers and they kissed, passionately, until both were out of breath.

"I don't think you have a choice," he said once his breath had steadied. "You have to know what's going on here. You picked a side, and I need you here with me. Until the end… Husam is collecting the staff's computers and phones. He'll take yours, too… he has to," he said, nearly apologetic. "One of your people is telling them everything."

Anna caressed his cheek, kissed his ear, and when she felt his swelling erection, slipped her hands into the copper handcuffs. Imad fastened the rings around her wrists and stroked her ass, the pace of the strokes quickening in tandem with his breath.

You picked a side, and I need you here with me, until the end. His words echoed in her mind when he ripped off her panties and smacked her ass with an open palm.

"Stop that, Imad, there's no intimacy in it."

"Intimacy my ass. Your ass, really. I'm going to tear it apart," he muttered, accentuating the words with another hard smack to her ass, which was already beginning to bruise.

"Come to me," she said. "Hard!"

Imad tried to squeeze himself inside of her. "I'll rip that white German ass to shreds, Doctor von Stroop."

Knowing that a complete lack of resistance would make him suspicious, Anna clenched her muscles, refusing him entry. Imad wiped the sweat from his face, pressed and pushed against her. When she remained closed, he began punching her. Stomach, kidneys, until the air was knocked out of her, and she groaned, surrendering. He brutally penetrated her.

"It's good, my Nazi whore." He grabbed her head between his hands, pulling himself ever deeper. "It's good, your white… flesh…" He kept thrusting until he came, with a loud cry, shuddering.

He slipped out of her, breathing heavily, and covered her back with gentle, conciliatory kisses.

"I love you." His voice was raw. "Was it good for you, too?"

"What the hell was that Nazi crap?"

"You've passed your test already." He kissed her neck and laughed. "Bunch of idiots, those Nazis. Try to build an Aryan empire, and instead create the Jewish fucking state. On our lands!"

He opened and removed the handcuffs.

"I need my passport back," she said, buttoning her shirt.

"Are you leaving me?" He pouted in feigned worry.

Anna smoothed her fingers over her face. "This desert of yours is bad for my skin. A hundred degrees in the shade… what shade?" She chuckled. "But really, I'll also need a hundred and fifty thousand dollars for a new ultrasound machine."

"You just bought one." He looked up at her, puzzled.

She stroked his head. "An X-ray, not an ultrasound. Also, that asshole Greek supplier of yours sent us an X-ray that was obsolete twenty years ago. Probably got it at Turkish bazaar."

"I'll handle him."

"I'm… booking a ticket for next week." She reached for her phone. "You can come, if you want. Please get the money and my passport ready. And another thing. Tell your idiot fighters that you're their commander, not mine."

Imad walked over to the espresso machine he got her for her birthday, made a cup and offered it to her before lighting a Gauloises cigarette.

"Your cigarette," he said, placing it between her lips and kissing her forehead. She hugged him. He collected her laptop from the desk, stroked her head and kissed it again.

"Husam will give you back your computer and your passport. Go next week, find a proper ultrasound machine and we'll get it for you. Get back soon. You have a hospital to run."

Imad slammed the door behind him and Anna crumpled into a fetal position on the floor. A tear escaped, then another, and then she was weeping bitterly, mumbling in German, a high-pitched, childish voice—"*Anna ist eine Putana, Anna ist eine Putana…*"

Anna is a whore. For a moment, she was fifteen again, a boyish, chubby, clumsy adolescent, with thick glasses and long blond hair. In the storeroom of the school in Charlottenburg, she was holding Francesca, the Jewish-Italian girl who was clutching her torn clothes, wiping her tears. Francesca acceded; she was kissing Anna's lips, leaned into her. They were locked in a tight embrace, kissing passionately.

Anna unraveled the remnants of Francesca's sky-blue shirt and kissed her small breasts. Francesca responded in kind...

A firecracker exploded near Anna's feet. Both girls backed away in alarm. Wild laughter erupted around them.

"Let's tie the whores up!" Five boys and a girl rushed them. Anna stepped in front of Francesca and grabbed the boy closest to her. Her hands were on his throat; she was squeezing as hard as she could—he grew pale, gurgling. The other boys pounced on her and slammed her to the ground. Francesca took advantage of the distraction and fled. One of the boys yelled—"Run, Jewish *Putana*, run—you're next." Four boys struggled to hold Anna down, one for each limb.

"Open your legs!" ordered their leader, Günter.

Anna spat, but it landed on her face and they all howled in laughter.

Charlotta towered above her. "Do that again, whore."

Anna didn't respond, and Charlotta kicked her in the stomach. "I told you to spit again... never mind. I'll get you wet myself." She lifted her skirt and urinated on Anna.

"Bravo!" cried the boys.

"Flip her over!" commanded Günter.

The boys released her momentarily to turn her on her stomach. The fat one covered her mouth with his hand, and Anna realized that now was the time to bite down as hard as she could. She placed her teeth around his hand but couldn't provide them with any strength. Her muscles no longer obeyed her. The fat boy knocked her away easily. Anna stared at the floor, astonished, trying to understand what was cutting into her flesh, as if the floor was covered in a million glass shards. White-hot pain sliced into her, and she didn't respond. Later, when her Auntie Hannah wiped her face and took off her shirt, she cried, "What happened, my Annuchka? Who did this to you?"

But Anna could not answer.

16.

The boiling water cleansed every inch of her. Anna used a hard brush, scrubbing red tracks into the white skin. She rinsed, then scrubbed herself raw again, soap, boiling water, rinse. She threw back her cognac and re-brushed her teeth. *It's better than I thought*, she convinced herself. *Husam will give me back my passport and laptop, and I'll be on my merry way, no drama. Avner's told me more than once that he'll get me out of here the second I get uncomfortable. Once I buy that ultrasound, I'll talk UNICEF into relocating me. This desert is giving me wrinkles. They have plenty of helpless refugee children in Germany.*

I won't exactly miss it when I'm gone, she thought and realized that she would in fact miss Abdu. And she would miss Imad, her cruel and exotic prince. *He should come in a compact version*, she giggled inwardly, *so I could fold him up in a suitcase and only take him out when I feel like it.*

She looked at her watch. Staff meeting in fifteen minutes. The desert sun was already harsh and cruel, and the blinding glow reflecting from the white dunes made it clear—there would be no refuge here, no mercy, for anyone.

She approached Imad's office, suddenly noticing a low mechanical hum, and low grunts, gasps of pain. It was getting louder. She thought she recognized the voice, and when she stood at the door, she was certain it was indeed Dr. Patrice grunting behind it.

There was no hesitation. She opened the door. Patrice was tied to a chair, covered in blood, groaning. Husam was holding an electric drill.

Much of Patrice's blood covered him as well.

"What are you doing here? Fuck off!"

A thin mist clouded her vision. Flashes of light whirled around her, dizzying. Husam twisted into a huge, cyclopean beast, bending over Patrice, sneering, about to sink its claws into him. More flashes, and Francesca's image rose from Patrice's body, crying, her clothes torn.

Anna didn't reply. She took a step toward Husam, hoping he attacked first. She had always been better with a defensive stance than with an all-out attack. Husam reached out with his right arm to block her. He failed to predict how quickly she would react. She batted his arm away and aimed a brutal kick at his testicles. Husam dropped the drill, recoiling in pain. Anna crouched down and snapped back up like a spring, the palm of her hand slamming against his chin, along with every bit of her upward inertia. Husam doubled over, breathing heavily. Anna knew that he would tell no one—especially Imad—how he was defeated by a woman.

She released Patrice from his ties and draped one of his arms over her shoulder, supporting him.

"Where are my laptop and passport?" she asked Husam gently, as if she were speaking to one of her patients.

Wordlessly, he indicated Imad's desk. Anna collected her things and shuffled outside, the injured Patrice leaning on her, toward the treatment rooms.

When she finished cleaning and dressing his wounds, she dialed Francesca. Her fingers shook.

"I need a vacation. White snow, a Mahler concert."

It was Code B. A request for extraction.

17.

Froyke struggled to stand as I walked into his sparsely furnished office. I hurried over and hugged him. He was so pale, it made no sense—that the healthy tan gained by decades of kibbutz and Flotilla 13 sun would be so easily wiped away by the pallor of this fucking disease. I knew that both Bella and the DM had tried to get him to take some time off, and that he'd refused.

"Of all people," he said with a weary smile, "it was my little doctor who convinced me to get back to my normal routine as soon as possible."

He went on to tell me that he received the director's approval for my "Pissed-Off Saudis" proposal and even handled Abrasha's auction bid with the MOD. So far, so good.

"Talk!" he said, leaning back in his chair. Few people can listen like Froyke. His eyes were shut, and you could almost think he was sleeping—that is, until he opened them and read you like an open book. He realized that my main concern was Anna's use of Code B—specifically B, which signified nothing urgent, nothing serious—just a request to get ready. It was possible that she used it, and not Code C, just to stop us from engaging in an urgent extraction that could blow our cover and harm our info on future convoys.

I told him everything I knew about Anna and Imad, focusing on my concerns that after the next convoy was neutralized, heads in Shabwah would roll. And it was easier when the head belonged to a foreigner. I recalled the profiler who'd worked Anna's case. She'd characterized two primary aspects of Anna's personality: a deep and uncontrollable urge to stand beside whomever it was she saw as an underdog, and a strong desire to bring satisfaction to those she loved, and who loved her. I wondered how this would affect things. Froyke took a deep breath and trained his gaze on me.

"The director refused to approve the operation. And before you say anything—he's right. Consider the cost-effectiveness... he's right, Ehrlich. This asset has already been milked for all it's worth, and this extraction you're planning... I can't tell if it's more expensive or more dangerous."

I got up.

"Ehrlich, sit," he ordered, his hand making a "down, boy" gesture. "Sit. Down. I know what you're planning. Go up to the office, grab that little bureaucrat by the balls and wring his neck like a chicken."

"That sounds more or less accurate."

"Be quiet. I'm approving a B-level extraction for you."

"Boss, there's no need for you to get involved—"

"I assume you got Abrasha to see to the rescue chopper," he added.

"What...? How—?"

A tired grin stretched his lips. "I've told you before, kiddo, any jackass can put two and two together. You've already decided you're going to get her, no matter what I said. You're not running this extraction on a camel, or a damn jeep. You didn't request a helicopter to Yemen, but you did ask me to arrange that auction for Abrasha. Fair enough, I know Jule. Hell of a pilot. Best there is."

18.

Over the past couple of days, Luigi had settled into the offices of the Rome-based power company, from where he began a series of random power outages in the solar farm array in Shabwah—outages that lasted as long as Luigi wanted them to. The idea had been conceived and implemented by Digital Albert. The Shabwah hospital spiraled into chaos. A constant stream of angry calls from both the UNICEF logistics chief and the hospital director, Dr. Anna von Stroop.

Luigi guaranteed that a team of engineers would be arriving in two weeks, but he would try to push it up, and asked if they could land the helicopter at the hospital. Anna received Imad's approval for the helicopter. Husam would assist her in marking the landing pad. A reserve team led by Ran would arrive at Djibouti in separate flights and hang back near the passage to Hadhramaut unless they were needed. All that was left was flight plans for Luigi and me.

One of the unbreakable rules I insisted on including in our combat doctrine involved approach through hostile territory. An Israeli agent is less likely to arrive from an Arab country on an Arab plane. Therefore, in order to arrive at Rome as the CEO of the Italian Green Energy Systems, I first flew from Tel Aviv to Vienna. This flight went smoothly—I winked at the bald, earring-adorned guy who checked my boarding pass, and slipped into an available seat in business class. In Vienna, in a facility run by the local Mossad branch, I switched identities. My new documents identified me as Dr. King Schultz, like the German bounty hunter from Tarantino's *Django Unchained*. I assumed Nora was responsible.

Dr. Schulz boarded Libyan Airlines flight 545 from Vienna to Tripoli, in a gray suit, a sky-blue shirt, and a red tie.

"As for the shoes—you should probably try them on and buy them yourself," said Johnny, the logistics guy from the Vienna branch. "I recommend Guccis. Soft like a glove. You won't feel them, even in… coach," he added, avoiding my gaze.

The one hundred and eighty seats crammed into the old Russian Tupolev airliner were spectacularly small, as if designed for the bony asses of Libyan punks and skinny Italians. My knees were fully implanted into the back of the seat in front of me. The poor guy sitting there fidgeted uncomfortably through the entire flight. At some point, he miserably turned around, intending to say something, but turned back upon glancing the two hundred and forty-five sweaty pounds squeezed in behind him. The slipped discs in my back were screaming. I swallowed my pain, wishing strange, excruciating deaths upon the Russian flight engineers and the mustached Libyan flight attendants.

We landed at Tripoli, Libya, where I spent the two hours of connection time fighting off flies, no-see-ums and militant mosquitos. I boarded Air Italy's 269 to Rome, bitten, stung and drenched in sweat. I sat with Bruno at the lounge in Rome for a few minutes, and once Luigi got there, we left for Djibouti, to meet Jule and fly to Shabwah.

If Bella were around, I thought to myself, this whole ordeal would be considerably more convenient. Bella had flown off to New York for her granddaughter's birth and abandoned me to the mercy of the system: according to the DM's orders, all flights, without exception, would be flown in economy class. This was unfit for humans in general, but especially for me and my four discs (which had apparently slipped sometime during my days jumping out of planes with a hundred pounds of platoon gear in my leg bag).

I thought to myself that next time the old hag went on vacation, the Mossad should probably go on hiatus. Bella, who had seen three directors come and go during her reign, had the secret power to upgrade any flight to business class for free. But this boon (and many others) were enjoyed only by a handful: the DM, Froyke, and most of all—yours truly. For some reason, I'd always been her clear favorite. Anyone else—rookies and veterans alike—was politely and smilingly abandoned to the mercies of their respective departments. According to hallway gossip, which had never been corroborated or refuted, in olden times, Bella served as a Kidon fighter—racking up a higher kill count than any other fighter in the Mossad.

The wheels of the aircraft hit the runway with a light jolt. I bolted out of my seat, stretched my legs and stood by the hatch, ready to escape as soon as it opened. The plane came to a full stop. Enthusiastic applause ensued. I barely stopped myself from bowing to the morons.

19.

Bruno spotted me the second I left the plane. He arranged quick passage and an empty, secure room provided by the airport administration.

After we extracted Anna, I'd have to partner with the Pissed-Off Saudis and get their approval to send in our planes and blast Shabwah camp off the face of the earth. This required that I convince said Saudis that the source of all their trouble was the same as ours—Shabwah.

"Are you still in touch with that Italian Al Jazeera reporter?" I asked Bruno.

"Affirmative."

"Good," I said and laid out the plan. The Saudis were pissed at Al-Qaeda, for obvious reasons—getting an explosive past the lauded security of their Royal Ministry of the Interior, turning it into smoldering ruins, killing and wounding dozens.

"I need another tiny pinch of international humiliation."

"Consider it done," said Bruno, who understood perfectly. In a deep, official-sounding voice, he said: "A major source in Israeli intelligence claims that the latest series of Al-Qaeda bombings in Rome and Saudi Arabia originated with an Al-Qaeda branch in Shabwah, Hadhramaut."

"Not an Israeli source. Anything but an Israeli source."

Bruno nodded. "You know Prince bin Nayef? He's their head of intelligence, and he absolutely adores O'Driscoll. If O'Driscoll vouches for you, consider bin Nayef on board." He smiled, adding, "Just get O'Dri to be your best man."

"Good thinking."

"All that aside, you'd do well to establish a relationship with the man," Bruno continued. "These royal families usually have several dozen princes. Trick is finding the right one to build a rapport with. Bin Nayef is a good pick."

I called O'Driscoll, who readily agreed. "Expect a summons," he said and hung up.

Bruno walked with me to the arrivals terminal, where Luigi was already waiting, wearing a driver's uniform and an admiral's hat. He held open the limo door, and I poured myself into the backseat. As I removed my shoes, I asked Luigi for a secure phone. He reached under his seat, retrieved a bag full of burner phones, and tossed me one.

"Hey, boss, you laughing at me again?!"

I never managed to keep from grinning when Luigi was around. Some people, rare people, are like that—the mere sight of them makes me smile. It was strongest with Eran, but I also felt it with Froyke, Bella, Verbin—granted, for them, it was a different sort of smile. Maybe gratitude, for the comfort and honesty that they radiated, allowing me a brief intermission from being constantly alert, on guard—a tension that accompanied me with the persistence of a shadow.

Luigi... Luigi was a child. Comforting. An explosion of innocent, youthful motivation, and a true joy he derived from simply being in the company of those he loved.

"I'm not laughing at you, Luigi. I swear."

Luigi was a smallish guy, around five foot seven, but solid and compressed like a Bavarian sausage. In another life, he could have been the heavyweight champion of the world (for under six feet). His head, constantly tilted forward, gave the unsettling impression that at any time he might deliver a crushing head-butt to your face, follow up with a brutal kick to the balls, and then vault into the air and land on top of you—all while flashing that childish, charming grin of his. Imagine a sort of mischievous Bob Hoskins.

Luigi Levi Napolitano, born and raised in Milan, had volunteered to join the IDF around his seventeenth birthday on the explicit condition that he serve in the First Golani Brigade—one of the most highly decorated infantry units in the IDF. After his mandatory service was done, he'd applied to the Mossad cadet course but had been rejected due to "difficulties with adapting to teamwork and accepting authority." On the Memorial Day for The Unit's fallen, I ran into Boaz—an ex-soldier of mine, and the current commander of the Yamam counterterrorist police force. He told me about the "Italian punk" that had been kicked from the Mossad exams and ended up as one of the Yamam's finest fighters. The day after that, I met Luigi in Boaz's office and decided to snatch him to myself. Some strong-arming with the head of human resources, subtle pressure from Froyke, a diplomatically blind eye from the DM and (possibly most of all) some cunning management on Bella's behalf—and the punk was ours.

I dialed Nora on the burner phone. She had finished scanning the security footage from Rome—airport, bus and train stations. Albert had apparently managed to isolate a single frame from the Leonardo da Vinci Airport footage. In said frame was an Arab guy in a striped brown suit, a red keffiyeh, and *agals* with a golden fringe—all of which screamed "I'M AN ARAB." Nora checked with her counterpart at Bruno's Agenzia. They'd missed him too. Albert had run facial and body recognition in all available databases. Nada. They'd passed it along to the Europeans—nada. "Until," she added after a pause, "we gave the file to your pal Ami, and... jackpot."

"Get to the point."

"This guy—his name's Qawasameh, you asshole. You knew all along."

"Ami noticed an unusually steep shahid grant... and did some digging," I mumbled by way of apology.

"Whatevs," said Nora. "Anyway, this Qawasameh is a terrorist from Balata camp. Did two years for membership in a hostile organization, then fled to Belgium. This much we got from Ami's intel. Then we took it to the Belgians. Apparently they found him in some dusty old visual database, under a different name. About six months ago, he boarded a flight to Pakistan, and then poof—vanished."

"Pakistan?"

"Yup."

It made sense. Ever since Osama bin Laden, the caves of Pakistan and Afghanistan had become the cultural center in world jihad.

"Excellent," I said. "And how did this fine gentleman get to Rome?"

"Through Frankfurt."

"Great! So now it's retracing-our-steps time. Follow him back through the Frankfurt Airport cameras, and from there back to wherever he was before that, and the one before that, and the one bef—"

"Yeah, gotcha." Nora cheerfully cut me off. "Let me get to work already, jeez."

20.

"Luigi, I'm starving. Feed me."

He parked the car in a lot crowded with trucks, taxis and motorcycles.

"*Osteria della mamma*," he presented.

"What? Your mom's place?"

He laughed. "Just say the word, and make my mother the happiest woman in Italy—unfortunately, she's in Milano. This is a small *osteria*, mostly truck drivers and porters, all look like they're related to you. You'll feel right at home."

The restaurant looked like a kibbutz mess hall thirty years ago: greenish laminated tables, silverware with plastic handles, water bottles recycled from old wine bottles. The place was jam-packed, and uncharacteristically silent for this type of Italian eatery. Most of the patrons seemed happily occupied.

We sat at one of the tables. "No menu?" I asked.

"Here you eat what they give you," said Luigi. I decided to submit—it's not like I had other options. A thin, stooped waiter around ninety years old placed a cold water bottle on our green Formica, followed by a large bowl of thick dark olive oil and a small tomato salad with crushed garlic and green chili peppers. We dipped our thick sourdough slices in the bowl and devoured the bowl in under a minute. I gazed at it mournfully, but Luigi made it clear that we would receive no more. The waiter returned, this time with a stainless-steel tray covered with translucent pink slices of prosciutto *crudo*, garnished with roquette and parmesan. It was by far the best prosciutto I'd ever had. The pasta ragù was nice. The house wine, served in a carafe, was excellent, no-frills and to the point, like a table wine is supposed to be.

Only when we'd arrived at the *secondo* did Bruno bother to inform me that this was, in fact, the house specialty. We received a beautiful *bistecca alla fiorentina*. Steak the size of a tablecloth. We stopped talking and joined the other patrons in their focused, joyous and now understandable silence. I was about to bid a sad farewell to the final bite, when some unrecognizable noises from somewhere behind me began to grow louder.

"Something up?"

Luigi pointed toward the old TV set hanging in the corner. Someone had turned up the volume. Sirens, the crackling of fire, cries for help. The GIGN—the French Gendarmerie's tactical unit, in their black combat gear and ski masks—were establishing a perimeter to fend off potential attackers, who by now were long gone. Various officials in bright yellow vests were running around, getting in the way of the firefighters and paramedics. The short clip repeated several times, until a terrified young reporter sent us back to the studio, where the anchor dramatically declared: "Paris is under attack, for the first time since the Nazi invasion in World War Two. And like it was then, this is an attack on the French culture and way of life." Cut back to the scene, where the young reporter had pulled herself together and fixed her hair. "Over twenty dead," she was saying, "among them children." She signaled to the cameraman to zoom out for a wide shot, and then picked up a crumpled teddy bear and broke into tears. Children this time.

I felt nauseous and pushed away the plate with the last slice of steak just when the broadcast cut back to the studio. The anchor solemnly spoke about a recent report from Al Jazeera, linking the bombings in Rome, Saudi Arabia—and now Paris—to the Yemenite Al-Qaeda division, operating from the Hadhramaut region.

"Two days ago," added the anchor, "the Israeli Air Force attacked in Sudanese territory, on the border of the Sinai desert, destroying a missile convoy apparently headed from Hadhramaut to the Gaza Strip."

Some degree of satisfaction mixed in with the nausea. Now that Bruno's leak was public knowledge, the Saudi prince would undoubtedly get the message. We silently drank our espresso. We waited for other diners who'd arrived about when we did to start leaving. We left the ancient waiter a generous tip and took off.

21.

By the time we got to the motel, the little bar had closed. The guy at the reception desk was happy to help. "This is exactly why I keep an electric *macchinetta*," he said. After a polite refusal, he agreed to take a tip for letting us borrow the coffeemaker. He even threw in a ten-ounce bag of coffee.

We made it to the room, I took off my shoes and we got to work. Although scenario B was the most appropriate response to Anna's request for extraction, I went over the other options again.

A—Non-urgent self-extraction. Anna would leave the country for some personal reason, possibly a medical convention we'd arrange. The problem here was mostly logistical in nature—Anna would need transportation to the Port Sudan airport, and that could only be provided by Imad—no time. This was no longer an option.

B—Immediate extraction (low-intensity)—we'd flip the kill switch on the solar farm's power supply. An "Italian" crew would be summoned, arriving via helicopter through Saudi Arabia, "fixed" the malfunction and left with Anna snuggled up in the chopper. This was our current plan.

C—Aggressive extraction (high-intensity)—two squads of five Matkal fighters each and an auxiliary extraction force in reserve. A full-blown combat operation on Yemenite soil. Impossible.

We both knew that plan B was the only real option, and we'd both familiarized ourselves with every single detail. There was just one problem—this was not a plan you would generally execute with a two-man force and a pensioner pilot. Luigi noticed my concern. "You and me, boss. We're gonna destroy those fucks."

In the face of this compelling argument, I could do nothing but lay out the plan of action and go over it for the sixth time.

Firepower: The deal was that the pilot would provide four 9mm Glocks with silencers and four MK-10 rifles, ten magazines for each firearm and another spare ammo crate, four frag grenades per person, four smoke grenades to provide cover during takeoff. Four flat, easy-deployment landmines. Four ceramic vests. The Italian punk insisted on a rocket launcher. Fine by me.

Schedule:

04:00—Takeoff, Leonardo da Vinci Airport. Qatar Airways flight 663.

09:00—Land at Djibouti-Ambouli airport.

10:00—Get to the American facility. Change into energy company coveralls. Equipment check.

14:00—Lunch. Another equipment check. Albert kills the solar farm's power supply.

14:25—Luigi calls Shabwah and lets them know we'll arrive at 17:30. The hospital's director, Dr. Anna von Stroop, is meeting us there—most likely accompanied by Husam, who's armed with a 9mm Glock, a MK-10 and a tactical knife.

18:00—Luigi strips one of the more distant panels and asks for Husam's assistance. Anna sprints toward the chopper. After I make sure she's safety aboard, I join forces with Luigi.

18:25—Luigi and I overpower Husam, disarm him, cuff him to one of the devices and tape his mouth shut. If he seems like too much of a threat, we neutralize him.

18:45—Sundown. Luigi deploys the landmines and blocks the access route.

18:53—Takeoff.

By the time we were done quizzing each other, it was 1 a.m., and we had an hour before we were supposed to be at the airport. The motel was thankfully within spitting distance of it. We had thirty minutes to nap and clear our heads. I lay back on the bed and Eran came, like he always did before an op, to go over the plan with me and wish me his usual "good luck, Dad." I closed his eyelids and kissed them.

Anna also came to visit. Her image was inflated into an extreme close-up, laughing gleefully, a thin trail of blood trickling from the right corner of her mouth. Just as I was finally drifting off to sleep, Verbin showed up, squeezing into my mind. *Honey*, I told her, *I have to finish this project first.*

"*Ristrrrrretto*," Luigi declared, drawing out a rolling *r*.

Opening my eyes, I saw him standing over me wearing a hardhat and a Green Energy Systems coverall. He handed me a steaming mug.

"Did Nora call? Any progress?" I asked, rising from the bed.

"We'll get out update once your fucking doctor is extracted."

"Say again?!"

"Her words, boss," he raised his hand defensively. "I'm just the messenger."

22.

By 3 a.m., we'd gone through tickets and passport control. I walked into the VIP lounge wearing Dr. Schultz's suit, a coverall and hard hat in my carry-on. The large espresso machine expelled a cloud of steam with a loud hiss. The drowsy barista had only just turned it on to face the day.

"*Ristretto*," I ordered.

"To go?" asked the barista, already holding a paper cup.

I glanced at my watch. "No, no cardboard. A cup."

He smiled, warmed the cup on the steam from the machine, and pointed questioningly at the TV. I nodded. The little guy turned on the TV, and the monitor burst into a cacophony of sirens, fire and black smoke. We both froze, staring at the screen; a Red Crescent ambulance whined as it entered the frame. The camera panned to the reporter, who was describing a bombing in the American embassy in Riyadh. Multiple casualties, including a security squad of Marines.

"Saudi Arabia this time," said the barista. His worried face seemed to relax somewhat, and he pursed his lips. "They recently blew up a restaurant, right here in Rome. Twenty-two dead, you've heard."

"Sorry," I said. "I didn't… I haven't heard."

"Twenty-two dead," repeated the barista, slapping his rag on the counter and rubbing frantically, as if he could scrub away the foulness that clung to the world. *My serial killer strikes again. Someone up there's looking out for me, keeping the Saudis nice and pissed. Knowing O'Driscoll, the minute he finds the bastards, he'll strangle them with his bare hands.* Honestly, I'd hoped they'd do more. The more they acted, the more likely it was that we'd catch them.

I left the lounge and boarded the magnificent, spotless Qatari airliner. I settled into my seat and went down the stairs for the customary tour of the plane. I smiled at Luigi, who was down in coach, reading an Italian newspaper and chewing gum. I went back up to business, collapsed into my seat and took my shoes off, mentally preparing for the utter boredom of a Muslim—and therefore sober—five-hour flight. Again, I went over the plan, thinking up unexpected secondary scenarios (these days they call them "ancillary"), and finding solutions. The further I dug into the smallest details, the clearer it became that, while God might be in there somewhere, it was I, Avner Ehrlich Ne'eman, father of Eran, who would determine the final outcome. The more troubling conclusion was that any dangerous surprises would, most likely, be Anna's doing.

Five hours passed, nearly imperceptibly, as I ruminated. The pilot thanked us on behalf of the crew for choosing Qatar Airways and took the opportunity to ask us to respect the local culture and customs. He also mentioned that a hot air current from the Sahara had caused a dust storm, currently swirling near the landing area. The locals refer to this storm as "the yellow devil"—local legend tells that a demon lives at the heart of the storm, and he will not rest until he is appeased with a proper sacrifice.

Despite the devil, we landed on time. By 11:00 we'd left the airport, ahead of schedule. A good start.

23.

A small Yemenite was waiting for us, holding a sign reading "Dr. Schultz and Mr. Napolitano, GES." We followed him into a Subaru taxi. He sliced through the thick yellow clouds like a getaway driver. About thirty minutes in, even the tips of antennae disappeared, along with the rest of civilization—we were deep in the bowels of the yellow cloud. The driver pulled a keffiyeh over his face, Luigi lowered his dust goggles onto his eyes, and I suffered in silence.

Suddenly, the driver broke right, off the road and into the dunes. I was terrified we would lose the time we'd gained. He stomped the gas pedal into the floor, and the taxi flew, skimming the dunes like a hovercraft. Occasionally we'd bump into the sharp crests of the dunes with a hard jolt, prompting the driver to laugh ecstatically, raise four fingers in the air and yell, "Four by four!"

We continued our mad joyride across the dunes, steadily gaining altitude, until we dove past the crest of a large dune and straight down a steep slip face, the end of which was obscured by the dust. Several more minutes of soaring in the yellow dust, and the Yemenite came to a screeching halt mere inches from a worn-down black helicopter, parked at the bottom of the valley with the rotor spinning. I noted our pilot's wise choice of location. We bid the driver farewell and boarded the chopper.

"You—Luigi." The pilot pointed, yelling over the racket. "You—Avner, me—Jule."

Crazy Jule was a small, bald fellow in his sixties. He wore round

John Lennon sunglasses and looked more like a schoolteacher than anything, although beneath this timid exterior lay tattoos of the Night Stalkers' centaur, and more impressively, the largest number of successful extractions in the Night Stalkers, working with the Navy SEALs, the Marines, Delta Force, and anyone better at killing than at being killed.

He gave a thumbs-up to signal takeoff, politely asked us to buckle our seat belts, and rose into the yellow cloud.

"As a general rule of thumb," said Jule, "we try to avoid flying when the yellow devil's around."

After about an hour of flying in the dense yellow dust, he took us down, landing his chopper above a beautifully concealed facility. The CIA doesn't fuck around. Even a close inspection wouldn't reveal the Predator UAVs hidden inside, waiting to be sent on their targeted assassinations. The roofs of maybe twenty hangars protruded just inches above ground level. We descended into one that turned out to be a mess hall.

A machine at the entrance wrapped our shoes with disposable overshoes. We went into the restroom and washed our hands and faces. The mess hall was well lit and air-conditioned, filled with both civilians and uniforms. None of them awarded the unfamiliar newcomers a second glance. Jule got us stainless-steel trays and silverware. We skimmed past the salads and loaded our plates with burgers, deep-fried chicken, home fries and little packets of ketchup and mayo. It all paired well with the Budweiser that Jule graciously provided. The coffee, unlike the rest, was awful.

When we'd finished eating, I changed into my green coveralls. Jule put my suit in a plastic bag and promised I'd get it back, cleaned and pressed, when I returned. In the meanwhile, Luigi set up a connection to Digital Albert and received confirmation that the power to the farm was cut. He and Albert went over the process to restore power, one last time. I called Dr. von Stroop and informed her in Italian that we'd arrive on time, maybe even early. She sounded cheerful and energetic.

We went back out into the valley between the dunes and unloaded the weapons and ammo crates from the chopper. Luigi commenced a quick function check, testing each weapon in turn. I walked Jule through the structure of the solar farm and the plan of action. Luigi was his usual strict self, insisting on also testing a randomly selected frag grenade and a landmine he'd triggered with a shot. I told Jule I didn't expect his assistance in case shots were fired, apart from self-defense. He smiled and nodded. I handed him an envelope with ten grand, as agreed. He refused. Apparently Abrasha had already handled his fee.

Jule nodded appreciatively as we collected and buried the empty shells and packages from the function check. Luigi asked for some more mines and rocket launchers. Jule shook his head, saying that we were already nearing the chopper's weight capacity, and this storm could cause low atmospheric pressure that would harm the engine output.

We flew south in the yellow mist. At 17:30, we were an estimated twenty minutes from target. Then, suddenly, a thud. The chopper shook slightly. I looked to Jule, who raised his hand to signal that everything was fine, adding that a bird had probably hit the rotor.

But then there was another thud, and the rotor stuttered. Not a good sound. Jule scanned the dashboard. Other alarms began to chirp and wail, and there was a great deal of orange and red among the lights on the dashboard—neither of which boded well for us.

The helicopter was losing altitude.

"Shit!" spat Jule. "Losing pressure in the manifold. I'm taking us down!"

Jule somehow landed the chopper like a leaf on a pond, softly and safely. He unbuckled from his seat, twisted around and raised a single finger. "Now, no questions. Do exactly as I say and we might actually make it on time. Avner, under your seat, there's a red suitcase, a diagnostic computer. Get it."

I bit down the bitter thoughts at the front of my mind and passed him the suitcase. He pulled out a network cable and plugged it in under the dashboard. Froyke had once said that the difference between a good fighter and a dead fighter was focus, the ability to concentrate on the mission, the enemy, ignoring everything else.

"Luigi, there's a blue suitcase under yours, toolbox, says SIGNET. Get it." As Luigi was pulling it out, Jule was switching through various windows and tabs on the computer. Luigi stood behind him, ready for his next task, and I went through alternate scenarios, including calling on Ran's reserve force. Each scenario was worse than the last. The thought of Anna being tortured for information kept barging in on my attempts to plan alternatives.

"Air sensor, fucking air sensor, the filter's blocked. Luigi! Blue cardboard box in the back, left side, air filter." Jule skillfully unscrewed and disassembled several layers of plastic and metal to pull out the old air filter, now rendered an opaque yellow, and shook some of the sand out of it before placing it in the new filter's box. "Green air pressure tank in the back. Left." I leaped into the rear of the chopper and brought the air pressure tank. Jule shoved it into the manifold and released air pressure in a loud, shrill whistle. He then lifted the tank and, without awarding it a second glance, tossed it to the back. I managed to catch the flying hazard. Jule reassembled everything and rebooted the diagnostics computer.

"*Shema Yisrael, adonai eloheinu, adonai echad*," he said, the Hebrew sounding strange in his deep Texas drawl.

"What?!" I replied, astounded.

"Pray," he said, still tracking the new diagnostics. "It might help. Okay, there we go, baby. Good boy. There's a good boy." He walked over to the dashboard and attempted ignition. Nada.

"I said pray, dammit!" he yelled and tried again.

The rotor groaned and stuttered before slowly stabilizing into a steady hum. Praise the Lord!

"Night stalkers never quit, huh?" I yelled gleefully.

"Put everything back where it was," ordered Jule, leading by example. "We might still make it on time, but we won't necessarily make it back out. We need to lose weight."

I immediately informed Anna that we were on our way and that we'd arrive on schedule. I couldn't stop thinking of his *Shema Yisrael.* Every once in a while, never for more than a few seconds at a time, I wondered if maybe there was a point in that sort of thing after all.

We were back in the air in moments and soon crossed the Bab-el-Mandeb Strait. Beyond the plumes of yellow dust, the black waters and tiny fishing boats looked like a child's drawing, hopeful and naïve.

24.

"We've arrived at Hadhramaut, en route to Shabwah," declared Jule, prompting us into action. We cocked the weapons and concealed them in the coveralls, along with the grenades. Jule was supposed to "miss" the marked landing space and fly over the camp to try and make sure we weren't flying into a trap. Conspiratorial thought was deeply embedded in each of us, and this was supposed to provide some sort of defense against the possibility that Anna had already been exposed and forced to broadcast the extraction code.

My complete confidence in Anna—whom I had recruited, trained and nurtured—allowed me to rely on this meager defense, but I could have been wrong. After all, when we'd recruited her, she'd been working at the Palestinian refugee camp in Balata. This disturbing thought tossed me back through time, a swift and agonizing recap of Anna's recruitment: a combined force of the Service, IDF commando and Border Police operatives disguised as locals, had entered Balata camp and engaged in a violent chase after suspects. At the time, Anna had been treating a six-year-old who'd shredded his arm with an electric saw working at his father's carpentry shop. One of the Jihadis managed to escape the attack force and make it to her infirmary tent. By the time Anna had applied a tourniquet and started treatment, a Border Police force tracked the blood trail to her tent. Anna tried to protect the wounded jihadi, who was still in danger of bleeding to death. She was arrested, following a struggle, and taken to a Service facility for undergo further investigation. She didn't cooperate there, either—insisting on answering all questions presented to her exclusively in German. Kahanov didn't manage to find any German speakers among the Service's available interrogators, so he called me for help.

I remembered it like it was yesterday. I was with Ya'ara, at Eran's officer course graduation. He'd graduated with honors, as usual. "Ami," I whispered angrily at Kahanov, "this is a bad time—the commander-in-chief's pinning his stripes on as we speak."

"Top of his class! No surprise there," "Uncle Ami" replied proudly, and I felt a tear sneaking down my cheek.

"Locally sourced kid," I answered with my regular, well-worn joke.

"So what am I supposed to do with her?!"

I signaled to Ya'ara and stepped back from the row of proud parents.

"What are you, high? Smack her, kick her around a bit, and she starts singing. No joy? Smack her twice."

"Well, you know I would," said Ami, "but the Supreme Court is really riding us, and besides, she's German—they build your boss's submarines. It'll be a whole thing. Just get over here, whisper some *Mamaloshen*[9] in her ear."

"Fine. Inform Nora." I hung up. Nora would prepare a concise report with everything I need to know about this fräulein.

The newly dubbed Second Lieutenant Eran Ehrlich, who knew that Ya'ara couldn't stand firearms, handed me his weapon to put his arms around her and then pulled me into our small, family hug. It was the last family hug I remembered, and sometimes I'd think of it, and it would pull me out of my misery; other times, it pulled me deeper in.

I walked into the interrogation room, uncuffed Anna and placed a cup of coffee in front of her.

"I'm the good cop," I said in perfect *Hochdeutsche*, smiling.

She smiled back, and I was stunned by her beauty.

"And if you don't want to be charged with crimes that'll keep you

9 Yiddish: "Mother tongue"—T.K.

locked in this dump for a decade or two, until you're not that pretty anymore, you should really start answering some questions."

Anna pushed the steaming paper cup in my direction.

"Good cop can take his coffee and shove it up his asshole," she said, still smiling.

I slammed my hand down on the table. The cup toppled over. I raised my knee, tipping the table slightly in her direction, so that the stream of boiling coffee ran down toward her. She didn't flinch. Another blow to the table, harder this time. This time, she flinched.

"Now strip!" I yelled.

"What?!"

"I said strip."

"You strip!"

I pulled a photograph from the folder—a line of women waiting for Dr. Mengele, naked in the snow.

"The one on the left, the tall one, that's my Aunt Mimi. Your Dr. Mengele attempted to mate her with a large German shepherd, a thoroughbred. We could go meet her, if you like. She's hospitalized not too far from here. Completely catatonic."

A visible shiver gripped Anna's spine. A placed a photograph of her grandfather on the table.

"This is Colonel von Stroop. He ran the camp. I assume you know him."

Anna stared at the photo. The shiver became a heart-wrenching sob. I left the photo on the table and left the room.

Outside, Nora asked if Mimi was the aunt's actual name. I had no idea, to which she responded by letting me know that I was a vicious, heartless creature. "You're definitely falling for her," Nora concluded and left.

The concentrated rat-tat-tat of small-arms fire by the chopper's nose tore me away from my thoughts. We were above the camp, having "missed" the solar farm, as planned, to perform a quick survey of the surroundings. The gunfire urged us back on course, and we complied. At 18:00 we landed at the designated landing point, right on schedule. We briefly "introduced" ourselves to Dr. von Stroop, and Mr. Husam, who surprisingly arrived with another armed man, named Hamid, supposedly to "assist with translation." The sun began to set, casting a dim red glow on the settling plumes of yellow dust. The skies looked like the Valkyries set at the Berlin opera. I was raised on Mahler—Mother would play him to me any chance she got—but I much preferred Coppola's Tarantinoesque use of the Ride of the Valkyries, with his insane colonel who loved the smell of napalm and reminded me so much of our own mad "Colonel" Mizrahi.

I picked up the laptop with the GES sticker on the lid and connected it to the farm's control system. Husam and Hamid observed this curiously, inching toward me. I tucked in my elbow, making sure the Glock was safely nestled in its holster. What if this Husam was the fighter Anna had saved back in Balata? I was suddenly troubled, and not for the first time, by the thought of her being a double agent. I nudged the Glock with my elbow again, trying to estimate how quickly I could draw it.

The laptop indicated a malfunction—of course—and I ordered Luigi to dismantle the circuit from the unit in the last solar panel, located about a third of a mile away, in the far-west corner of the farm. I requested that one of the armed men join him, because he would probably need help removing the lids. To my surprise, they both left with Luigi. When the three of them left our line of sight, growing ever shorter with the setting sun, Anna slammed into me, holding me in a tight embrace. This was not the time nor the place. According to the plan, we had fifteen minutes to take off once we'd neutralized Husam, fixed the "malfunction," and covered the access route to the chopper with landmines. But Anna, wearing the Valentino blouse I'd given her, clung to me tightly and wouldn't let go. I clenched my jaw and somehow managed not to smack her. I reminded myself that she was, after all, a child.

"Anna, sweetie, get on the helicopter and stay there until I get back. I'll go help Luigi wrap things up and we're out of here, okay?"

But Anna wouldn't let go and oddly started to turn me around, toward the camp. Only then did I notice the small, bandaged figure limping toward us from the camp. Fuck me, now what?

Luigi signaled me with his walkie. I was fairly confident in his ability to overcome two targets instead of one even without my help, but who knew—nothing else seemed to be going according to plan.

"Hurry, hurry!" Anna was yelling in French at the bandaged man, who struggled to waddle faster. I told Anna to board the chopper while I talked to him. She refused and explained that this was Dr. Patrice, a Jewish physician from Paris, who'd been tortured by Husam with an electric drill because he was suspected of supplying us with info.

"He's Jewish," she reiterated and added that she wasn't going anywhere without him.

I radioed Luigi and told him he needed to dismantle another circuit.

"This helicopter does not have the capacity to carry another adult person," I told Anna.

"Then go," she said calmly, "and come back with a bigger one."

I shook Dr. Patrice's hand and took a deep breath. Anna and I supported his weight as he limped toward the chopper as fast as he could. I tried to calculate if the ammo and weapons could be discarded to make room for him but soon realized that I lacked the technical knowledge. I needed to check with Jule, who was smoking a cigar outside the chopper, his hand absently leaning on the rocket launcher. His eyes widened when he saw the company I'd brought, and he raised his arms in frustration.

"Another extraction," I said. "Once we deploy the mines, we'll be lighter."

"Yeah," said Jule, "exactly forty-five pounds lighter, and this guy weighs..." He scanned Patrice with an assessing glance.

"One hundred and sixty pounds," said Patrice. "I'll manage," he added and turned to leave, collapsing before he managed a single step. Anna and I helped him sit up. At times like these, systematic thought is useless. Each step, I knew, must be solved independently.

"Wait here. I'll go get Luigi." I signaled Jule to stay on high alert and headed toward Luigi. He was still examining the printed circuit when I got there. Hamid hovered over him, holding a flashlight. I started to take apart another board, about fifty yards from them, and called for assistance. Hamid gave Husam the flashlight and started walking toward me. I nodded at Luigi.

Hamid suddenly stopped and looked back at Husam. He seemed to suspect something. I drew the Glock and hid it behind the open laptop lid. "Hurry, please!" I called out to Hamid. When he approached, I handed him the laptop, while my right hand pressed the Glock's barrel against his temple. For the last time in Hamid's life, he felt surprised. Shot at point-blank range, like a mob hit. I was the one who told my men never to execute, other than in cases of mortal danger. He was a risk to Anna. The execution was justified.

Things didn't go as well for Luigi—when he lowered his eyes momentarily to reach for the Glock, Husam lunged forward, ramming him in the stomach. Luigi dropped to the ground and Husam drew his weapon. Luigi fired from the ground, a split second before Husam had the chance. He got to his feet and fired another, confirming the kill.

We each tossed a corpse over our shoulder and shuffled toward the chopper, our feet sinking into the fine sand. I explained the new situation to Luigi as we walked.

When we got there, Anna was gone. I looked inside the chopper, around it—nothing. This wasn't Murphy's usual bullshit. This was a straight-up kick to the balls. Patrice was inside, sleeping. Anna must've pumped him full of anesthesia. Jule told us that once Anna had become convinced there was no way to carry the weight of another person, she'd smiled and said, "When they find out that Husam and Hamid are dead and Patrice was taken, there'll be no doubt anymore that Patrice was the spy."

"She helped me get him into the chopper, kissed me on the cheek and walked away," concluded Jule. "Hell of a girl!"

I seriously considered taking the helicopter into the camp, tossing Patrice out the door and taking Anna on board by force. Luigi and Jule looked at me expectantly.

"Want me to go in the camp and get her crazy ass back here?" asked Luigi.

I didn't know what to tell him.

"I think she's right," said Luigi eventually. "If we extract Patrice, it'll clear her of any suspicion. She could continue working."

We unpacked the landmines and placed the corpses behind a small mound of sand. Luigi took the rocket launcher and headed out to deploy the mines as I attempted, unsuccessfully, to contact Anna. I understood where she was coming from, but this little stunt of hers had two snags: for one thing, Patrice would now be forced into hiding for several years. Also, though she couldn't possibly know this, my plan with O'Driscoll and the Pissed-Off Saudis included bombing this camp into the dust, which meant that another extraction would be required before we could engage.

On the way back, I asked Jule if he was Jewish. He laughed in response.

"I have this Jewish buddy," he said. "*Shema Yisrael, adonai eloheinu, adonai echad*, that's what he says every time your boy Omri Casspi stands on the Golden State Warriors' free-throw line."

He picked up the chirping satellite phone from its housing and answered with a cheerful, "Hey, old man. It's all good." He twisted back and handed me the phone. "It's for you. Line is secure. Calls may be recorded for training and quality purposes up at Fort Meade."

Froyke was on the line. "Who's this nice Jewish boy you're bringing back with you?"

"Long story, boss. Can it wait?"

"Negative," he replied, and I was wondering how the hell he already knew about Patrice taking Anna's place on the chopper. Had he hitched a ride on a satellite, or did he have other sources, unknown to me? I hadn't even finished the story when he cut me off impatiently.

"Is Bruno in Rome?"

"I think so."

"Goodbye." He hung up. And slowly, far too slowly, the old bastard's plan was beginning to dawn on me.

From Djibouti, we flew back to Rome, where we waited for the meeting with bin Nayef.

25.

Anna was sitting on the sofa in the corner of Imad's office. He sat at her feet, his head between her knees. They sat there smoking in silence. Imad's jaw tensed as he straightened out the newspaper, which had been crushed into a ball, and looked again at the front page. A large image of three men, cuffed and blindfolded, lying on a gray concrete floor. The headline cried, "ISRAELI TERROR AT THE HEART OF ROME." According to the article, three representatives of GES, the Italian energy company—a German engineer named Schultz, a technician and a helicopter pilot—had been kidnapped and restrained by Hebrew-speaking agents. The team had been about to fly to Hadhramaut to fix a solar farm at the UNICEF children's hospital. Their documents and IDs had been taken and apparently used by their kidnappers (perhaps the Mossad) to book a Qatar Airways flight to Riyadh. The Rome Police Department was investigating the bizarre affair. The writer also mentioned that only a week had passed since the bombing at Ambasciata d'Umbria, associated with the jihadi underground...

"I knew something was off about him, right from the start. Then I thought—they couldn't possibly be dumb enough to plant a Jew as a spy... and that's probably what they were counting on. Fucking Jew, fucking Jews," Imad spat and recrumpled the newspaper.

Anna had never felt so safe in his company. First the death of his brother, Nasser, and then Patrice's extraction by the Israeli commandos posing as solar farm technicians—which had proven beyond doubt that Patrice had been the mole supplying the intel on the convoys...

something had changed in Imad, and he had become more open, more attentive, and more in need of her attention. Oddly, the deaths of Husam and Hamid seemed to contribute to this change, as if he had accepted his fate. The fact that Anna had managed to narrowly escape the Israeli team of assassins had only strengthened his faith in her and the sense of camaraderie and partnership they shared.

Imad had told Anna that a large shipment of rockets and missiles should arrive at the camp any day now, including the Russian anti-aircraft systems sold to the Iranians at subsidized cost, intended for Hamas and Hezbollah.

"The fighters on the front lines are desperate for ammunition. A recent Israeli bombing campaign has destroyed their reserves. It's time for a change of approach," he said with a sudden, astounding openness. "I was wrong, thinking we could defeat and subdue the West. In the meanwhile, more and more Muslims and Arabs are murdered by other Arabs. No enemy has been as destructive to Arabs as the Arabs themselves. On 9/11, in a single day, we erased centuries of humiliation—and for what?! Now the Americans are tearing through Afghanistan and Pakistan, they control Iraq, they're swarming all over Saudi Arabia, they're arming the Jews—the Europeans cooperate, of course, and once again we are the black sheep of civilization."

Anna took a drag from her Gauloises, her other hand stroking his hair. "Impressive speech. Did you practice just for me?"

She flinched slightly, expecting retaliation. It never came.

Instead, Imad laughed. "You're smarter than a good woman should be," he said, smiling, and added that in several days, he would head out to Riyadh to meet the sheikh and inform him that he was retiring from the global front. "I'm getting back to the real work. The real cause," he said, explaining that his new goal was not only attainable but slowly gaining recognition by the West as well—taking back Palestine.

"What?" asked Anna. "How?"

Imad rose to his knees and his eyes bored into her. "I need you with me."

Anna nodded in agreement.

"A good friend of mine, Dr. Taissiri, should be arriving at any moment," said Imad. "He's a great guy, a physician and chemist. He'll need to use your operating room for an hour or so, maybe longer. I'll let you know."

He offered her his fist. Anna giggled and awkwardly bumped her fist against his. Imad left. She remained there for a while, trying to come up with plausible explanations for this Dr. Taissiri's sudden need of her operating room. She could think of none.

She returned to the hospital, disinfected her hands and put on her white coat. A loud knock on her office door startled her. Imad walked in, followed by an older man in a wrinkled gray suit whose disheveled hair failed to conceal an expansive bald spot. Behind him stood a quiet, withdrawn adolescent, about seventeen years old.

"Dr. Anna von Stroop, Dr. Taissiri." They shook hands.

Anna smiled at the boy and went to shake his hand. He shied away from her.

"I… would be happy to help. What does the patient suffer from?"

Dr. Taissiri shot a wary glance at Imad and mumbled, "It is… a personal matter. A family matter. He… we prefer… I thank you for your good intentions, but this must remain within the family… extremely personal matter…"

"Okay, of course. What do you need?"

"Elementary surgical instruments… local anesthetic only, an efficient nurse to assist, a sewing kit. Most importantly, I require antiseptics and a clean, hygienic environment, which to my understanding are much more achievable in your hospital than in our usual clinics…"

They followed Anna into the modest, but impeccable, operating room.

"As you can see, Dr. Taissiri, it's no Mount Sinai, but…"

Taissiri briefly scanned the room. "It's more than adequate for my needs, much more than adequate. My compliments, Dr. Anna."

"Thank you."

"Thirty minutes and you'll have it back. I only need local anesthesia and an X-ray after the procedure."

"An X-ray, after the procedure?" Anna repeated, surprised.

Taissiri looked up at Imad questioningly, receiving only a glare in return. "I'm not a doctor, I don't know what's going on," Imad said. "Just let him use the X-ray machine, please."

"When?"

"Right now," said Imad bluntly.

"Sure thing, boss. Nurse Hamid is unfortunately missing. Will you manage?"

Taissiri eyed the machine, concealed behind a screen at the corner of the room, and nodded. He began to unpack a small heating tank from his bag, plugged it into a power outlet and spilled a large bottle of paraffin oil inside.

"Good luck," said Anna and left for the staff room. Imad hurried after her.

"What the fuck was that?" she snapped at him once they were outside.

Imad laughed. "You know I don't know anything about this stuff. It's a family thing, let him do what he wants. Now, can I get you a cup of coffee?"

She looked at her watch. "Too late. I have a staff meeting," she said. But the paraffin emulsion Taissiri prepared, along with the odd request for a post-op X-ray, caused her to stay and observe through the one-way mirror.

The patient—Abdullah, Taissiri's younger brother—was already anesthetized on the bed. Imad walked back into the operating room. "Turn his head to the side and hold him there."

Imad held Abdullah's limp head as instructed. Taissiri made a long incision across his lower abdomen. "Imad, hold his head! And insert this tube—suction, suction!"

Imad moved the suction tube to remove the pooling blood. Taissiri spread the warm paraffin around the incision, lining the pocket he'd created in Abdullah's gut. He waited several seconds, applied another coat, and repeated the process several more times. After the fifth layer of paraffin had dried, he ran his finger along the incision. "Good, good separation with the emulsion," he said.

Taissiri picked up a large Tupperware box with a blue lid. Inside was a grayish gel-like substance. PETN—a liquid explosive, a gel version of which had been developed in Dr. Taissiri's laboratory in the outskirts of Kabul—had already been proven both effective and invisible to Western scanning equipment: in Rome, Saudi Arabia, Paris and Riyadh.

Abdullah mumbled incoherently and tried to turn his head. Imad tightened his hold, forcefully pressing the boy's head to the sheet. His other hand stroked Abdullah's forehead. Taissiri filled the pocket with the gray gel. Layer after layer, he patted them down to compact the substance and remove any trapped air, then piled on more. When the pocket was full to the brim, he began to close up, sewing the flesh back over the gray gel.

"It looks fine." He stroked his younger brother's head and kissed his forehead.

"Forgo the X-ray so the German doesn't get curious. This'll work, no question."

There was a knock at the door. Taissiri shot a glance at Imad, who failed to react in time. The door opened and Anna peeked inside.

"I assume you're finished by now, Doctor," she said to Taissiri. "Has everything gone smoothly? Does your patient require anything?"

Taissiri shook his head adamantly. "Thank you, Doctor. We're done here. Thank you, again, for your help."

Back at her office, Anna downed her glass in a single gulp. The surgery she had just witnessed had stretched the borders of human viciousness to new lengths. Lengths unheard of since, perhaps, Dr. Mengele—and Auntie Hannah, as well. Avner was the only one she knew capable of analyzing and containing such evil. Back during her training, in a London basement, they had spoken of the shahid bombers, and he'd explained: "These terrorists have no country, no air force, no tanks.

They have people, though, in abundance. Under these conditions, using these people is an extremely reasonable strategy."

Imad owed her an explanation. Anna calmly pressed 1 on her phone to start a recording and placed it in the lower shelf of the letter tray on her desk, along with the patient release forms, just as Imad came into the room and approached her. It was the first time Imad had ever appeared without warning, and she was not afraid, and she did not shudder, and no cold sweat ran down her spine. Just the slight tremble of her right eyelid, the subtle myokymia she'd had since she'd arrived in Shabwah.

"Why my operating room?" she asked him.

Imad circled around, pushed aside the letter tray and sat on the edge of her desk.

"His Kabul clinic blew up. A work accident. Or maybe not. There are Jewish doctors in Kabul, too, right? Who knows?" He smiled.

Anna tried to smile back. "The manager in Kabul is a Pakistani, Hisham, and he's every bit as much of a terrorist as you are, possibly more so. I heard him say that it if were up to him, he'd slit the throat of every single infidel—barring the blond female ones."

"Aren't you going to ask why I need a clinic? First in Kabul, now here? Aren't you curious?"

"I'm not the least bit curious about Kabul. But I would like to know what you're planning on using my clinic for." Imad smiled understandingly, and Anna added, "And I won't ask you about that, either, for two reasons—"

"I'm all ears," he interrupted.

"The first step in keeping a secret is to hide the fact you have a secret." She was expecting a response, but he seemed to be waiting for her to explain. "If you tell me about the secret, it means you no longer want to hide it."

"I told you, you're too smart." Imad sighed. "What's the other reason?"

Anna smiled. "That I'm about to find out anyway." She lightly kissed the tip of his nose.

"You've heard of the recent bombings? In Rome? Paris? Riyadh?"

"I've heard, yes. I haven't been following it too closely, to be honest."

Anna didn't know what was coming, but she knew it was big. She knew it would be something Avner would appreciate. She placed her hand on the letter tray and casually pushed it closer to Imad.

"Wait, did you have anything to do with that?"

Imad nodded. "And that was just the beginning." He went on to talk about the decades of humiliation and the tens of thousands of casualties, and Nasser, and Baba. "The Jews have their tanks and fighter jets and missiles and submarines," he said, "and we have people. The people are our weapon." She was momentarily thrown by the resemblance to Avner's explanation but quickly asked, "And what's all this have to do with my clinic?"

Imad patiently explained, with unbridled pride, the chemical process and operation which could turn a fighter into a human bomb, capable of safely passing any security screening. He spoke of Jerusalem and the Al-Aqsa Mosque, and mostly about himself, soon to become the first man in all of history to unite the millions of Arabs into a single, unified force.

He stopped, then, and closed his eyes.

Anna noticed a tear sliding down his cheek and kissed it away.

Imad slid off the table, grabbed her shoulders with both hands and held her close.

"I need you with me," he said.

Anna nodded, raised his hand to her lips and kissed it.

"I have to go," he said. "Taissiri will perform several more operations. During the evening, of course, only after you've finished with the operating room for the day. After that he'll leave for Riyadh, and you'll go with him, and from there to wherever you like—just return to me happy, with a shiny new ultrasound machine." He kissed her eyelids.

Anna pushed the letter tray into place and was surprised to "finally" find her phone as it clanked in the bottom shelf. She slipped it into her coat pocket, relief washing over her.

A loud, whining growl—the type usually associated with a cat in heat—suddenly sounded, startling both her and Imad. She removed the phone from her pocket, and the whine grew louder.

"That's Francesca's ringtone—the friend I told you about," said Anna, answering the phone and almost dropping it when Avner's voice asked how she was. She told "Francesca" she'd call her back.

"Should I be worried or jealous of this kitten?" asked Imad, smiling.

"Worried? No. Jealous? Absolutely."

Anna pressed against him and hugged him at length. She wondered whether—and to what extent—she would miss him.

"Well," she said eventually, "I'm going for a run."

When Imad left, Anna changed into sweats and wore the armband with the running calculator. The recording she had just made should find its way to Avner; too partial, and in dire need of clarification. She was well aware of technology's occasional failure in dealing with obstacles such as bad weather and magnetic fields.

When she was done stretching behind the large mound near the farm, she punched in the code for the departure of an "extremely large" convoy in two to four days. It was inaccurate—Imad had mentioned more missiles coming in, but Anna had no code to convey arrival, only departure. It was the best she could do under the current conditions. She badly wanted to speak to Avner, apologize for the mess with Dr. Patrice and tell him about the gruesome operation. She was certain that when she revealed the information about the operation, the Kabul clinic, and the other operations about to take place in her operating room, Avner would forgive her.

26.

Anna's stunt with Dr. Patrice had been so unexpected, so empathic and selfless, that I couldn't even bring myself to be angry. We relocated Dr. Patrice to Karmia, a kibbutz in which we'd found some distant relatives of his. The icing on this clusterfuck of a cake was that, though it demanded some creative thinking and a quick response on Froyke's behalf, if she hadn't pulled said stunt and remained there—thereby strengthening her already-intimate relationship with Imad—we wouldn't know about the source of these stuffed shahids, or how they seemed to completely ignore any known scanning equipment. *I'm close, Froyke, so close to serving you these assholes on a fucking platter, just like you asked.*

But first, there was the matter of the missiles, and the Russian antiaircraft batteries. Neutralizing the Shabwah nest had just climbed back to the top of the EEI—the operational priority list dictating the actions of the entire intelligence community. In order to make sure this operations went as smoothly and quickly as possible, Bruno and I took a borrowed coast guard chopper to the Pissed-Off Saudis meeting with O'Driscoll and bin Nayef. Bruno had already heard about the attack on the US Sixth Fleet destroyer, which had killed seventeen Marines, including Lieutenant Eric O'Driscoll Jr., John's only child. After a brief mourning period, John had left his post as head of the Marines' guerilla training center and started the Bureau of Counterterrorism. The USS *Mount Whitney* became his base of operations, from which he coordinated the war on jihad throughout the Arabian Peninsula.

But Bruno didn't know the rest. Six months after the attack on the destroyer, one of our agents in Yemen had spotted Abu al Hariti, who had planned it. I was a young, unfamiliar officer at the time. I landed on the *Mount Whitney* without invitation or warning, in a fashion some might describe as "violent," and handed the intel over to O'Dri. That November, al Hariti and five of his men were killed by a missile fired at their vehicle from a Predator UAV, sent by O'Dri from a concealed CIA facility in Djibouti, and I sent my agent in Yemen to fetch al Hariti's DNA for confirmation. In this business, you need as much credit as you can get.

"And we've been drinking bourbon together ever since," I told Bruno as the helicopter approached its goal.

"No shit!" he said. "Wow."

This reaction made me unusually talkative. I told Bruno about the anniversaries of Eran and Eric Jr.'s deaths, which we usually spend together. I told him how, on the first anniversary, I brought a twenty-four-year-old Macallan, and O'Dri offered his Kentucky straight bourbon in its place, calling the Macallan a "whiskey for British homos."

Bruno, who was openly gay, laughed until he nearly choked. When he'd recuperated, he placed a hand on my shoulder. "It's a wonderful thing, that you helped him find closure. Amazing... how small this world is, sometimes."

"Small, round, stupid world," I mumbled, knowing that this supposed closure supplied John with no comfort or consolation whatsoever. That he lived on the brim of a deep abyss, and as the days elapsed, the abyss only grew deeper and darker. Just like mine.

"Oh," said Bruno, "I almost forgot." He passed me his phone. The video on the screen showed three men from Bruno's task force, in a large gray warehouse. They were changing into GES coveralls. Froyke, the sneaky old bastard, entered the frame along with Bruno. They cuffed the men and blindfolded them before unceremoniously lowering them to the ground. There was some laughter and scattered profanity, and white camera flashes as the "media" snapped some photos.

The video ended.

Good people. Good people.

The pilot pointed down at the water, where the *Mount Whitney* shone brightly upon the waves, and we began to descend. The smell of the salt air was invigorating, and I was feeling uncharacteristically optimistic. All things considered, O'Driscoll and bin Nayef had plenty of good reasons to cooperate. After the latest attacks at the Saudi Royal Ministry of the Interior and the American embassy in Riyadh, it felt safe to assume that they'd both be nice and pissed.

The helicopter tilted down and we hopped out like two young, strapping infantrymen, which neither of us were anymore. Bruno waved a kind of two-fingered salute at our pilot, who waved back, smiled, and soared back into the sky.

A young Marine officer in a spotless blue dress uniform saluted us as we arrived, and we followed him into the bowels of the ship. We reached a heavy steel door, and he lowered his head toward a biometric eye scanner. The steel door clicked open, and we walked into an operations room equipped with plasma screens, lots of electronics and a vigilant staff. We crossed the room quickly, forced to return the salutes of the sentries securing each door and turn in the ship's intelligence deck. At the end of a long hallway, the swanky Marine officer finally stopped and rang a doorbell.

"Mr. O'Driscoll," he said, "this is… Mr.…?"

I awarded the master of ceremonies with a bone-rattling smack on the shoulder.

"Mr. Big. Thank you," I said.

"Thank you, Lieutenant," drawled O'Driscoll.

The Marine saluted and closed the door behind him. O'Dri was dressed impeccably, as usual, in a three-piece suit and a gleaming tailored shirt. Whenever we meet, I'm overcome by the need to fix my rebellious shirt, which always seems to sneak out of my pants. I stared at him, unable to ignore his resemblance to Eran. Tall and wiry like a capoeira dancer. He held out his hand, and I grabbed it and pulled him into a hug. He placed his hand on Bruno's shoulder, who seemed to be feeling left out.

"Let's get to work. Hungry?"

"Always," I replied, placing my left foot at the heel of my right shoe and popping it off. Its sister soon joined it.

O'Driscoll pulled over a serving cart and unveiled a tray of ham and cheese sandwiches and three Budweisers.

"Strictly Kosher," he said, pointing at the sandwiches. I removed the cheese and ham from two sandwiches and wrapped them in a slice of bread. Bruno stared at me, amused. We clinked our beers. O'Driscoll let out a "*l'chaim*," and I responded with, "*saluti*," leaving Bruno with "cheers."

I handed O'Dri the small memory card. We listened together to the recording from Shabwah. They didn't seem too interested in the part where Imad informed Anna of the arriving missile convoy. But the description of Taissiri's clinic evoked a very different response.

"Catawampus!" declared O'Dri with his deep Southern twang, making me laugh and once again recall *Django Unchained*, where the mention of this imaginary demonic beast was used to terrify the slaves. I had seen the film during Tarantino Week at the cinema. I'd dragged Froyke to a marathon—*Inglourious Basterds*, *Pulp Fiction* and *Django*. He snuck away at some point, and the next day I returned with Nora to watch the *Kill Bills*. Around when Daryl Hannah tries to poison Uma Thurman, Nora decided oral sex was in order. After that, we went to her place, and there in her bed I confessed that as a boy, I'd wanted nothing more than to be a filmmaker, and if I could make movies, I'd make them "just like that guy Tarantino does."

"Are you telling me you know who pulled off these bombings? And how?" O'Driscoll grumbled, his voice a mixture of anger and astonishment, as Bruno chuckled.

"If we assume the intel is good, then I'd say the answer is yes."

"Mind telling the rest of the class just how the hell you have access to this girl's intel?"

It was obviously a rhetorical question.

O'Dri's phone rang. He picked up, hung up again, and informed us: "The prince just landed on deck one."

"Put on your shoes," Bruno whispered at me.

"Please. Like that Bedouin's gonna bother wearing shoes," I said, when O'Dri decided to retort.

"Glad you got to fly with Jule," he snickered. "He's the only pilot I'd trust."

Scheisse. Of course, Abrasha also worked with the CIA. Froyke had once told me, "In this business, everyone works with everyone, and everyone's a piece of work."

Would the prince prove to be a piece of work? I hoped not. When lying is involved, politicians have the home-field advantage.

27.

O'Dri's officer soon arrived, accompanied by the prince. I looked up and saw a guy more or less my age, holding a thin, elegant titanium briefcase, who wouldn't look the least bit out of place leaving a business meeting on Bond Street. I was momentarily surprised. A part of me had expected an extravagant sheikh in a gleaming white *gallabiyah*. O'Dri warmly shook his hand and introduced us. The prince offered me a limp handshake, then smiled and asked, "Which of you is the primary source?"

Bruno and I simultaneously pointed at each other.

"Mr. Ehrlich." The prince turned to me.

"Avner," I corrected.

"Mr. Avner, you are the first man I've heard of who decided to take a tiny helicopter into the yellow devil and lived to tell the tale."

He smiled appreciatively and apparently expected me to carry the conversation from there. I was horrified by how freely this info seemed to have gotten around. I glanced at O'Dri, perplexed. He was the only one who could've informed the prince, and he wasn't supposed to know, either. The prince's sharp gaze missed nothing.

"You are correct in your suspicions, Mr. Avner. Mr. O'Driscoll shared this information with me. But please be assured, he had nothing but good intentions. He is certain that we Arabs always appreciate heroic tales of men who ride a mighty steed into the heart of enemy territory—specially to rescue a beautiful woman. Shall we proceed?"

O'Driscoll and Bruno smiled, and I decided to stop beating around the bush. I handed over the memory card, which contained a concise presentation on activities in Shabwah, but the prince waved it away.

"No need for a presentation. We're not starting a business together."

I was getting worried. This prince didn't seem like a pissed-off Saudi in the slightest.

"This deal is between you and me, and we will seal it with a handshake. Do you agree?"

"I'd be honored," I replied and went on to outline the primary findings that had led us to Imad and the Shabwah camp.

"To my understanding, you are requesting a clear air corridor, for as much time as is required by your air force to wipe Shabwah off the face of the earth, along with several hundred Arabs."

"Several hundred Arabs who mostly kill Arabs," I blurted out, unable to stop myself.

"And what motivates you to invest time and effort in killing Arab-killing Arabs?" His eyes shifted toward O'Driscoll and Bruno. It was time to deliver the goods, set the bait.

"The camp serves as a base for missile convoys, sending out Iranian missiles to the Gaza Hamas and the Hezbollah Shiites. They're creating a route for the Iranians leading all the way to the Mediterranean. According to our latest intel, they're about to receive a large shipment of Yakhont missiles and SA400s. You don't want that, any more than we do." I tossed the seasoned politician his mostly accurate carrot.

Now came the stick. I spread my arm in a wide arc to include O'Driscoll and Bruno as I concluded, "We would all be exceedingly happy if the Saudi Royal Air Force would handle this assignment."

Bruno and O'Dri suddenly seemed very pale. The prince decided to deliver the knockout punch. "That is precisely our intention," he said. "The Royal Air Force will solve this problem to everyone's satisfaction."

An awkward silence settled over the room.

O'Driscoll shattered it, eventually. "Hang on, let me get this straight. Are you refusing our request for a clear air corridor for the Israeli Air Force?"

"Not at all, just the contrary," replied the prince. "We will supply you with a secured corridor, and the Royal Air Force will handle the assignment."

I felt like we'd begun to establish an understanding and said that, while the corridor was open, I expected the Royal Air Force craft to remain grounded. The prince objected, "reminding" me that even if we did receive the air corridor, this did not mean that the Kingdom of Saudi Arabia was relinquishing its sovereignty, and continued to quietly and confidently describe what he assumed would be our distributed force and plan of action.

"Two F-16 bomber quartets, similar to those flown by the Royal Air Force. One fuel tanker, one electronic jammer, two rescue helicopters." He placed the titanium briefcase on the desk and opened it. Inside were standard-issue Royal Air Force stickers, a memory card and some diagrams.

"I assume that your 'primary sources'"—he added air quotes, smiling—"will inform the appropriate parties that the Royal Air Force performed the bombing."

"You have no reservations about taking responsibility for dozens, maybe hundreds of Muslim Arab casualties?" I asked.

The prince shook his head. "Power begets respect," he replied decisively.

I tried to wrap my head around the new situation. I wasn't willing to take the risk of one of their pilots suddenly snapping, deciding to take the opportunity to shoot down some Jews. I knew Froyke wouldn't risk it, either. But the weathered politician read me like an open book.

"Our Royal Air Force will not be grounded. However, your electronic countermeasures could, most likely, neutralize any nearby radio and radar systems."

The prince got to his feet. We all followed. He offered me his hand, and this time he shook forcefully, confidently. "You must know, these Arabs—all they understand is force," he said, smiling. "So be sure to give them hell."

28.

Imad's black Range Rover pulled into the sandstone-lined driveway next to a dingy blue truck. Najib's Café, deep in the desert in Atbara, Sudan, seemed to float in midair, carried on the dusty heat rippling up from the baked earth. Najib came out to greet them, his rotund form wrapped in a brown pinstriped suit, a thin Iraqi mustache adorning his upper lip, and a set of golden teeth gleaming under it. From his left ear down to his cheek, the skin was strangely smooth and oily, indicative of a cheek transplant—compliments of an Israeli phosphorus bomb. He hurried over to hug Imad and offer his condolences for Husam and Hamid. A large waiter with jet-black skin arrived, carrying a golden tray with a coffeepot and cups. Najib waved over a young man who approached them and stood next to Imad. The resemblance—at least in height and body structure—was striking. Najib nodded, and the young man and Imad took their clothes off. Imad handed over his clothes to the double, instead wearing his red keffiyeh and gold-embroidered black *agal*. When he was done, he looked at his watch.

"Okay! Twenty seconds, give or take, and it's time for our photoshoot. Smile, everyone."

The group left the café, smiling. Imad's double led the way, with the bodyguard—Hamid's replacement—at his side, followed by Yasser the driver. Imad stayed behind, in the entrance to the café.

"Now!" Imad ordered, and the group collectively looked up, as if they could see the satellite. Yasser took off his pants and bent over, mooning the heavens. "*Tilhasi tizi*—lick my ass, *ya America*."

"*El-anza*—you jackass," said Imad from the doorway. "They need to see your face."

"Sorry," apologized Yasser. "My bad."

"Fuck it, never mind. Your face, your ass—same difference..."

Yasser turned to the double. "Walk straight, stomach tucked, like you've got a massive stick up your ass."

Imad laughed as the double got into the car in his place. The Range Rover headed out, toward Khartoum. The blue truck waited a beat, then discreetly followed. Both vehicles vanished into the yellow dust, leaving a fading cloud of dust in their wake.

"This is for you," Najib cut through the silence, handing Imad a small travel bag with a flight ticket, a new passport and the keys to a new, white Range Rover that was parked under the pavilion in the café's backyard.

Imad shifted the car into sports mode, hardening the suspension. Five hundred and ten horsepower in a light, strong chassis, with air suspenders—it felt wonderful, like gliding on a cloud. He lowered the window, letting in the desert night's chill, and took a long drag from his Camel cigarette. These were his moments with Baba. His and his alone. Five hundred and ten noble, winged Arabian steeds, harnessed to Baba's old Mercedes, pulling it through the air. The velocity slowly diminished, the horses moved in a sort of slow motion. Then the Mercedes was gone. So were the horses.

Imad floated alone, in a vast, curving sky. His arms were spread and he rolled, like a skydiver, toward the quickly approaching ground. Would his parachute open? Baba's good hand stroked his head, wiped the sweat from Imad's brow. Baba was there now, and so were the horses, and they were pulling Baba's run-down Mercedes. Mom was sitting in the back, along with his three sisters and little Nasser. Baba was at the wheel. Imad was sitting on his lap, "driving" the car, which bounced wildly at every crack in the pavement. Each bounce banged the little ones' heads against the roof of the car, to the sound of Baba and Imad's laughter.

The family reached the Rafah border crossing, and Mom got off with the little ones. The taxi was already waiting to take them to Cairo. From there they would travel to Mom's parents, in Saudi Arabia. The little ones waved goodbye from the other side of the border. Baba and Imad waved back. And now they were finally alone, just the two of them.

"I have a question for you, *ya ibni*. How do you get inside the car when the doors are locked, the window is open, and you don't have your keys?"

"I reach in through the window..."

"You can't, *ya ibni*, there a big *Kalb* inside. Grrr..." Baba growled and barked, and Imad laughed.

"What are you laughing about, little *Kalb*? Big *Kalb*'s gonna eat you." His father picked him up and gently bit him on the cheek. Then he tossed him through the open window. "That's how you get in."

Imad bounced on the worn upholstery, sat by the wheel and growls, "Grrr... woof. Woof! *Ta'al, ya baba*, get in."

Baba plopped into the driver's seat. "Now drive."

They drove back to Gaza. The horses were back, and they were galloping with them above the orchards of Khan Yunis, Deir al-Balah and, finally, Jabalia. Baba breathed deep, large breaths of the citrus-blossom-scented air.

"Breathe, *ya ibni*, breathe. This is the smell of angels."

They arrived back home. Imad had already fallen asleep. Baba carried him in his arms, gently tucked him into bed and kissed his forehead. Then, suddenly—an explosion!

The house shuddered. Baba hurried to Imad's bed. The butt of a rifle collided with his face, and he spat blood and teeth. The soldiers tied his hands behind his back, tied a blindfold over his eyes, and shoved him. Imad burst into tears. The intelligence sergeant took a photo out of his vest and examined Baba's face.

"Yeah, it's him... face looks a bit different, though." The soldier laughed. "He's so much prettier now, ain't he? Confirmed ID!"

Baba tried to say something, looked up at Imad with eyes Imad would never forget. They seemed to cry, "*Ya ibni*, my brave Imad, why won't you save me?"

The soldiers shoved him to the front of the house, urging him on with the butts of their rifles. A large young man with a kind face, who seemed to be in charge, handed Imad a chocolate bar with a red cow on the wrapper.[10] "Sit over here, quietly. Someone will pick you up in the morning."

There was a sudden burst of gunfire outside. A large explosion, yelling. The soldier ran outside, Imad on his heels. Baba's corpse lay on a field stretcher. The large soldier gently turned Imad around and herded him back into the house. And Imad was filled with shame, and remorse, and not a single drop of fear.

---

10 The logo of a popular Israeli chocolate manufacturer. -TK

29.

The shrill voice of the announcer at the airport snapped Imad back to reality. He chewed on his lower lip. If he could just find that gigantic Jew who had murdered his father.

Dr. Zechariah el-Masri quickly passed through passport control and the exhaustive security checks and boarded Nova Airways flight 920, from Khartoum to Riyadh. The airplane he boarded was empty.

"This way, please, Doctor el-Masri," said the stewardess politely before taking him to business class. A security guard built like a tank was guarding the entrance. Imad slapped him on the shoulder, and the tank, who'd known Imad from Shabwah, smiled and invited him inside. Imad approached the sheikh, hugging him and kissing him on both cheeks before taking the sheikh's hand and kissing it as well. The sheikh turned a smartphone screen toward Imad.

"Look," said the sheikh.

The camera that was shooting the video was mounted on the landing skid of a Mi-24 helicopter, which kept popping into the shot. The battered blue Unimog truck was slowing down on a thin strip of asphalt cutting through the golden dunes. It turned around and came to a stop, positioned across the road. Imad didn't know what was coming, but he was fairly certain he would hate it. Silence surrounded him when the video came to an end, the final frame showing both the blue Unimog and Imad's black Range Rover on fire, charred bodies littering the asphalt around the wreckage. It took Imad several seconds to digest.

"Imad Akbariyeh al-Nabulsi is dead," said the sheikh. "Long live

Doctor Zechariah el-Masri." He handed Imad a briefcase, a business card for Dr. el-Masri, CEO, whose company imported and marketed medical equipment, and the keys to a Porsche, adding, "The newest model. You've earned some fun."

"My men?"

The sheikh was silent.

"My men?" asked Imad again.

"No one survived. Not even you. You died in an aerial assault. Your DNA was scattered at the location—it's already on its way to the American labs. And you... you are as free as a bird..."

Imad's hand moved toward that gun that wasn't there. He took a deep breath, wondering if the sheikh had taken advantage of the opportunity and eliminated Yasser and his security team just to weaken him. That was probably the case. He noticed that the sheikh didn't offer the appropriate condolences for the deaths of Husam and Hamid, who had served as the sheikh's eyes and ears.

The sheikh seemed to read his mind, as usual, saying, "The cause is bigger than either of us. I'm getting off in Riyadh, and from there I'm off to Islamabad. You stay here until the dust settles. Najib will take care of anything you might need. When the time is right, we'll send you to Berlin—Doctor von Stroop is already there, by the way. You can keep her busy."

The sheikh flashed a dirty little grin. "Impressive girl. Excellent lineage."

Desire fluttered through Imad's body. The sheikh went on, "Doctor Taissiri will be waiting for you there as well. They're looking for him up in our caves. I scatter breadcrumbs around, they keep looking."

The sheikh smoothed his face from the traced of the grin, fell silent for a moment, and then looked straight into Imad's eyes. "You are now in charge of our most significant operation since 9/11. We will flood Europe with these stuffed shahids, and any other country that harbors infidels. After that, if you decide you want Palestine, I will personally support you—financing, men, ammunitions, anything you want."

"When do we start?" asked Imad, hoping the sheikh would leave him time to meet the sultan before Berlin.

The sheikh smiled cheerfully. "*Tawil sabrak, Tawil sabrak... il-ajaleh min elshitan*. Extend your patience—haste is the devil's work. First we let your death sink in. Rest for a week or two, maybe a month. I'll let you know when you can go see your fräulein."

Excellent, thought Imad—*this is my chance*. And he hoped that the sheikh would fail to read his mind, just this once.

In the middle of the night, Imad got into his Porsche and drove to Atbara. There, in a junkyard in the middle of nowhere, he was supposed to set the car on fire, burning the final forensic evidence on earth of the existence of Imad Akbariyeh. The sheer elegance of this beautiful machine gave him pause. There might be another solution. Najib, perhaps, could give the car a thorough cleaning and look after it for him.

He soon realized that he had no choice. Burning this car could be the only true end to his former self. He sadly inserted a tube into the gas tank and sucked. The fuel came in a hesitant trickle, at first, which grew into a steady stream, soaking the ground, pooling around the car. He took a long drag and tossed his cigarette into the puddle. The machine burned, marking the beginning of a new era, a momentous era—and Palestine would be the opening chapter, and he'd have revenge, undo the humiliation.

He then briefly coordinated with the ever-loyal Najib and boarded a flight to Cairo. From there he would fly to the Sultanate, where he could finally share his vision with the sultan.

And then it was back to Berlin, to make some stuffed shahids. He couldn't afford to disobey the sheikh.

30.

O'Driscoll phoned just as I was stepping out of the shower, and requested—ordered, really—that I postpone my flight to Tel Aviv. "Stay put," he said, "I'll be there in thirty."

Thirty minutes later, on the dot, he arrived at the motel, pulled out an iPad and placed it in front of me.

"Look!" he ordered.

It was satellite footage, medium quality and badly edited.

When I'd watched the whole thing, he offered me a glass of bourbon.

"Again?"

"Affirmative. From the top, at Atbara."

At the bottom of the screen was yesterday's date. The time was 14:05 plus some serial number. Bird's-eye view of Imad's Range Rover parked beside Najib's Café, near a blue truck. The party left the café, led by Imad. One of them flashed his ass at the estimated location of the satellite.

The Range Rover sped down the winding Route 38 from Atbara to Khartoum. The driver, probably Imad, took full advantage of the rear-wheel drive, drifting through the curves. There was a cut to the blue truck, which left the road momentarily to turn and position itself across it. The shot widened.

Imad's Range Rover arrived at a sharp curve. The rear of the car broke right, the front swerved left, and Imad was forced to slam on the brakes hard to avoid hitting the truck blocking the road. Too late. The jeep, and Imad with it, collided violently with the truck, spun through the air three times and eventually landed upside down. The camera panned slightly to the right. A Mi-24 attack helicopter hovered above the demolished Range Rover, waiting. One of the passengers—impossible to identify—tried to climb out of the crushed window. The helicopter fired a missile at him, then another. the Range Rover exploded and went up in flames. The helicopter ascended, stabilized, and fired another missile—a kind of pointless confirmation.

An armed figure hopped out of the truck and ran toward the blazing remains of the jeep. He prodded the heads of the bodies with the tip of his shoe, apparently confirming the kills, and raised his head toward the circling helicopter. The pilot signaled with a thumbs-down, and the man on the ground nodded, took out a box of cigarettes and lit one, tossing the box on the sand. The helicopter seemed to be making a final round before departing. On the left landing skid, a knee was visible, as well as two hands holding a camera. The men on the ground waved goodbye, and then, suddenly, the helicopter turned, heading back toward the truck. It stabilized and fired another missile, then another. The truck exploded. The helicopter rose and droned away, and the desert was silent once again.

"What the fuck is this?"

"Wasn't us," said O'Dri. "Wasn't y'all, either. Who else around there has Mi-24s?"

"The Iranians, the Libyans and the Somalis. Some other ones lying around the free market. The KGB Russkies can probably get them, too... did you see the guy from the Unimog who confirmed the kill? Got instructions from the pilot, then got executed? Like a goddamn mafia execution? They're insane..."

"You can't expect abnormal people to exhibit normal behavioral patterns," said O'Dri.

"You got anyone over there?"

"Yemenite police forensic team is down there, collecting evidence."

"Do they have DNA testing?"

"Affirmative. They'll pass along their findings."

Apparently, we weren't the only ones after Imad. We raised our glasses in the name of the dearly deceased, and I tried to explain the subtleties of the Hebrew expression, "The work of the righteous is done by others." Along with this minor satisfaction, however, I felt a much greater frustration. As if my quarry had been snatched away from my fingers.

31.

At noon, Froyke, who was looking much better, came to visit me in Agur, along with G. They both successfully passed the entrance exam performed by my dual monstrosities—Garibaldi and Froyke got along famously, while Adolf maintained a respectable distance.

We went over the checklist again. G's pilots and navigators had been grinding the simulators to dust. The concluding exercises, carried out in a training area in east Azerbaijan, were a success. I was still worried about the sensitive Saudi material, the Royal Air Force stickers—we couldn't afford a leak. One of the navigators on the assault team had some design experience; we made sure he applied the stickers himself, with no eyewitnesses, no matter their rank.

The skies had also been cooperative and the weather seemed promising, perfect for an aerial assault. When we were done, Froyke asked to see Eran. He leaned on the gravestone and muttered something. G observed from a distance, shifting his weight uncomfortably. Froyke parted from Eran and came over to hug me.

"So today's your big day, huh?" he said at some point. It was uncharacteristic, and I was caught off guard. And the old geezer had more up his sleeve—before they headed back to Tel Aviv, he casually mentioned, "The little doctor asked about you. She expressed a great deal of interest, in fact," he added with a mischievous smile that assured me more than anything else that he was back to his old self. "A great deal of interest!" he finished with his standard reiteration.

Five p.m. The setting sun dyed the clouds crimson. Ten hours to

H-Hour. That was a lot of time. I lit a small Cohiba and dialed the hospital. I asked to speak to Dr. Verbin and hung up before they managed to transfer me. What would I tell her? That I loved her? Our shared history consisted of all of two minutes, and I was in love? Ask her how she was doing? Idiotic. After several seconds I called again, asked for Dr. Verbin again. The call was transferred and landed in her voicemail. I whistled the main theme from *La Donna è Mobile* and hung up.

"He's an overly sentimental crowd-pleaser. And he's off-key," my mother would say whenever I played Pavarotti, who was my main link to classical music. My mother taught at the Music Academy and had perfect hearing, but I couldn't care less that Pavarotti was off-key, or that Bob Dylan was "grating" and Mick Jagger was "all over the place." I loved every moment of it. It was different, missing my sharp-tongued, opinionated mother, or the father I'd never known. It was so much calmer than the slicing agony of missing Eran and Ya'ara.

My vertebrae were in dire need of attention, so I took off my clothes and dove into the pool. An hour of Ironman front crawl and another thirty minutes of butterfly stroke later, my back should be back to a tolerable state.

Garibaldi and Adolf came running once I jumped in and proceeded to patrol around the pool. I had been trying for years to convince them that I knew how to swim. Nothing seemed to work. The second I was in the water—there they were, patrolling. As a puppy, Garibaldi had fallen into the pool once. It was winter, a cold day. I jumped in to get him and we dried him with Ya'ara's hairdryer. He hadn't set foot in the water since, and he ran whenever someone turned on a hairdryer. During my swim, I thought I heard the phone ring, but I kept swimming. When I finally left the water, I found myself hoping it was Verbin, but it was O'Driscoll, calling to wish me good luck.

On my way to the Pit, I attempted to put my thoughts in order: *today I destroy the camp at Shabwah.* Other than that, Imad had been executed, Taissiri had vanished, and Anna was busy opening a new children's clinic in Berlin. I wanted her to come back to Israel. I thought we could give her a clinic for Ethiopian refugee children in some kibbutz. She'd adamantly refused. I asked Luigi to join our Berlin branch and watch over her, her security measures and her debriefing regarding Taissiri's operations in Shabwah. When I asked him if he wanted Nora to join him there, he practically licked his lips in response. I wished them both a great deal of fun. Tomorrow, when it was all over, I'd finally take Garibaldi to get his teeth cleaned, and read the new Ken Bruen novel. Froyke's voice appeared in my head, quoting his father—*Mensch tracht und Gott lacht*—reminding me not to overindulge in expectations. Man plans, and God laughs. *Just please, please don't let Him laugh at my operation. He won't get away with it, this time.*

32.

At the Pit, I went over the checklist again with Froyke and G. The jets had been adorned with the emblems of the Saudi Royal Air Force, and no one had been informed of this other than the parties directly involved in the operation. At my request, G drastically reduces the number of entry permits, resulting in an uncharacteristically empty Pit.

02:00—Recheck all systems. I went out to the small smoking balcony and indulged in another Cohiba. It had been one of those days. I realized that, more than anything, I was expecting a sort of catharsis. Once this was over, I was taking some time off. And Miss Doctor would definitely be coming with me. When I checked my phone, I saw a missed call from Verbin. Overjoyed, I dialed back and immediately realized it was the middle of the night. I hung up.

02:30—The Pit, which we'd emptied so meticulously, was now quickly filling up. The commander of the air force was first to arrive. He shook hands with me and Froyke like we were the mother and father of the bride and then went to huddle with G in some corner. Then came the head of the intelligence corps, the director of operations, the commander of Unit 669, and the head of the Cyber Defense Directorate. Half of the general staff was already there by the time the chief of staff finally made it, accompanied by the minister of defense, the director of the Mossad, and the prime minister's bureau chief. The DM came over to shake my hand and congratulate me with a "Good job, Ehrlich," before finding a corner to hook up his laptop and obsess over the risk management program he'd developed.

02:45—The prime minister walked in. The generals rose to their feet as a single mass. I had no choice but to join them. He nodded in greeting, then sat down to exchange whispers with the defense minister and his bureau chief.

02:50—G assumed command. The pilots in the air reported locations and readiness. All small talk hushed. A tense silence took its place. Ten minutes to H-Hour. A cache of hundreds of missiles would be destroyed. The coordinates the pilots had fed into their smart bombs were accurate. This was what Anna had spent a year in the desert for. I tried to predict from which angle Murphy would strike.

My Eran appeared suddenly, to say everything looked good. "Kiddo," I said, "we crush this Shabwah today, there's a new Shabwah tomorrow." An insane scene flashed before my eyes, thousands of brightly glowing ballistic missiles, cruising through the black skies, from every direction—Gaza, Lebanon, The ocean, so many, all at once. The Iron Dome[11] computers broke down under the pressure, and the missiles kept coming, their movement oddly slow.

Eran kissed my cheek and vanished. I loved that kid so much.

02:55—The pilots reported one hundred and eighty seconds to target.

02:58—The pilots were ready. Visibility was good. Targets identified.

02:59—G glanced at the air force commander, who looked to the prime minister. The PM nodded. The commander nodded at G, who addressed each of the pilots in turn with an order to "engage!"

03:00—The director of operations, an infantryman through and through, blurted out an enthusiastic "Fire! Fire! Fire!"

How puny we infantrymen looked when compared to a fifty-million-dollar aircraft. The massive technological infrastructure. The bunker busters weighing a literal ton. There would be no catharsis. There was never any catharsis in this line of work.

---

11 A mobile all-weather air defense system designed to intercept and destroy short-range rockets and artillery shells fired at a populated area. -TK

We watched the plasma screen, following the descent of the heavy bombs. Flyby after flyby, bomb after bomb, the bunkers were crushed, exploded, burned. The secondary explosions looked like Fourth of July fireworks. One camera, I had no idea which, managed to get closer to the destruction. Vehicles were visible, along with burning tents, and dozens of frenzied black grasshoppers, running, burning, falling. Infantrymen.

03:03—G informed us of a perfect execution. The commander of the air force quipped, "I've always said our Royal Air Force was the best in the world." People began to laugh.

"You've done great work, which has and will continue to have crucial strategic and historic repercussions. We have struck at the heart of the axis of evil..." The prime minister was spewing his standard political prattle. I was suddenly troubled. I tried to capture the DM's attention, but he was too deeply focused on his laptop screen. Froyke shot me a curious glance. I realized that at the first sign of political difficulty, our prime minister might use this victory for his own needs, destroying the trust our fragile new coalition was based on.

I raised my hand like a good boy.

"Yes?" said the PM. "Ehr—uh—Ehrlich, right?"

Out of the corner of my eye, I noticed the sudden tension in the director's face. Froyke seemed amused. "Yes, your honor," I replied. "For over forty years now, Avner Ehrlich. I'll just take twenty seconds, if it please your honor." I gestured at the room.

His puzzlement quickly morphed into a smile. "Please, be my guest, Avner. You're the guest of honor, after all."

"Friends, I'd like to take advantage of the prime minister's presence to stress a crucial matter. This operation was carried out by the Royal Saudi Air Force. We had no part in this, nor any prior knowledge. Thank you."

The prime minister waved goodbye and made his way toward the exit. The chief of staff winked at me and the air force commander, who hugged my shoulder and tipped his head toward the PM's entourage as he whispered, "Think he got the message?"

I nodded. "Of course he did, and of course he'll do whatever he wants to, regardless. We're just the dog's tail," I replied, grinning when I imagined a happy, tail-wagging Garibaldi. Froyke approached me along with the director and winked at me.

"Good job, Ehrlich," said the DM, shaking my hand. "Good job."

BOOK 2

33.

"Good job, Ehrlich," said the director, and with that, another chapter in my life concluded. I had noticed that with each ending of a chapter in my life, someone else's life seemed to end entirely. What did that make me?

I was too exhausted to muse at the moment. I took off my shoes, peeled off my socks, and got on Highway 1. I set the cruise control to one hundred miles per hour, stuck my head out to dry the sweat off my face, and hoped not to encounter any cops.

I'd been in this business long enough. I should have known that no joy would come from the demolished camp and the burning, scattering grasshoppers. No sense of victory. No, it was empty and metallic, like after a bad fuck. A full year of work, of tension and fears, and Anna, that maniac who risked herself day after day, just because she was born to the wrong family. A 180-second light show, and *voilà*! They were gone. Now I just wanted to go home, to my Eran, my golden blue-eyed boy.

When I got to Agur, the sky was already brightening, and the yellow metal gate was ajar. I took my clothes off as I walked, and dropped into the deep end of the pool. I stayed down there as long as I could. Ya'ara used to say that my greatest aspiration was to return to the womb, and I'd destroy whoever gets in my way back there. Adolf and Garibaldi were patrolling the poolside when I popped back to the surface like a cork out of cheap champagne. I decided to make the best of the situation and take a swim. Forty minutes of front crawl and twenty minutes and butterfly stroke, and I was as good as new.

The camp at Shabwah had been destroyed, along with its missile bunkers. It'd take them at least six months to reorganize. Imad Akbariyeh was dead. An unknown number of PETN-stuffed human bombs were still walking around. At the moment, it seemed they were keener on exploding in Europe and Saudi Arabia. They'd probably come our way when they felt better prepared. Our intelligence-gathering agencies, and those of our colleagues, had analyzed every crumb of intel. R&D had been working 24/7 to develop monitoring and scanning equipment that could recognize the stuff, but R&D took time—and I was the one who was supposed to buy that time. This was my next mission. I'd provide this precious resource through three main channels. The first, and most urgent, was to prevent the stuff from leaking into our neighborhood—a move requiring exceptionally accurate intelligence and an immediate, even spontaneous, reaction. The way things usually went, we wouldn't know until it was too late, too close. Froyke had managed to move this task to the top of the intelligence community's priority list. The second move would be to locate and dismantle the supply routes, providers and distributors. The third and (so far) final move was also the costliest, and the most complex: neutralizing the Chernobyl explosives factory, deep in the heart of Putin's Russia. At that point, the politicians would waltz in and do their best to turn absolutely everything to shit. Life, unlike what they teach us, is a black-and-white sort of ordeal: Good vs. Evil, black pawn takes white pawn. No grays. Either kill, or be killed.

Okay, then what? I needed to catch up on some sleep. See Dr. Shahaf for Garibaldi's teeth appointment, which had been postponed far too many times. Then the crazy Irishman's book. Unless I was distracted, I could finish it by the afternoon, including a lunch break, as Paleolithic as possible. For the grand finale, I had schemes of a dinner with the lovely Dr. Verbin, and so I called the hospital and asked for her. She was taking the day off, they told me. I soon discovered she wasn't listed, either. I dialed the hospital again, and they predictably suggested to take down a message.

"I need to speak with her urgently. There's a problem with the dosage she prescribed my uncle, and she told me I should call—that I have to call, really, if there's trouble, twenty-four hours a day."

"Sir, if you'd leave your contact information…"

"Fine, thank you," I said. I hung up and called Nora. After fifty-four seconds, I had Verbin's number.

"Doctor Verbin?"

"Excellent diagnosis, Mr. Ehrlich. How are you?"

"Great, thanks. You?"

"The usual. How's Froyke doing?"

"Fine, I think. Are you hungry? I mean, will you be hungry, later? Can I ask you to dinner?"

"I'd like you to, but I have a shift starting at seventeen hundred."

I was silent.

"Mr. Ehrlich? Are you still with us?"

Seventeen hundred, both looks and attitude. She was a catch, this one.

"Ehrlich?"

"Yes." I tried to sound as tough and businesslike as possible.

"I'm delighted by this invitation. Really. Very gentlemanly of you. Please try it again, or I will. Thank you. Goodbye," she said and hung up.

Good conditions—shitty outcome. My disappointment was understandably great. "*Try again.*" Of course I'd try again.

34.

I indulged in another hour's swim and deliberated whether to send her roses, and risk seeming like an overeager child, or wait for her to call. The phone suddenly vibrated, but it was playing the Takbir—a keening "*La ilaha illa Allah; Muhammad Rasul Allah.*" Ami Kahanov's ringtone.

"If you ask me, it seems you've taken a day off."

"And you took it upon yourself to ruin it."

"You wound me. I wanted to cook you a Paleozoic dinner."

"What do you want, jackass?"

"I have a fascinating tale for you." A "fascinating tale," in our code, was the sort of tale that required immediate attention.

"Where are you?"

"Tel Aviv. Want me to stop by Zalman's in Jaffa?"

"Affirmative. Get a nice cut of rump cap. About three pounds. And about two pounds of ribeye. We'll make some *Yudalach*. Get parsley, too, and some onions."

"Fire up the grill," said Ami. "I'm on the way."

I renewed the supply of coals in the grill. They'd be white-hot by the time Ami got here. The smell of the citrus coal tossed my mind back to Eran, who loved these dinners with "Uncle Ami."

Five years had passed.

It had happened in the middle of the week. The kid was with his team at facility 500 down in Tze'elim. Urban warfare exercise. At the end of the exercise, he was supposed to get some R&R, and we'd planned, barring any of Murphy's usual bullshit, that we'd take the ATV and finish the southern stretch of the Israel National Trail.

I was sitting under the pergola, barefoot and free. Ya'ara was performing a pipe organ recital at the Abu-Gosh church, and I was supposed to pick her up at midnight, when it was over. In the meanwhile I was listening to Pavarotti and friends—James Brown was singing that it's a man world, but it wouldn't be nothing, nothing, nothing without a woman. *Nulla ha più senso te si vive solo per sè,* agreed Pavarotti—nothing makes sense when you live only for yourself. Mom would probably say it was an opera for football players. I leaned back, puffed at my cigar, and expelled fragrant blue smoke rings at the reddening sky, imagining the moment when I'd have them back in my arms—my angelic Ya'ara, and Eran. Life could be truly beautiful, when it so pleased.

"W...what? What is this?"

A group of people were approaching. Kahanov at the lead, followed by "Colonel" Mizrahi in dress greens, and Froyke and Bella bringing up the rear. A surprise party? I wracked my brains and could find no meaningful dates, nothing. More people were coming up the path. Dovik, then commander of The Unit, in his usual battered fatigues, along with Dr. Agranat, who had been The Unit's medical officer back in my day. He'd been discharged from the military years ago—what was he doing here? Probably reserve duty[12]. And Leibowitz, our own staff physician. What was going on? I choked.

"Eran?"

Something had happened to Eran. That had to be it. It was the only possible explanation. *No. No. No, I won't have it.*

---

12 In reserve duty, Israeli residents who have completed military service are assigned to the IDFs' military reserve force to provide reinforcements, both during emergencies and as a matter of routine course (e.g. for training or reinforcement). -TK

"Oh God," I said. God, a word I hadn't uttered since kindergarten. God, make it be something else—not Eran. God, no. What the hell did he have to do with anything?

Kahanov leapt past the steps leading to the terrace. I tried to hand him my glass of Macallan. He placed it on the floor and hugged me forcefully. The rest of the group stopped in their tracks. I tried to wriggle loose, but Kahanov held me there. My mouth was pressed against his sweaty shoulder.

"Eran?" I spoke, an odd, strangled grunt. Kahanov nodded. Bella broke into tears.

"Sit him down," ordered Dr. Agranat. Froyke and Kahanov lowered me gently into the chair, as if I were a child. When had I gotten up?

"RP"—Agranat pulled out a syringe—"I'm going to administer something to calm you down." He fiddled around with a small bottle.

"No!" I said. Agranat retreated with the syringe.

"What happened to Eran? Will someone fucking say something?"

Dovik approached me, knelt, brought his head next to mine and whispered, "Eran jumped on a grenade, Avner. A Mills 26. He saved his team."

It sounded like an apology. Dovik's forehead pressed against mine. "His father's son."

Bella couldn't stop crying. She occasionally managed to pause briefly and take some deep breaths, and then a new wave would hit. Froyke was rubbing her shoulder, avoiding my gaze. She referred to herself as "Grandma Bella" whenever Eran was around. They had this adorable grandma-grandson thing, despite the lack of any blood relation.

"Where's Eran? I want to see him!"

Mizrahi shook his head, crossing his arms in an "emergency stop" gesture, as if to say, *There's nothing to see. You know what the aftermath of a grenade looks like.* I sank into the chair. Agranat took the opportunity to jam his needle into my arm. I either fell asleep or blacked out. When I came to, Kahanov was sitting on the floor next to me. He waved a nearly empty bottle of Macallan in front of me and shoved a glass into my hands.

"Drink, drink now." I did, and collapsed again. This time, I definitely blacked out.

A cloud floated into my brain. Something pricked my arm and fell into a hazy abyss.

I woke up the next evening, twenty-four hours later. Kahanov told me that the Mossad shrink defined my long sleep as "temporary catatonia." Bella handed me a cup of coffee, her eyes raw.

"Ya'ara, where's Ya'ara?"

Bella squeezed my hand. "She'll be okay. She fainted and we took her to the hospital. She's going to be okay."

I later found out that Ya'ara had suffered a nervous breakdown, from which she'd never manage to truly recover.

"The funeral's at five, at the military plot at Mount Herzl. The prime minister is probably coming with the director. We arranged for the cemetery to be closed, they're preparing a full military ceremony and a firing squad and—"

"No! No ceremony," I cut her off. "No prime minister, no cemetery. Eran will have a plot right here, with me, where I can look after him. Where I can finally do my job and look after him."

After thirty days, Eran came home. And we talked every day, even when I was out of the country.

"Generous and chaotic and painful—the spring is so brief around here." Grossman's lines cut into my consciousness, as they occasionally did. "Brief and abrupt and heartbreaking.... It was mine for a moment, then taken away.[13]"

The poem shattered into a million pieces, and I along with it. Five years had passed, and time didn't heal shit. The abyss just grew deeper.

---

13 Both lines are from the poem "spring is so brief around here" by David Grossman, written about his son Uri, who was killed in the 2006 Lebanon war. -TK

35.

When Ami arrived, the coals had whitened, and the smoke rising from them was thin and white.

The rump cap cooked slowly, giving Ami time to tell his fascinating tale. "So old Qawasameh from Balata, the one who got the thirty-thousand-dollar grant from the Iranians, set up a mourning tent. Some of my guys came over to offer their condolences and pay their final respects to the shahid. His name was Bassel, and guess what—he's the guy we identified from the da Vinci Airport security footage."

Ami fell silent, chewing on a small slice of rump cap. I knew him well enough to know something big was about to follow this pause. "After some lively poking and prodding—we're forbidden from anything more, as you know"—he grinned—"we discovered that when the deceased—may Allah rest his soul in peace—came back to visit his hometown, he let slip that after Pakistan, he's being sent to Yemen, to serve a tour of duty in Shabwah."

Despite myself, I let out a low, appreciative whistle. Ami shot me a smug glance.

"And he let slip another thing, too. Turns out your buddy, Imad Akbariyeh al-Nabulsi, was his direct superior."

Finally! The holes were still pretty big, but I could make out the vague shape of a net being woven. The motherfucker who had blown up in Rome and killed those pensioners was working for Imad—concrete, specific confirmation for Anna's more general intel.

I took the rump cap off the grill, peeled off the layer of fat with a knife, and we dipped the slices in chimichurri with hot sauce à la Ehrlich.

It would be wrong to say that life is beautiful; it is not. But it has its moments. The pups appeared, seemingly out of thin air, and stood beside the table with their muzzles in the air.

Ami threw each of them a slice, on the condition that they both leave immediately afterwards, as "this is highly classified information. Shake on it?" he said. The dogs did not budge. "I see your word is worth nothing," Kahanov reprimanded them.

"This Imad Akbariyeh, by the way, has since found peace in the bosom of Allah," I said and told him about the assassination.

"Praise the Lord. I guess when you're as righteous as Avner Ehrlich, your work is done by others." He pointed two thumbs at his own chest. "But wait! There's more!"

I made several impatient gestures.

"*Tawil sabrak*, my brother, *Tawil sabrak... il-ajaleh min elshitan.*" Be patient. Haste is the devil's work. And when Ami started with the Arabic, he was building for something big.

"Abu Seif reports that Hezbollah just acquired one thousand and five rocket launchers. Guess who the seller was?"

"Victor the Chechen," I said, ruining his big reveal.

"I'm glad the cholesterol hasn't clumped up your brain yet," he responded dryly. "But that's not the point. The Chechen's regional representative is a guy named abu Nawata. Do I need to wag my fucking tail to get a fucking steak around here?"

I placed some rib eyes on the grill and covered them with the slices of fat wrapped along with them, courtesy of Moyshe from Zalman's. Ami opened two beers.

"*Na zdarovje.*"

"*Na zdarovje*," I replied, anxious to see what bombshell would follow this pause.

"A while ago I told you that this Chechen might also supply that stuff you're looking for, but it's just a shot in the dark."

He had told me that. I nodded.

"Well, if you ask me, it's not a shot in the dark anymore," he said, fixing his eyes on mine. I tensed. This could be it.

Sensing my impatience, Ami took another pause to play with the dogs a bit. He then shifted the steaks around to a safer location on the grill, poured some beer on the small flames that flared up, and tossed the rest of the fat and cartilage to the dogs. They each hopped to grab the pieces from the air.

"Abu Nawata, remember?"

I nodded, but he seemed compelled to build up instead of just getting to the point. "He's the Chechen's local representative, and he asked abu Seif, my guy from Ghajar, to see if any of his clients would be interested in… a tanker truck full of PETN liquid explosive. When abu Seif asked what the stuff's even good for, Nawata presented a veritable family tree of bombings, in Rome, Paris and Riyadh, explaining that it's the only known explosive to pass every single type of security screening."

I watched as Ami peeled the last slice of fat from the grill and swung it from side to side. The heads of both dogs followed the motion, left and right, left and right, before he tossed it into the air, smack between the two of them, like a basketball ref. The dogs both lunged into the air after it, banged their heads together and landing on top of Ami, who crashed to the floor along with his chair. I helped him up, laughing. There was something fascinating about tracing a tangled web, spreading from bombings in Rome and Riyadh, and who knows where else, passing through Afghanistan to Hadhramaut, and it turned out to have started right here, in your own backyard.

"I'm calling Froyke," I said, already dialing.

Ami pointed at his watch to remind me how late it was. I briefly wondered if he wasn't aware of the importance of this new info, or was just underplaying it like a bashful adolescent.

Froyke, unsurprisingly, knew exactly why I was calling. "Have you found the schmucks?"

"Affirmative," I said. "Tomorrow—well, today, I guess—at oh six hundred?" I addressed the question to Ami as well. He nodded.

"Good night."

I tossed Ami some towels and sheets, and as he got settled in Eran's room for the night, he received an alert from up north—abu Seif was gone. He'd missed a meeting with his handler, wasn't at home, and wasn't answering calls. They'd activated the location on his phone to find it abandoned at his house.

Ami washed his face and took off.

As I desperately tried to use the few remaining hours for some sleep, a phone call from Abrasha woke me up. He eagerly informed me that he'd received a message from the chatroom we'd visited together. It took me a second to realize he was talking about the secure darknet chatroom.

Abrasha didn't wait for my response, and I had to whistle several times to grab his attention and stop him from rambling into the phone. I told him I'd wash my face and get back to him. I gave my face and neck several minutes under the cold water and called him back on the secure line.

Abrasha's theory was that Victor Zhdaniev was antsy, because he had a large quantity of the stuff that he'd gotten from the manufacturer, but Imad—being dead—was no longer buying it. Now Victor was stuck with a tanker of liquid PETN, without a potential buyer, and without the cash he was due to pay the Chernobyl factory. And no one wanted to fuck with the Chernobyl mafia; "not even Victor the Chechen."

Abrasha drew a deep breath and continued, "You have a chance to buy the stuff now, at a good price. I recommend you do so, ASAP, before it gets snatched up by some other bunch of assholes. If you need help with funding or anything else, you be sure to tell Papa. Good night."

"Good night," I replied, knowing there would be no more sleep for me tonight.

36.

Ami and I got to the prime minister's office at 06:00. We met up with Froyke and then sat there and waited, as per usual. We were all still forced to wait there for a few minutes. No one really talked at the waiting area by the prime minister's office, because he might pop out at any minute and catch you in the act, so I spent the time thinking. While it was extremely fun to cross intel from two different, reliable sources, which had arrived within two hours from one another—it was also disconcerting. Someone could be feeding us misinformation. Still, I couldn't afford the assumption; I had to chase this lead, and I had to chase it now. Who knew when that unidentifiable, explosive-filled tanker might show up? If Nawata had offered it to abu Seif, it was already in the neighborhood. Most likely in Lebanon or Syria. The dozens of warring factions there made for an excellent marketplace. But Jordan was also nearby, and sometimes, the unlikely option was the likeliest. The tanker could be in Sinai. It could be in Iraq.

The prime minister called us into his office. Ami laid out his intel, and I added the news from Abrasha. Locating the tanker was raised to the top of the EEI. My adrenaline was pumping. Nothing gets you focused like a clear, distinct target.

The prime minister was apparently in the mood to provide some leadership, because he contacted Colonel Dudi, commander of Visual Intelligence Unit 9900, who appeared on the ridiculously huge screen to assure us that, "if this tanker is anywhere in the neighborhood, we'll find it. What gets past the satellites will be caught by the drones, and what gets past the drones will be picked up by our aerial scouts."

Froyke and I exchanged skeptical looks. We were both considering the possibility that the tanker might be hidden underground, or in some warehouse—there were plenty of ways to avoid detection from the air.

When we were done there, Ami went back to his office, and I escorted a limping Froyke back to his car. Suddenly he grabbed his prosthesis and doubled over. I lunged at him and grabbed his shoulders.

"Deep breaths."

Froyke leaned on the car, panting. "Bring me a cigarette, please. There's a pack in the car." He tossed me the keys to the Land Cruiser.

I found a green pack of Noblesse cigarettes in the glove compartment and lit one for him. Froyke took a long drag and slowly managed to steady himself. "It's not the prosthesis that hurts, you know. It's the missing leg."

"Well, imagine how much it would hurt if it was still with us."

"What's going on with that Taissiri? Haven't the Yankees found him yet?" Froyke always referred to Americans as "Yankees." I couldn't help but smile.

"The Yankees seem to be getting closer. They estimate he's hiding out around the Taliban caves."

I waited for Froyke to finish with his usual reiteration—instead, he grasped at his chest and suddenly fell, writhing voicelessly on the pavement.

At first, I froze. Then all of the blood in my body seemed to rush back into my face. I shoved him into my jeep, turned on the siren and sped out of there like a maniac, sailing past red lights, flying over sidewalks, taking any shortcut I could think of. On the way, I called Bella and told her to inform the hospital of our arrival.

The glass doors of the emergency room were saved only by the grace of a screeching emergency stop. Two paramedics emerged, running, and placed Froyke on a stretcher as a third yelled to "clear the entrance."

I nudged him aside and left the jeep and the whining sirens in place until I was certain that Froyke was the ER's top priority.

The nurse was already removing the electrodes from Froyke's chest when I swung aside the curtain around his bed.

"Cardiac arrest," the doctor told me. "He's okay now."

Froyke was as pale as a sheet, but breathing regularly.

I went back outside to properly park the jeep. The hospital administrator was there when I got back—Bella must have terrified him into coming—along with Dr. Verbin.

"We'll keep him here overnight, just in case," said Verbin, and without waiting for a response, she began to wheel the rolling bed out of the ER. Two paramedics hurried after her to take over. Verbin walked at Froyke's side, I took up the rear. I was certain I could hear my pulse, thumping and thumping.

"You're exceptionally stubborn." She smiled at me. When she looked back at the bed, her smile froze.

"Stop!" she ordered the paramedic pushing the bed, and placed her hand on Froyke's neck. The little green line tracing his pulse was running flat.

"Machines are too far. Basic resuscitation, now! You, pinch his nose."

She placed two hands over Froyke's heart and massaged it vigorously while the paramedic pinched his nose shut. Froyke was unresponsive. She didn't stop, even when the paramedic spread his arms helplessly to the sides. The look she shot him was murderous. She closed her hand in a fist and struck Froyke's chest with the heel of her palm. The paramedic ran down the hall, kicked an inoperative resuscitation cart in frustration, kept running. Verbin struck Froyke again. He did not respond. She looked at me.

"Get over here!"

I approached. She indicated the location of his heart. "Now you hit him, right here. Hard." Her eyes bore into mine. "Don't be afraid. Strong—not strong enough to break the bones, but strong." She laid her hand on Froyke's chest, palm up. "Now, hit my hand."

We'd practiced this resuscitation maneuver many times over the years. I'd never thought I'd use it, certainly not on Froyke. I took Verbin's hand and moved it away.

"I love you, Froyke," I whispered. I raised my fist and lowered it with a force neither too strong nor to weak. Froyke's body jumped, and then twisted and squirmed as if he was being electrocuted. He cracked opened his eyes and looked up at us, puzzled. I kissed his forehead.

I turned around into Verbin's hugging arms.

"You're not so bad. And he isn't doing too bad now, either," she told me and smiled sweetly. "Now, you can…you know." She waved her hand at me dismissively. I realized, after several seconds, that she was getting rid of me—just like I had gotten rid of her when we'd first met. Tough lady.

37.

Froyke had been placed on anesthesia and life support and declared "stable." Verbin was finishing up her shift. I was exhausted and soaked in sweat. It wasn't like I could do anything to help at this point. I decided to head home and come back tomorrow, first thing in the morning. I went out to the parking lot, and when I climbed into the jeep, there she was, unlocking a shiny red Volkswagen Beetle.

My heart was pounding again.

"Do you need a ride?" I solemnly asked.

Verbin turned around, smiling. "Not really," she said, jiggling her keychain. "But I think you might need a passenger."

"Come on," I told her. She held out her hand, and I helped her climb into my Cherokee.

"Here I am. Where are we going?"

"Agur, to park the jeep."

"Agur?"

"Agur. A worker settlement in the Judaean Mountains. Founded 1950 by immigrants from Kurdistan. Currently houses eighty-five families, and me, and... my son... Adolf, and Garibaldi... and the most beautiful sunset in the country. A thousand feet above sea level, at winter the temperature—"

"Okay, sold." She leaned her head on my shoulder, and I drove slower than usual. Twenty minutes later we turned from Highway 1 onto Route 38.

"Can we stop somewhere to pick up a bottle of wine?"

"There's probably one at the house..."

"That's fine, but what kind of guest shows up empty-handed? My Jewish mother would be horrified."

"I'll give you a bottle, and you give it back to me. How's that?"

We drove past the yellow gate, into my little cul-de-sac that ends with an electric gate. I clicked it open with the remote and progressed toward the second gate. When the first gate closed behind us, the second one opened. The two monstrosities lunged at the jeep, barking maniacally. She flinched slightly.

"It's fine, they're just letting me know how happy they are to see me."

"What about me?"

"I guess we're about to find out."

They escorted the jeep, happily barking, until we parked it by the small shed. I grabbed Verbin around the waist and lowered her from the jeep. "Introductions: this is Garibaldi the mastiff, the son of a friend from Rome, heir to the Italian royal family. This is Adolf, who graduated from Oketz summa cum laude and was discharged after his handler was killed at the Kasba."

"Adolf? That actually his name?"

"Yeah. Long story."

I crouched to pet them. Garibaldi interpreted this as a desire to kiss and slobbered all over me. I wiped the drool off and cleaned my hand on his fur. "Garibaldi, you are an absurd creature."

They approached Verbin, who bravely stood her ground, and sniffed at her feet until I scolded them. We walked into the refrigerated shed. I pulled a bottle of red wine from the shelves and handed it to Verbin, who seemed captivated by the heavy wooden shelves covered in tagged, dated bottles. I took a ball of cheese and a jar of cracked Syrian olives from the old Philco refrigerator in the corner.

"Come on," she said, "we'll miss the sunset."

"Not a problem, I'm all about missing out on things. All we need now is some bread."

I placed the goods in a green plastic crate.

"I'll carry this to the terrace." I pointed at the pergola at the end of the small vineyard. "Could you grab some bread from the kitchen? Basket on the right. The puppies will go with you."

"Other way around," said Verbin and lifted the crate on her shoulder before heading out to the pergola.

I walked behind her and looked at the house, enjoying what I saw: a single-story elongated rectangle, built from rough-hewn Jerusalem limestone. An open staircase shaded by a large, twisting vine led to the roof. Some of the walls were built from dark, massive Canadian logs that had been added as an extension of the old stone structure.

I passed through the kitchen, got bread and some silverware, and met her on the terrace. Verbin was looking westward, spellbound by the reddening view of the hills.

"Fantastic view. You're clearly a professional seducer."

"It seems to work only if the subject is looking to be seduced."

I poured wine into the glasses and swirled mine around before shoving my nose in the glass.

"To Froyke."

Verbin touched her glass to mine. "He'll be okay. He's strong."

She sliced off some cheese and nodded her head toward the narrow, elongated pool.

"The pool is amazing. I've never seen one like it."

Eran used to call it The Dungeon. "Would it be okay if I hop in?"

"Sure. Hang on, I'll get you a towel."

By the time I came back, she had already stripped down to a black bra and panties. I was thrown, and slightly flustered by the perfect, curving shape of her. I kept my distance, tossing her the large towel.

"Is this supposed to keep me chaste?" She tossed the towel at my head and jumped in the pool.

The sound of her hitting the water alerted Garibaldi and Adolf, who rushed over to perch on the edge of the pool like a couple of lifeguards. I poured myself another glass and looked at her. It wasn't like I had any choice in the matter—I was mesmerized. She moved in the water like a pro, round, tight motions. The water flowed over her smooth back, and a small, sculptured ass protruded from the water whenever she plunged her head in. I forced myself to get up. I went into the house and turned on the sound system. "*'O sole mio*"—Pavarotti rolled out of the speakers like soft waves lapping at the shore.

The song was beginning its final verse—"*Quanno fa notte e 'o sole se ne scenne, me vene quasi 'na malincunia.*" Night comes, and the sun has gone down, and I am struck by melancholy, and then—an annoying buzz from the pager, followed by a message: "Nora wants you on the Rose."

I picked up the bulky, yet secure Mountain Rose[14] device just as it rang. Nora was on the other side.

"Hang on, finding a secure location," I said and headed toward the vineyard, away from the pool.

"You're at home? With company? Good for you, man. Female company, I'm guessing. Listen, Dudi from 9900 called. They combed the whole neighborhood, couldn't find it. They asked if there were any identifying marks."

"I wish."

"They tracked several dozen tankers—none were deemed relevant."

I was about to ask about the criteria used to determine said relevance, but Nora was already explaining—they were looking for a specific heat signature. Which meant that the satellites would be useless if the tanker was underground, or even just in an air-conditioned structure. I wanted to ask if she'd applied pressure to the other potential sources, if she'd told 9900 to continue their tracking efforts. At some point, someone would move that tanker.

But Nora already knew what to do. I was starting to turn into Froyke, always reiterating, always double-checking.

---

14 Mountain Rose is an encrypted cellular network used by the IDF for some sensitive communications. -TK

"Okay, Nora. Thanks," I said.

"Enjoy the company," she concluded, hanging up.

When I got back to the pool, Verbin was no longer there. The towel was laid out to dry on the green lawn chair. I whistled and Garibaldi came running. He rubbed up against my legs and led me into the house. I followed him down the hall, until he stopped at the bathroom door. Verbin was just walking out, her wet hair framing catlike green eyes which were usually obscured by her horn-rimmed glasses. I relaxed.

"Where are your glasses?"

"Do you prefer me with glasses?"

"I think… I don't know. At this point I can only say that I prefer you."

She came closer and took my hand. "Contacts. At the hospital I need the glasses to look a bit older, more trustworthy. Hold on a minute." She went back into the bathroom and retrieved her wineglass. "Get the dishes from the pool, I'll wash them."

"You know something my dishwasher doesn't?"

"Good point. Now pour me more wine, you huge bastard."

"Happily. I'll get the dishes, you choose a bottle."

She raised her eyes questioningly.

"There's a little wine cooler in the study. All the bottles in there are ready to drink."

Verbin turned and went to the study.

Scheisse. The study? You idiot.

I hurried out to the terrace, collected the dishes and stacked them in the dishwasher. I wondered if it was really an accident, or maybe I had done it intentionally, pointed her straight to my open wound. So she would know. So she could comfort me.

When I turned around, she was standing in front of me, holding a bottle. It wasn't a wine bottle. It was bourbon, and two glasses.

"This is the strong stuff, right? Open up, please!" she asserted.

"Drink." She held the glass up to my lips. "Drink!"

I gulped down the bourbon like it was a glass of vodka. This was not how bourbon was meant to be drunk. Verbin downed her one glass and then grabbed my hand and led me to the study. She nodded toward the photos of Eran. Dozens of them, framed, different sizes, from different times. They were everywhere. Eran nursing in Ya'ara's arms. Baby Eran in a carriage at the beach in Tel Aviv. A small, golden-haired child, dressed as a cowboy. Eran in a judo uniform and a white belt, surrounded by his peers, a tall kid, his hair had darkened into a chestnut brown, big blue eyes and an athletic build. The judo uniform gave way to a karate uniform. The belts also traded colors, from white all the way to black. Martial arts certificates in English and Japanese, one of them signed by Mas Ōyama. The two of us leaning against the battered ATV, at the edge of the cliff on the edge of Ma'ale Vardit, arms around each other's shoulders. Eran in his paratrooper uniform, receiving his wings, receiving his officer stripes. Graduation reports for outstanding performance from every course he ever took in the IDF. A photo of Ya'ara, beautiful, calm, leaning back in a straw chair. Older. Her hair was tied back. In the background was a large garden, and people frozen by the photo mid stroll. A big close-up of Eran I'd enlarged out of a year photo of his unit. I stood there, facing the wall of photos, facing her, and didn't quite know what to say. I noticed a tear sliding down her cheek.

"I knew Eran. He was an amazing guy. A really, really good guy," she said.

"What? How?" I stared at her, lost.

She poured us both another drink and raised her glass. "To Eran and Gil."

"Gil?"

"My baby brother. I raised him, pretty much, after…" She paused for a moment, then continued, "Anyway, Gil was in field intelligence. He told me that Eran led them into the Gaza Strip one night to do some reconnaissance. They had special night-vision gear, confidential equipment. When they got back, it turned out that one of the lookouts left behind some classified equipment. Eran never reported it. In the middle of the night, he went back out there by himself, deep into enemy territory, and came back with the missing equipment. No one knew. Later, it turned out that…"

"And your brother, Gil, how's he? Is he okay?"

"My brother, Gil… my baby brother, he's at Loewenstein."[15] She slowly shook her head. "A vegetable, and that's that. My baby brother's a vegetable, and there's nothing anyone can do about it."

"Take the glass with you."

We left the room, holding hands, with the bottle and the glasses. We crossed the terrace, heading toward the pool. The motion detectors activated the outdoor lighting, trapping us in two bright beams of light, like rabbits caught by a hunter's torch. Verbin shielded her eyes and I guided her along. The hunting lights went out. A column of small solar garden lights led us westward, toward the small cliff. I tightened my grip on her hand and took her to the black slab of rock.

The words "Captain Eran Ehrlich Ne'eman" were carved into the rock, simple white letters. A garden sofa sat by the grave, and some empty wine bottled were scattered around. I picked them up and placed them in the wooden crate to the side. "Sit."

She sat and poured us another round.

I sat beside her. "When Abrasha, who was the GOC[16] at the time, gave Eran his captain stripes," she said, "he was talking, very calmly and quietly, about the time some lookout had left behind some heat-vision equipment, and how Eran went into the Gaza Strip to retrieve it, by himself, the following night. He told us how he and Eran's battalion commander weren't sure whether to reprimand him or give him a goddamn medal… then he pulled Eran into a fierce hug, like he was his

---

15 Loewenstein hospital and rehabilitation center mostly treats patients who were injured during their military service. -TK

16 General Officer Commanding (Central Command). -TK

son. I was there—Gil had just made first lieutenant."

I was silent for a while, not knowing what to say. Eventually I opted for my default question at times like these. "You hungry?"

She nodded, her eyes glittering. I tried to remember what I had in the kitchen—most of it was probably intended for my paleo diet. This might constitute a problem. I somehow found it difficult to imagine her biting into a bloody steak.

Her phone suddenly rang. "It's the hospital," she said and picked up. It was a short call.

"Okay, excellent, thank you" was all she said before she hung up.

"Froyke's blood pressure and blood count look fine. He's recuperating," she said. "You know, back in med school, we practiced that thump on a CPR mannequin. None of us managed to save the poor doll. One or two of us broke her ribs, and the rest didn't hit hard enough. Your accuracy, it saved his life."

"You—you saved his life, I just… you're wonderful!" I told her. "And I'm going to kiss you," I declared, like one declares a tossed grenade. I leaned in and kissed her until we were both out of oxygen.

I thought I saw the hem of Ya'ara's floral dress fluttering out of the corner of my eye. But that was impossible, I realized. Her hologram was back in the Bavarian sky, where parents tended to die before their children. Eran didn't show up, either. I hoped they'd love Verbin just as much as I did. She would certainly love them.

38.

Muhammad bin-Yaakov, the son of a renowned Tripoli architect, had finally finished his architecture degree and received his diploma from the Rossetti Facoltà di Architettura at the University of Ferrara, Italy. He bid his friends farewell and flew to Pakistan, where he received a basic combat course at the Al-Qaeda training camp. He joined the secret elite squad, the Al-Quds Shahids, mostly owing to his fluency in English and Italian, coupled with his remarkable religious fervor—which only seemed to grow, fanned by his arrival at the camp and proximity to the sheikh.

In a small hospital at the Pakistan camp, Muhammad became Dr. Taissiri's final patient. His generous size allowed the good doctor to stuff him with an exceptionally large amount of gel. The entire unit, along with Dr. Taissiri and the rest of the shahids, was then transferred to the Shabwah camp, into the command of Imad Akbariyeh—the visionary behind the stuffed shahids.

After Imad's tragic demise, communications among the members of the units slowly wilted into nothing, and they found themselves scattered around the world, adrift like satellites without planets, waiting for the order to come. Muhammad returned to Ferrara and renewed his relationships with his university friends, and particularly with Emmanuella, his ex-girlfriend. Occasionally, living with the spirited, carefree Emmanuella, Muhammad would feel the prickly weeds of heresy growing within him—he attempted to nip them in the bud, but there was also the pain, the bleeding, pus-filled wounds that had become of his surgical stitches, the nausea he'd suffered from since his surgery. Water and sunlight for Muhammad's little garden of heresy, eating at the remnants of the motivation left over from his time in Pakistan. He began to wonder about a surgical procedure to remove the explosives from his gut, allowing him to build a new, less painful life for himself. He managed to convince himself that removing the explosives had no bearing on his true faith. After all—he had never heard of any sheikh, not even the holiest and most devout, who walked around with explosive charges in his belly.

Emmanuella convinced him to join her on a tour of his architectural roots—observe Spanish Muslim architecture in all its glory at the Great Mosque of Córdoba, and finish up at the Alhambra music festival. Her unending optimism allowed her to brush off any concerns about Muhammad's sudden bouts of nausea and vomiting, and he let her, jokingly proposing that she must've knocked him up.

They boarded a direct flight to Córdoba. Muhammad knew for a fact that the substance in his stomach was effectively invisible to security screening, and true to form, they passed smoothly through the Ferrara and Córdoba airports without incident. Any suspicion or hostility melted away in the warm glow of Emmanuella's smile.

The massive pillars and colorful arched dome of the Great Mosque lifted Muhammad's spirits. This glorious architecture, he told Emmanuella, stemmed from a deep familiarity with the movements of the sun and wind, the climate and colors of the Mediterranean. Emmanuella was captivated by the openness and spaciousness of Muslim architecture, so different from the defensiveness of Christian architecture.

By the time they headed to the Alhambra music festival, his sickness seemed to vanish completely. His mood improved considerably. For the first time, Muhammad allowed himself to embrace Emmanuella, even kiss her, in public—where everyone could see.

When they got to the Carlos V Palace, they were greeted by a long, arduous queue. The police officers responsible for the security procedure were slow but gave no one the benefit of the doubt. Six people had been killed in the last ETA[17] bombing, dozens injured. Each bag was opened and thoroughly emptied and searched. A pair of sniffing dogs pulled at their chains, eager to approach the crowd, their police handler struggling to restrain them. Muhammad shuddered, cold sweat dripping down his neck. The thought of being contaminated by the impure animals was unbearable. When he collected his belongings back into his bag, one of the animals rubbed against his leg. Muhammad cursed in Arabic and kicked it. The handler, enraged, slapped Muhammad in response.

The slap was not a powerful one, but the humiliation of it slammed into him like a ton of bricks.

Muhammad was furious, prepared to respond, but two of the policeman's colleagues approached, armed and threatening.

Emmanuella saw how offended Muhammad was and attempted to downplay the whole incident, laughing as if it were a joke. She hugged Muhammad, telling him this cop was an idiot, and they could go file a complaint against him later, if he liked.

Muhammad eyes flashed around. The ambient noise became an insufferable buzzing. The empty soft drink cans and food wrappers scattered around by the infidels swarming the palace charged him with an uncontrollable fury. He felt as if his head would explode. The words of the sheikh rose from the depths of his soul: "*There is no resistance, no resurrection, save by striking the infidels.*" Muhammad suddenly felt sick and ran toward the restrooms. He didn't make it and ended up vomiting on the tiled floor of the entrance hall. A group of nearby teenagers recoiled, exclaiming in disgust, fanning the fires of his humiliation.

Muhammad leaned against the wall. "There is no resistance, no resurrection, save by striking the infidels," he muttered. "No resistance—s-save by—"

---

17 The "Euskadi ta Askatasuna"—a terrorist organization of leftist Basque nationalists and separatists. -TK

Emmanuella finally caught up with him, breathless. “Where did you run off to?” she asked, and when he couldn’t answer, she dabbed at his face with a wet wipe and kissed him.

Muhammad pulled his cell phone from his pocket. His hand shook as he dialed the activation code.

“Who are you calling?” she asked, baffled.

“My Allah.” Muhammad embraced her and dialed again.

The sizable charge in his stomach went off—thirty-four dead, including Muhammad and Emmanuella.

The local press associated the bombing with the previous actions of the Basque ETA. Emmanuella’s father, who identified her corpse, said that she had been traveling in the company of a friend, one Muhammad bin-Yaakov. The search that followed, led by the local security service, led them straight to the University of Ferrara. Bruno Garibaldi, head of the Islamic terrorism department in the AISI, was summoned. In the room Muhammad had rented, they found three passports, cash, a book by the sheikh with a personal inscription, and documentation for a great number of flights—Tripoli, Libya, Pakistan, Yemen, Rome, Córdoba. The most meaningful find was a huge enlarged photo of the Al-Aqsa Mosque, at the Temple Mount in Jerusalem. In the foreground were ten masked men, and the words “the Al-Quds[18] Shahids” in black, swirling Arabic letters. A red arrow marked one of the masked men, who seemed large enough to be Muhammad. Bruno examined the material, endless profanities spilling from his mouth at Allah and all of his Muhammads.

---

18 “Al-Quds” (lit. “The holy one”) is the Arabic name for the city of Jerusalem. -TK

39.

Two days later was the thirty-day anniversary of the Rome bombing, and Bruno flew in for the ceremony as the Italian representative. Usually I avoided these kinds of things. When the sad ordeal at the cemetery was over, we drove back to Agur, where I promptly removed my nice Guccis.

"Kahanov isn't coming?"

"If Ami hasn't answered yet, he's probably still looking for his missing informer."

I uncorked the bottle of Munch, made by Ze'evik in his boutique vineyard in Bar Giyora, not far from here. The cork smelled promising. I passed it to Bruno, who nodded his approval.

"Excellent nose. Why Munch?"

"Why Garibaldi?"

"*Testa di cazzo*," he replied. "I didn't choose Garibaldi—he chose Munch. What's Munch?"

"Munch, like the crazy painter. My buddy harvests a ton of grapes and makes six different wines—each named for an artist. There's also Fellini, Antoine, Camus, Lennon. The white is James Joyce, I think."

We swirled the wine and shoved our noses into the glasses.

"*L'chaim*," Bruno said with his rolling Italian *l*.

"*Saluti*," I said and inquired if he thought the wine would pair well with a carbonara.

"Only if the carbonara is as good as the wine," the smart-ass replied, and I went to handle the food.

Garibaldi on his father's side, Ventura on his mother's, and despite the years of friendship and professional cooperation, I still didn't know if the names were real or self-chosen, and if *Ventura* hinted at Jewish roots. Two years ago, after the bombing at the Great Synagogue of Rome, we'd just taken out what the local press nicknamed "The Little Jihad" in a joint operation. We celebrated at Roberto's, at the Ambasciata d'Umbria—Bruno's home away from home. We drank like the fancy restaurant was a trucker dive bar. Roberto was happy to oblige. Bruno, who had hated Arabs ever since his tour in Libya, insisted that every single one of them "is a primitive and an idiot. And they all smell."

"You're exaggerating," I said. "It isn't all of them."

Bruno agreed and we raised another glass of Centerbe, the drain-cleaner liqueur—seventy-six percent alcohol by volume.

"Not all of them, just around ninety-six… no, make it ninety-eight percent," he said and asked Roberto for yesterday's *Corriere*.

Roberto wiped his hands on his apron and vanished into his office by the kitchen, returning with yesterday's edition, featuring an interview with Oriana Fallaci.

"Motherfuckers are turning this place into Euro-Arabia," he said, paraphrasing Fallaci. "Do you know what she said? Let me read it for you: what you fail to understand, is that these fuckers, these bin Ladens, they think they're allowed to kill your children because you drink wine, go to the theater and enjoy classical music. *Fanculo*, goddamn primitive motherfuckers. You, Ehrlich, you're a dissident. If I were you, I'd round them all up and *smack*. Voilà! No more Islamic problem. You guys fuck up your one job—you have one job! Kill them when they're young. Historically, it is your responsibility—but you're sloppy, and so they make it to Europe and fuck it up for us, too." Occasional points of this tirade were highlighted by Bruno banging the bottle against the table.

"Have you ever considered a career in Israeli politics?" I suggested, adding that nothing would get him elected faster than that exact kind of rant. Probably as the minister for Arab Affairs.

The angry whistle of the boiling teapot snapped me away from Rome, back into my kitchen. I poured the boiling water into the pasta pot and patiently waited for Bruno to reveal whatever news he most likely had for me. He seemed in no hurry to do so. I decided not to squeeze so that the intel didn't come out with a deformed head.

"You like those shoes?" I pointed at the nine-hundred-dollar Guccis on his feet.

"Of course. What am I, a peasant?" he answered, nodding at my Blundstones, which lay under the table. "Why do you ask?"

"I bought the same ones… nine hundred dollars. Damn things are unwearable."

Bruno laughed. "Nine hundred dollars? You could've bought the whole store for that. Probably a fucking Arab. You got ripped off."

I received my scolding silently, deciding not to mention that the shoe salesman was an Israeli expatriate who had insisted on sharing his IDF war stories.

"*Yalla*," Bruno said, seeming to enjoy his skillful pronunciation of the Arabic word. "Business before pasta."

He started from the top, telling me again about the results of the investigation following the Alhambra bombing, leading them all the way back to Ferrara. He took out his phone and showed me some photos of Muhammad bin-Yaakov's passports, which seemed to have carried him all over Europe.

This, while troubling, was no longer surprising. Old news. But that was when Bruno pulled the rabbit out of his hat, sliding his finger dramatically across the screen to reveal a group photo of masked shahids standing in front of the Al-Aqsa Mosque at the Temple Mount.

"Oh." My excitement was evident by the fact that I whistled inwardly, like a child first learning how. Bruno informed me that the photograph was undergoing identification processes, but so far only in Rome. They feared a leak and shared the material with no one—"except for you, *cazzo*. I guess you'll find more than anyone and tell less than anyone."

We tried to guess whether the name of the group—"the Al-Quds

Shahids"—and the Temple Mount in the background were there merely to reinforce the religious link and their sense of vision, or if they referred to concrete targets. There was no way to know. Figuring that out would be up to the researchers and threat assessors. Down in infantry, we focused on eliminating the assholes.

The kitchen timer magnetized to the exhaust hood finally beeped.

"Bruno, move the pasta to a bowl."

He stopped the beeping timer and transferred the steaming pasta into a large bowl.

"Carbonara with strozzapreti. You know what that means? Priest-stranglers, we call them."

"May they strangle the rabbis as well. Amen," I prayed, remembering the rabbi who had insisted on converting Ya'ara and Eran to Judaism, and beat four eggs, pouring them into the pasta bowl. I added parmesan shavings, black pepper and some cream and mixed it all with the fried chunks of bacon. I added some cubes of smoked goose to deepen the flavor. The carbonara, cooked à la Luciano Pavarotti, was a brutal deviation from my paleo diet—but it had its advantages. An impressive capacity to soak up alcohol was one of them. "Another Munch, or something new?"

"The Munch was excellent," said Bruno. He took the second bottle lying in wait and uncorked it. He happily sniffed at the cork, then at the bottle.

"*Na zdarovje!*"

"*Na zdarovje!*" I sipped and held my glass up to the kitchen light. The white halo was thin and delicate, and the wine was perfectly ripe.

"Bruno, do you think everything would be different if the Muslims just drank some wine occasionally?"

"Oh, they drink, don't you worry. Those fuckers drink. In the dark, where Muhammad can't see them…"

He raised a finger. "*Neshama sheli*," he said with his rolling Hebrew. "My soul, *mia anima*—you know I love you guys. Truly. But I need an honest answer. All of Europe is shitting its pants over these bombings, and here, at the center of the conflict—nothing?! You should know, word around the community is that you sneaky fucks have found some screening tech and you're not sharing it with anyone, so the enemy won't find out you have it."

"No new technology," I quickly assured him. "For now. Our people are working on it, along with everyone else from the Engineering Corps to Technion[19] professors. Once we'll have the tech, you'll know, because we'll be selling it to you. These technologies are the backbone of this country's economy."

Bruno kept his eyes on mine. "How, then?"

"Elementary, my dear Bruno. Our security people are trained to smell an Arab from a mile away. Anyone suspicious—anyone 'nearly' suspicious"—I added the relevant air quotes—"we put in a locked, armored room, pass through an X-ray, and subject to an intimate bodily search. Procedures that would never be approved in your 'Euro-Arabia.'"

"And that's it?"

"Yeah, it's a simple solution. It's only your hypocrisy that's stopping you from implementing it."

His face crumpled, and for a moment he seemed on the verge of tears—like an indignant child, shocked and insulted. I couldn't help but start laughing.

"Hypocrites? Us?!" He slapped his chest. "There is no hypocrisy. Financial interests, sure. Cheap energy, and a market of—oh, two billion Arabs? More than all of Europe combined, paying full prices for our tycoons' merchandise... but hypocrisy? How dare you."

Bruno was getting worked up. A small blue vein pulsed visibly at his forehead. "Have you ever seen a tycoon or a politician at the scene of one of these bombings? Never. Because it never happens. Only the poor get fucked. The people out on the streets. *Puta de madre.*"

It was a sort of epiphany. Unfortunately, the very rich and the politi-

---

19 The Israel Institute of Technology. A prestigious science and technology research university.

cally inclined never seemed to be the victims of the bombings. "Unless you see this as the war that it is and start acting like it, you're going to lose," I said.

"The Americans estimate twenty, twenty-five Arabs still sneaking around, we have no idea where, any one of which could pass any security check and explode whenever, wherever they want. These fucking bastards… got us hoping they'd go ahead and blow up already, spare us this… fear…"

The smell of the carbonara attracted the other Garibaldi, who stalked quietly into the room, placed his head in my lap and made a soft, rumbling sound. Bruno watched the behemoth, beaming fatherly pride, and then stretched and turned to me. "And now I give you the crème de la crème," he said, pinching his fingers together.

"I have a guy, small-time mafioso—medium-time, maybe—who sells expired meds to the Arabs and imports opium at half price. I give him a little breathing room, he gives me information."

Just like Kahanov and his abu Seif.

"Now you listen to me, *cazzo*, you listen well. This Mafioso *cazzo*, he swore to me on his mother's life. A Sicilian mafioso does not swear on his mother's life for nothing. Someone in south Lebanon is offering an entire tanker of PETN for sale, *capisce*?"

He slid his finger again. A large red tanker appeared on his phone screen, covered with Arabic text reading "caution, flammable; hazardous materials."

I stood up with the full intention of kissing him, but then he had to go and slide another photo, and another—there were apparently three, nearly identical red tankers.

"Three?" A chill crawled up my spine.

Bruno nodded. "One real, two decoys. They're primitive assholes, but they're not dumb."

"You could blow up a city with that much stuff," I said.

Bruno raised his eyes at me, frowning. "You're pale. Everything okay?"

"Almost," I said. "And what isn't will be."

Bruno nodded.

Afterwards, the conversation returned to the usual topics. Bruno tried to take a photo of Garibaldi, but every time he clicked, the slobbering monstrosity turned its head to the side.

"*Hijo de puta...*" muttered Bruno.

Around 2 a.m., I drove him to the airport. We hugged and I promised to keep him updated. I summoned Froyke and Ami to an urgent meeting before I'd even left the airport.

40.

At 5 a.m., Ami showed up at my office, and together we went to see Froyke. He seemed a bit ashen but kept insisting that he was fine. The director was out of the country—Froyke, who'd been filling in, made sure that every available resource was devoted to the task. Exposing and neutralizing the tanker was now the top priority of the intelligence community. Nora's situation report painted a bleak picture; 9900's satellites had located only two out of the three tankers reported by the Italian source. Thermal analysis of the two tankers had shown them to be full of water—meaning that the third, which most likely contained fifteen thousand gallons of liquid explosive, was still ticking away in some hidden location. Unless we found it in time, it would literally blow up in our faces. Observation and reconnaissance teams, some disguised as Arabs, had been sent out to perform searches, along with 9900 airborne reconnaissance. Our main assumption was that the tanker would be hidden in a heavily populated civilian area—maybe near a school, or a hospital—to prevent us from carrying out an air strike.

Ami, who'd been frantically texting during Nora's briefing, seemed extremely unhappy. He reported that abu Seif had stopped responding to his calls. This Abu, as we'd begun calling him, was our only connection to the truck; then again, Abu was also a collaborator, and collaborators are notoriously fickle. Living under the threat of the Shin Bet on one hand and Hezbollah counterintelligence on the other can make anyone a bit unstable. Therefore, Ami decided to raid Ghajar, Abu's village, and find the little pissant, alive or dead.

An undercover team of disguised border guard soldiers entered the village and secured the perimeter. Three drug enforcement bureau squad cars came in immediately after them and raided the clan's central complex as noisily as possible. Ami's team—men from the Service in blue police uniforms—located abu Seif in a hidden cellar at his parents' house and arrested him. We all breathed a sigh of relief. At Froyke's request, he was flown back to Tel Aviv in a police helicopter.

Later, Ami and I drove to a snug and secure apartment in Tel Aviv's old north and found Abu terrified to the point of hysteria, and starving. When Ami asked if he was okay with hummus and falafel, Abu grimaced and responded, "Thai House—the best Asian food." And a small, mischievous smile flashed past his face.

Abu continuously switched stories as to why he'd suddenly lost contact. Each excuse was more ridiculous than the last. Ami kept applying pressure. The security guard we sent to the Thai House came back with enough takeaway to feed a battalion. Abu ate and calmed down a bit. After coffee, Ami hugged him like a brother and thanked him for his loyal service to the state of Israel. Abu—perhaps expecting increased compensation—hugged him back, smiling. Ami's voice was amazingly soft as he began to explain, still tightly embracing Abu, how Hezbollah counterintelligence would most likely react once they discovered that Abu had betrayed them, reported their comings and goings in south Lebanon to the Shin Bet.

Abu's smile remained for as long as he managed to convince himself that this was some kind of joke, but once it had cracked, his face quickly crumpled into horrified, bitter tears. Ami still held him as he calmly described what they would do to Abu's wife, his children, perhaps his elderly parents.

It wasn't long before Abu was begging for "a thousand pardons" from Ami, who was now apparently his "best friend, brother and father." He then, finally, confessed: the Shiite clan, his drug suppliers, had kidnapped him and demanded to be paid a blinding amount of money after accusing him of an act of lowly deception he swore he had really had nothing to do with. He added that the matter had been solved by a "judge," a local Qadi[20], who had ruled that Abu must leave them his brand-new Mercedes-Maybach. Ami sent a team to corroborate.

Ami informed Abu that he would inject a dog tracker chip in his goddamn neck, and on the other hand promised him a new Maybach on the condition that he behaved. He questioned Abu about his relationship with Nawata, again and again, until he was certain that they'd never met face-to-face, and that Nawata couldn't recognize abu Seif.

Froyke, who arrived soon after that, looked at me, then at Ami, and a slow, wicked grin pushed the sickness and exhaustion from his face.

"So Nawata has never actually seen abu Seif, huh?" he said, raising his finger. Funny that it was the so-called responsible adult among us who was the first to figure it out. Wordlessly, Ami and I caught on.

---

20 A Qadi is the magistrate or judge of an Islamic Shari⊠a court, who also exercises extrajudicial functions (such as mediation). -TK

41.

We left abu Seif with one the babysitters and went to sit at a small neighborhood café hidden in an inner garden. We were excited, talking quickly. A military raid, at a scale of a single company, seemed to be the way to go—but there was no contingency plan for the spotting and capture of an enormous ticking bomb with the face of an innocent tanker. Therefore, this ran the risk of becoming a slow, convoluted process of information gathering and meticulous planning. Every little thing would have to be approved and confirmed all the up to the prime minister. A pain in the ass, really. All three of us agreed that there was no time for this. Time is a key player in cases like these, and right now it was playing against us. And so, bit by bit, a plan was coming together.

Ami spoke perfect Palestinian Arabic. We decided he would pose as abu Seif, and we'd head out to meet with Nawata, with me posing as Abu's bodyguard. We shared our plan with Froyke, who was apprehensive, to say the least. Honestly, so were we—it was far from perfect, but it was the best we had under the circumstances. Ami sent the security guard to the nearby mall to buy a change of clothes and asked Abu if he had any particular preference. The jackass answered, with all seriousness, that he preferred Tommy Hilbiger.

"If Abu wants Hilbiger," said Ami, "Abu gets Hilbiger." Another security guard was given abu Seif's old clothes and sent to the dry cleaners, ordered to pay double and come back with the clothes as soon as humanly possible.

When the guard left, Digital Albert came in and set up his workstation. Abu, thrilled by the fact that everyone seemed to be friends again, sat on the old floral sofa, under a framed old certificate of appreciation from the Jewish National Fund, blatantly expressing his enjoyment at smoking my Cohiba. Albert finished planting his computer's IP somewhere in the Syrian battle zone, near Halab, and informed us he was all set.

Ami dialed the Lebanese number Abu had provided and left Nawata a voice message in abu Seif's name. The number, according to Albert, was listed under the pharmacy in the Beirut teaching hospital. Twenty minutes later, Abu's pink cell received a call from a phone number Albert recognized as the result of a number-generating app. Abu Seif nodded at me excitedly, covering the phone's microphone with his finger. "Nawata!"

Ami signaled him to keep talking, while Albert tapped his keyboard like a concert pianist, trying to trace the call.

Abu, following my instructions, told Nawata that his clients were interested in purchasing a small, initial sample of the untraceable explosive. Nawata explained, with seemingly infinite patience, that the substance could be turned into said explosive by changing its state from liquid to gel. "The process," he explained, "is very simple, but the formula will cost you extra."

He also made it clear that he did not deal with samples. "It's all or nothing. There is only one of these tankers in the neighborhood, and no shortage of potential buyers. So let me know in an hour. Nine hundred thousand dollars, and not a cent less."

Not exactly pocket change. I was certain that this demand would raise a shitload of red flags, but similarly confident in Froyke's ability to somehow make it work.

Albert sent the recording to the lab. They also failed to identify Nawata's location. However, voice pattern analysis revealed that Nawata believed everything he said. Froyke handled the banker. Apparently, the size of the required sum had rattled him—Froyke managed to assuage him by quoting the late JFK: "The Chinese use two brushstrokes to write the word 'crisis.' One brushstroke stands for danger; the other for opportunity."

I chimed in with one of my personal favorites, Thucydides' classic mantra: "Fortune favors the bold."

"Fuck protocol," Ami said, contributing his own two cents, and we concluded the historic session.

Soon after that, I received an alert that nine hundred thousand dollars had been deposited in a Zurich bank account. A biometric scan of my iris was the only way to transfer funds to or from this account. I registered as an authorized signer and, several failed attempts later, received the bank's confirmation. Only then did I think of adding Ami as the second authorized signer—a kind of insurance policy, to make it difficult for the Victor/Nawata party to attempt to gain control by separating me from Ami.

As per Nawata's instructions, we transferred five thousand dollars in advance, divided between three accounts, in the Cayman Islands, Adams Island, and New Jersey. Apparently Victor was exceedingly cautious. In the meanwhile, Ami's team up north confirmed abu Seif's kidnapping alibi. In the midst of all this uncertainty, it was surprisingly comforting.

Okay, I said to myself. *Here we go*. The first step to eliminating their production and distribution chain.

42.

With the exception of Eran, there is nothing I love more than these moments, just before the shift; combat-readiness mechanisms snap into action, adrenaline swells and widens the arteries, more oxygen filled the lunges. The muscles stretch, the senses sharpen, and the mind empties from all things unrelated. I am sharp and full of purpose and see nothing other than what is required for the accomplishment of the task ahead.

"A person," Froyke told me once, "is sixty percent water, and forty percent past." And certainly, before my combat-readiness armor engulfs me and seals me off from the outside world, I am usually hurled into the past, almost always to Eran. But this time was different.

I recalled that mission in Beirut. Guli, my partner, was shot in the throat; the tourniquet wasn't working. The extraction team was telling me to retreat without him. Guli, who was astoundingly lucid, asked me to put a bullet in his temple and get it over with.

I came home with my tail between my legs.

I sat before Ya'ara and couldn't stop the tears from falling.

She was sitting by the pool, barefoot as usual, strumming a German requiem on her harp. When she was done, she asked me what it was that I wanted from life.

I didn't know what to say, so I said nothing.

Today I know that I am most likely an adrenaline addict who suffers from a chronically enlarged sense of duty.

"I don't know anyone," she said, picking at the strings, "who loves Michael Kohlhaas and sympathizes with him more than you do."

Heinrich von Kleist was my father's favorite writer; though he shared the title with Goethe, Nietzsche and Hermann Broch. The massive library he left behind contained hundreds of nonfiction books, most of which had to do with quantum physics, and one shelf of fiction. On the day of my bar mitzvah, Mother took me to his study, which she had kept exactly as it was.

"Read the books your father loved, and get to know him," she said, and I devoured them, desperately, book after book. I liked Nietzsche, especially his cryptic humor. Hermann Broch failed to hold my interest back then, but I learned to love him years later. One line of his stayed with me to this day—"The heaviest costs are imposed by the merciful." But I fell in love with Heinrich von Kleist. I saw myself as Michael Kohlhaas, burning down the kingdom that killed my father, burning and murdering without mercy.

"You are a cripple. And someday, I know, you will leave me," Ya'ara said to me.

43.

The air force helicopter that Froyke arranged was waiting at our landing pad, but the security officer wouldn't let us bring abu Seif into the compound.

"I can tie him to a rope, have him run after the chopper," said Ami. The security officer realized she really had no alternatives, so she blindfolded Abu and put him on the helicopter.

On the way, we received word that the Shin Bet's undercover team had been in a car accident. Froyke alerted the GOC, who brought in a replacement undercover team of Unit 217 commandos. Fast response always comes with a toll, and this time it was the risk of an info leak. Too many different parties were involved.

Froyke began to seem hesitant, again reminding us of the DM's suggestion—to wait, and better prepare. But Ami and I were adamant.

"We have a brief window of opportunity here," I told him. "We can't afford to miss it." He seemed to be convinced.

Abu Seif was mostly petrified during the flight, only piping up occasionally to ask if we were there yet.

Around midnight, we sat down with the command team from the Egoz guerilla and special reconnaissance unit. The unit commander was there, along with the intelligence officer, the deputy G3, and the captain of our extraction team. There was something, I thought, about this captain's posture and speech patterns that was reminiscent of Eran. I asked Froyke and Ami, and neither of them seemed to notice the resemblance. They just stared at me sympathetically instead.

Froyke briefed them on the materials relating to the operation, ever since the first bombing in Rome.

"I'm sure you all realize that whoever has control of this substance holds the key to open all kinds of doors that we would very much prefer remained closed."

The captain, who reminded me more of Eran with each passing minute, asked why we didn't just blow up the factory where they made the stuff.

Froyke shot me a half-smile and said, "We're looking into that option."

The answer made it clear that the option had been rejected with no room for discussion, either by the DM or the prime minister.

We went over the predicted scenarios with the Egoz fighters, marked the coordinates of contact points, reviewed communications procedures and codes. They were excited, eager. It was understandable. If the operation had gone through the usual channels, passed through the Intelligence Corps Special Operations and our own operations branch, either Matkal or Flotilla 13 would most likely have gotten this rare treat.

I requested for a UAV to be at our disposal until the operation was concluded, at least one experienced bomb squad, and an antitank team. I also asked for a chopper to be on standby in case we managed to take prisoners.

We got it all.

The GOC provided us with his personal ceramic vests. A technician from the Service hooked us up with minuscule, nearly invisible communication systems, and tuned them to the relevant frequencies for the Egoz unit and command.

Before we went our separate ways, the unit commander walked up to me, looking like a man desperate to get something off his chest. "You—you're RP, right?"

I nodded, and Ami couldn't help but add, "The very same, he and no other."

The young commander eagerly shook my hand. "We took first place at the special units joint exercise," he said, as if to put our minds at ease despite it being them, not the Matkal units, who would be covering us.

"We know," said Froyke. "And around here, no one can do the job better than you."

The scouting party was briefed and left toward the meeting point. Froyke joined the command post. The undercover Unit 217 commandos arrived—they seemed like nice kids, and they cheerfully got to work on our disguises. Ami changed into abu Seif's dry-cleaned clothes. They were a perfect match. When he wore his dark Stevie Wonder–style sunglasses, he looked like a perfect, textbook Arab—apart from his bulging Romanian Adam's apple.

They had a harder time with me, mostly because of my shoe size. They took away my Blundstones, and after a brief argument we agreed on Palladium boots, but there weren't any in my size, so I got the Blundstones back, after they'd been torn up a bit and smeared with something black and disgusting.

They'd also arranged for a battered old Subaru pickup truck with Lebanese plates. A tracker was installed in the pickup, and the three of us were off to Ghajar, to Abu's house. Abu seemed to be quite comfortable in the midst of all the chaos. He asked me for another cigar and lit it, puffing happily and pompously.

When we reached the arabesque-adorned iron gate of the clan complex, two armed men signaled us to stop. After recognizing Abu, they opened the gate and jogged after the car until Ami stopped, upon which they could conduct their exhaustive hugging-and-kissing ceremony.

We went inside, and while Abu went to arrange some refreshments, Ami and I sank into the old sofas and silently stared at each other. I checked my wristwatch. We left in fifteen minutes. I went into combat mode, sliding a bullet into the chamber, just as Ami did the same, as if we'd coordinated. As we smiled to one another, two short, decisive bursts of gunfire sounded outside.

We jumped to our feet, weapons cocked, but it was too late.

"Where's that fucking Abu?" Ami hissed as the front door crashed open, along with two windows. Black, threatening rifle barrels were pointing at us from each one.

"Which one of you is Ehrlich?" the man who entered through the front door asked in Arabic, returning his gun to its shoulder holster. He was squat and thick, like a German sausage. Ami and I stood together. The Sausage approached Ami and held out his hand. Ami glanced at me and surrendered his Glock. The Sausage shoved the gun into his belt, his eyes trained on Ami.

"You must be Kahanov," he said.

There was no longer room for doubt. Abu had sold us to the Hezbollah.

In the meanwhile, one of the other two men relieved me from my own Glock and surprisingly settled for that, not frisking me any further. We weren't the only ones playing it by ear, apparently.

"Cuff them!" he told the other one.

"Hands and feet?" asked the younger one.

"Just hands, unless you want to carry them. They're not going anywhere. Let's go."

44.

The one thing we had going for us, the only reason we were both still alive, was that they knew they needed both of us to authorize the money transfer. This meant we had to find a way out of there before the transactions took place. Ami was hurled into the front seat of the Ford Transit that took the lead, with the Sausage. I was tossed into the refrigerated box of an Isuzu truck. I found myself cuffed, lying on a pile of green wooden crates enforced by thin bands of metal. RPG-32, antitank rocket launchers. I wondered if this was the shipment they had gotten from Victor and set to figuring out my next step. I was still wearing the tiny transmitter installed by Ami's technician, which had fortunately not been activated yet. Even better, they hadn't taken away my Blundstones. A small leather pouch was sewn into my left boot, and nestled within was a small knife with a folding steel blade. A gift from Eran, who had written to me then that "no organizational consultant is complete without his letter opener."

I estimated I had no more than five or six minutes. I hugged my knees, pulling them as far up as I could. For some reason, I was struck with the ridiculous notion of pulling the knife out with my teeth. Once that failed, I folded forward and reached toward the boot with my cuffed hands. It took me four attempts, but on the fifth I managed to pull out the compact knife, dangling between my two pinkies. Now I had to somehow move it into my palm and fold out the blade.

As I began the process, the asshole driver hit a speed bump and the knife clattered away from my hands. I threw myself on the floor, picked it up, held on to it for dear life, and managed to pull the blade out with my teeth. Once I'd achieved that, cutting the cable tie was a cakewalk. The first thought that came to me was that I needed to contact Froyke. The second was that by the time the cavalry showed up, the bad guys would have finished us.

Were we headed for the same fate as Ron Arad[21]? Panic gripped me momentarily. His last-known photo appeared in my mind—bearded and sunken. I decided against the attempt to contact Ami and risk exposing myself. I would not be Ron Arad. The metal strip hugging the wooden box beside me was thin and sharp. I wrapped my hand in my shirt and leaned into it with every ounce of mass I had, until it gave.

This was the turning point.

I pulled an RPG out of one of the crates and armed it. Then I reconsidered and pulled out three more launchers, armed them and placed them on the floor beside me. Then I waited. If I blew the door now, I'd be putting Ami in immediate mortal danger. I tried to activate the radio and whisper to Froyke, but the thick walls of the refrigerated truck blocked the transmission. Several more minutes elapsed before the vehicles came to a stop and I could make out the sound of approaching steps. I tightened my grip on the launcher and tried to recall the last time I'd fired one of these.

The lock on the door rattled, and an armed young hostile opened the back of the truck, his jaw dropping when he found himself staring down the mouth of the launcher, a rocket trained directly on his face.

"Shut up, and you'll live," I whispered.

He offered no response.

I raised my shoulder and the barrel inched closer to his face. "Shut up," I repeated, "and you'll live."

---

21 Lieutenant Colonel Ron Arad, was a weapon systems officer in the Israeli Air Force who is officially classified as MIA since 1986, but is widely presumed dead. He was lost on a mission over Lebanon, captured by the Shiite group Amal and later handed over to the Hezbollah. -TK

He nodded, eyes wide.

"Now hand over your weapon and get in the truck."

He surrendered his short-barreled Kalashnikov and held out his hand. I grabbed his elbow and his wrist and twisted, flinging him inside and slamming his head against the wall of the truck. He fell silently. I checked his wrist and failed to recognize either a pulse or the lack of one. This was no time to take prisoners. I broke his neck, just in case.

They had Ami, and the possibility of catching up with the tanker seemed to grow more distant by the second. I had no time to figure out what to tie him with. I recalled the words of "Colonel" Mizrahi, something along the lines of, "It's a real bitch, dealing with a death of an enemy you killed in close combat. But trust me, it's a lot harder when you're the other guy."

I slid out of the truck, hefting the pair of armed missile launchers and the short-barreled Kalash'. I needed to act quickly, before they came looking for him. Contacting Froyke and mounting a rescue would have to wait until I got a grip on the situation and prepared for the encounter with Nawata and his tanker.

I got under the truck and crawled to a better vantage point. The Sausage was standing by the Ford Transit furthest from me, smoking a cigarette and holding abu Seif's pink cell phone. The other hostile was leaning against the front of the van, the barrel of his gun pressed into the back of Ami's neck. Any move I made at this point, I realized, would get Ami executed.

The Sausage was tossing worrying glances at the direction of my truck. The distance I'd have to crawl across to get a clean line of fire was too great. I considered getting into my truck, quickly and discreetly disposing of the driver, and then using the truck to charge into the other van. Every alternative I found seemed to leave Ami at the mercy of one of the two armed men beside him. I estimated that shooting the younger one would cause the Sausage to take Ami out before checking on him. On the other hand, a nonlethal shot at the Sausage would probably cause the kid to drop everything and come to the aid of his leader. That, most likely, was my best option.

I shuffled around on my belly until I was facing the Sausage. I pressed the barrel of the rocket launcher to the ground, upside down so that the trigger guard pointed upwards. This still allowed me to fire but rendered the sight useless. I tilted the launcher slightly to the side, setting both the trigger guard and the sight on the other side at a forty-five-degree angle to the ground. Now the mouth of the launcher was trained right on the legs of the Sausage, who was yelling at the guy in the truck to "move his ass."

I engaged, taking the oddest shot of my life. The rocket singed the ground, sand billowing around it, taking his right leg. The Sausage went down, wailing horribly. The other one pushed Ami away, diving for his superior as expected. The other two rockets, I fired from a much more convenient crouching position, and the world lost two more saints. I hurried to cut Ami out of his cable ties. He looked around him, amazed, and, upon realizing what had happened, raised an imaginary hat and bowed deeply and theatrically.

Abu's pink phone had fallen from the Sausage's dead fingers. I picked it up and tossed it to Ami.

"Nawata. Call him—now!" I yelled at him and raised Froyke on the comm. He expelled a sigh of relief and told me that half the Lebanese army was struggling to hold back a large Hezbollah force approaching our location.

"I'm sending in the extraction team!"

"Negative, Nawata isn't here yet. Wait, I repeat, wait. Out."

"Let's go!" yelled Ami, leaping into the driver's seat. I hopped inside and we headed back onto the road. "I talked to him. He changed the location. Twelve miles north, at the abandoned village. He won't wait more than fifteen minutes. The army is on its way there."

I made some quick calculations and realized that we were exiting the area agreed upon with the scouting team that was supposed to provide us with cover and extraction. Also, in all likelihood, we were driving into a trap. I comforted myself with a timeworn IDF mantra—"It is what it is, and it'll have to do."

Ami pushed the engine to its limits. The speedometer showed 112 miles per hour, and the tachometer was well into the red.

"If the engine doesn't explode, we'll be there in eight or nine minutes, and…"

He nodded, and his foot went all the way to the floor.

45.

The sky was beginning to gray. We would lose the cover of darkness in about an hour, at which point we would find ourselves in the middle of Lebanon, in full light, outside the area defined for our scouting team. Ami was asked to call Nawata again so that the UAV could identify his vehicle. Three Lebanese military APCs passed us, probably on their way to where we had just come from. Some distance behind them was a Toyota pickup with a heavy machine gun mounted in the back and a small green-and-yellow Hezbollah flag—only then did I notice that a similar flag was tied to our own radio antenna. I waved at them, and they waved back.

I received a transmission from the intelligence officer. The UAV identified the tanker. "The heat signature seems to be a match," he said. "'Seems to be' is the shitty cousin of 'maybe.'"

"Check again," I hissed.

Ami-Seif brought the van to a screeching halt next to a black Mercedes, and he and Nawata engaged in the local sequence of kissing and hugging. I stood in the back, my weapon cocked and ready—as abu Seif's bodyguard, I was expected to. I scanned the perimeter and noticed some movement in the windows of the abandoned houses surrounding us.

We contacted the bank. Froyke informed me that the heat signature was approved as a match, and we were okay to proceed. We each brought an eye to the camera of his laptop for the biometric scan. One hundred and thirty nerve-wrenching second later, Nawata received electronic conformation for the rest of the payment, four hundred thousand dollars. I hoped Albert managed to get into his account as planned. Nawata handed us a folder with the vehicle license and registration, along with the keys. He then drove away, along with the four snipers he had hidden in the houses around us during the exchange. We removed the camouflage net from the tanker and headed out. Ami took the lead in the van, and I drove the tanker.

"They're laying out roadblocks on the southern roads, including yours. When you approach, we'll take it down," reported Froyke, sounding stronger and happier than he had in a long time. I laughed, despite myself, when I was suddenly struck by the image of him charging the roadblock and smacking the Hezbollah around with his prosthesis. There was nothing funny about our situation, however. They'd recognized us—and they were concentrating their forces. I slammed on the gas pedal and sped past Ami's van. According to Froyke, they were preparing another Egoz unit to fly in for backup. I was driving too fast to plan anything properly. I told Ami to pull over, then asked if he knew of any way to blow up the tanker. He did not.

In the distance, we could just make out the APCs and Toyotas that made up the roadblock, a combined effort of the Lebanese military and Hezbollah. We decided that I would turn the tanker around and drive it in reverse into the roadblock, hoping that their fire would ignite it, and then run to Ami's van and we'd drive back north, away from the roadblock and the possibility of being stuck in crossfire between them and the incoming Egoz team.

About five hundred yards from the roadblock, I took some small-arms fire. A barrage of mortar fire, 52 and 81 millimeter, was immediately returned from the direction of the supporting Egoz fighters. I exploited the resulting decrease in gunfire to turn the tanker around to face north. The radius of the turn was too small, and the tanker rocked alarmingly from side to side before steadying. I straightened it toward the roadblock and put it in reverse.

Ami drove behind me in the van. Around two hundred yards away, I pinned down the gas pedal with the Kalash' and jumped out. The tanker lost speed but kept rolling toward the roadblock. Ami sped toward me, also in reverse, and I had to leap to the side to avoid from getting hit. When I climbed in, he grinned at me and told me he'd spoken to the bomb squad. "We need to heat the inside of the tanker to detonate the stuff. Now, MacGyver, any idea about how to generate that much heat?"

"Yeah. Stop the car."

We stepped out of the car, each holding a rocket launcher.

"Focus fire on the engine and the gas tank," I said. "We need to ignite the gasoline."

The tanker had come to a stop in the meanwhile and was now surrounded by Lebanese soldiers and Hezbollah. The UAV circled above us. I fired the first rocket at a Hezbollah Toyota that made it way toward us, and the second one at the tanker's engine, which was destroyed but did not burn. Ami fired and gas started flowing out. He fired once more and the gas ignited.

Now all we could do was wait.

The UAV suddenly made a sharp turn and dove, nose first, with a force that tore the tanker open—there was a loud crash, but the PETN still didn't ignite.

The fire grew taller, bluer. Hotter. And…

The explosion was magnificent.

Finally. Flames rose into the air like fiery snakes, burning anything they touched. They were getting closer to us as well, and we drove away. Five hundred yards from the explosion, Froyke told us that they were bringing down smoke, a hundred behind us and ahead of us, and ordered us to hold our position.

I managed to hear the commander of Egoz barking orders at the backup team. They created a thick wall of black smoke masking us from the roadblock, and another one around a hundred yards to our north. I felt like Moses, walking in the rift on the floor of the Red Sea.

"Move, I'm coming down." Froyke's voice sounded practically giddy on the comm. The CH-53 Sea Stallion helicopter landed at our feet, with Froyke standing on the landing skid like goddamn Colonel Kilgore.

46.

The chopper took to the air once we were safely inside, and after a hug from Froyke and a handshake from the Egoz commander, "Colonel" Mizrahi lunged at me out of nowhere and, upon noticing Ami, pulled him into his arms as well.

"My boys, get in here, my brave boys! RP and Kahanov, I planted these beautiful flowers," he proudly announced to anyone who would listen.

"Aren't you supposed to be in the West Bank?" I asked.

"Affirmative. But I heard my boys were here and I came right over."

I tried to imagine the winding, unsecure route that the intel had taken, all the way from Northern Command to the West Bank. The helicopter crossed the border, distancing itself from the fire and the plumes of black smoke that rose up from the site of the explosion, obscuring the sun.

"This is what I call high-intensity conflict," chuckled the Egoz commander. Mizrahi shook his head.

"No, this is what they call RP. Two hundred and thirty pounds of rage and power."

The words took me back to Ya'ara. Brahms's German requiem played in the background, and she was half-singing, half-reciting an odd *recitativo* in her low, sincere alto:

"To achieve the cruel and absolute justice he demanded, Michael Kohlhaas, our brave protagonist, burned the mansion of the evil nobleman Wenzel von Tronka, and then the entire kingdom." And suddenly, barefoot and floating, Ya'ara was gone.

Ami suggested we head to Babai's, but I was already sinking, deeper and deeper into my abyss. Seeing them together, Ami, Froyke and Mizrahi, threw me back to that terrible day, when they came up to my porch in Agur.

That night I sat beside Eran. I uncorked a bottle and told him that I had only managed to get out of the cable tie thanks to the small Browning knife he had given me. Eran smiled and said nothing. At Eran's bris—a procedure I had initially objected to, and it was Ya'ara, of all people, who'd insisted—our friends came to celebrate. I didn't invite them; Ya'ara and Bella had become close friends over the years, and this was most likely their doing. The DM came, and Froyke, the "Colonel," Ami, Bella, Nehemiah—who had come all the way from Princeton—and even Amaziah, the organization's rabbi, who came for his pound of flesh. He did circumcise Eran, eventually, but only after an exhaustive array of warnings delivered first by me and then by Ami, who threatened violent retaliation in case of "even the smallest damage to the goods."

When the uninvited guests scattered, the rabbi approached me and asked to speak privately.

"Ya'ara must be converted to Judaism," he said. "Otherwise Eran will not be acknowledged as a Jew."

"I won't put her through that Mikveh bullshit with the frogs. She's happy the way she is, and that's enough."

The rabbi spoke at length about the problems Eran might encounter for no fault of his own. I explained that Eran was not, nor would he be, a Jewish criminal in need of the Law of Return[22].

"Rabbi," I said, "am I a Jew, as far as you're concerned?"

"Of course. A good Jew, even."

---

22 An Israeli law which gives all Jews the right to come and live in Israel and to gain Israeli citizenship.

"If I'm a Jew, so is my son. Let's leave it at that."

"It doesn't work that way," he persisted. "The authorities—"

"Authorities my ass. Look, Rabbi… here's a Talmudic conundrum for you. What determines the quality of a loaf of bread?"

The rabbi shrugged, and I said, "A good baker uses good flour, right?"

"I suppose."

"And the good baker makes good dough, and he molds it and shapes it well, and he puts it in the good oven. Right?"

The rabbi caught my drift and set his eyes on some point behind me.

"I'm the baker. Eran is made out of me. I put him in the best oven I could find, and nine months later, I took him out. I'm Jewish, so he's Jewish, *capisce*? You've got connections up there; you make it work, you hear me?!" I was furious.

Bella placed a hand on my shoulder. "He'll make it work, don't worry," she said, and I didn't know which of us she was talking to. "If any problems come up, we'll help." She kissed the stunned rabbi on the cheek. I wiped away a tear. Every time I remember Eran's face voicelessly contorting during the circumcision, I wipe a tear.

***

Garibaldi brought me back to the present, licking my face thoroughly. He sat back and then stretched majestically. I struggled to stand up. My right arm fell asleep, and a sharp series of aches and pains stabbed every inch of flesh in my stiff limbs.

I dropped into the pool and probably fell asleep in the water. I was woken by Garibaldi's angry barks. Adolf was glaring at me reproachfully. I sloshed out of the water, took a quick shower and collapsed into the bed. I slept like a bag of bricks.

When I woke up again, I smelled coffee. Strong and fresh, right under my nose. Verbin's face peeked at me from behind the little espresso cup. I drank the coffee and rolled over on my stomach, so that the heat radiating from her could seep into the slipped disks and the stiffness in my neck. Her fingers moved over my back, pressing gently into the pain, until it had melted away. When I rolled back over, she was gone. I fell asleep again.

After some unknown period of time, I managed to get out of bed. I looked for Verbin and couldn't find her, in the house or outside. I was aware of the mostly virtual character of my relationship with Eran and wasn't too eager to have a similar one with Verbin. I touched the espresso machine and found it still warm. The cup I had drunk from was on the dresser and still smelled faintly of coffee. I calmed down and went out to the garden. The two monstrosities were happily barking, loping at her side as she came up the path to the house. She was carrying a heavy-looking basket in one hand, a baguette in the other.

When she was done feeding me, she fed the dogs while I loaded the dishwasher. Afterwards we jumped into the pool together. Pool sex is nowhere near as comfortable as movies make it out to be—especially with the dogs patrolling around and having opinions about everything. We moved to the shower, and then to the bed. We lay there, calm and entwined. This was a perfect time for a cigar on the balcony, and maybe Campari with orange juice, like I used to drink with Eran.

"RP..." Verbin's twin lakes stared at me. "Why do people call you RP?"

"It's kind of a long story," I said.

"I have all the time in the world."

"Long and really boring. And unimportant."

"Ehrlich!"

"Yes, my dear."

"Fuck you."

"*Avec plaisir.*"

"No story—no fuck," she said with a comically coquettish French accent and kissed my eyelids. I realized there was no getting out of this.

"Okay, so once I told this asshole team leader—and possibly threatened him, just a bit—that I was two hundred and thirty pounds of rage and power, and after that the guys started calling me 'Rage and Power,' and later it just became RP, and that's it, pretty much."

"Ehrrrliiiich!"

"Okay, um. It was during an operation. We got our asses kicked, and then we kicked back. When they asked how we did it, I said the rage and power thing… it kind of stuck."

Verbin leaned on me, slid her hand up my face and spread open my right eyelid with her fingers. She peered into my eye curiously. "You're a fatalist, aren't you? The kind that thinks every bullet has an address."

"Nope."

"Good," she said, smiling. "That's good."

"I know every address has a bullet."

"Okay. And the rest of the story?"

"That's… pretty much it."

"I see. And they give you medals for that kind of crap?" She didn't wait for a reply, adding, "Was there an investigation after the operation?"

"Sure."

"And no one thought to put you in an institution?"

"Doctor…" I used the most threatening tone I could muster and grabbed her by the hips, lifting her in the air like a child. She tried to wriggle free, kicking and pulling on my nose. I lowered her on top of me, gently, and kissed her. We clung to each other with no intention of ever detaching.

"It's a good thing you aren't obsessed," she told me when we woke, still locked in an embrace.

47.

The war room constructed by abu Bachar—head of the Mukhabarat, the security service, and the sultan's personal assistant—was buried forty feet underground. It lay just under the massive greenhouse, where thousands of colorful butterflies fluttered amongst saw palmettos and budding geophytes. The war room was equipped with top-of-the-line computer and control systems. Once the run-in period was done, abu Bachar gathered the British engineering team that had constructed it—he held a brief ceremony and gave each of the engineers an ornate mahogany box containing a gold bar: a bonus for their hard work.

"A nostalgic bit of memorabilia—not money, and therefore not taxed." He smiled and suggested that they leave their bonus at the compound, "until you return." He then escorted them to the private jet that would take them on a weeklong vacation, where they would enjoy all that the exotic Sultanate had to offer.

The jet's black box, which was found intact several hours after the unfortunate crash, pointed at a critical failure originating with a pressure drop in the engine manifold. While the black box was examined, no one thought to check the reliability of the data, which had been entered prior to the flight. Abu Bachar noted in his log, with some satisfaction, that the only possible source of a leak regarding the secrets of his war room had been eliminated. It helped that they were all infidels.

"First the stick, then the carrot—that's the strategy that seems to work best," abu Bachar told Imad, who was sitting beside him, staring at the plasma screen. Cassius, the youngest of the Shabwah stuffed shahids, had passed the security check at Gatwick about two hours ago and had now been seen walking undisturbed out of Schiphol.

Imad glanced at the golden Rolex he had received from the sultan. In about an hour, the sheikh's loyalists would assemble at the Great Mosque at Molenbeek. Imad lit a Camel cigarette and watched, for the third time, the short video abu Bachar had sent to his secure Telegram account. The video showed Anna walking through the Tiergarten Park in Berlin, with Francesca and the Sudanese boy, Abdu, the amputee. Anna had taken the kid from Shabwah and officially adopted him in Berlin. She seemed happy.

"I see you miss her," said abu Bachar, not knowing how right he was. While thoughts of his father and Nasser filled Imad's head with a thick, heavy fog, his thoughts of Anna cut into flesh.

"No wonder I'm missing her, with what you're offering here. Fat, boring-ass Russians. The Turkish girls are even worse," Imad responded dryly. "Speaking of which, the Turk who shot the video—is she capable of something more?"

"Depends on the more. What did you have in mind?"

Imad shrugged. "Before I come back from the dead, I need to shake Anna's confidence in her current life." After a small pause, he added, "First the stick, then the carrot, right?"

Abu Bachar promised that after the meeting at the mosque, he'd check with Tilda's handler to see what could be done. The red light beneath the screen started to blink, signifying that H-Hour was nearing. Cassius went through the security check at the entrance and took off his shoes to join the mass prayer.

"He seems too far away," said abu Bachar.

"I won't activate until he's right on top of them," said Imad, and as though Cassius could hear him, he began to progress slowly toward the front rows, where the sheikhs prayed.

"Here, you do the honors—type in thirteen," said Imad, passing the phone to abu Bachar.

He did—nothing happened.

"Try again," said Imad, and then Cassius exploded. Horrified cries and shouts of *Allah hu akbar* filled the mosque.

"Good job. How many more of these shahids have we got?"

Imad shrugged again. "Nine left. After Rome, Paris, Riyadh and Córdoba, and before the Saudi bombing."

"Saudi bombing?!" Abu Bachar roared with laughter. "Those assholes couldn't bomb a dead donkey. The Israelis did it for them."

"*Kul kalb biji yomo*," said Imad, staring at the plasma screen. Belgian police and rescue teams were carrying away the bloody remains of the sheikhs. *Every dog has its day.*

"You should have looked after your little brother," Baba said to him and smiled. Imad remembered the time he and Nasser had spent together at Uncle Mahajna's house in Nablus, after Baba was murdered. It was November, just around the olive harvest, and little Nasser had vanished. The entire clan went out to look for him, terrified that the masked Israeli settlers might have harmed him. Eventually they found him asleep on a large sack of olives near the olive press. Uncle Mahajna laughed and picked Nasser up, placing him in Imad's arms. Nasser awoke and burst into tears, wailing "Baba, Baba," and Imad embraced him tightly and swore to protect Nasser until his last breath, hoping that Baba could hear him.

"Now, after the stick"—abu Bachar was smiling—"they'll come running to do business with us." Imad nodded and quickly pushed Nasser and Baba from his mind.

48.

Froyke seemed better. It was evident that the operation in Lebanon had supplied his body with some vitamin or mineral he had been sorely missing. We started that morning with the exasperating weekly staff meeting/inquiry. The DM opened the meeting with congratulations on a job well done, adding that "the cooperation with the counterparts[23] was also executed perfectly. However, risk management"—a new term he had recently grown fond of—"left much to be desired, and was extremely lacking in consideration for human lives. Not to mention"—he failed to swallow a small smile—"a certain degree of infantile behavior."

Froyke attempted to draw the fire, but the rest of the table seemed keen to expand on the subject of my irresponsible and childish behavior. At some point, the director turned to me. "Ehrlich, anything you'd like to say? This is your show, after all."

"Is it a strip show? Is that why everyone here's so eager to fuck me?" I said, and the muttering ceased.

"I'm glad you're getting in touch with your feminine side," said the director. "But still, we'd appreciate your input."

"Look, boss…"

"Call me Moshe," he said. "And keep that to yourself."

"Sure, boss," I said and reached into my pocket to pull out the monthly paycheck I had gotten from Bella that morning. I removed it

---

23 The Mossad and Shin Bet often refer to one another as "the counterparts."

from the envelope and looked at it. The silence grew thick enough to hear toes wiggling inside shoes.

"If you really want my opinion, I'd say that for this bottom line"—I raised the paycheck—"you've gotten more than your money's worth."

The director blinked several times, scrambling for something to say. Froyke folded into his chair, and the rest were buzzing amongst themselves like busy bees.

"Look," he eventually said, apologetically, "you know we have hardly any control over… that. It's a collective agreement… the lesser of two evils."

I shoved the paycheck back in my pocket. "That's exactly my point, boss—I mean, Moshe. Some things we can't control, and whatever we can get… it's the lesser of two evils."

The director smiled. So did Froyke. The rest of the putzes retreated to their respective lairs. I joined Froyke down at his office.

"So, did we get the director's approval?" I asked, removing the lid from the ceiling smoke detector so we could smoke in peace.

Froyke nodded. "Under the condition that they aren't there," he added, referring to Victor the Chechen's Spetsnaz buddies.

I cut the wires connecting the small sensor to the board and replaced the lid. "Good as new."

When I hopped off the table, I glanced at the photos on the desk. Near a photo of Froyke in diving gear next to the Flotilla base in Atlit, there was an old group photo of Froyke's father among a group of other adolescents in light-colored khakis. They were standing in front of a large flag reading "The Hebrew Secondary School in Vilna-Lithuania." One of the kids in the photo looked just like Eran.

I lit my cigar. Froyke pulled out a twenty-five-year-old cognac and poured.

"Well, this is new. Since when do I get the good stuff?"

"When's your flight?"

"I leave for the airport in an hour."

He handed me the glass. "You've earned it," he said and slid a grainy photo across the desk. A body I couldn't recognize was suspended from the end of a large crane. "Taken in Ghajar. The dangling corpse is abu Seif. This is how they do business up there," he said and passed me another set of photos, colorful magnifications of the burning tanker.

"And this… is for the soul. Compliments of the GOC. Now"—he leaned back—"on for phase two?"

The primary goal of phase two was neutralizing the substance's supply routes. Imad had thankfully dropped dead, but undoubtedly some other asshole was already popping up in his place. In these circles, supply creates demand—if the explosives are out there, there will be buyers.

The practical implication of this was that I needed some way to rein in the Chechen. The wheels were already in motion—Victor Zhdaniev had been spotted in Frankfurt. Luigi had taken over from the local team and made arrangements. The skilled technical team from Nevi'ot[24] had outdone itself, providing us with high-quality eyes and ears. Froyke took the trouble to remind me again that the operation would only take place if Victor's ex-Spetsnaz bodyguards are not present, leaving us to deal only with Victor and Sveta, his "secretary."

Froyke looked at his watch. "Doctor Anna von Stroop. Her Berlin clinic. Is that her final decision? Is this what she wants?"

"UNICEF already rented and renovated the space," I said.

"Is there anything we can do to help? She earned it, she really did. Did you offer to bring her to Israel? We'll get her a clinic here, a good one."

"I did," I replied. "She refused."

"Strange lady." Froyke rubbed his chin. "On the one hand always looking for poor Arab kids to help, on the other hand, helping us out."

"She's pragmatic," I said.

---

24 *Nevi'ot* (lit. "spring") is an operational wing of the Mossad which deals in infiltration and information obtainment through the installations of surveillance equipment. -TK

"Pragmatic?"

"In her own way. She does exactly what she thinks is necessary to make up for crimes she didn't commit."

"And that little file you compiled on that Nazi schmuck, von Stroop, with the photos of the children at the concentration camp… that probably didn't hurt either. Okay. Next on the agenda: I found an opening—well, Bella found an opening for your guy Luigi." He frowned. "How certain are you about this kid?"

"He's creative, assertive, and completely obsessed. He gets the job done with no bullshit, and no politics."

"Sounds like someone I know," said Froyke, and he signed the promotion papers. "There, along with my blessing."

After a brief pause, he added, "She's cute, my little doctor. You two have been getting to know each other."

"Just what the doctor ordered."

"You must realize that you are well and truly fucked this time," he said, smiling, and I completely agreed.

"Need anything else?"

"Could you scratch my back with the prosthesis? Right in the middle." Froyke raised an eyebrow, and I cleared my throat. "Look, boss, after I shut down Victor's shop…"

"Negative," Froyke cut me off. "Chernobyl is not approved, and probably never will be. The prime minister refuses to even consider it. Let it go and—" He suddenly let out a hushed, pained cry and grabbed his leg. I got up, reaching for him.

"Do you know what a phantom pain is?" he ground out.

"Yeah, boss. Been having them for the past five years."

Froyke looked up at me, puzzled at first, then nodded.

"Yes, I suppose you have," he said. "Okay. Victor Zhdaniev. Are you good? Anything else you need?" he asked, for the third time that day.

I told him I was good. "Nora told me the goddamn Chechen is a vegetarian. Who'da thunk it, huh?"

Froyke shrugged. "So was Hitler. Are you and Nora still…?" He trailed off.

"Fucking?" I asked, to be as clear on the subject as I possibly could. "Absolutely not."

"Okay. Well, if they're there with him, the whole thing's a no-go. It makes things a great deal trickier, this Chechen along with a whole gang of ex-Spetsnaz." He reiterated, again, for good measure, and we were done.

Before leaving for the airport, I managed to pass through Bella. The old crone was the only one capable of sending Froyke to his check-ups—or, if necessary, bring the doctors to him.

"What do you need, *bubinke*?"

"Could you handle the old man? Keep him from expiring on us?"

Bella shook her head. "I'm doing everything I can. So is that professor from the hospital and your adorable doctor, and Moshe… everyone's doing their best, but… things don't look too good, and your old man thinks he is twenty years old."

"Look after him. Please."

"I am. They're coming in tomorrow to do some tests."

I blew her a kiss. "Who loves you?"

"You do. Conditional love," she said and went back into the office.

49.

On the plane, Luigi texted me that Uncle Victor was already waiting for us and was getting impatient. I was also expectedly impatient, with the target flashing in front of us and adrenaline flooding my brain.

The Frankfurt apartment Zhdaniev rented was in a luxury apartment complex on Schifferstrasse. The building could only be entered from the lobby, which was guarded by a sharply dressed concierge and an impressive surveillance system. The building's owner was an amiable Jew who asked no questions when we requested he fire his previous concierge and hire Luigi in his place for a weekly salary of nothing.

We also rented an apartment in the building across the street, owned by the same cooperative Jew, for the purpose of surveillance and a command center. Everything seemed to be going smoothly. Visuals and audio of the apartment was excellent. We found that Victor's Spetsnaz buddies were currently away killing some poor sap in Abidjan. Africa was far enough for comfort. Noam from the Mossad branch gave me command over a small local team—now I had Ran and Uzi, in addition to Luigi. We now outnumbered them, just like Froyke insisted.

I set the H-Hour. Tonight, 03:00.

At midnight I met O'Driscoll, who had come all the way to Frankfurt to tell me that they were extremely interested in the information Victor could provide, adding that Jones's team was stationed nearby, primed for action.

"Jones is a good guy. Trustworthy," I said, realizing this is my chance to pay O'Dri back for the Pissed-Off Saudis arrangement, as well as dumping the tedious hostage care on him once the operation was concluded.

02:15—Luigi phoned me from the concierge desk and brought my attention to the screen showing Dima and the Colonel, from the Spetsnaz team, on their way up to the apartment.

"*Scheisse.*" There went our advantage. We could still pull this off if we used Jones's team for reinforcement—but that would require Froyke's authorization, and Froyke had told me, several times, that the operation was only approved if the Spetsnaz bodyguards were away.

It would be a clear violation of orders, but one I was willing to live with. I muted the audio link to the operations room back home. Luigi and I reexamined our assets and options. We no longer outnumbered them, but we still had the element of surprise. We'd just have to be sneakier.

***

Someone banged on the door, loudly and urgently. More knocks followed. "Mr. Zhdaniev! Mr. Zhdaniev!"

The Colonel stared at Victor. "Sounds like the new concierge, that idiot Italian."

"I'll go," said Dima and went to open the door. Luigi stood there in his blue concierge uniform, yelling excitedly and waving his arms in the general direction of downstairs.

"*Machina, machina* fire! Auto—boom!"

Dima tried to get him to talk English, but Luigi didn't respond. Dima grabbed him by the ear and dragged him toward Victor, who asked him what he wants, this time in Italian. Luigi again flailed his arms around in response. "Your car. Downstairs. It's on fire!"

Victor ran to the window to see smoke rising from his Audi. He yelled at Dima to come down with him and ran out of the apartment. Luigi remained in the apartment, his eyes scanning the room. Victor and Dima's steps continued to echo down the hall. Luigi rubbed his injured ear, drew his weapon and aimed it at the Colonel. "Colonel Sokolovsky," he said, "I suggest you avoid moving without permission. I'm not Spetsnaz, just Golani, but from three feet, I never miss."

The Colonel, despite having spent around forty of his sixty years in some of the more daring operations by the Spetsnaz, seemed stumped. Golani? Israelis? What were they doing here?

Victor and Dima were charging out of the building toward the smoking car, when the way out was suddenly blocked by three rather large men, all aiming weapons at their centers of mass. Victor raised his hand, halting Dima. He stared at them in disbelief.

"*Guten Morgen*, Mr. Zhdaniev. How are we doing this morning? Please hold your hands out in front of you," I said in German and, switching to Hebrew, added, "Dan, cuff them. Uzi, search."

I provided cover while Dan and Uzi collected the weapons, including Dima's hidden arsenal—a Scorpion submachine gun, a .22 Beretta concealed at his ankle, an ice pick on his right shin and three star-shaped shurikens.

"Shall we head upstairs?" I politely suggested.

We went back up to the apartment. The Colonel was also handcuffed, as was Sveta. Luigi was admiring the Japanese dagger he had taken from the Colonel—"perfectly balanced and sharper than your brain, boss."

"Colonel Sokolovsky, I presume. Nice to finally meet you. We've been waiting for you to come visit for years… a shame."

"Mossad?" Sokolovsky calmly inquired.

"That's right. We have work to do, comrades."

"Who are you? Who sent you?" asked Zhdaniev.

"The state of Israel sent me. My boss sent me, to shut down your business. Fifteen hundred Stingers for Hezbollah, three thousand RPG launchers, five Cobras for the Somalis, liquid PETN for Imad Akbariyeh, another tankerful at Lebanon. I'm afraid this is unacceptable. By the way, we destroyed the tanker three days ago. Oh, and we pulled back the transaction you were waiting for—nine hundred thousand, remember that?"

A twisted smile stretched his lips.

"You move to America," I said. "Full board for the rest of your life. You help me back into the Chernobyl factory and I try to be nice. This is the deal."

Jones came in with his team and started loading Victor and his buddies onto the truck. And then I received a call I would have given anything not to.

"Froyke's in bad shape," said Bella. "Doctor Verbin is with him. Get down here as soon as you can."

I transferred command to Luigi and left to the airport, trying to fathom the meaning behind the words "bad shape." Was Froyke leaving me, too?

50.

An airport police patrol car drove by the plane when it touched down on the runway at Tel Aviv and waited under the ramp once it came to a stop. I sprinted toward it. The sergeant driving the car yelled, "Ehrlich?"

"Go," I said, and he hit the gas before I closed the door.

"I'm taking you out directly through our station," he said. I thanked him and he added, "There's a driver already waiting for you outside with one of your jeeps. Do you need an escort to Jerusalem?"

"No need. The jeep knows the way. But thank you for all your help."

The car screeched to a halt and I sprinted to the jeep waiting outside the police station with the engine running. Verbin was at the wheel.

"Move over, I'll drive," I said. I drove out and turned on the siren, and soon we were at 140 miles an hour, the tachometer creeping into the red. Verbin seemed a bit alarmed but said nothing.

"I've missed you so much, but… how is he?"

She squeezed my shoulder. "It isn't good, but it isn't hopeless. Professor Fleishman is with him."

"Who's Fleishman?"

"Our senior oncologist. He's very good, at the top of his field. He… Froyke's recovering from surgery. He's still sleeping, hooked up to a ventilator. You can drive a bit slower. He's in the best possible hands, I promise. Stable and asleep. Nothing is going to change over the next couple of hours."

I flicked on the emergency lights and stopped at the side of the road near Motza, on the edge of Jerusalem. I pulled Verbin into a hug, as tight as the car seat allowed. “I’m sorry, I…”

She placed a finger on my lips and smiled. “You’re just incapable of doing anything properly, aren’t you? It’s either speeding like a maniac or standing on the side of the road like a klutz. Drive.”

“I really did miss you.”

“I did, too. Now drive.”

I drove. After a minute, I asked again. “So what’s going on with him, exactly?”

“He was in a meeting in Jerusalem—they brought him in a prime minister’s office car. At first they thought it was a heart attack. Turns out it was aggressive pancreatic cancer. Problematic… but there are patients who have managed to recover. Professor Gorni, for example…”

“Verbin, sweetheart, speak Hebrew. How long do we have?”

“We don’t know. We need to wait and see how he responds to the surgery, see if Fleishman managed to get all the damaged tissue… or if it’s spread.”

She stroked my arm. “Does he have any family?” she asked. “Bella only told me when they brought him in…”

“He has family. One son left the country; he’s somewhere in Alaska now. They’re not in touch. The other one found religion, along with Froyke’s wife. They’re extremely Orthodox now, and not really in touch, either.”

When we got to the hospital, Verbin leapt out of the jeep and hurried inside. I remained behind, leaning on an overgrown hedge, postponing as much as I could. When Froyke’s old squad members had begun to wither and die one after the other, he’d told me, “It’s stalking me, too…”

“What’s stalking you?”

Froyke had smiled. “The Kishon cancer,” he’d said and made spooky sounds, wriggling his fingers.

Verbin came back and took my hands in hers. I pulled myself together and we went inside. One of our guys was sitting in the hallway by Froyke’s door, a small earbud in his ear. He stood up the minute he saw me, and I signaled with a small nod that he could sit back down.

Froyke was hooked up to sensors and machinery, seeming to have shrunk to half his size. The prosthesis lay beside his bed. I placed a hand on his forehead. It was cold. I stared at the dark brown bloodstain on his green hospital gown, and for a moment, it seemed to spread, growing lighter and larger. I braced my hand against the wall to counter the sudden dizziness, and then the images flooded my mind. The bloodstains spread, filling my vision. I heard the voices of Eran and Ya'ara.

51.

We were at Dana, the children's hospital at Ichilov Medical Center in Tel Aviv. I was with Ya'ara and little Eran, waiting for the doctor. The name "Prof. Agranat" was written on the door. I remember thinking it couldn't possibly be the same Agranat.

"Ehrlich family, you're next," the nurse declared and saw us in.

"RP? RP! Unbelievable... how many years has it been? Get over here and give me a hug!"

After the hug, the professor crouched and held his fist in front of Eran, who happily bumped it.

"So this is my little fighter? Strong, aren't you? Come here, sweetie, open wide."

While Agranat examined Eran's throat and went over the X-rays provided by Ya'ara, she whispered, "What's RP?" in my ear.

"An old joke," I said. "I'll tell you later."

Agranat finished the examination and said, "Polyps are inflamed. We need to remove them." I appreciated that he chose the word "remove" rather than "surgery" or "cut."

"We were expecting this," I said, patting Eran's back. "Right, little man? We found the best polyp remover in the world for you, and he's a friend of mine from the army—we trust him."

Eran was peacefully wandering the professor's office, seemingly entirely disconnected from the exchange, and only opened his mouth upon encountering a large Transformer on the small cabinet behind Agranat's desk.

"I have two questions, Professor Garganat," he said.

"Agranat," I corrected.

"Thass fine," replied Eran. "Tell me, Garganat—why'd you call my dad Arpee? And question number two is what are you doing with this Optimus Prime?" He shook the Transformer. "This is for kids!"

Agranat laughed. "Like father, like son. Look, young man. You'll have to ask your dad about the first bit. Regarding Optimus Prime, he's yours—if you behave."

Eran approached the professor, his little fist raised in front of him. The professor obediently bumped it. "I recommend removing these polyps as soon as possible."

"Whenever you say, but ideally when Avner's home. When's your next flight, *RP*?" Ya'ara asked, smiling.

"In a couple of days. I'll be gone for about a week."

"Actually, you know what?" Agranat pointed at the timetable he had opened on his screen. "What are you doing right now? Another patient just canceled his… removal. I have an open slot, if it works for you."

"You mean you want to operate right now?" Eran asked. "Thass fine with me. What do you think, Daddy?"

I hoisted him into the air and pressed my forehead against his. I whispered that I loved him more than anything in the world, and there was no doctor I trusted more than this Garganat.

Ya'ara went with Eran into the operating room. I waited outside.

***

"These fighters," Agranat told Ya'ara while he checked Eran's blood pressure. "It's all well and good on the battlefield, but when it comes to their children, they're terrified." He smiled. "Everything looks good. A couple of hours in recovery and he'll be as good as new."

"Why RP?" Ya'ara asked before they left the operating room.

"That jackass, he really never told you? I will, then. RP stands for rage and power," said the professor, and in a deeper voice, he added,

"Avner Ehrlich Ne'eman. Two hundred and thirty pounds of rage and power." He signaled one of the nurses to move Eran from the operating table to one of the rolling patient beds.

"Could you clean the blood, please? It would be better if Avner didn't see it," Ya'ara asked.

"No problem, lady," said the nurse and carried on with whatever he was doing. Aganat went to the sink and sterilized his hands.

"We were raiding a Syrian observation post. Suddenly we were taking heavy fire, a barrage from an unknown source. They had a heavy machine gun positioned somewhere, probably a new post, because there was nothing about it in our intel. We didn't have time to react. Two dead, Ra'anan and 'Loco' Moshiko, who was a volunteer from Argentina, no family. He and Avner were close. Ido, who was the commanding officer, ordered a retreat. Avner refused, said he wasn't going anywhere until he took down the machine gun operator. There was no love lost between the two of them, to say the least, and Ido asked what a smart-ass like Avner was going to do against an invisible, heavily armed opponent who had the clear tactical advantage. RP answered in short: 'With rage and with power.' Then he loaded his rifle and sprinted up the hill, alone, yelling and firing like a maniac, like those Indians in the old movies. I don't know if it was the fire or the yelling that killed that Syrian with the machine gun, but he got him. We took down the rest of their force with pretty much the same method. It was insane. Insane! The team started calling him 'Rage and Power,' RP for short. But it was just the team—no one else was supposed to know. But you know how these things are. After that, the way that team acted out in the field—they thought they were, like they were unlisted in the bullet address book… they gave him the Brigade Commander Citation—should have been the Chief of Staff Citation, but those assholes said that on account of the insubordination—he essentially disobeyed a direct order—he got the next best thing. Idiots. You know, that team… other than Avner and Ami Kahanov, I think there's no one left."

Agranat and Ya'ara came out to the hallway.

"Where's Eran?" I asked.

"There's nothing to worry about. Everything went perfectly," said Agranat, and then the nurse came, pushing Eran's rolling bed, and there was dark blood on Eran's chin and it had poured down the sheet covering his sleeping body, and I felt the floor slipping away from under me. Everything was far too white.

"RP, what's going on with you?" was the last thing I heard, and I didn't know who it was that spoke, because the voice sounded like it was rising from a deep, bottomless well. The last thing I remembered was feeling the chill of the floor, but no pain.

***

"You faded out for a while. Where were you?" asked Verbin, dabbing my forehead with a wet wipe.

"I'm fine. When is he going to wake up?" I nodded toward Froyke.

Verbin looked at the monitor. "He's stable. I estimate he'll be awake in an hour or so. Let's go to the cafeteria. He needs his rest."

When we got back, Professor Fleishman was there, arranging the pillows to better support Froyke's raised head. "He's strong. Our hero, really. He'll make it. Are you his son?"

"Almost," I said. "A colleague. He's my boss."

"Your father's an impressive man. I'll get going. He'll be fine," he said and handed the chart to Verbin. "Doctor, tell him he'll be fine."

Verbin read diligently, and I went to Froyke and held the hand hanging out from under the blanket.

"Phase two?" Froyke rasped.

"Yeah, boss. The Chechen is closed for business."

"Good." A hoarse whisper. "Good."

"Let him rest," said the doctor. I leaned in, wiped the sweat from his forehead, and whispered, "Come back soon, boss. It's time for phase three."

"What's phase three?" he croaked.

"Chernobyl!" I said, grinning.

Froyke turned his back to me and fell asleep.

52.

Imad was dead. We'd destroyed the ticking tanker. Victor was buried in some black site in Arkansas for the rest of his life. The only link still active in this shit-chain was the Chernobyl factory. The road there passed through the eternally festive Santa Claus Village in Lapland, located just three miles from the North Pole, and about the same distance from Rovaniemi Airport, where I was supposed to meet Boris—our man in Saint Petersburg.

The prime minister had yet to approve an active operation. However, Putin's utter refusal to stop the deliveries of antiaircraft "tie-breaker" missiles to Iran—and from there, to Syria and Hezbollah—had at least nudged the prime minister into granting approval for preliminary reconnaissance and planning. A good start. Much better than the complete ban I'd had to face before.

The plane landed roughly and bumpily on the frozen runway. The fingers of my right hand were aching with paresthesia. I was desperate for either a long swim or a chiropractor, maybe both. My legs, which the economy seating had crumpled into origami, were also due a long vacation, or flat-out retirement.

I checked into the hotel as quickly as possible and threw myself into the steaming indoor pool. The heat, and fifty minutes of aggressive breaststroke, did the trick. After I showered, I went down to the lobby and waited for Boris, holding a stack of brochures presenting a selection of photovoltaic panels from GES Energy—which really should have been erased from existence after the Shabwah camp had been destroyed but, probably due to some clerk's typical negligence, hadn't been.

While Boris "read" the brochures, I asked him whether we should sic our excellent cyberwarfare department on the Chernobyl gang. The same cyber department had grown the Stuxnet worms that had collapsed the centrifuge computers at the Iranian reactor in Natanz.

Boris literally howled with laughter. When he calmed down, he said that he doubted the bookkeepers up there even had digital calculators and went on to confirm the rest of the intel provided by Victor. The Chernobyl factory, as it turned out, was not so much a factory as it was an array of bunkers stocked with Red Army weapons, ammunitions and explosives. The facility had been abandoned after the Chernobyl disaster and captured by a gang of ex-KGB operatives, which had proceeded to sell its contents to the highest bidder. According to Victor's intel, there were three PETN tankers parked at the "factory," which Zhdaniev had already agreed to purchase.

Although Victor's interrogation had been conducted with the help of a polygraph, it was reassuring to have the intel confirmed. I was certain that Spetsnaz and GRU had been trained to fool polygraphs, just like we had. Sixteen hundred dollars in cash had bought Boris the factory's schematics and inventory list, which included over thirty thousand Stingers, ten thousand RPG launchers, small-arms ammunitions, and of course the liquid PETN, which was stored comfortably in the three rusted tankers.

"Truth is"—Boris smiled—"I already have everything I need to create a work accident."

The problem, as he quickly acknowledged, was the collateral damage—the workers who might be hurt, and the possible effects on dormant radioactive remnants from the reactor explosion.

"Not good enough," I said. "We'll never get approved for something like that."

"Either way, here's what I'd recommend," he said and raised his glass of cognac. "*Na zdarovje.*"

"*Na zdarovje*," I said but decided to forgo the drink. "What would you recommend?"

"Fuck the assholes up. Fuck 'em up as hard as possible. If we don't get on top of this, some new Imad will."

I'd mentored Boris back when he was a cadet. He was a quiet kid who mostly spent his free time listening to Stravinsky and trying to solve the Clay Mathematics Institute's Millennium Problems. Had working with us turned him into an uncouth *muzhik*?

His constantly drumming fingers suddenly froze. "Got it!" he said.

"Got what?" I wondered.

And he leaned in and whispered, "The liquidators, they're even more motivated than we are."

"Who?"

The liquidators, Boris explained, were the thousands of political prisoners who had been put to work cleaning the remains of the radioactive explosion at the Chernobyl No. 4 reactor and had come out dripping with cancer. Many of them had been Chechen captives.

"Chechens never forget. Find them, or their children, and we'll find our volunteers," said Boris and downed the last of his cognac.

"Good. See what you can do," I concluded, hoping for the best.

53.

"*Ich hab' noch… einen Koffer in Berlin*," Anna hummed Hildegard Knef's homesick words, and kissed Francesca, who blushed in response. *I still have a suitcase in Berlin…*

It was Francesca's birthday. She was sitting in the passenger seat of the red Mini Cooper; Anna was driving.

"The café on Ku'Damm?" Anna half-asked, half-informed her, and Francesca nodded cheerfully.

"Definitely Ku'Damm."

"Still have a suitcase back there…" sang Anna, a slight variation on the lyric. Seeing that Francesca remained oblivious, she nodded slightly toward the backseat. "You still have a suitcase back there."

Francesca turned around and let out a small yelp. Seven tightly monogrammed Louis Vuitton creations rested on the backseat, ranging in size from a tiny coin purse all the way up to a large suitcase.

"You're insane," she said, leaning closer to Anna. Anna tilted her head toward the kiss, and there was a sudden crashing sound, a screech of metal—Francesca's head bumped against the windshield and she shrieked in alarm. Anna quickly pulled over, calming down only when she saw that Francesca was safe, that she was only startled, not injured.

Anna got out of the car and faced the large black Mercedes G-class jeep that pulled over behind her. The red-faced fat man who drove it apologized profusely, admitted his failure to maintain a safe distance, and asked for Anna's details so his insurance company could cover the damages. He even suggested driving Francesca to the hospital, just in case. Anna calmly provided him with her details, accepted his business card, thanked him for his concern and assured him that she was a doctor and she'd handle it from here. The fat man apologized again. Anna examined the lightly dented rear bumper.

"It doesn't look too bad," she said. The fat man apologized one last time and got back into his jeep.

Once he'd gotten back on the road, he paused his dashcam and dialed a number. "Berlin carried out successfully. Sending the video now. The opera tickets were also delivered."

The fat man's handler forwarded the video to abu Bachar, who immediately sent it to Imad. He'd wanted to rattle Anna, even slightly, before his arrival.

The brunch at the Ku'Damm café was excellent as usual. Anna examined Francesca's head, tilting it gently from side to side, kissing each side in turn. Francesca was loving every second of it. If it weren't for the fat man, it would've been a perfect day—a perfect week, really, thought Anna. Yesterday they'd officially broken in the new equipment in the top-of-the-line operating room UNICEF had recently added to her clinic. The European UNICEF representative cut the ribbon and praised Dr. von Stroop's hard work and dedication. Life in the absence of Imad and Avner was calmer, more peaceful. The thrills inherent to those two seemed like they belonged in a distant, negligible past—as they should. And in any case, the responsibilities of parenting—which they had both committed to upon adopting little Abdu—demanded a calmer life. Anna's depleted mental reserves were slowly recharging. They were approaching better, happier times. She'd talk to the secretary tomorrow about the insurance thing.

"Today's for celebrating," she said and hugged Francesca, who seemed surprised to find something in her new purse. She pulled her hand out and stared at the two tickets that had somehow been waiting inside.

"Tickets to the Valkyries. Wagner and Barenboim," she announced.

"What? When?" whispered Anna, who considered the Valkyries, Wagner and Barenboim to be the holy trinity of music.

"Tonight," said Francesca, still puzzled, and the word was swallowed by Anna's soft lips.

They picked up Abdu from the kindergarten, and after their daily walk through the zoo, followed by a Ku'Damm falafel, a *schlafstunde*, a shared shower and an espresso, they were ready to head out. The doorbell rang and Francesca went to get it.

"You're not Olga." She smiled.

"Olga's sick. She asked if I could fill in for her," said the girl at the door, a tall, brawny teen with light brown skin.

"What's your name?" asked Anna.

"Oh, sorry. I'm Tilda. Olga's friend. She told me Abdu is the sweetest kid. Can I see him?"

"Cesca, could you show Tilda around?"

Anna went in to the study and dialed their usual babysitter. "Olga? Everything okay? The flu, huh? Yeah, yeah, Tilda, she's here. Yeah, she seems nice. Okay, good night. Thank you for finding a replacement. *Tschüssi*."

Francesca showed Tilda the house, made sure she knew where the coffee machine and the bathroom were, and explained that Abdu was an amputee and needed assistance standing up.

"Your bag," Anna said, staring at it. "Beautiful! Turkish?"

"Yeah," replied Tilda, handing it over. "Handmade—my dad works with leather."

Anna inspected the bag appreciatively. "Is it okay if I look at the lining?"

"Sure," said Tilda. She opened the bag, and it slipped out of Anna's fingers, spilling its contents on the floor. Anna apologized and carefully collected the innocent items back into the bag, with Tilda's help.

"We'll be back by midnight. Is that okay?"

Tilda smiled. "Nice house, adorable kid—I'll stay here as long as you want. If you want one, by the way, I could ask my dad..."

"Yes, please do. I'll buy two, I think—it's a gorgeous bag. Here's my number—the other one's Francesca's, in case mine is busy. See you later, have a good night."

54.

Darkness descended on the hall. The orchestra musicians took their places. Applause. The last to take his place was Daniel Barenboim. The applause grew louder, then reached a crescendo when Barenboim bowed to the audience. The strings whined a tense whisper, dark storm clouds covered the slowly descending screen behind the orchestra, thunder rolled. The contrabass swelled louder and louder. Sigmund was running helplessly under dark, stormy skies. He found a door, set inside the stone, and knocked on it loudly and desperately. Anna opened the door. The brass progressed in a military attack formation. Sigmund looked just like Imad.

"I'm cursed," he told Anna. "I'm cursed, and now I must go from here."

"Not now, don't go yet…" pleaded Anna Sieglinde. "We're all cursed… I have a mission."

The timpani drums thrummed and rumbled, and Anna didn't understand how a squadron of helicopter gunship came to be on the screen of the Berlin opera. Colonel Kilgore was standing on the edge of a helicopter that was raining hellfire. The string section battled the brass section. *This can't be the Ride of the Valkyries*, she thinks; *we're still in the first act.* Anna wiped her sweaty brow. On the stage, on the mountaintop, Sieglinde and Brünnhilde were on horseback, leading the dead to Valhalla. Act Three—the Ride of the Valkyries boomed at a volume that threatens to bring down the walls. Kilgore's helicopters rained death and destruction, creating a horrible, fiery ring. Anna was alone on the summit, surrounded by flames, unable to move. Robert Duvall was laughing his ass off. He sounded just like Eli Wallach when he said, "You're my friend. I'd kill you for nothing."

Francesca, who was holding Anna's hand, suddenly noticed that it was sweating.

"Are you okay?"

"No," said Anna. "Something is very much not okay. I feel, I… sorry, I need to go home, I'm scared." Anna got up and, without waiting, jogged outside.

"Taxi!" she ordered the terrified doorman.

"Corner of Blumen Strasse, now!" She shoved a hundred-euro note into the driver's palm. "Hurry! Go! Now!"

The taxi sped away with a screech of rubber.

Anna sped into the building and summoned the elevator, only to realize that the elevator was open in front of her. "Oh God… just let the kid be okay… please, Abdu, please be okay…"

There were no lights on in the apartment. She ran to Abdu's room in the dark, found him sleeping soundly, his breathing calm. Anna gently stroked his cheek and kissed the top of his head.

Francesca arrived, breathless. "He's fine. No need to wake him, he's fine," Anna said, calming her.

"Abdu's fine, but where's Tilda? The lights are off. There's no one here."

The cabinet doors in the study were open, and the large gym bag that held one of her go-bags was on the floor, empty. Anna signaled Francesca to stay where she was, took off her shoes and carefully crept into the kitchen. She pulled out a large chef's knife and stalked into the bedroom. There was no one there. On the floor, she found the ornamented, empty jewel box.

"It's okay, babe. No one's here. Keep an eye on the kid? I'll be right back."

55.

The tires shrieked their discontent at the sudden force, and Anna eased her foot slightly off the gas, allowing the car to accelerate. Two thousand rpm, three thousand rpm—the turbo kicked in. Anna sped past the Platz der Republik, entered Moabit, drove down the boulevard, took a left, then a right—the townhouses, the foreign workers' housing projects. She screeched to a halt in front of Olga's house. A beat-up Fiat Panda was parked in front of her with the doors wide open and Turkish music blaring from the speakers. The backseat was covered in piles of clothes. Tilda folded her tall form out of the car and stood with her legs spread apart, fists on her hips.

"Olga, get out here," she yelled. "Your fucking doctor is here. What, you wanna fuck me? You wanna fuck this ass? No problem, but in the ass is extra. Fucking dyke."

Olga arrived, pressed against Tilda's back and kissed her bare shoulder. Anna nodded toward the backseat, covered with what used to be her wardrobe. "Keep the clothes, keep the jewels. I need the gun and the papers."

"Or what?" sneered Tilda. "What the fuck are you gonna do? Send over your little nigger to hop at me?"

Anna took a step and a half forward and planted her heel—backed by her entire body weight—on the tips of Tilda's toes. Tilda folded forward, groaning in pain, upon which her center of mass met Anna's rising knee. She collapsed to the ground. Olga fled.

Anna rummaged through the backseat and pulled out the go-bag, containing her documents, her Beretta, and a thick stack of bills in a yellow envelope. She then started her car and for a while just sat there, trying to collect the pieces of her calm new life. After several minutes, she turned off the engine and walked back to Tilda, who was still lying on the ground, wheezing. She lifted her shirt and examined her ribs, then took her pulse, which was normal. Tilda raised her head slightly and spat in her face.

"The Arabs are coming to tear your ass apart, you cunt." She laughed wildly. Anna wiped the spittle from her face and pulled five hundred euros from her stack of bills, placing them wordlessly by Tilda's head.

In the shower, Anna submitted to the heat of the water. Francesca cut through the thick cloud of steam to hand her a glass of cool, dry Riesling. Anna didn't move from the stream, drinking the wine along with the hot water pouring into it.

I'm scared, she wrote in the steam on the glass door.

56.

Abu Bachar's strategy was proving effective. After the bombing at the Molenbeek Mosque, the sheikhs had acceded to a *tahdiya*—a ceasefire. The sultan had requested a reconciliation and received it; Imad and his stuffed shahids would officially leave Al-Qaeda and enter the service of the sultan. Finally, Imad was standing on the path that would lead him to his destiny.

"Israel is a foothold," he was saying. "The American fort within the Middle East, within our territory. It supports interests of the American oil companies, which in turn are bleeding us dry."

"True," said abu Bachar. "But how is any of this relevant to us?"

Imad crushed the butt of his cigarette. "Take down the fort and we're free to charge forward. Nothing will stand in our way. All we need is a foothold."

Abu Bachar stared at him blankly, and Imad realized the time had come for practical demands. He stressed the importance of acquiring the PETN at all costs. Tupolev and Schwadron, the two remaining PETN distributors, had gone underground following Victor Zhdaniev's arrest, vanishing not only from the darknet, but apparently from the face of the earth.

"There are three tankers left at the Chernobyl facility, under guard twenty-four seven by the Russian mafia. There are a few more pounds of the stuff back in the old Kabul clinic," Imad said, "but we have no way of bringing them here. We need the PETN and we need a clinic, in Sultanate territory, where no one'll bother us."

"No clinic on Sultanate ground." Abu Bachar's refusal was final. "I won't have the American dogs sniffing up my ass, not to mention the Jews."

And so, the remaining PETN made their way through the Pakistani diplomatic mailing service all the way to the Sultanate's embassy in Berlin, where Anna had recently opened her new clinic.

57.

Anna's new, untroubled life, Imad's death, taking out the tanker in Lebanon and Zhdaniev's business—it all left an emptiness inside of me, and in this emptiness, the sense of danger from the Chernobyl tankers rang clearer and louder than ever. Being my usual obsessive self, I continuously pestered Froyke on the matter, and he pestered the DM, who pestered the prime minister, who in turn refused vehemently given the level of risk that would be involved—until, eventually, he didn't.

I had no way of knowing what prompted the change—perhaps the realization that some other jihadi would inevitably take control of the tankers, or perhaps the fact that Putin insisted on continuing to provide the "axis of evil" with advanced antiair missile systems, making it difficult for the prime minister to present any politically meaningful progress. Either way, we were now approved for an actual operation, subject to a final authorization on D-Day, and also subject to the DM's guarantee that the operation could not be traced back to us.

"And that," the director said, "is an unbreakable condition. Not by the department"—he indicated Froyke, who nodded—"not by me, and not by the prime minister himself." I thought to myself that Bella could probably break it, if she wanted to, but said nothing.

Chechen liquidators, Boris told me. Find them, or their sons, and you have your volunteers. He then bought a list of said liquidators for half a million dollars and, for another five thousand, another list of the commissars who had sent these political prisoners to their cancerous forced labor. Fortunately, the authorities had kept these commissars from wandering too far away, and most of them still lived in the rural village of Novi Yarylovychi, near Chernobyl. This presented a golden opportunity. Boris came up with a pretty decent plan, involving Dragan Ismailov, the head of one of Grozny's top gangs. His men were Chechen Islamic resistance, born and bred to hate Russians. His father, Bruno Ismailov (yes, really), one of the founders of the Islamic resistance, had been imprisoned by the Soviets and sent to liquidation forced labor. When he had become sick, the Russians had sent him home, to die in the arms of his eldest son, Dragan.

Boris planned to recruit the Dragan gang to a fully funded mission, during which they were to steal the PETN tanks from the facility and blow them up at the center of Novi Yarylovychi, with the goal of killing as many commissars as possible. His assumption—and it was a reasonable one—was that the Russians would see this as a clear-cut act of revenge, initiated by Islamic Chechen terrorists. I liked the plan, and its inherent poetic justice. But it still wasn't as tightly sealed as we needed it to be—it could still be traced back to us, and neither the director nor the prime minister would approve it.

And so, I found myself on a plane from LaGuardia to Arkansas, in the company of John O'Driscall and Colonel Sokolovsky, who we'd taken from the bosom of his newly rediscovered family in Bat-Yam.

The CIA detention facility was a black site in the middle of the forest, which appeared at first glance to be nothing more than a farmhouse. Victor was pleased to see the Colonel, and even more so to receive the bottles of Stoli and jars of beluga caviar that accompanied him. After lunch, an exhausting negotiation regarding the conditions of Victor's imprisonment and some reluctant quid pro quo, we handed him a satellite phone.

He dialed Dima, who was in Somalia at the time, and recruited him to the project. The Colonel listened attentively and at the end of the call told me he was fairly certain this would work. Any attempt to trace the operation back to its designer, no matter how thorough, would come to an abrupt halt once it reached Arkansas.

This satisfied both the prime minister and the director. The third and final phase was officially underway.

58.

The reddish haze of the afternoon sun shrouded the Tiergarten in Berlin. Little Abdu was happily skipping along, getting used to his prosthesis. Anna had his right hand in hers, and Francesca took his left. He counted out loud, "*Eins, zwei, und…*" Anna and Francesca took a large step, swing him up in the air, and the three of them cheered, "*Ka—ka—du!*"

Another long step, and Abdu shrieked, "*Eins, zwei, und…*" Another swing through the air. "*Ka ka du…*"

"*Eins, zwei—*"

A phone rang, annoyingly, and they stopped. Francesca pulled a phone out of her bag. "It's yours," she said to Anna, handing it over.

"This is Doctor von Stroop. Hello. Hello…" No response.

Across the small pond to their left, a couple of joggers appeared from between the trees and waved at the three of them, who waved back. Abdu was laughing, overjoyed.

Anna glanced at her new running calculator. "Okay, guys, time for my run. You'll be at the zoo?"

"*Ka-ka-du, kakadu!*" Abdu nodded excitedly.

"Say hi to the *kakadu* for me." She smiled. "I'll see you at home in… two hours?"

She kissed Francesca's lips and Abdu's forehead. They both took a right toward the zoological gardens, and Anna headed toward the forest in a light jog, shortly joining a large group of other runners. One of them, his face obscured by a hoodie, stopped and tied his shoes, then increased his speed, passing her. She stared curiously at his back. Something about his movement felt familiar. He broke into a sprint and vanished. Anna ran the four-mile route circling the pond and then jogged up the stairs to the Gold Else monument. The first of the city lights gleamed through the red mist. Anna examined her running calculator, stretched her legs, and looked at the muscular form of the man standing at the lookout point with his back to her, shrouded by a hoodie. Was this the same runner who'd passed her earlier?

Her cell phone rang. "This is Doctor von Stroop… to whom am I speaking?"

"To me," said the man and turned to her, removing his hood and reaching out his hand. "How do you do, Doctor von Stroop?"

Anna's heart skipped a beat.

"Imad?" she whispered.

"In mind and body, it is I and no other." He smiled.

She ran her fingers down his face, and they hugged tightly and silently. Anna wiped away her tears and examined him from head to toe. Then she shoved her hand in his pants and cupped his package.

"Yeah, it is you… definitely."

Imad grinned and pulled her back into his arms. "Let's see what this resurrection did for my cock."

Anna pulled down her sweatpants and wrapped her legs around him. He slowly penetrated her.

"I missed you, lady SS." Anna gave in, surrendering to the sensation. Imad increased his pace and came almost instantly. She remained fused to him, her legs squeezing his waist.

"Was it good for you?"

"Resurrection…," she breathed. "Let's get dressed before—"

"My guys are down there. No one's getting through them."

"What about Gold Else?" She glanced up to the golden statue.

They sat at the edge of the lookout, and Imad offered her a Camel cigarette.

"I quit."

"Couldn't you find some doctor to tell you it's fine?"

Anna stroked his hair. "Tell me."

"It's a long story," Imad said, placing a finger on her lips. "Let's go home."

"My place?" she asked, feeling the old fears, the ones she'd almost managed to shed, balling back up inside of her.

"Your place? And what are we supposed to do about your girlfriend, and the little Arab you stole from us? No, my place, obviously."

"Back to Shabwah?" she asked innocently, already beginning to reconstruct her shell, the shield of confidence that allowed her to safely lie.

"I'm living in Berlin right now. But I actually have some urgent business that needs handling. I'll see you tomorrow morning, at your clinic."

"At my clinic?" she echoed. A sudden panic gripped her. How long had he been following her?

"The one on Nürnberger Strasse, in case you forgot." Imad smiled.

"There's no getting rid of you, is there?"

"If you really want to get rid of—"

Anna hushed him with a deep kiss.

"You leave first," she said. "Men always come first in this country."

He kissed her lightly, then ran down the stairs and disappeared into the darkening dusk. She leaned against the railing, trying to organize her thoughts. Imad's death had wounded her. Not a mortal wound, but still a deep one, one that threatened to reopen with each careless motion. While his death had freed her from the constant tension—the constant companion of spies—she had missed him. Unlike most people suffering from bipolar disorder, Anna was fully aware of hers and occasionally managed to suppress the symptoms. When the sorrow overwhelmed her, she needed Avner, his broad shoulders and the confidence he gave her, in herself and in her abilities. During her rarer manic episodes, she needed Imad, and his cruel love, to slam her back down to reality.

She lived in constant unease—cold sweat on her back, warm sweat on her brow, the fear of the unexpected, the creak of a door, the whistling of a teapot, the screech of wheels on asphalt, the thousand sounds of everyday life—these were a perpetual threat, unaffected by the passage of time. Trembling prayers to someone or something, to keep the fragile ground from crumbling away from under her. But ever since Imad's death, the sharp tension had given way to a mist of vague worry, soft like a spongey cloud. The myokymia, the nervous twitch in her lower eyelid, had almost disappeared. Even the worry lines seemed to smooth away. And alongside all that fear, there was love. As much as she detested the violent sex her "exotic prince" favored and forced on her, she was also irresistibly drawn to him. She had found her lost comfort in Francesca's arms.

Imad had left the park but still lingered in her thoughts. After he would conquer and penetrate her, Imad would usually become talkative, cooperative. He would be at his most revealing. Hooray for oxytocin! Anna shook the thoughts away. Time to focus. What she needed right now was concrete action. Let Avner know about Imad's resurrection.

Anna searched around the lookout point for his cigarette butt but couldn't find it. She took a small burner phone from her pocket and texted:

"Sigmund is in Berlin. No error. Sigmund is in Berlin."

She headed down from the lookout point. When she'd reached the bottom of the winding stone stairway, she bent over to tie her shoelaces and noticed the crushed butt of the Camel cigarette, right in front of her. She carefully collected it and then jogged to the lake and threw the small burner phone into the dark waters.

59.

I was on my way to Italy to make final arrangements with O'Driscoll. Victor would receive temporary access to a phone in his Arkansas farm, for the purpose of leaving a message on a voicemail we acquired in Tunisia and ordering Dima to engage. The third and final phase to eliminate the threat was in motion.

My pager beeped. I was expecting a message from Froyke, reiterating the need for caution. I was most certainly not expecting: "Sigmund is in Berlin. No error. Sigmund is in Berlin."

I read it a second time, then a third, but the message refused to change.

"Sigmund is in Berlin. No error. Sigmund is in Berlin."

I stared at the single line of text that had been passed from Anna to the control center at Ramat HaSharon, and from there some young and alert duty officer—probably some university student working half-time—had bounced it on to me and Froyke, who had undoubtedly passed it on to the DM.

I sipped my cognac. It wouldn't hurt—at most it would restore the sugar level of the Mossad's best analytical mind. Could Anna be mistaken? Everyone made mistakes, but it was unlikely. She'd lived with him at Shabwah for over a year, knew every square inch of him. Could she be intentionally misleading us, providing misinformation? It wouldn't be the first time an asset had switched sides, and I couldn't ignore her history, forget who she had been when we'd found her, caring for the injured terrorist. On the other hand, prior to recruitment and training, we'd put her through a finer comb of tests and interrogations than anyone had ever undergone before her. The entire staff had approved her unquestionably. Could she have still tricked us? And why not, when that fucking Bedouin Imad apparently had…?

The head psychologist in charge of her case had stated that Anna was not a left-winger, nor was she a right-winger—and more importantly, she was not anti-Israeli. She was motivated by something much simpler—an overwhelming sense of guilt, leading to a powerful urge to support those she deemed to be underdogs, and to satisfy those she loved. I had taken her to a guided tour at Yad Vashem[25], where she'd "happened" upon repeated mentions of the crimes of her family: Colonel von Stroop—who, among other things, had supervised Dr. Mengele—and photographic evidence of her "Tante Hannah," the baby-smasher. Anna had passed out, and just as the lead psychologist had expected, requested to return there and see everything there was about her family's crimes. At the psychologist's behest, we'd exposed her to the rest over several shorter, easier visits. When that angle had been milked dry, we had taken her to Lohamei HaGeta'ot[26] to personally meet some Mengele alumni. The treatment had succeeded beyond expectations, creating an inexhaustible fountain of guilt that we were free to exploit.

"Sigmund is alive…"

Who profits from this news? The Jihadis? Imad himself? Probably not. He has nothing to gain from our renewing the hunt for him. Why am I finding this resurrection business so hard to believe?

Because then I would have to admit that they had fooled us with a

---

25 Israel's official remembrance center and memorial and to the victims of the Holocaust. -TK

26 A kibbutz whose founding members include surviving fighters of the Warsaw Ghetto Uprising, as well as former Jewish partisans and other Holocaust survivors. Its name (lit. "The Ghetto fighters") commemorates the Jews who fought the Nazis. -TK

bullshit handheld video, which had bought them a significant amount of time to advance their goals. These fucking Bedouins had tricked me, and O'Driscoll, and all of our fancy intelligence systems, and all of our ineffectual European partners. And the DNA samples, found at the site of his death, tested and confirmed… Assholes!

I called the duty officer who had processed the message, and confirmed that the entire chain had been checked. There was no doubt. The message had come from Anna. I canceled my meeting with O'Driscoll and made arrangements to fly to Berlin as soon as possible. Imad's resurrection took precedence.

During the flight, I tried to think, analyze the new data, but my brain wouldn't cooperate. The thoughts pelted me in quick succession, exploding in my mind like homemade missiles. I took a deep breath and exhaled. In and out. In, out. Slowly, some sense started to emerge from the chaos: I had to comfort and debrief Anna. And I had to arrange tracking for Imad so he didn't slip away again. Figure out what he was up to. Construct a response strategy. Then came the annoying thoughts about the need to properly allocate our limited resources. Why was Imad in Berlin? For how long? Was he still a ticking bomb, or had he mellowed into a vaguer threat? Perhaps he had just come to fuck Anna a bit. Perhaps we should leave this to our ineffectual European buddies. He was in their backyard, after all. The bigger question was this: why would they invest so much effort, resources and ingenuity in creating this deception?

The more I ruminated on the subject, the clearer the answer became. Imad was a pivotal piece of some elaborate plan. A project high up in their priority list. And this time, we hadn't the slightest idea when and where it would blow up in our faces.

60.

Noam from the Berlin branch rented a room for Dr. King Schultz, in a family-owned inn named Pariser Ecke near Ku'Damm. Luigi, this time as a Turkish taxi driver, drove Anna over, took her to her room and secured her until I arrived. She threw her arms around me, sobbing, the moment I opened the door. I stroked her hair until she calmed down a bit.

"Hey, *Schatzi*. I'm here..."

Anna smiled weakly. We went over the account of their meeting under the Gold Else, then went over it again.

"Is there any chance this was someone other than your prince?" I asked. Anna wiped away a tear with the back of her hand.

"Is this protocol, or do you also think I've gone crazy?" She took a small evidence bag containing a cigarette butt out of her purse. "Here, test it yourself."

I put the bag in my pocket. "Protocol, *Schatzi*. I have to ask. Who's crazy enough to think you're crazy?"

"I am!" she said and suddenly laughed. "I'm crazy enough to think I'm crazy."

She was on the brink of collapse. We had to find this asshole, now. Finally free her from this shitstorm.

"Did anything else happen when you met? Anything you haven't told me?" I forced myself to ask.

"Something that you need to know about? No, I don't think there was. Maybe that I fucked him on the Gold Else lookout, two hundred feet above ground," she said and searched my face for a reaction.

"And he didn't mention anything about his plans?" I asked. She usually got her best intel from him postcoital.

"It ended too quickly. Oxytocin didn't get a chance to kick in."

Oxytocin, as Dr. von Stroop had explained to me earlier in our relationship, is the so-called "love hormone." It is produced, among other things, during orgasm, and assists in creating a feeling of trust and companionship.

"Are you pleased with the debriefing, or would you like to have me examined?"

I couldn't help but ask the final, pointless question, although I knew the answer. "Do you have any idea where he is? Where he came from, where he'll come from? A phone number, anything?"

Anna shook her head.

"You'll be at your clinic tomorrow? I assume he'll be visiting you."

Anna nodded. "Come here, *Schatzi*..."

I came closer and she put her arms around me.

"Give me the keys to the clinic."

She handed me a key, and I imprinted it into the soft wax pad I'd brought with me.

"Luigi will be working at your clinic."

She smiled. "He's a sweet kid. And you... you're leaving?"

I embraced her. "Don't worry, *Schatzi*. We have you under guard twenty-four seven. You're safe. The clinic, the apartment, it's all secure."

"Come with me. Let's go now..."

"You know that makes no sense."

Her chin crumpled, like a child trying not to cry.

"Have it your way," she said, pressing against me. I stroked her hair, and she pushed harder against my chest, as if trying to disappear inside me. I gently tried to cool her down a bit, and she placed a finger on my lips. "Come here."

I obeyed. She guided me to the sofa, took off my shoes and lay down beside me.

"I know you can't… I know it's wrong." She turned to me, kissed my forehead, my cheeks. When she reached my lips, I kissed back. I found it difficult to stop. The kiss grew deeper.

"Just for tonight, just this one night, I can't be on my own… just this night, and that's it."

I took off my shirt, and she suddenly threw back her head and laughed wildly.

"Ha! Some tears from the blonde, and there you go, giving in. Fantastic. The Israeli hero cracks like an egg. I love you, *Schatzi*." She got up and held out her hand. "Now get up, and let's go our separate ways."

I ordered the taxi. Luigi picked her up, and I drove after them and returned only when I watched her safely reach her apartment. On the way back, I made arrangements to have Digital Albert and his team flown in, to tap every security camera in Berlin.

A year before that, we'd been in London. Three months of intensive training—surveillance, communication protocols, withstanding interrogation, body language. Other than that, we'd spent every free minute fucking. We were staying at a basement apartment that I'd rented on an alley just off Kilburn Road. Our only tape was Bob Dylan's *Highway 61 Revisited*. We must have listened to it a thousand times. A Greek called Spiros would arrive twice a day to bring us "fish and ships" for two and examine our security arrangements. At the end of those three months, I'd decided that she was ready. She'd accepted my offer and started her new job as the administrator of the UNICEF children's hospital in Shabwah.

61.

The operations room that Noam had arranged for us was in central Berlin, on the twenty-first floor of the Sternbach Towers, in the offices of the Initiative for the Development of Alternative Sustainable Energy Sources. I preferred to keep tabs from a surveillance car we'd parked at the corner of Anna's street. Her building's concierge had been replaced by Nathan, one of our guys, granting us another foothold.

Just as Nathan reported that Francesca was on her way up to the apartment, Anna's phone rang. Imad, on the other end, told her that he'd sent a car to take her to the restaurant. He was cautious, not mentioning an address, calling from an untraceable phone. I felt an odd stab of excitement at the sound of his voice. I alerted Uzi, another one of ours, who was patrolling the surrounding block on a BMW bike. Nathan reported that Anna had entered a Berlin taxi. Uzi followed her on the bike for a while and at some point was replaced by Keren, from Noam's team, driving a modified Smart. Twelve minutes later, she reported, "Restaurant Margaux, Unter den Linden 78."

I asked Albert, back in the operations room, to tap into every camera he could find in the restaurant's vicinity. Uzi joined Keren and we tried to get them a table at Margaux. There were no available tables, but we insisted and eventually got them a couple of bar seats. This would have been optimal, if it weren't for Imad's two covert bodyguards who also came and sat by the bar.

"For the main course, Chef Hofmann recommends the salmon. The salmon is absolutely spectacular—it is flown here in a special aquarium specifically developed for the restaurant, steamed in a local Riesling and served with white asparagus in a clarified butter sauce with black lentils and porcini flecks."

"Anna?" Imad held her hand and tilted his head toward the head waiter, who was waiting for her reply.

"Yes, sorry, I spaced out. That sounds wonderful. How about you choose, and we'll just eat?" she suggested, fixing her glasses, which had a small transmitter embedded within the frame. She pushed them up her nose, reminding herself that Avner could hear every word, and that he was close.

The head waiter bowed, smiling. "I'm certain you will be pleased." He clicked his heels and returned to the kitchen.

Imad squeezed Anna's hand and proceeded to ask a question which had never before come up. "Do you love me?"

"Do you really love me, baby?" Luigi's mocking voice suddenly blared through. "Can you believe this asshole?!"

I was momentarily horrified, but thankfully, the sound link from Anna was one-way. Anna decided to bring the ball back to her court. She slipped off her shoe under the table and gently slid her foot under Imad's testicles.

Imad reached under the table and gently stroked her foot. "Anna, I'm serious..."

"Do I *love you*? The truth?"

"Yes. This is important to me."

"Oh, it's so important to me, baby! *Testa di cazzo*, important to him... fucking Arab." Nathan was giggling uncontrollably at Luigi's second outburst, and Uzi was demanding an exact translation for *Testa di cazzo.* I was forced to shut them up.

"I don't love you."

"Yes!" yelled Luigi triumphantly.

"I'm..." Anna sighed. "I'm addicted to you. I hate you, but I'm addicted to you. I thought I kicked the habit, and suddenly you're back and I'm so happy... like a junkie that suddenly found a pound of crack on her doorstep."

"I couldn't call sooner, not with them listening—Anna, they're after me... the Americans, the Israelis, Interpol..."

The audio link fell silent. Nothing but distant background noise.

"But you're so adorable," Anna cooed eventually.

"Jeez, lady, tone it down," muttered Keren from her seat at the bar.

The waiter arrived and placed the entrées in front of them—two plates with large truffle slices, soaking in fizzy champagne. The sommelier arrived shortly after, brandishing a wrapped bottle.

"Just pour, please," Imad cut him off. The sommelier uncorked the bottle with a loud *POP* that startled both Anna and me, then poured a tasting sample, which Imad drank and approved with a nod. The sommelier seemed frustrated by the lack of a more appropriate response for his Dom Pérignon.

"Anna, I need your help..."

Anna took a large gulp from her glass, stood up and rounded the table to embrace Imad, who had gotten up as well. She kissed his neck, his forehead, his cheek, and eventually his mouth. Luigi's melodramatic groan extracted hushed giggles from everyone. Imad tried to say something, and Anna placed a finger on his lips.

"I'll do whatever it takes to keep you with me. You're mine, and I'm greedy and possessive as you well know. Just, please, don't hurt my work at the clinic..." Anna was sticking to the pattern I had trained her to follow. Only accede after reasonable resistance.

"I promise. We won't use the clinic until you say you're done for the day. Thirty operations—"

"That many?"

"Two a night. Two weeks, and it'll be done, over. We'll start tomorrow night, and after we have ten, we'll take a break for a week or two."

Just that sentence alone would have been worth this hassle. They had ten shahids' worth of explosive stuffing—fifteen gallons of gel, give or take.

Anna returned to her seat and refilled their glasses. "It's dangerous, *Schatzi*. If they close my clinic, these kids… they have nowhere to go. They'll stay sick. Some will be permanently crippled. Why not rent a clinic? It's not difficult—I'll help, if it'll keep you safe."

"I'll help… *porca Madonna*." Luigi spoke with genuine anger, a true classic among Italian curses, again inciting giggles.

Imad gazed into her eyes.

"Your clinic presents the perfect opportunity. Arabs are always coming and going—anywhere else, this sort of activity would be monitored, but who would even consider monitoring Dr. von Stroop's UNICEF children's clinic?"

"What about the people looking for you? The Americans, Interpol?" She didn't dare say "Israelis."

"They think I'm dead. And we'll keep it that way."

Anna finished another glass of champagne. "Shall we go?"

Imad smiled and rose from his seat. "By the way, this new nurse, Stephan—what do you know about him? Check, please," he added to a passing waiter.

"You're about to find out, *cazzo*," Luigi hissed, his voice an odd mixture of joy and malice. More scattered laughter.

I was momentarily concerned, but Anna simply ignored the question and kissed him again, deeply. The asshole did his homework and was again proving to be a thorough, dangerous professional. I decided that it was time to end this. My dance with Imad, from the Little Jihad in Rome all the way to Shabwah, had gone on for too long. The trail of bombings, injuries and deaths he'd left in his wake was even longer.

Chef Hofmann arrived at the table and pointed at the champagne truffles, frowning. "Was the food not to your liking?"

"Oh, not at all—it was delicious. It's just, we have… urgent matters to attend to." Imad winked. "Another time."

Hofmann smiled. "Yes, the entire restaurant shares your happiness. I'll pack the meal for you, you can eat at home."

"You are gracious as usual. Thank you. Please send over the waiter with the check."

Hofmann shook his head. "On the house. When you have a proper meal, pay a proper bill. It will be soon, I hope."

Uzi and Keren were kissing passionately when Imad and Anna passed them on their way out, and so it made sense when they got up and followed them outside to wait for the chauffer.

"*Guten Abend*," Uzi greeted Imad, who nodded back. "Good evening."

A calculated move, to remind Anna we were right there with her.

The Porsche arrived. Imad held the door open for Anna and signaled his bodyguards, who got into a black Lincoln Navigator that seemed to appear out of nowhere and blocked the view of the Porsche until it disappeared from sight.

"Your place?" Imad asked.

"His place, Anna, please! Go to his place!" I muttered to myself, but Anna directed him to her apartment, perhaps out of concern for Abdu. Imad sent his bodyguards away for the night—he apparently felt safe enough without them.

The temptation was great, but I had to hold back, stick to the original plan. We needed him alive. A kidnapping, right under the noses of his bodyguards, let alone flying him back to Israel without incident, required meticulous planning and logistics. Far more logistics, unfortunately, than a quick bullet to the brain.

62.

Noam coordinated the night shifts, and Luigi joined me for a cognac and an espresso at a nearby bar.

"Remind me again why we aren't just executing the *cazzo* along with his pair of gorillas," he moaned.

I told him that I'd rather give Imad the freedom to hopefully lead us to Taissiri. It wasn't an all-out lie, though the truth was that we were not authorized to execute Imad, and that didn't seem likely to change in the near future. Nahum from foreign affairs has been scolding us daily about the Germans—and the rest of Europe, for that matter—who were "extremely pissed at our crude and invasive actions within their borders." He also made sure to remind us that the use of European passports during the recent operation to assassinate al-Mabhouh[27] in Dubai "did nothing to increase their love for us."

Luigi remained unconvinced. He raised some other arguments supporting an immediate execution—from an operational viewpoint, they all made perfect sense. I couldn't help but notice that I'd made each and every one of these arguments before, to Froyke, to the director. We clinked our glasses, this time drinking for healthier, yet considerably shorter lifespans for all spiteful politicians and bureaucrats.

---

27 Mahmoud al-Mabhouh was the chief of logistics and weapons procurement for Hamas's military wing. His assassination in Dubai is widely seen as an operation by Mossad, and triggered a diplomatic crisis after Mossad agents allegedly used forged foreign passports to carry out the killing.

Luigi's final argument was one I hadn't yet considered. According to him, "This Mabhouh, he grew up in Jabalia, with our buddy Imad. They were probably friends."

"And…?"

"And nothing. Isn't that reason enough?" he concluded the subject. I imagined Nora and him—the intel had undoubtedly come from her—giggling in bed after a cheerful fuck and making bets as to who could justify the assassination more creatively, tickling each other to death. I chose not to tell him that the primary obstacle was the continuing negotiations to fund the German submarines—this has become a personal obsession of the prime minister, who was unlikely to approve anything that might sabotage it. I suddenly recalled all the scheming and plotting I'd carried out along with Froyke and Bella in order to bring Luigi to The Unit, despite the ardent objections of the HR clerks.

"Why are you laughing?"

"Not laughing, just smiling."

My pager beeped. Now what?

But this time, it was a welcome beep. O'Driscoll, who'd been keeping an eye on Victor back in Arkansas, informed me that Dima was ready. We hurried to the operations room, currently ruled by Albert's iron fist. Froyke received approval from the DM, who'd received approval from the prime minister. I sped things along as much as I could, before anyone got a chance to change their mind. Froyke pulled some strings and got Unit 9900 to redirect a satellite and provide us with real-time coverage.

I spent the time remaining till H-Hour with Luigi, rechecking Anna's security and the surveillance on Imad. Everything seemed to be in order, but something was troubling me, a vague uneasiness I couldn't pinpoint. I needed Eran, but I was too troubled to communicate with him. The first images from Chernobyl were filling the screens. I found myself idiotically wishing for a large tub of popcorn to go with this movie night. The night was clear and the satellite images were clear and sharp. The plan ticked along like clockwork. The guard in the front showed the expected amount of enthusiasm toward the blond prostitute that approached his booth; within seconds, he was lying in a pool of his own blood, gushing from a slit throat. The three guards on patrol had a few seconds to stare blankly at the spike strip that slashed their tires before they were taken out with silenced bullets.

Dima approached them to confirm the kills, and I think I saw him smiling skyward. Three large military ZIL trucks entered the scene. Someone was directing them to position themselves on top of the railroad tracks, each stopping about six feet before its designated PETN tanker. Dima's men linked the trucks to the tankers with red-and-white tow bars and started towing them down the railroad, gaining speed as they went. After about an hour of driving, the first truck suddenly came to a screeching, rattling emergency stop, causing the tanker to rock dangerously from side to side. This was a cause for concern, to say the least. Luigi was swearing in several different languages. It didn't affect the tanker, which continued to sway alarmingly. Albert later claimed it rocked thirteen times before finally settling down. The other two trucks behind it were approaching fast, dangerously fast—why the hell wasn't anyone warning them? I asked Albert to zoom in. Dima's minuscule form could be seen on the tracks, waving his hands at the trucks which continued to hurtle toward him.

"*Puta madre*, the *cazzo* cut corners with the radio. One hundred grand, and the *cazzo* goes cheap on communications," Luigi swore, just as Dima pulled out a pistol and fired at the first truck. It was a smart move. The driver heard the bullet ting against his right wheel cover and began a controlled emergency stop. The driver behind him, however, failed to notice in time. The brakes shrieked with compressed air, the sound something between a hissing snake and an approaching missile. The tanker's metal wheels vomited clouds of sparks against the rails. It was becoming clear that this would not end well. The driver, who had apparently come to the same conclusion, jumped out of the truck and fortunately had enough wits about him to turn the wheel before his escape. The truck swerved off the tracks and flipped on its side. The tanker, still attached to it, rolled off the tracks as well. I had the option of an emergency link to Dima—I wanted to order him to blow up the tanker and move on, or possibly blow up all three, but any such contact would leave a digital footprint. As I considered the options, a call came in from Froyke, who unsurprisingly knew exactly what I was thinking and warned me to avoid contact. Dima figured out what needed to be done. He and two of his men approached the tanker and set up a few charges, then moved away to activate them. The explosion and resulting flames would not have looked out of place in any Hollywood action blockbuster, and the operations room burst into applause and exclamations. If only I had that damn tub of popcorn…

The two remaining trucks continued until they reached an unexpected gap in the railroad—they had most likely been confiscated by the metal merchants of the new Russian economy. The convoy headed for the 61K-012 regional road. Dragging the tankers' metal on asphalt was a trying, arduous task. The steel wheels would occasionally dig into the road and become stuck. The trucks moved in low gear, milking their massive diesel engines for all they had. After an hour of this dreadful ordeal, the two ZILs came to a halt in the middle of rural Novi Yarylovychi's only road. Small explosive charges ignited the gel, and the small village was burned away from the earth. The wooden houses blazed in ever-growing flames. We could smell it all the way from Berlin. The rookies in the operations room applauded again, and I thought of Robert Duval in his cowboy hat, smoking a Havana cigar on the chopper's landing skid and destroying the Vietnamese village to the sound of the Ride of the Valkyries, giving that speech of his—the smell, you know that gasoline smell, the whole hill. Smelled like . . . victory.

Not for the first time, I thought to myself that this Tarantinoesque scene should surely be considered the very peak of Coppola's filmographic record. I approved Albert's request to transfer the rest of Dima's pay.

The next morning, Russian and Ukrainian newspapers reported the attack carried out by Muslim terrorists, who had murdered thirty-two victims in cold blood, most of whom were retired commissars. The Grozny newspapers, on the other hand, joyously informed their readers of the long-awaited revenge of the liquidator families. The photos portrayed celebration. Free candy was had by all. Phase three had been executed successfully.

63.

Now it was time to settle things with our walking dead, this time in a permanent manner. The prime minister, however, was worried about the Germans' reaction and wouldn't succumb to the DM's pressure and approve Imad's assassination within German borders, instead suggesting that we hand Imad over to the Germans. This was also an unacceptable solution—the Germans would release him the first chance they got. Less than two months after the Munich massacre[28], the German authorities had released the three murderers in their custody for a pinkie-swear from the terrorist organizations that they would avoid activity in Germany. Politicians are a bad breed. It's just a matter of time until they fuck you over.

Then again, politics, my ass. A small Beretta, a .22 bullet. Point-blank, like we did in the old days, and no more Imad. The DM would throw a tantrum and Froyke would call it a "violation of orders that we can live with," and the director would say that Ehrlich's entire career consisted of violations that he decided we'd be able to live with. And then… Bella would talk to him, and he'd calm down, or he wouldn't.

I had to find some way to calm down. I transferred command to Luigi. The little punk had grown up to exceed each and every one of my

---

28 A terrorist attack during the 1972 Summer Olympics in Munich. The Palestinian terrorist group Black September took eleven Israeli Olympic team members hostage and killed them along with a West German police officer. -TK

expectations. Before my very eyes, he'd transformed from a wild and fresh-faced war machine to a sophisticated, calculated one. I allowed myself a mental pat on the back.

The small neon sign that glowed with admirable modesty on the street that intersected Anna's pointed to a small dive bar, which seemed like a fitting place to raise my serotonin and blood sugar levels back to normal. I was hoping it would help pass the nerve-wracking wait, and my unending frustration from this spectacular stunt they'd somehow managed to pull on us. I remembered the heritage stories about the military commandos of yore, which my old team had considered heroes. According to the stories, when those fine soldiers needed to unwind, they would go into Jordan, raid some Bedouin settlement, slaughter a bunch of them and come back in a far calmer mood. Shit like that no longer flies in today's military—let alone the Mossad—so when I needed to blow off steam, I went into the nearest bar and ordered a Kentucky bourbon. It used to be Macallan, but O'Driscoll had changed that.

When I entered the bar, I realized that it was in fact a watering hole for skinheads. Everyone seemed to be wearing brown or black leather suits. There were swastikas on the walls.

Fine, I thought. *So be it.*

I ordered a beer and a schnapps. The bartender did not appreciate this invasion, and neither did his little Nazi patrons. I felt their hostile eyes on me.

"You have five minutes and then *heraus*, we're closing."

"Okay," I answered and lit a cigar. "Then make it a Kentucky straight, *bitte*."

The bartender pointed at a sign forbidding smoking in public places. I looked around and saw that nearly everyone was smoking.

"You're quite the *Arschloch*, aren't you?" I said, blowing a ring of bluish smoke in his direction.

"What did you say?"

"I said, you're an *Arschloch*."

He pulled out a long crowbar from under the bar and waved it around threateningly. Out of the corner of my eye, I saw the group of approaching skinheads. I leaned toward the bartender, who took the bait and swung his crowbar. My left hand diverted the swing and my right rose quickly toward his chin, my open palm colliding with his chin. A familiar *crack* signaled that his jaw had been broken. He went down, whimpering. The rest of his Nazi buddies were still steadily approaching. I gripped the crowbar and headed toward the exit, which happened to be on the other side of their main thug. He was massive, with a body-builder physique, arms the size of utility poles. The sleeves of his tight black T-shirt were like tourniquets. He crossed his arms and smiled sweetly at me, licking his lips. A gold stud glinted at the tip of his tongue. If only I'd had a pair of pliers, I'd relieve him of both of them. His fellow patrons were closing in around us, watching the show, and perhaps waiting for the right moment to jump in. I swung the crowbar, and the schmuck charged at me like a bull; I shifted half a step to the left and swung my shoulder back for momentum, striking his solar plexus with my right elbow. I brought the crowbar down on his mouth, breaking his front teeth, and swooped my leg in a wide arc. He was on the floor now, coughing up tooth fragments, so I put out my cigar in his open mouth and turned to face the exit. They parted before me like the Red Sea. Outside I noticed that the steel doors had two large rings welded to them, meant for a padlock. I slipped in the crowbar. If there was no rear exit, the little Nazi bunch would be enjoying each other's company for a while. As unprofessional and irresponsible as that was, it did wonders for my serotonin.

64.

Tracking Imad was becoming exhausting. Apart from Anna, he made no calls—cellular or any other digital medium—at least, none that we'd managed to intercept. He wouldn't go anywhere or do anything without first checking for surveillance. His armed bodyguards were just as meticulous. This meticulousness forced us to keep our distance and rotate our lookouts as much as possible. If it weren't for Anna and her clinic, we never would have come close. Imad seemed to have grown more paranoid since their dinner at Margaux, and I decided not to risk Anna by planting cameras and tracking equipment. There we'd settled for simple audio transmitters. The Nevi'ot technicians went a step further and planted the same type of Siemens bugs used by the German security service.

"Doctor Taissiri will arrive at the clinic this evening, to make some arrangements," Imad informed Anna. I considered that to be our go-ahead. We performed communication checks and checked with Albert, who confirmed his access to just about every camera and CCTV in Berlin. The Siemens microphones were responding perfectly. An IDF Lockheed C-130 military transport plane, which had been loading ammunition at an American air force base, received instructions to sit tight. To avoid either of them warning the other, I planned the operation on three simultaneous fronts.

First front: Both of Imad's bodyguards would be neutralized by four fighters provided by the local Mossad branch, and set free once Imad and Taissiri were safely on their way to Israel.

Second front: Luigi would take control of the clinic operation, where he was stationed undercover as Stephan, a part-time Chechen nurse. This would be his first time performing as a team leader, and he was excited and determined. He had chosen Ran to serve as his number two and had personally handpicked the means and equipment. He and Ran should have no trouble detaining Dr. Taissiri, and I had no doubts whatsoever in Luigi's ability to deliver. I knew that as we approached H-Hour, he would grow less excited, and more focused.

Third front: The cherry on top. Uzi and I, assisted by Anna, would detain Imad. This had to be coordinated perfectly with Luigi and Noam from the branch. I'd decided that if worse came to worst, I would shoot Imad with the intent to kill. Let them yell at me afterwards.

Anna shot a wary glance at her watch. She should be meeting Imad in under an hour and still had no idea where. I went over the details with her one more time. When Imad called and suggested a meeting place, she would suggest another, and try to bring him to her apartment, but would not insist too much—what was important was the timing. We took Abdu to Francesca's apartment, just in case.

When Imad arrived, she would attempt to initiate sex with him as soon as possible. That should be easy—especially with the help of the incapacitating agent, similar to Rohypnol but slightly more potent, which waited in a small perfume bottle in her bag. One spray should suffice. When Imad started scratching his ear, she'd know he was near the breaking point and primed for seduction.

It was at this point that Anna stopped me and raised her large, pleading eyes at me, asking for my personal guarantee that Imad would not be assassinated. I gave it, telling her that even if I wanted to, I didn't have authorization to kill Imad—and either way, his strategic value was in what he knew, so we were all similarly motivated to keep him alive. It wasn't the whole truth, but it seemed to calm her.

Anna was lost in her thoughts, and I went over the details again and again in my head, once again coming to the conclusion that if anything went wrong, I had no choice but to neutralize Imad and deal with the fallout later.

I could already see Froyke telling me off like an insubordinate child, see myself responding the same way I always did—"It was an unavoidable violation of orders, one we can live with"—and him telling me, "Sure, Ehrlich, you can only live with the violations you can live with… I'm too old for this, Ehrlich. What do I tell them upstairs?"

"That an alteration was necessary due to unexpected conditions in the field," I would say, "and that Ehrlich is an uncontrollable asshole and a slave to his whims."

"That's fairly accurate," Froyke would probably say, then smile slightly and sigh.

65.

Stephan the nurse finished disinfecting and prepping the operating room. He looked at his watch. H-Hour was approaching. A car sped down the road nearby, blasting Hare Krishna at full volume. That was Nathan, letting him know the bad guys were coming. The music grew distant and died out. Now Nathan was supposed to wait and follow Taissiri into the clinic. Luigi had no way of knowing that a Bavarian traffic cop, deeply distraught by the Hare Krishna, had pulled Nathan over, thoroughly checked his papers, called to check with the station, all while an increasingly impatient Nathan stood there and waited.

"Good evening, Nurse Stephan!"

"Good evening. Doctor Taissiri, right? I'm just finishing up the OR and I'll be out of your hair."

"Could I ask a personal favor?"

"Of course," replied Stephan. "Anything I can do to help."

"I need assistance with this evening's operation, and I'd appreciate it if you joined me."

"This evening?" Stephan wondered. "I just finished prepping it for tomorrow."

"Yes, I see," said the doctor. "And you've done a fine job. However, there's been an emergency… of course, you'll be paid overtime. One hundred and fifty percent."

Luigi couldn't help but think that Nathan was supposed to be here by now. Where was he? *Calm down*, he said to himself. *Calm down and be patient. You're overenthusiastic. Take it slow.*

As he considered his response, two large men in scrubs entered the room, pushing two smaller men in wheelchairs.

He needed to think quickly, now. Where the fuck was Nathan? Avner had warned him against operating alone, but there was no other option—he would be pissed at him, but ultimately happy with the results. Dr. Taissiri was still waiting for his reply.

"Two hundred percent for every extra hour or part of an hour," said Luigi.

The doctor held out his hand. "Deal."

A small lopsided smile appeared on Luigi's lips. He imagined the surprise on Dr. Taissiri's face after the operation. His two thugs would probably wander off somewhere; they had nothing to do here. The other two would be confined to the operating tables. He just needed to overpower Taissiri. That wouldn't be difficult. *Then the guys from the branch'll get him on the transport plane, and we'll fly back to Israel, along with Imad. It'll be great.*

He smiled inwardly, anticipating Avner's fatherly scolding, which always carried with it a note of appreciation for Luigi's determination and ingenuity. After that, Avner and he would sit down and share a bottle of grappa di Romano Levi.

"Be right back," he said, feigning coyness. "Need to take a piss."

He walked into one of the stalls in the restroom and took the old Japanese dagger he'd confiscated from Colonel Sokolovsky out of the toilet tank. It was the only weapon he'd allowed himself to bring into the clinic. Nathan had the Tasers and the guns. Luigi flushed and attached the dagger to a Velcro strip on his leg. Should he phone Avner? No, now wasn't the time to bother him. *We'll move along with the bad guys, neutralize the fuckers.* Avner will be pleased with him.

When he got back to the operating room, Taissiri was standing by his two patients, stroking the head of the one nearest to him, speaking quietly in Arabic.

"Blood pressure," Taissiri ordered, pointing at a cart. As Luigi turned around to take out the blood pressure monitor, Taissiri pulled a loaded

Beretta from his white coat and yelled, "Now!"

The two large orderlies lunged at Luigi and confined him. Each shoved his hand under one of Luigi's arms and grabbed a wrist—an old-fashioned lock, favored mostly by cops, but an effective one. One good squeeze was all any either of them needed to snap Luigi's arm. The two idiots in the wheelchairs were clapping. Taissiri hushed them and filled a large syringe. Luigi stopped struggling—any resistance at this point would only serve to exhaust him. Taissiri returned the Beretta to his coat and approached Luigi, wielding the syringe.

"Calm down, Stephan. It's just some mild anesthesia."

The time was now. Luigi raised his foot and brought it down on the toes of the orderly on his left, who recoiled in pain and released one of his arms. He quickly spun around and shoved two fingers into his eye sockets, and the orderly fell to the floor, moaning and blind. The other orderly, still holding his right arm, was pushing Luigi's elbow upward and leaning his entire weight on his wrist. Luigi's arm broke with an audible crunch, but he managed to break free from the orderly's grasp and bent into a defensive stance, his dangling arm cradled against his stomach. The orderly inched forward, eyeing Luigi's broken arm. Luigi turned his right shoulder toward him, seemingly exposing it, and when the orderly reached for the arm, Luigi snapped open like a spring. His open left palm connected with the orderly's chin, breaking his jaw. A final kick to the testicles and he was down, neutralized.

"Come on, motherfuckers!" Luigi cried out hoarsely and moved toward Taissiri, who was pale, sweating, and steadily moving backwards. Taissiri dropped the syringe and pulled out the Beretta, yelling commands in Arabic. One of the surgical candidates sprung out of his wheelchair, and the other rolled back into the corner of the room. Luigi managed to draw his dagger and retreated slightly, reevaluating. "Move as slowly as the time frame allows," Avner always told him. *But I have no time frame*, he thought. *I need to slow down, but where's Nathan? Where the fuck is Nathan? I can't think, can't focus.*

The patient that had left his wheelchair was running toward Luigi with his head lowered, apparently attempting to ram him. Luigi let him come closer and stepped aside at the last second, bringing his elbow down on the back of the attacker's neck. He exploited the moment of stunned confusion to slide his dagger across his throat. The patient fell to the floor, dead. Taissiri's shaking hands failed to extract a shot from the Beretta. Luigi moved toward him, his dagger at the ready. Taissiri began yelling desperately, and the other patient left his corner and rolled himself toward Luigi. Taissiri finally managed to squeeze the trigger, firing at Luigi's center of mass. Luigi fell, struggled to get back up. Another shot and Luigi sprawled on the floor, unmoving.

Taissiri, breathing raggedly, stood above Luigi's corpse, his gun aimed and shaking. He kicked Luigi's head, watched it rock limply, devoid of muscle tone and of life. He then walked toward the blinded orderly who was whimpering on the floor and shot him as well.

66.

Murphy was also working overtime tonight and had apparently pulled out all the stops. Imad was gone. Gone! The little shit had canceled his meeting with Anna due to an "urgent issue that required his attention" and vanished without a trace. Even worse, I was the idiot who had ordered the local Mossad branch to drop their surveillance; I didn't want to spook him. Well, it fucking worked—he was so un-spooked that he up and left. I could only hope Taissiri knew where he was. And to top it all, the line to Luigi and Nathan was down. The Siemens surveillance system, which had responded perfectly during the tests before H-Hour, had fallen completely silent. The Nevi'ot technician, who was operating it for the first time in his life, couldn't seem to reactivate it.

I hopped on Uzi's bike and we sped to the clinic. Everything seemed quiet when we got there—we kicked down the operating room door, weapons drawn. I didn't see Nathan, or Luigi, at first; Taissiri, however, was standing in the middle of the room, attempting to aim the gun with shaking fingers. I fired two bullets into his right shoulder, and he dropped the Beretta and crumpled to the floor. Uzi charged the hostile in the room, who was sitting in a wheelchair, wetting his pants.

I kicked away the Beretta, which Uzi picked up, and noticed Luigi lying on the floor. I hurried to check his pulse, childishly and pointlessly hopeful.

"What?" Uzi said, stunned, as I rose from Luigi's lifeless corpse. "What, he's dead?!"

He raised the gun toward the man in the wheelchair and fired a single shot into his brain.

"Cuff him," I said, pointing at Taissiri, who was writhing and groaning on the floor. Uzi cuffed Taissiri, added a kick to his injured shoulder, and seemed to think one kick wasn't enough. I was forced to pull him away. I wondered where Nathan was during all this. Later I found out that he had been detained by some asshole traffic cop, and taken in for questioning at the local police station when he'd responded aggressively. The entire plan had shattered into a million pieces, and me—I had to pick them up. Froyke rose in my thoughts, quoting his father—*Mensch tracht und Gott lacht.* This is how the bad thoughts begin.

If I'd taken out Imad when he was at Anna's, like Luigi had begged me to do, I'd have a dead Imad right now, and a breathing Luigi. If I'd agreed to risk Anna, just a bit—and why not, really?—and installed proper surveillance at the clinic, Nathan wouldn't have had to resort to his fucking Hare Krishna and could have assisted Luigi when this whole thing had started, and then I'd have a captive Taissiri, and a breathing Luigi. I was at the epicenter of a massive, roiling shitstorm, and it just kept piling up. The entire plan had gone to shit. Now I had to do damage control and plan for the rest of it.

I dedicated every available digital and human resource to the search for Imad, alive or dead. Budget was no longer an issue. All restrictions had been removed. I called in O'Driscoll, Bruno, anyone who owed me even a sliver of a favor. Noam's team arrived in an ambulance. No one dared touch Luigi's corpse, until Noam snapped out of it for long enough to lift Luigi up on his shoulder and head out to the air force base. The four Arabs Luigi had killed would be transported to the pathogenic waste incinerator in Wannsee.

"Our little *cazzo*," Uzi tried to comfort the rest of us. "He took out four hostiles single-handedly before the fifth one got him."

I ripped off the band of electric tape that covered Taissiri's mouth. He gagged out the rag shoved in his mouth, breathing heavily.

"Where's Imad?"

Taissiri didn't answer. I slapped him hard enough to knock him to the floor. Uzi picked him back up, signaling me to take it easy when Taissiri spat out two teeth. I nodded back. Uzi fixed the bandage around Taissiri's shoulder and, while he was there, shoved his thumb in the bullet wound. Taissiri made strange squealing sounds, like a butchered calf. I looked up at Uzi, signaling him to calm down.

"Cooperate, and we'll take you to Israel for the remainder of this interrogation. You'll spend some time in a luxurious government-run facility, and at some point, someone'll decide to release you for some emotionally significant corpse. Why did you kill Stephan?"

"We didn't know if we could trust him, so Imad ordered me—"

"Where is Imad?"

"Out of the country, I don't know where!" he quickly added.

I backhanded him, and he fell to the other side this time. He wheezed and gurgled, blood welling in his mouth. Uzi went to pick him up again and I raised a finger to stop him. Let him lie there. I placed the heel of my shoe on his wounded shoulder.

"Doctor, outside, there is an ambulance that will soon transport our pathogenic waste to the Wannsee incinerator. There's a lake there, and a beautiful forest. Green everywhere." Taissiri shivered and I went on. "Six million Jews passed through the crematoriums, and with zero complaints—we can only assume it wasn't that bad. The thing is, when we lower the temperature of the furnace, you're going to burn very, very slowly. The fire moves from the feet up, you know, so those are always first to go, and then… well. I think you get it, Doctor. I think you understand what it is I'm offering you here. You get to see the end coming. This is huge, Doctor—huge. All of humanity wants to know when it will end, and no one does. You get to know, precisely." I squeezed his shoulder again with the tip of my shoe and let go, to let him think. After a few seconds, I asked again.

"Where is Imad?"

"Imad left the organization. He left the sheikh and swore allegiance to the sultan. They're trying to create a united Arab coalition and attack the Jews."

"Please. You've been spewing this bullshit for years. I asked you where he is. Where is he?!" I didn't wait for a response but pressed my heel deeper into the wound. Taissiri was making those sounds again. His bulging eyes seemed to nearly pop out of their sockets.

I relieved a bit of the pressure and Taissiri gurgled, "I'll tell you, I'll tell you," and I pressed harder. His eyes threatened to spill out of his face. When I could take it no longer, I moved my foot away.

"Speak!"

Taissiri was breathing shakily through his mouth, his chest rising and falling like a bellows.

"Now!" I yelled. "Talk now, or I swear—"

"London! In London, he's in London with abu Bachar..."

I realized that there wasn't much more I would get from him right now and kicked him in the mouth with my heel. His jaw broke and dropped, dangling. He passed out.

"Take this piece of garbage to the incinerator."

Uzi gave me a puzzled look.

"Take him to the incinerator, see if you can get anything else out of him about Imad and their communication protocol. I doubt he knows much more than that."

"And..."

"And then burn him."

"Sir... Avner, you... you..."

"What? I what?!"

"You said, more than once, that killing without the intent of saving lives cannot be justified. You said that would never happen under your command."

"This motherfucker killed Luigi. And someday, some idiot politician will decide to release him for a corpse, or some asshole drug-smuggling officer. Killing him will save lives, I guarantee it." *At the very least, whatever's left of mine.* I imagined Luigi's grave sprouting from the earth, right next to Eran's.

"If you can't do this, Uzi, tell me now." I took a deep breath. "I doubt he knows any more, but either way, take him down there, put him in the oven, light a fire under his ass. If he knows any more, he'll talk."

The oven delivered. Taissiri revealed that Imad had been urgently summoned to the Sultanate embassy in Bayswater—though he didn't know why. He also disclosed the names of the remaining nine stuffed shahids, and their last-known locations. Uzi tried to question him about their destinations, future attacks, but Taissiri kept saying that only Imad knew. He flooded them with details, making me wonder if this was some kind of survival strategy. Time to fly him to Israel. If he was still hiding anything, they'd get it out of him.

I mounted Uzi's bike and let it take me where it wanted. I ended up on the Autobahn, and the BMW was quickly gaining speed. The helmet's visor kept away the wind but failed to keep away the thoughts. Luigi appeared before me, smiling. "Hey, boss. I didn't get the chance to thank you. For trusting me."

A tear snuck out of my tear duct and, with nowhere else to go, poured into my eye, down my cheek. Other tears came, and soon I couldn't see the road. I tore off the helmet and flung it away and let the cold wind dry my face. The helmet bounced once and smashed on the asphalt. I thought of Eran.

On the one-year anniversary of Eran's death, I'd finished placing the basalt tombstone over his grave, facing the view. Nehemiah came to visit—a close friend who was heading the psychology department in Boston back then.

"You're just reinforcing the pathology of your bereavement," he said. Pathological bereavement, the professor explained, constantly enables the sense of loss and impairs recovery. "You don't want to go there. This isn't you."

"I didn't want to go here, and it isn't me, but here I am. I'm here to stay. I'm never leaving him again, not ever." I concluded the discussion.

Ya'ara and Nehemiah, Eran and Luigi—gone. *I'm alone.*

67.

"Anna's gone," Albert told me warily back in the operations room. "She called in an hour ago, I told her about Luigi, she hung up on me, and… that's it. She's not at her apartment," he added before I could ask, "not at the clinic, not answering her phone."

I drove the BMW back to the city.

Albert and his technicians were sitting at their screens, examining the satellite images. I started to create possible scenarios. None of them boded well for us.

Scenario 1: Anna and Imad ran off together. Where would they go?

Scenario 2: Imad exposed Anna's cover and killed her. How did he find out? Where is the body? I'll kill him.

Scenario 3: Imad has tortured Anna and she revealed everything she knew. What does Anna know? She can ID me, and the whole team. Doesn't matter, I'm killing him anyway.

Scenario 4: Imad is still torturing Anna. She is naked and tied up, and he approaches her with a large syringe, jams it into her chest. I went to the restroom and washed my face.

Scenario 5: More optimistically, Imad might have exposed Anna and taken her hostage, to trade for Dr. Taissiri. I agree to the trade, most likely disobeying my orders, and then kill them both, Taissiri and Imad, probably also in violation of orders.

"Yes!" yelled Albert.

"Imad? Where? Who?"

"Anna! At the bank—"

I ran out and hopped on the bike. Of course. Her primary go-bag was in a safe deposit box.

"Doctor King Schultz." I showed my papers to the clerk in charge of the vault.

"Herr Doctor, your wife was just here..." He glanced at his watch. "Fifteen minutes ago."

"Yes, *danke*, I know—she forgot one of the papers, so of course I get sent over..."

The clerk smiled sympathetically and escorted me to the safe. I waited for him to leave and whispered into the microphone, "She left about fifteen minutes ago. Take a forty-mile radius."

The handgun, the passports, the credit cards, traveler's checks and two hundred one-hundred-dollar bills were gone. In their place I found a yellow envelope.

"To Avner," it read. Inside was a letter in handwriting I knew well.

> I can't do this anymore. I'm leaving. Don't look for me, you can't find me (I had excellent teachers—I know how to disappear). And even you do, it wouldn't help. I'm done. When I finished med school, I swore to do whatever I could to save lives. And for a while, I did—and I was happy. And working for you also made me happy—as much as a confused pervert like me can ever be happy. You were clever enough to provide me with the father figure I needed, and to leverage my guilt over my family's actions during the Holocaust. I was proud of my work, and satisfied—no less than I was by helping those Arab kids. Perhaps I thought that it allowed me to redeem myself. My soul is horribly messed up. I know this, you know this, and you used this knowledge perfectly. I loved you like a father. And I loved Luigi like a brother, though I hadn't known him long. I imagine he was the son you adopted, to fill the space left behind by Eran. I loved Imad, too, as a lover. I love all of

> you, and you all hate each other.
>
> You killed Luigi, and soon either you or Imad will kill the other. I can't stand it anymore.
>
> Avner, I know that if you choose to, you'll find me, wherever I run.
>
> I love you. Don't look for me... please.

It had been two days. I'd lost Luigi, I'd lost Imad, and now, finally, I'd lost Anna.

When I'd finished the letter, I knew what I had to do. I contacted Jones, O'Driscoll's guy. After he had gotten back from his tours in Afghanistan, Jones joined the Marshals Service until O'Driscoll had plucked him out of there, and for good reason—Jones was a sort of an American Luigi. Clever, determined, and born with a rare lack of bullshit. I was very fond of him.

I gave Jones the details of Anna and Francesca's passports, credit cards and bank accounts. I asked if he needed photos, and he replied that it wasn't necessary. I could almost hear him smiling.

"*Semper fi*," said Jones.

"*Semper fi*," I replied, knowing that I'd just accumulated one more debt—but one I would gladly pay.

68.

Bayswater, London. The meeting went swimmingly. The sultan, ever courteous, apologized to Imad for bringing him in from Berlin in such short notice.

"The world's leaders are about to assemble in New York for the UN General Assembly. I called a summit for the heads of the Islamic states, and I wanted to listen to your proposal again, face-to-face, before I meet them."

Imad nodded and repeated the main points of his vision, strategy and operational plan. The sultan listened intently and occasionally stopped Imad to take notes.

"First, Al-Quds—that is my creed, and my strategy is for all forces to converge on the focal point," Imad concluded.

"Impressive," said the sultan. Abu Bachar nodded his agreement, then took the notes and excused himself from the room. The sultan fixed his gaze on Imad.

"Come closer," he said.

He approached, and the sultan took Imad's hand into both of his. "Stop worrying. Abu Bachar has Gertrud with him, and they are operating with an unlimited budget, provided by me. Have no doubt—they will find Doctor Taissiri, and your German doctor. Just keep it in mind that abu Bachar and Gertrud are... well." He pinched two fingers together and smiled suggestively.

Abu Bachar returned with the printed speech and an official diplomatic passport of the Sultanate, which he proudly handed to Imad.

Imad flipped through his new passport and thanked them both. They parted.

On his way back to Berlin on one of the sultan's private jets, Imad found himself troubled by thoughts of the years he'd wasted with global jihad. He would have liked to push these thoughts away, focus on the bright, promising future—but someone had intervened with this future, changed the rules. Dr. Taissiri, his key player, had disappeared. So had Anna. Without the two of them, he had no way of producing more stuffed shahids—and worse, either of them could have turned or defected altogether, revealing the names of the active shahids. This sort of damage was beyond repair. Imad realized that from this moment onward, he had to create the change himself. He had to take back control. It was his turn now, he thought. He could do this.

69.

At the very fringe of the Berlin international airport, there is a dedicated landing strip for the Israeli airplanes. The airport workers have nicknamed it "the Jewish ghetto." This relative remoteness allowed the German and Israeli security forces to supervise, and operate if need be, without putting everyone else at risk.

At 02:30, Zacharia Mizrotzki, the Israeli security officer responsible for the "ghetto," phoned Gerhard Schwager, the airport's head security officer. Schwager was a colonel (res.) in the Bundeswehr's special paratrooper operation division; Mizrotzki was a company commander (res.) in the IDF's Paratrooper's Brigade Unit 55. Mizrotzki and Schwager were old friends. Mizrotzki did his best to nurture this friendship, at first because he had been ordered to by his superiors—employing for this purpose many pints of beer, fancy meals and free trips to Eilat and to the luxurious casinos in Antalya and Bulgaria (most of which were Israeli-owned). The fact that Schwager's father had been a senior Gestapo officer had only strengthened the friendship between the two ex-paratroopers.

"*Jawohl, Herr Kommandant*," Schwager sleepily answered his phone. "What have I done to deserve this questionable honor in the middle of the night?"

"*Mein Herr*," replied Mizrotzki. "We're having some issues with the defense system of one of the Israeli government jets. Technicians are on the way, and I'd like to close off a remote defense perimeter, so that no harm would come to your brave Wehrmacht troopers."

"You plan on blowing some shit up in my airport?"

"God forbid. Just a reboot of the system. But regulations state we have to clear the area."

"We do love our regulations here," yawned Schwager. "I'll talk to Franz, he's the officer on duty. Good night, and be careful. This isn't the Levant. If something happens, it's the shower for you, Mizrotzki." He laughed hoarsely and hung up.

Four minutes and forty-five seconds later, the airport guard security force had outlined a perimeter ring around the Israeli jet. The soldiers distanced themselves as much as possible. A yellow maintenance tractor arrived, towing three large wooden crates. Mizrotzki and three technicians in white coveralls followed it in a Mercedes G-class jeep. The technicians opened the cargo hold doors and wheeled the large crates inside. The pilot and another crewmember pulled them in and wheeled them toward the back of the plane. The technicians tested the defense system and reset it.

Mizrotzki radioed Franz. "All clear. You can cancel the alert."

He then headed to the terminal, where I was just finishing up with security.

"Your package is in there. Everything okay?" he asked. "You seem troubled."

"It'll be fine, Mizrotzki, everything will be fine. Or it won't. Thanks, either way, for your help."

The stairs pulled up and the jet started preparing for takeoff. I went to the back to check on our cargo.

"Why's he still in the box?" I asked the guard.

"You want 'im outta the box, he's outta the box…"

He pulled out a Leatherman multitool, cut open the metal bands hugging the crate, and lifted the lid according to the arrow drawn on it. Dr. Taissiri was lying inside, sedated. Fresh bandages covered his shoulder, face and legs.

"Keep him cuffed at all times, but take out the gag. If he so much as peeps, kick him in the face. But don't kill him, you hear?"

"I heard he took out one of ours… can I fuck 'im up a little?"

"Nope. He still needs to undergo further interrogation. Just, if he peeps, you know, kick to the face. You can break some teeth, if he still has any. You know what? You come get me, I'll kick him in the face."

"No problem, boss, you got it."

I walked back to the front of the jet, pushed off my shoes and tried to get some sleep.

"Passengers are requested to fasten their seat belts, turn off all electronic devices, and keep their shoes on their disgusting, smelly-ass feet at all times," spoke a jeering falsetto. I cracked open an eye. Moti was standing in front of me, a bottle of Macallan in his right hand, two glasses in his left, swinging his arms around in a ridiculous imitation of a flight attendant pointing out the emergency exits. Moti could always make me smile. He was the first openly gay combat pilot and had spent a great deal of his career smashing up preconceptions about masculinity. We'd started at the same course in the Air Force Flight Academy. I had gotten kicked out later for fucking around with the Fouga Magister above the female officers' quarters—it's how I'd ended up at The Unit. Moti plopped down beside me, shoved a glass in my hand and poured.

"Hang on to that glass, RP. It's 1932 Macallan. Each drop costs like two Avners. You look like shit, man. Can I help?"

"You've helped already. Pour another one and go see to your flying machine. I guess the boss sent someone up here to badger me?"

Moti nodded toward the cockpit, where the DM had just emerged.

"I'm afraid it's the head badger himself," he said. Moti shrugged and sauntered away, and the director sat down next to me.

"Where's the doctor?"

I pointed toward the back of the jet.

"No, Doctor von Stroop."

I poured the whiskey and handed one glass to the director.

"Here's to Doctor von Stroop's new life in… Indiana? Or Wyoming, or New Hampshire. Wherever the US Marshals Service decided to put her."

The director slowly sipped. "The Marshals Service?"

I nodded.

"O'Driscoll. And... Jones, was it? Okay. Okay," he said, rubbing his chin.

I tried to decrypt the meaning behind his double *okay*. Okay? And not a word on my blatant violation of procedure, of explicit orders. I suppose that's the true power of seniority—it allows you to be generous, kind, where others can't. I shuddered to think how I would respond to this level of disobedience from one of my own subordinates. But Anna had done everything she could to get out of this life, and I felt compelled to provide her with a safe haven, secluded enough so that no one could find her—not Imad's people, nor ours.

"Look, Avner," said the DM, "Froyke's in bad shape. He seems..." He hesitated, searching for words. "He seems tired. Your Doctor Verbin is taking good care of him, but I want... I ask that you bring him back. You're the only one who can. We can't have him following in Motta's footsteps[29]."

"Verbin? She didn't say anything to me."

"She's been keeping Bella updated."

Scheisse. "If Froyke's already made up his mind..."

"It appears that he has. Your job is to stop him."

The DM finished his glass and switched to a more businesslike tone. "The NSA have spotted a three hundred and fifty percent increase in communications between the Sultanate palace and the estate in Bayswater, as well as a significant increase in aerial activity."

"Makes sense," I said and nodded toward the back of the jet, where Taissiri lay tied in his box. "He told us that Imad was headed to Bayswater. Slipped right out of our fingers."

---

29 Mordechai "Motta" Gur was a legendary Chief of Staff of the IDF who committed suicide after being diagnosed with terminal cancer. -TK

"Another interesting tidbit, courtesy of Nora," said the director. "Apparently, the sultan's been funding Imam al-Qaradawi, who's been publishing fatwas[30] calling for reconciliation between the Sunnis and the Shiites—a collaboration to achieve common goals. Apparently the sultan wants to be the next Harun al-Rashid."

"And how does Imad fit in?" I asked, although I'd pretty much guessed the answer.

"Imad is currently working for the sultan. Are you familiar with the phrase, 'first, Al-Quds'?" asked the director.

I wasn't. The director was happy to oblige, explaining that a fan of ours in MI5, who didn't want to get in trouble, had passed the intel along to O'Driscoll, who'd passed it to us, along with an invoice for an IOU to MI5. The intel didn't provide any operational insight, but it did give us their main strategy. The Al-Quds Shahids—that is, the stuffed shahids—were just a trial run. The main goal was to use the Al-Aqsa Mosque as a focal point for global change. Get the shahids in there, blow up the mosque, then blame the Jews for the explosion. The pan-Islamic coalition would unite during the aftermath and attack Israel—one big, final attack.

"*Endlösung der Judenfrage*," said the DM and fell deep into thought. A final solution to the Jewish problem.

I considered reassuring him—things had changed since the *Endlösung*, after all—but decided not to. He seemed to be concerned about the historic aspect of the plan. I was much more interested in the operational aspect.

"So where's our MI5 fan now?"

"Pushing daisies," said the director with a nonchalance that suited me more than it did him. Apparently, among the casualties of the "plane crash" designed to eliminate the British Engineers who planned and built the Bayswater war room, there was also an "antisurveillance

---

30 In Islam, a fatwa is a legal opinion or learned interpretation, issued by a qualified jurist (a *mufti*), pertaining to Islamic law. -TK

expert" from MI5, who was kind enough to bug the war room with a microscopic surveillance system that transmitted straight to the basement of the Thames House.

"As to your question," said the DM, although I hadn't asked it yet, "after thirty days of broadcasting, the bugs stopped transmitting. The engineer in charge would have reentered the activation code if he hadn't died in the plane crash."

He stood up. "I have some business to take care of," he said and headed to the front of the jet. Before he went into the cockpit, he pointed at the back, toward Taissiri. "Good job, Ehrlich," he said and disappeared inside.

I thought of my own little focal point, back home, and promised myself a great deal of Verbin, lots and lots of Verbin, just Verbin—without Imad or any other intrusions.

BOOK 3

70.

The lights dimmed in the Sultanate estate's private screening room. On the screen, thousands of aircraft obscured the sky; fighter jets arriving from air bases and aircraft carriers, bombers emerging from underground hangars, cargo planes brimming with bombs, and hundreds of civilian planes, booby-trapped with flammable and volatile substances—flying Molotov cocktails. With every passing second, less of the sky was visible, until the entire frame was a black, sparkling mass of machinery. And out of this dark mass, the golden dome of the holy mosque slowly rose. It was replaced with a close-up of Sheikh al Qardawi, the greatest Muslim jurist of his generation, reading a fatwa endorsing the necessity of full cooperation between the Sunni and the Shiite—"A collaboration which will enable us to eradicate the enemies of Islam, whoever they may be," he said.

The image was replaced with a picture of the sultan's new mosque, a perfect replica of the Al-Aqsa Mosque. The rays of the sun struck the golden dome and shattered into a million golden sparks. The lights in the screening room came back on, and an immaculately dressed waiter entered the room bearing an ornamental gold tray and poured dark, thick Bedouin coffee into small cups decorated with the Sultanate crest.

"Perfect," said Imad, "perfect—this is exactly how it's supposed to look!"

"We plan on opening the summit with it." Abu Bachar smiled. "Would you like a rerun?"

Imad assumed that the sultan was listening in but couldn't ignore the gentle sarcasm wrapping abu Bachar's words. He decided to give the sultan his pound of flesh.

"Israel is a foothold," he said. "The American fort within the Middle East, within our territory. It supports interests of the American oil companies, which in turn are bleeding us dry. Take down the fort, and we're free to charge forward. Nothing will stand in our way."

"Interesting. Go on," said abu Bachar, as if he was hearing the pitch for the first time.

"For the first time in jihad history, we have an operable strategy, not just idle talk about some 'global caliphate.' This is the strategy led by the sultan and me. It will expunge the humiliation and return hope, comfort and honor to the Arab world. After we destroy the Jewish state, we will have a continuous bloc of Arab nations—from Iran, Turkey, Syria and Iraq all the way to Jordan, Palestine, Egypt, Sudan and the Emirates. A united force, equal in influence and rights to the Western, Chinese and Russian blocs. Two billion believers against a nation of eight million, including the old and the very young—two million of which are ours. No one"—he fixed his gaze on abu Bachar—"no one, not even those of the smallest possible faith, can say it's impossible."

"The summit will convene in twenty-nine days. Until then, you have to deliver on your words without all this…" Abu Bachar spread his hands. "Without this, the whole thing is meaningless."

"I'm positioning all our forces at a single, pivotal target. The mosque is our foothold. With it, we will change the world. The Al-Quds Shahids are standing by for orders. Please give the sultan my blessings and gratitude. Without him—"

"There is no need," boomed a benevolent voice from the screen, where the sultan's face suddenly appeared. "I embrace you, Imad. You will continue with your holy works. I have decided—from this day, you are my eldest son. We shall celebrate the memory of your father, the holy shahid Mustafa Akbariyeh al-Nabulsi abu Imad, may he sit in the grace of Allah. Abu Bachar will make the necessary arrangements. I also have a humble gift for you." The sultan smiled and added, "Gertrud!"

71.

"Yes, sir," said Gertrud, entering the screening room. "I'm here." She clicked her heels in a German salute and quickly typed something on the screen of her golden smartphone. A close-up of a face, taken recently, appeared on the large screen.

"This is the Jew responsible for either the kidnapping or murder of Doctor Taissiri and Doctor von Stroop. Avner Ehrlich Ne'eman, deputy chief of operations in the Mossad—"

"Where can I find him?" Imad instantly asked.

Gertrud didn't have a chance to reply to the intrusion, and the sultan reappeared on the screen, smiling amiably. "Let her show you."

Imad nodded and Gertrud tapped her phone. A series of photos quickly appeared on the screen, flickering quickly. In each photo, Avner looked younger. The photos flew by faster and faster, little black crosses and numbers flitting across them, until the screen eventually settled on a photo of a much younger Avner. Imad could not tear his eyes from it. The screen split in two; beside Avner's recent close-up appeared a much older photo of him in uniform, wearing a red beret[31]. The two photos slowly merged together.

Imad grew pale.

"Ninety-six percent match," Gertrud said triumphantly.

"How did you get this?" Imad finally said.

---

31 Red berets in the IDF are worn by paratroopers, and several commando units, such as Matkal. -TK

Gertrud smiled. "I ran facial recognition software on our Israeli data. I found this image in the archive of an Israeli newspaper."

An image appeared of a small segment from a newspaper, the headline reading "PROMINENT TERRORIST MUSTAFA AKBARIYEH AL-NABULSI KILLED BY IDF FORCES IN JABALIA." Imad's heart skipped a beat. A photo of Baba's face, taken postmortem, appeared under the headline. The subtitle presented him as "Mass murderer Mustafa Akbariyeh al-Nabulsi, responsible for the deaths of over thirty Israelis." Gertrud translated the text to English, and Imad remained silent.

Another photo appeared—a squad of Israeli soldiers in full battle gear. When it zoomed in on the leading soldier, there was no longer room for error. Avner Ehrlich Ne'eman.

"This one reads, 'IDF troopers returning from a raid in the heart of the Jabalia refugee camp,'" said Gertrud, still clearly pleased with her findings.

"I don't need a translation," Imad said.

"I know," she replied. "But Mr. abu Bachar does."

Abu Bachar placed a hand on Imad's shoulder. "This is our small gift to you. Your father's killer, your brother's killer. The Jew that's been after you. From now on, we'll be the ones after him."

Abu Bachar slid a finger across his throat. "You'll have your revenge, and it'll be sooner and sweeter then you could have imagined."

"I need a moment," Imad said and left the room, tears clogging his throat. He crumpled into the carved wooden bench in the palm greenhouse, trying to replace the image of his dead father's face with a memory of his living face, unsuccessfully. Baba's face remained dead in his mind, swollen and blue, his mouth open, as if gasping for breath. Tears flowed freely from Imad's eyes, and for the second time in his life, he fully wept, uncontrollable, bitter tears.

A small flame ignited in the corner of his eye. Gertrud crouched in front of him, handing him a lit cigarette. He took it and drew the smoke into his lungs. She sat down next to him.

"How did you find him?" he asked flatly.

"Are you all right?"

He nodded. Gertrud gently plucked the cigarette from his lips, took a long drag and put it back. "The Berlin police. I have some friends there who gave me access to security camera footage." She looked up at Imad. "I isolated him and ran him through every database, including Interpol and the German intelligence service. *Null*, nothing. So I changed tactics. The Mossad usually gets its killers from the special units, IDF commandos. We have a photo database of their officers and soldiers, from the Jews' newspapers and television and social networks, and that's where I found him. He was an officer in Matkal and had his share of operations. I went over them, one by one, until I got to the raid in Jabalia..."

"He gave me chocolate."

"What?"

"This Jew, he... they came in through the wall, blew a hole, blocked the door and snatched Baba. I was sleeping next to him, and when I woke up... he gave me chocolate and said someone would pick me up..." His voice cracked.

"They blew a hole through the wall?" asked Gertrud, attempting to channel the conversation elsewhere.

"A tactic they've developed for the refugee camps, to avoid alley fires. Go through the walls, move from house to house, avoid the streets."

Gertrud grabbed his hand. "It's only a matter of time now... as we speak, I have people looking for his home address. Abu Bachar suggests that we start with his woman. She's an oncologist at Hadassah Hospital in Jerusalem. I haven't found any children yet—if they're out there, we'll get to them too, and kill him after."

"I'll kill him," said Imad. "Only me. And right before I do, I'll give his dog a chocolate bar. And then I'll..." He fell silent when abu Bachar arrived and joined them.

72.

"So," said abu Bachar after a while. "Do you really think you'll be able to get the shahids into the mosque and complete the operation before the end of the summit?"

"The real explosion won't take place in the mosque itself but under it, in the tunnels, where the foundations are. The shahids in the mosque are mostly a photo op."

"I'm not sure I follow," said Gertrud, and abu Bachar seemed to share her confusion.

"The bombing in the mosque will be meaningless without real-time, widespread media coverage," said Imad. Abu Bachar nodded. "After my shahids enter the mosque, they'll wear kippahs and keffiyehs dyed like Jewish tallits. They'll have blue Israeli IDs in their pockets. When I activate the PETN charges, the world will see a group of Orthodox Jews attempting to destroy the holy mosque. This is phase one. When Professor Barghouti receives this broadcast, Haj Kahil will activate the main charge, in the tunnels under the Temple Mount. This is phase two—fifty or sixty kilos of military-grade Semtex that will bring down the mosque. This humiliating act will force the rest of the Arab politicians to fall in line. Anyone who won't join the sultan will be ostracized."

"A creative plan," said abu Bachar. "But not without risk. Tell me, how do you think the Jews will react to our attack?"

And as Imad tried to think of an answer decisive enough to nip this philosophical hypothesizing in the bud, abu Bachar provided his own answer: "They'll have but one option left."

"A nuke? They wouldn't dare. They'll be pariahs, condemned by the entire world."

"And yet," insisted abu Bachar, "the Jews are used to being the world's pariahs. Wouldn't you rather be a live pariah than a dead prince?"

"The Americans won't let them," Imad bit out impatiently.

"The Americans?" Abu Bachar chuckled. "The same ones who dropped two nuclear bombs on Japan, not even as an act of self-defense, but of revenge?"

"Fine," Imad snapped. "So the Israelis drop a nuke on… what, Syria? Too close. Iran? The Iranians would retaliate, the Americans would threaten, and the Russians would be overjoyed. And from this clusterfuck, a new world order will emerge—that's still our goal, isn't it?! A new world order!" He stood up and his tone was commanding when he added, "You'll locate Anna and Dr. Taissiri. I have some things I need to take care of."

73.

Ibrahim heaved and gagged into the toilet but only managed to produce a bitter yellow fluid. The nausea grew worse every day, and so did the bloody, puss-laced discharge from his stitches. When he left the bathroom, the doorbell rang. Ibrahim glanced at the feed from the security camera and his heart dropped into his stomach. Imad Akbariyeh was standing there, accompanied by another young man. Ibrahim scurried out the back service door, unaware of the damage wrought on the London Mossad branch's surveillance efforts by his decision to leave his banged-up Toyota parked by the curb.

Ibrahim ran as fast as he could but was soon cut off by a black Ford Escort. He collided with the bumper and fell. Bassel, the man accompanying Imad, leapt from the car, grabbed Ibrahim and tossed him into the backseat. Imad started the car in reverse and must have hit a nearby drunk, who kicked the car and yelled extremely impolite Irish-accented slurs about the mothers and fathers of "all those fuckin' Jews and Arabs and blacks."

Imad raised his eyes to the rearview mirror and stared at Ibrahim.

"You're coming with me to Jerusalem, now."

"Today? But… my boy. His mother's dead… cancer… he's all alone," he wept.

Imad stopped the car, turned around, grabbed Ibrahim's throat and squeezed until he started to gurgle. Bassel glared at Imad, and he released Ibrahim and changed tactics.

"Your son, Muhammad. He'll live with the imam and his wife until he finishes college. How're his studies going? Computer science, right?"

Muhammad's future was all Ibrahim cared about, and he visibly calmed, smiling. "Actually, he's recently gotten it into his head to study music… he's very talented," he added, noticing Imad's skeptically raised eyebrow. "He really is, he's just passed the entrance exam for the Royal Academy…"

"Let's make a deal, Ibrahim. First computer science, then music."

"Oh, if only. He's so stubborn… maybe… could you talk to him? I'm sure he'll listen, if you say something."

Imad reached his hand between the seats and shook Ibrahim's. "Deal. I'll talk to him. Ibrahim, when was your most recent contact with Dr. Taissiri?"

"Nothing since the operation. Sorry. Is he all right?"

"He's fine. Must be something wrong with his phone… who were you partnered with?"

"Latif. He lives nearby."

"I have some things I need discuss with abu Bachar. Take me back, then go pick up Latif and meet me at the airport."

The alarm light from the cameras tracking Latif's house was blinking. The Israeli student working part-time at the surveillance station, trying for the ninth or tenth time to perform a proper regression analysis, ignored it completely. "Fucking Arab can wait a couple of minutes," he grumbled.

After several minutes, he raised his head at the screens and saw that Latif's alarm had gone quiet, but, glancing at Ibrahim's screen, he noticed that the Toyota was still parked. He noted in the log that Ibrahim had stayed in the garage to work late, and then got back to studying to his statistics exam tomorrow morning at the London School of Economics. The regression problems, specifically, were quite the bitch.

Bassel, Ibrahim and Latif then drove to a real estate office in Stamford Hill and picked up Anwar. The desperate student groaned at the digital buzz and blinking red light, eventually raising his head at the screen displaying the entrance to Anwar's office. He saw Anwar leaving the real estate office, accompanied by Bassel, whom he did not recognize. This was an extremely regular occurrence—Anwar would often accompany Arab clients to view properties, and so the student logged, "Anwar—business meeting, out of office."

74.

"Coffee? Another round?"

Imad nodded vaguely, deep in thought. Abu Bachar signaled the waiter.

"How many shahids do we have who are ready for action?"

"Anwar, Latif and Ibrahim, here in London. Another one in Frankfurt, three in Brussels, two more in Paris."

"So, nine total?"

"There used to be fourteen," Imad replied and counted them off on his fingers. "The first one was activated in Rome, second one in Paris—no, wait—Riyadh first, then Paris, then Córdoba, then the last one when I was with you in Norwich."

Abu Bachar promised to collect the other four shahids within forty-eight hours and fly them to Amman. From there he would arrange transport to Palestine. Imad warned abu Bachar not to use any digital form of communication. "Those Israelis hear everything," he said.

Abu Bachar burst into laughter. When he noticed Imad's puzzled stare, he explained how hilarious he found the fact that getting into Israel was so difficult. "They train their dogs to smell Arabs, not just explosives. But once you're in there… weapons, ammunition, explosives, you name it, they got it. Just place an order, the Bedouins will get you everything you need. The Jews in the settlements also sell, mostly small arms and grenades." Imad nodded. His cousin, Uncle Mahajna's son, had already contacted a Bedouin named Ayach to provide the Semtex they required. The same cousin, who regularly smuggled illegals into Israel, would also be responsible for setting up the safe house in Balata, to which they would escape after the explosion and lie low until the dust settled.

They decided that Imad would head to Amman immediately, with the three London-based stuffed shahids. The three of them would cross the border from Jordan to Palestine through the Lynch Strait in the Dead Sea and wait in the safe house until the arrival of the other shahids, which abu Bachar would collect from Frankfurt, Brussels and Paris.

Abu Bachar provided Imad with three official diplomatic passports, each from a different Arab state, for Ibrahim, Anwar and Latif.

A phone call cut their conversation short.

"Gertrud," abu Bachar answered. "Wonderful. Yes, excellent... Bavarian TV, excellent. Good luck," he concluded and hung up, raising a victorious smile at Imad. "She found Ehrlich's house."

Imad didn't react. They went over communication protocols again, and when they arrived at the airstrip, the three London stuffed shahids were waiting for them. The flight plan was confirmed, and the Sultanate jet took off, headed to Amman.

75.

Two and a half miles of breaststroke, just like the Ironman ordered. I was slicing across the pool when Verbin arrived with my *ristretto*.

"Come out of there, you huge ball of rust." She smiled, and I melted, tried to reach out and drag her into the water, coffee and clothes and everything, to wetly and happily entwine with her. The little minx took a step back and laughed at my look of childish indignation, informing me that old iron rusts in water. As I planned my countermove, an urgent call came from the phone lying by the pool.

"You need to come in," I was told. "Now."

Nora was waiting for me.

"What's up?" I inquired. "What's the rush?"

Nora was uncharacteristically grave, and slightly pale, and I was officially concerned. She reported that at 06:00, Shula Greenbaum had arrived at the London branch control room monitoring the Sultanate Bayswater estate. She'd examined the surveillance log, as she did every other morning, and realized that none of her three targets were where they were supposed to be. After quickly debriefing the student who was manning the station that night, she'd put out an urgent alert.

The DM arrived, along with Froyke and Nahum from foreign affairs, and we went into the meeting room. I wanted to ask Froyke how he was feeling—looking at him, I couldn't be sure—but decided to wait.

"According to the reports from Dr. Stroop," Nora started, giving me the stink eye, "apart from the three Londoners, there are at least six other stuffed shahids, each holding five to seven pounds of the stuff.

Three in Brussels, two in Paris, one in Frankfurt. All of them are under surveillance twenty-four seven. They never use cell phones, never use computers, and travel only by public transport—"

"If even one of them goes off," Nahum cut her off, "even accidentally, and the locals find out we knew they were there and didn't report it, we're in deep shit."

The director nodded. Froyke seemed to have trouble speaking. He cleared his throat, sipped some water and addressed Nahum quietly.

"How long do you think they'd be willing to wait?"

"Who'd be willing? What are you talking about?" Nahum snapped, clearly on edge.

"The locals," I explained. "We need them to wait until Imad contacts one of the shahids."

"Forget it. Won't happen. The minute they find out, they'll arrest them." He added that either way, he planned on delivering them to the custody of the locals by the end of the day and letting them handle it however they saw fit.

"It's their business," he said. "It's their territory, and if something happens, God forbid, we can kiss any chance of future collaboration goodbye. Not just there, too."

Nahum looked at the director and intoned, "The damage would be irreversible."

The director stared at us intently. "I… we… can't take responsibility for this kind of fiasco. Nahum, handle it immediately. Get the ball in their court as soon as possible."

He momentarily fell silent, frowning, then muttered to himself, "Frankfurt. Brussels. Paris. All in the same time zone…" He raised his voice. "Recommend that they coordinate, operate at the same time in all three cities so the targets don't have a chance to warn one another. Ehrlich, be ready to fly out there if they request assistance."

Nora placed a set of photos on the table. "Ibrahim, Anwar and Latif. The three who got away in London."

The photos were passed around. "Bella," the director said into his conference phone, "are you available? Be nice..."

"I'm always nice," came the tetchy reply.

"Please be even nicer than usual and have our lunch delivered here...?"

"It's already left the kitchen. You'll get it in five seconds."

"I swear, the old hag is supernatural," the director muttered, glancing warily at the door. The guy from the kitchen came in with a serving cart with sliced vegetables, hamburgers, ketchup packets, and bottles of water and orange juice.

"*Bon appétit,*" he said and left as quickly as he had come.

The second we started eating, Nora received an urgent alert on her phone and hurriedly excused herself. The DM and Froyke munched on the vegetables and I shoved two burgers into a bun.

"Did Dr. Taissiri have any new information?"

"May he lay peacefully in the bosom of Allah," I replied.

"Oh? How?" The director raised his eyebrows.

"Heart attack, down at the facility."

"Who interrogated him? Was it Maxim?" The director sighed. "Oh, well..."

"Well, Godspeed," muttered Froyke. "No rest for the wicked."

I grinned, thinking of the famous line attributed to General Schwarzkopf. Forgiving the terrorists is God's function. Our job was simply to arrange the meeting.

Nora returned with Anne-Marie Claire, a petite woman I'd always considered to be the very embodiment of professionalism—ageless and expressionless. She used to be a profiler for the FBI, before she had become the Mossad's star assessor. She didn't wait for questions, instead firing away in her heavy American accent as soon as they entered the room.

"There are three crucial points that must be addressed."

We all stared at her expectantly, and she went on.

"Point A is the sultan's recent acquisition. He took al Qardawi under his wing—the most respected imam in the last decade. Al Qardawi's call for an historic conciliation between the Shiite and Sunni fits perfectly with what we know of Imad Akbariyeh's philosophy and grasp of Islam.

"Point B—the sultan built a new Al-Aqsa Mosque. I believe he intends to destroy the old Mosque in Jerusalem, thus shifting the center of the Muslim world to his territory. Points A and B point to the sultan's intention of becoming a new Calipha—a pan-Islamic leader."

This information was not, in the strict sense, new to us—but I'd never heard it presented this clearly and sharply. We all knew that Imad planned to bomb the Al-Aqsa Mosque. We all knew the sultan had built a replica of the mosque in his backyard. But no one had yet to combine this knowledge into a meaningful insight.

Nora, who apparently knew what I was thinking, nodded with unrestrained pride and signaled me with several complex gestures that Anne-Marie's head was as big as the rest of her was small.

"Now pay attention," Nora mouthed at me as Anne-Marie continued to the next point.

"Point C is Imad Akbariyeh, an old friend of Avner's," she said, glancing at her laptop. "Imad studied math and computer science with Professor Hamdan Barghouti in Bir Zeit and then went to study systems analysis at Stanford, just like our very own Ehud Barak[32]. He speaks fluent English, and Hebrew..." Anne-Marie raised a single finger. "One thing is of particular concern. By all indications, Imad was extremely attached to his father. A truly close connection." Her sharp eyes met mine, and she seemed to address me alone when she added, "I find it very likely that he'll stop at nothing to take his revenge."

"What revenge?" Froyke demanded angrily.

"Revenge on Avner," she replied and sat down. "Nora will take it from here."

Nora stood and brought up a large photo on the screen behind her. It was a close-up of a dead man's face.

"This is Mustafa Akbariyeh, Imad's father. He was killed in a Unit

---

32 A former prime minister of Israel (1999-2001). -TK

operation in Jabalia, and of course, commanding the operation was none other than our very own"—she theatrically indicated me with both hands—"Captain… *Avner*… Ehrlich."

Nahum's low whistle tore through the silence following her statement. Froyke drummed his fingers on the table, and I struggled to remember. Jabalia had been the "terrorist capital" of Gaza, and we would operate there often—even daily, when the situation called for it. Nora switched the image and her laser pointer drew a red dot on the forehead of the young man that appeared on the screen.

"This is Nasser Akbariyeh," she said. "Imad's brother. He died recently, in the bombing of the final convoy to leave Shabwah. He led the convoy and was the first to die."

"This is serious business," said Froyke, coughing a bit. "The Jordanians also tell us that Imad and his buddies are looking for you. At this point, it's either kill or be killed."

"Imad is already in Amman." Nora finally pulled the rabbit out of her hat. "We showed the security footage from Bayswater to some workers from Gatwick. They recognized Imad, abu Bachar and the London trio, who all apparently boarded the Sultanate jet. Flight plan shows it landed in Amman last night."

"So where are they?" asked Froyke.

"The local branch is working on it. Trying to place them," said Nora. "As you know, their embassy has been under constant surveillance for a while now."

The director seemed to finally emerge from his thoughts and spoke. "This summit of theirs will come to nothing. Saudi Arabia, the Emirates, Jordan and Egypt are out. We're still working on the others. But this business at the Temple Mount is very disturbing. Bella!" he barked into his conference phone. "I need to meet with the prime minister, today. I would like this revenge issue addressed by Anne-Marie to receive full consideration." The director looked at Froyke and me. "Kahanov and his team are on their way, have them handle the security detail for him"—he nodded in my direction—"and that doctor of yours."

I started laughing. Froyke had a brief coughing fit into a handkerchief. I poured him a glass of water, and he sipped, cleared his throat and glared at me furiously.

"*Vhat* the hell are you laughing at?" he scolded me, his sharp Ashkenazi *w* momentarily escaping him. "You must realize they are gunning at you, personally! They want you dead! Weren't you listening? The schmucks are coming after you!"

"I come after them, they come after me… the only difference is the direction of the asses." I shrugged. "Instead of chasing them around, they show up right on my front porch. Isn't that a good thing?"

Froyke waved his hand, a sharp, dismissive motion, and then leaned toward me and spoke too softly for the others to hear. "I know what you're worth, Avner. I know better than anyone. That doesn't mean you can ignore that fact that, as far as Imad is concerned, you murdered his father and his baby brother. And Taissiri. And Anna. We both know he's no amateur. Don't talk back to me. Tell my little doctor I said hi," he concluded, and I suddenly realized the sheer idiocy of what I'd been saying.

I decided to ask Kahanov to post his best men on guard, knowing that he would have anyway.

As for me, I would remain at her side 24/7 and brutally murder anyone who got too close.

76.

Nahum did everything he could to present the intel he shared with his European colleagues as fresh, recently discovered information. However, their initial gratitude soon became a cold, silent fury. The Europeans, still reeling from the recent wave of bombings, had realized that while they had been running around like headless chickens, the Israelis had withheld information about walking, ticking human bombs walking freely in their territory. Jean-Pierre Baptiste, from the French service, who had frankly always loathed the Israelis, had even spoken with his German and Belgian colleagues about the possibility of an Israeli plant within the team responsible for stuffing the stuffed shahids. The DM had offered our help and resources during the operation and had received only a hostile silence in reply. Nahum and his team were unceremoniously removed from the loop, and the European operation commenced. Despite the convenience of all three of the capitals being in the same time zones, the French managed the "trivial error" of raiding the hideout a full thirty minutes before the agreed-upon time.

The GIGN—the French antiterrorist police force—broke into the apartment in the 19th arrondissement, near the Stalingrad Métro station. The first hostile opened the door holding a gun and was immediately shot in the head. The other one, Mustafa el Hariri, managed to send an alert to his colleague in Frankfurt before jumping out of the second-story window and getting himself severely injured and arrested. The German team breached an already-deserted hideout in the Sachsenhausen district in Frankfurt. Having been warned by el Hariri, and being familiar with the Germans and their search methods, Hisham simply walked down the hall to his girlfriend's apartment. From there he calmly watched the Germans search for him and called to warn his friends in Brussels. True hilarity, however, didn't ensue until Molenbeek: the Belgian SWAT team barged into the hideout, stun grenades blazing, to find one miserable, bound and battered Arab, who told them that his friends had beaten him when he'd decided to turn himself in to the police. During his interrogation, he also revealed that the remaining two had escaped in a red Polo GTI, heading for Eindhoven in the Netherlands.

All pursuing teams were then sent after the red Eindhoven-bound Polo, while the two remaining stuffed shahids calmly made their way in a white pickup truck to Dunkirk, in the opposite direction, where they then boarded a fishing boat.

In Paris, the shahid who had jumped from the window was taken the emergency room of Saint-Pierre University Hospital. There were about thirty other patients in the ER. When Mustafa el Hariri activated the charge in his stomach, twenty-one people were killed.

77.

A cardboard sign reading BAVARIAN TV—PRESS had been stuck to the windshield. The rented minivan climbed up from Route 38 and onto Road 353, eventually stopping in front of the yellow metal gate at the entrance to Agur.

Ahmet, the Turkish cameraman, sporting platinum-blond hair, large sunglasses and pierced ears, attached a dashcam to the front of the windshield and turned it on. Gertrud, the team's senior reporter, a tall and reedy woman with a bald head, pushed a pair of black-rimmed glasses up her nose. The golden phone that hung from her neck like an overgrown amulet was equipped with a camera—two twelve-megapixel sensors.

Gertrud asked Alon, the Israeli production manager, whether the gate actually operated or was it more of a symbolic gate? Alon asked Shabi, the driver who seemed to know everything.

"Sure, it operates. It stays closed from midnight till five a.m."

Alon translated, and the Turkish cameraman interrupted to ask, "What happens if a resident of Agur arrives after midnight? Or has company over late at night?"

Shabi, who required no translation, said, "You can tell Sinéad O'Connor and her faggy little cameraman that each resident has an entrance code for his cell phone that opens the gate by remote."

Alon translated, and Gertrud took some notes on her yellow legal pad.

***

At an aerial distance of about three hundred yards from the gate to Agur, Verbin was standing barefooted on a small stepladder, and on the very tips of her toes, she managed to reach and unscrew the old showerhead. She sadly noted to herself that the taller the ladder owner, the shorter the ladders—this might present a problem when she attempted to screw in the new rain showerhead. Avner's need to be covered in water was nothing short of an obsession. Verbin's diagnosis had been "a desire to return to the womb." She laughed when she imagined her giant man crumpled into a fetal position in a soft, pink womb.

Adolf's angry barks drew her attention to the cloud of dust raised by the minivan that parked next door, at Shuki's. She returned to her efforts with the huge rain showerhead and failed for the third time. With a resigned sigh, she went to the kitchen and put on the pumps she had taken off before her first attempt. The additional two inches did the trick. She moved the small stepladder and turned the water on. A brief rattle from the pipes, followed by an enticing stream of water. She entered the shower and melted into the torrent of warm bliss surrounding her from all sides.

Then, of course, her phone rang. "Waltzing Matilda"—the ringtone she set for the medical staff. The iPhone slipped out of her wet grasp several times, and just when she managed to grip it, the ringing stopped and she received a WhatsApp notification.

"*Mazal tov*, honey!" the message read, along with a smiling emoji and another one of a small bouquet. "Just in case you were wondering," came another massage from Limor, her friend from the OB-GYN department, "there is a ton of HCG!"

Verbin turned the water strength up as far as it would go and grinned into the gloriously warm current.

"When's he getting home, huh?" she mumbled, smiling. "When's your daddy getting home?"

The thought suddenly struck her that Avner might not be as delighted about this. She hurried out of the shower, threw on a robe and sat at the computer.

Honey bear, **I'm pregnant**!

Don't panic! I have no intention of stealing your premium, high-quality sperm. If you aren't into this, we'll terminate. I'm really hoping that's not what happens, though. For so many reasons:

A. While I'm certain that having a child at a young age would've been a terrible idea, by now I'm getting close to the point when having babies starts becoming difficult. I'm right on the brink of menopause, and I know what you'll say to that—"menopause schmenopause." But, from a purely medical point of view, every day that goes by is... well, you know.

B. And anyway, it's not like I could have given birth to anything worthwhile before I met you. Huh? There's something you can definitely get behind. I think he'd make a great brother to Eran and Gil, and I'm sure that if we could ask them, they'd tell us that they're so excited they can hardly wait.

c. You know what? Fuck it. I don't need to lay out reasons for you. I want to have your child, a child that's ours. There's nothing I want more in the world, and you should know that when he's born, you'll be second only to him, and that's a good enough reason already.

D. Applying pressure—I sat down with Eran today and opened the '67 Château Margaux. I didn't wait for you, because I'm sick of waiting all the time. Come back to me, honey bear, and don't worry your pretty little head over the Château Margaux. I took the bottle over to Shuki, gave him a teeny-tiny sip, and he corked it back up with the argon pump.

E. Applying attitude—by this point I'm sure Eran wants this to happen, and so do I, and if you don't yet, I'll make you. I'm crazy about you, you giant teddy bear. Say yes and come back already. I have little faith in the argon's ability to preserve the Château Margaux, and I intend to have a glass every day until you get back here. So you should really get a move on. There, you see? I've "divided my forces," I've "applied leverage"—I know all your damn tricks. I deserve to be the mother of your child—just come back, babe. Come back before I shrivel up and fly away from shorting for you so much. Yeah, that's right, shorting. It's better than longing, I think. I don't want it to take long.

Eff. Always a good idea. Come back to me already, shorty. We're shorting for you.

Best regards, Dr. Rosa Luxemburg-Verbin.

Verbin took a final look at the draft and pressed delete.

78.

Shuki the winemaker indicated the stainless-steel vats. "Miss Miller, welcome to 'New World' vineyard, located in the region where the very first wines in human history were produced, here in the Judean Mountains—one of the world's oldest cultures, with its most cutting-edge technologies."

"Oh, excellent speech! I'd like to film you saying exactly that for the introduction."

"I'm… not sure I remember it exactly." Shuki smiled timidly.

"Shit, man, an opening line like that?" sniggered Shabi the driver. "C'mon, must've took you a week to put that together. But don' worry, they're gonna play the audio back for you, you can write it down, hehe…"

Gertrud asked Alon what they were talking about.

"Shabi's taking care of business," he laughed. "He's telling him we have a recording."

"Okay," she smiled. "Rehearse the text with him for a moment, and Ahmet and I will look around for a spot to take some wide-angle shots of this fantastic view." Gertrud raised her hands in the air, her thumbs and forefingers framing a section of the westward view. "A wide shot of the sea and hills, then slowly pan toward the vineyard. A hundred and twenty seconds, music, some titles, then cut to a close-up of Mr. Shuki and his Old World/New World spiel, okay?"

"What's this house, across the fence?" Ahmet pointed at the house next door, his eyes scanning for security cameras and perimeter sensors.

"Just a neighbor," said Alon. "Shuki told me he's out of the country most of the time—a diplomat, or something."

"Whoever he is, his house is higher up—on top of the hill. Do you think you could get us access to take the B-roll shots from there?"

Alon said he'd ask Shuki, and that it'd probably be fine by him—this wasn't Europe, after all.

"Ooh, look over there," he added, pointing at the fence. A huge Neapolitan mastiff was standing by the fence, observing them curiously.

"If the neighbor isn't here," said Alon, "someone else must be feeding that beast. Maybe Shuki has the keys. Or maybe the neighbor's home?"

"He's not," said Gertrud.

"How do you know?" he asked, noticing that Ahmet was also confused, even angry, at her confident reply.

Another dog, maybe a Belgian shepherd, came running and lunged at the shaky fence, barking madly. The film crew retreated, and both dogs now stood on their hind legs, leaning against the fence. The smaller dog let out a threatening growl, and the mastiff hesitantly joined him.

"Let's go pay this neighbor a visit," said Gertrud.

"Baldi, home! Adolf, Baldi... come home." The voice belonged to a woman who had come from the direction of the house, a towel wrapped around her dripping hair. She scratched the dogs' ears and they settled down and sat beside her, flanking her.

So this is his whore, I suppose, the Turkish cameraman thought to himself and shoved his hand into the camera's lens bag, grabbing a small polymer pistol that had the appearance of a small camcorder and could fire two consecutive shots.

Gertrud cast a victorious glance at the cameraman, and her heart dropped when she saw him rummaging through the lens bag. *If Imad shoots the bitch now, it's all over.*

"No shooting, Ahmet! We're just checking, no shooting!"

Imad tightened his grip on the small pistol. A shiver crawled up his arm and he dropped it into the bag. The German was right, this wasn't the time. He reminded himself that they were just doing recon at this point, for the purpose of careful, meticulous planning. *Tawil sabrak*, he repeated inwardly, like a mantra, *Tawil sabrak.* No cutting corners on this one. *I have a plan and I intend to execute it perfectly, step by step. The little doctor's time will come, too.*

Imad removed his hand from the bag and nodded slightly at Gertrud, who instantly calmed down.

"I'm sorry if they scared you," said Verbin, gesturing to the dogs at her sides. "They won't do anything without being commanded to—they just look scary. Really they're just a couple of puppies." *Like their father*, she added inwardly and smiled.

"It's fine," said Gertrud. "I grew up with dogs. We're filming a documentary about the vineyard. We were hoping maybe to film from your house, if it's not too much trouble. I'm looking for a high vantage point, trying to capture the entire hill."

"Um... I'd be happy to help, but I'm just a houseguest. The owner will be available tomorrow and I'm sure he'll be happy to help you."

"He'll be here tomorrow? Good, excellent—could you give me his name and phone number?"

"His name is Avner. Give me your number and I'll pass it along. I prefer not to put him on the spot."

Tomorrow. He's coming tomorrow. Imad took a deep breath and tried to conquer the turmoil in his head. He quickly walked back down to the minivan, opened the trunk and shoved his head inside, pretending to look for something. It was better if she didn't remember his face.

"Thanks anyway," said Gertrud and turned around to head down. "Bye."

"Wait, Miss Miller, your phone number?"

"Oh, you're right, I'm all over the place today. Sorry, my mind's on the film..." She gave her a local number.

Gertrud looked around, and when she was certain that only Verbin could hear her, quietly said, "I had an... I was sick," she said softly, indicating her smooth head, "and for more than a year now, I've been...

really out of it..." Her voice seemed to grow fainter by the second. "It's been so long since I've been given the chance to make another film, and now finally..."

She slowly approached the fence, so that her frail voice would reach Verbin. "And the script is lovely, about the world's most ancient wine industry. This shot of the scenery puts us right in the middle, between modern Tel Aviv"—she pointed west—"and ancient Jerusalem"—she pointed east—"with its historical, theological and political significance... tomorrow morning I'm flying back."

Gertrud came close enough to lean against the fence. Under her breath, she let out a soft, high-pitched whistle. Adolf leapt up and slammed into her through the flimsy wire fence. Gertrud let out a yelp and fell to the ground. Both dogs were now jumping at the fence, growling furiously.

"Dogs, home!" Verbin commanded. The dogs slowly backed away but stopped several feet behind her and remained there, waiting.

"Don't move, you two," Verbin told them and then yelled, "Hey, you, camera guy, come help me!" She started lifting the bottom part of the fence. Imad ran up, slightly more composed than he had been, and helped her pull up the fence enough so she could squeeze under it. She crawled toward the apparently unconscious Gertrud.

"Bring me some water, now," said Verbin, cleaning her hands on her pants.

"Water! Get some water over here," yelled Alon, who'd been away on his phone. He crouched beside Gertrud. Verbin waved him away.

"I'm a doctor," she said. "Just bring me water, and wet wipes if you have them..." She rubbed her hands on her thighs again in an attempt to clean them and gently tipped Gertrud's head to the side before unbuttoning her blouse and jeans and elevating her feet.

"Hold her legs. Someone bring a crate or something to hold them up."

Shabi the driver came running and screwed the cap off the water bottle he'd brought, preparing to spill its contents on Gertrud.

"No!" ordered Verbin and held out her hands. "Here."

Shabi poured the water over her hands, looking skeptical. Verbin cleaned her hands as best she could.

"Wet wipes!" Shabi announced and handed her some.

"Oh good, these have alcohol in them." She meticulously cleaned her hands and opened Gertrud's mouth with her fingers, moved her tongue out of the way and started gently dabbing at her mouth. "Everyone, give her some space. You're blocking the air."

Gertrud opened her eyes and blinked. "Did I black out?"

"Kind of," said Verbin. "You passed out when the dog jumped at you. You need to get some rest now." She looked around. "Where, though? Okay, let's go into the house… away from all this mess. Bring the car."

Shabi ran off to get the minivan.

"There's no need, really… I'm fine…"

"I'm your doctor now. Do as I say."

Shabi arrived with the car, and Imad hurried to open the passenger door and help Gertrud in before getting in the backseat. Verbin went to the driver's seat, asked Shabi to get out, and then peeked into the back, visibly embarrassed. "Just me and the patient, please."

Shabi and Imad got out, and Verbin drove the minivan to the entrance to Avner's property. The dogs ran beside the car until she parked. She helped Gertrud out and took her to the couch under the pergola, looking out at the view. "Rest here for a couple of minutes, then I'll examine you."

Verbin's phone rang. She ignored the call, as she always did with blocked numbers, but it rang again, this time from a cell number she knew but couldn't place. She picked up. It was Marciano, from Ami Kahanov's team. He sounded cheerful as usual and told her he was on the way there and they needed to talk, "in person." Verbin assumed they were preparing some surprise for Avner and told Marciano he was welcome to drop by. She walked back with a glass of cold water, a bottle of orange juice and her medical bag. She handed the glass to Gertrud, who slowly sipped, and pressed a stethoscope to her chest, listening intently.

"Good, everything seems fine. Thirty minutes of rest and you'll be good as new. Drink your juice. And, Miss Miller—I'd like to apologize for the dogs' behavior."

"Oh, don't worry about it… I got too close, they must've felt threatened."

"Drink the rest of the juice. Right now you need plenty of glucose."

"Thank you. Of course, thanks so much. I hate to bother you like this. Is it okay if I wander around a bit, look for the best angle for the shot?"

"No wandering required—the tallest point is right up there. Take the stairs"—she pointed to the roof and the external stone staircase leading up to it. "Can I get you a cup of coffee? Espresso?"

"I'd love some, thank you. Are you sure this isn't too much trouble?"

"Absolutely," said Verbin. "I've been… pretty much on my own up here." She smiled a bit.

"Thanks, anyway. I'll try the roof, then, if that's okay?"

"This way. Watch your step, and don't let their barking get to you."

"You called the dog… 'Baldi'?"

"Yeah, short for Garibaldi. The other one, the jumper, he's Adolf."

"Adolf?!"

Wandering the roof, Gertrud photographed every possible angle of the gate, the fence, access routes, the dogs, the motion detectors and security cameras.

"Coffee's ready! Do you take sugar?"

Gertrud didn't reply. She considered kicking the little doctor down the stone staircase. She'd likely break her neck, and if she didn't, Gertrud was happy to help. That would make such a beautiful shot for Imad, she thought. On second thought, it was too soon—escape routes weren't ready, the crew would testify that Gertrud was the last person to see her. No, bad idea. Later—they'd do it later, and properly.

She smiled broadly at Verbin when she joined her on the roof. "Thanks again, you're so kind. You've helped us so much. The view from up here is astounding." Verbin walked toward the western edge of the roof and pointed southwest, at the sunset.

"The chimneys down there are the Ashkelon power plant," she said. Gertrud snapped more photos.

"It supplied power to the entire region, as well as the Gaza Strip." Verbin turned to her right. "And those chimneys are the Reading plant, in Tel Aviv. Over to the north, that's Herzliya."

"Herzliya," mumbled Gertrud. "Interesting."

She placed her hand on Verbin's shoulder. When Verbin turned around, surprised, Gertrud planted a kiss on her cheek. "You've been so kind. Can I ask, what kind of doctor are you?"

"Oncology," replied a still-startled Verbin.

The little whore's a doctor, she thought. *I guess Imad's not the only one who's got a thing for doctors. One kick, and I make this oncologist Jew a shahida.*

The setting sun colored the mountains a hot, reddish pink.

79.

At a gas station not far from Agur, Gertrud and Imad got rid of the Israeli film crew. Gertrud headed out to Tarqumiyah, on her way across the border and eventually to Amman. Imad waited for the film crew to get out of sight and joined Professor Barghouti, who was waiting for him in a white Mercedes with yellow Israeli plates. They made their way to Jerusalem. This was their first meeting since back when the professor had recruited Imad a decade ago and groomed him all the way to Stanford.

Imad didn't talk much, but the professor, like most professors, was exceedingly fond of the sound of his own voice. At first, he told Imad about the servers at his university, which were ready to receive and transmit the footage from the mosque. "From us it'll go to Al Jazeera, Al Arabiya, CNN—also Facebook, Twitter, Instagram…" He went on to speak of the Almoravids—Al-Aqsa loyalists who would flood the Temple Mount, armed with high-resolution smartphone cameras—and then plunged headfirst into a flowery, sentimental description of the combined Arab attack on the Jewish state—"An attack that will take place immediately after the world watches the destruction of the holy mosque." Imad realized from the professor's descriptions that he had also watched the video, and he wondered who else had. Though he knew professor was a close friend of the sultan's, and perhaps because of this, he decided to share some of his reservations. He told the professor that, while the sultan was generously providing the technical means and financial support, Imad often got the feeling that this was all a game, a spoiled child's ego trip. "If he could buy a plaque reading, 'Look at me, Dad—I'm the Calipha of the entire Arab world,' he would have." He added that abu Bachar was also, oftentimes, difficult to read.

The professor tried to put him at ease, telling him that these feeling and doubts were perfectly normal—after all, Imad was at the heart of a historically monumental task.

"But you can't let them distract you. We're closer now than we've ever been to bringing about real change. You, Imad, you are the seed of that change. It all comes down to you."

Imad didn't respond. The excitement that had gripped him near Ehrlich's house resurfaced; he envisioned Avner handcuffed and humiliated, begging Imad to release his tortured and bleeding woman and child in exchange for his own life.

He immensely enjoyed imagining how thorough he'd be with them, chopping off bit after bit as Avner watched. *He will undoubtedly offer his own life for theirs, but I will have no reason to comply*, thought Imad. *I will have him already*. They already knew that he had a son, Eran—annoyingly, Gertrud hadn't managed to find him yet. He would have to urge her.

"Is Mahajna ready?" Imad asked after a while.

"Of course. Normal procedure—one from him, one from you, three short howls from him. I don't believe you'll really need him, though."

Imad remained silent.

"I'm dropping you off at Haj Kahil's," said the professor. "This is the place. Look out for the old man." Imad raised an eyebrow, and the professor explained, "Haj Kahil is one of our activists. He coordinates the Almoravids whenever we need to kick up some intifada[33]. He's aware of the plan. But the old haj, he's the spiritual leader, and he gets word that

---

33 *Intifada* is an uprising against oppression. In the Palestinian context, it refers to attempts to "shake off" the Israeli occupation of the West Bank and Gaza Strip, ranging from strikes and protests to violent acts and attacks on civilian population. -TK

someone plans to so much as scratch his holy mosque, he'll slaughter that someone like a lamb."

***

Haj Kahil's halal butcher shop sat on the corner of Ha-Shalshelet and Suq El Qatanin, in Jerusalem's Muslim quarter. The blood drain in the meat cutting room, chocked with animal corpses, could be pulled up to reveal an entrance. Iron rungs were set into the wall leading down from the drain, leading into the hidden basement where the Almoravids' weapons and ammunition were stowed.

Aïcha, the haj's wife, gave the Almoravid wives their salaries when she handed them the change from their purchases. Over the past couple of days, dozens of women had arrived at the butcher shop laden with bags and handed Aïcha black-and-gray UNRWA blankets, thick and woolen. According to Imad's instruction, the blankets were nailed to the ceiling of the hidden basement, to absorb the noise of the jackhammers drilling away at the wall. Right beyond the western wall of the basement was the complex network of tunnels that lay below the Old City. After nine hours of digging, the breach in the wall was widened enough to allow the passage of the explosives and the rest of the equipment into the tunnel on the other side. The tunnel, less than fifty inches in height, was a combined effort of sorts—its western wall was built by the Muslim waqf[34], to keep Jews from entering the Temple Mount, while its eastern wall was built by the Jewish Temple Association, to keep Arabs from entering the Western Wall Tunnel.

Digging through the waqf wall was relatively quick work—it had been constructed with little concrete and plenty of sand, and it easily succumbed to the jackhammers. The original contractor had filled

---

34 In Islamic law, a *waqf* is an inalienable charitable endowment, usually the donation of a building, plot of land or other assets for Muslim religious or charitable purposes.

in the wall with piles of wooden planks, wire and random garbage; the engineers pinched their noses and shifted it all to the sides of the tunnel. Imad's instructions had been clear: not a single ounce of debris would see the light of day.

Nine metallic knocks on the metal drain alerted the engineers to the arrival of Ayach the Bedouin.

"The merchandise is here," he told them. From the back of the cooling truck parked at the rear entrance of the butcher shop, Ayach, Imad and the two engineers moved sixty packages of regulation IDF Semtex into the tunnel.

Evening came to Jerusalem, scattering its dwellers off the streets and into evening prayers in synagogues, mosques and churches. The protective din of the busy market streets had died out, and despite his impatience, Imad decided to halt the work rather than risking discovery. He'd also decided against returning to Balata that evening, thereby wasting precious time. He ordered his men to prepare to sleep there that night and regain their strength. The young Haj Kahil, who at the age of thirty had already received acknowledgment as an imam, arrived as planned. Imad made sure that he was fully informed and ready. The collapse of the mosque must be seen as a direct result of the Jewish bombing within—therefore, the haj mustn't act before Imad's go-ahead.

"Where will you be?" inquired the haj.

"On the Mount," said Imad, "and then back here. Is my bike ready?"

"Just where you asked it to be," said the haj, slightly distracted by thoughts of his father, and how he would react upon realizing what had happened. Father would understand, he reassured himself. Certainly, he would understand…

Imad was ordering him to procure some more gear—three IDF uniforms and regulation rifles, preferably M-16s.

"Oh, that won't be a problem," said the young haj. "We have plenty of those."

80.

The discussion at the Ministry of Public Security had gone exceptionally quickly, a blessing prompted by the heavy sense of imminent danger. Nora, who had been assigned to a multiagency team including the Shin Bet, the IDF, the police, the Mossad and a representative from the Ministry of Public Security, reviewed the intelligence we currently had. I had the disorienting sense of knowing both everything and nothing at the same time. We knew they were targeting the Al-Aqsa Mosque, but neither when nor how.

The DM had just returned from Riyadh, where he'd been forming a coalition with the Saudis, the Egyptians and the Jordanians. More than half the Jordanian population was comprised of Palestinian refugees who considered the Jordanian government responsible for the Temple Mount and the Al-Aqsa Mosque. This made them every bit as motivated to avoid this catastrophe as we were, and they therefore provided some fascinating intel: they handed over to us a supervisor from the Allenby bridge border crossing, an Israeli resident, who would apparently grant passage to anyone or anything for the appropriate sum. It turned out the Jordanian intelligence agencies had been employing this asshole's services for a while. He was interrogated, and he confessed. At least now we knew when and where Imad's shahids were. Kahanov's team began to trace their paths from the entrance points. Photos of Imad and the three shahids were passed along to all field teams. Civilian and Border Police bolstered security, setting up barricades and roadblocks. Teams of undercover operatives from the Shin Bet, Border Police and Unit 217 patrolled around like hungry dogs. Unit 8200 increased phone tracking and the seemingly impossible task of tracking the Almoravids activities on social media and their university intranet networks.

Like the CIA, the Mossad doesn't operate within Israeli borders, and so I was brought in as a chief consultant, with no operative role and no properly defined assignment. This suited me well. I was less pleased about the inflated security detail forced on me by Kahanov.

A car from the Service clung to me the moment I left the ministry, and I wondered what good they would be if these purported assassins set up an ambush on the side of the road and fired a shoulder missile, or attacked from the air with a UAV. I almost picked up the radio and asked them but decided against it. If I displayed so much as a sliver of concern, they'd latch on even harder. I would never get rid of them. I dialed Verbin and got her voicemail. I called the landline, and the lady at the hospital let me know that she was indisposed.

I injected a great deal of concern into my voice and asked her when the doctor would be available for an important conversation of a personal nature, an intimate family matter of great importance and urgency. It worked—the lady promised to ask the doctor to return my call as soon as possible. Several minutes later, Verbin called me back, saying that she did not recall any intimate personal business she had with me, "and if you'd like there to be any, you should really get your ass home and make a dinner worthy of a woman as positive as me. I'm talking mussels, you hear me? Mussels."

"Positive, what… what do you mean, positive...?"

It took me a few seconds. *The test. The test came back positive!*

I screeched to an emergency stop and pulled over and gripped the steering wheel as if holding on for dear life. A sequence of broken images flashed through my mind with terrifying speed, Mother and Father and Eran and Ya'ara and Guli, Kahanov, Agranat, Eran, and Eran and Eran and a blinding white light. I took the deepest breath I was capable of and wiped my forehead.

"Boy or girl?" I asked.

Verbin burst into her rolling laughter. "They're still deciding."

"Who is?"

"My ova. Currently in the midst of negotiations with your sperm."

"Get home quick," I told her, "quick! I have to 'consecrate you according to the laws of Moses and Israel,' before we pop out a little bastard..."

"I'll do my best."

She hung up, and I invited Pavarotti to share my joy—"*La donna è mobile*," he roared for the rest of the way to Agur, singing of his own fickle woman, and I conducted him with large, enthusiastic gestures. At a time like this, even Mother would excuse those sour notes I could never hear.

81.

I nodded at Marciano, who'd been posted at the front gate, and made a quick trip to the house to bring him a beer and two ham and cheddar sandwiches. He took off his kippah and ate.

When Verbin's Beetle stopped by the front gate, the two monstrosities charged the inner gate, barking and wagging ecstatically. Verbin replied with similar enthusiasm, and the barking reached a crescendo. Marciano, who functioned as the responsible adult among the Shin Bet kids, dismissed the car that was following her.

"Good evening, Miss Verbin." Marciano smiled.

"I told you, Marciano, no more Miss. It's Verbin, okay? How's your mom?"

"She's doing much better." He grinned. "Much better. Thanks so much, Miss Verbin."

"Good. I'm glad to hear it. Okay, then. Am I on the list?"

Marciano nodded and radioed me. "Avner, a Miss Verbin here to see you…"

"A who?" I replied with excessive bafflement.

"A Dr. Verbin, sir."

"A what now? Oh… her." I sighed dramatically. "Fine, let her in. After a full cavity search, of course."

"Avner, come on, man—" I could practically hear him blush.

Verbin grabbed the radio from his hand. "Keep this up, mister, and I'll come in there and perform a rectal colonoscopy, sans Vaseline. *Capisce*?"

Marciano opened the inner gate, and Verbin parked and headed up the path to the house, the two puppies leaping around her. I have no idea why, but watching her approach, I found myself thinking of her father. Professor Verbin had come to Israel fresh from the Nazi camps and landed a teaching post at Tel Aviv University. They'd fired him when they'd found out he was a member of Maki, the Israeli Communist Party, and he had gone on to teach at a high school, from which he was also fired. He was a true underdog, constantly angry, exceedingly brave. Verbin was, in many ways, the opposite—her ferociousness and courage were hidden underneath a kind, pleasant demeanor. Anna had that kind of toughness, but it had always been unstable.

When I was done kissing every square inch of her, paying special attention to her belly, the positive lady asked me, "So how do we clean the mussels?"

"It's pretty easy." I grinned at her. "Take them out of the net. If they're open, toss them. If they're closed, scrub them under the tap and throw them in the colander."

As she took over the mussels, I melted a slab of butter in the high-sided sauteuse pan. I added chopped shallots and a third of a Riesling bottle I had acquired from Doron at the Sphera Winery.

"Now, when it's simmering, mussels, parsley, black pepper. Simmer again. Cover, leave it for two minutes, stir once with a wooden spoon. Take the lid off. Chopped tarragon, and a shot of Pernod is always welcome. Ta-dam! All done. Butter. Baguette. Wine. That's it."

Verbin tore off some baguette, dipped it in the mussel sauce, and chewed with her eyes closed, absorbing the flavor of the sea. I thought to myself that I'd cook the entire planet just to watch her eat. I grabbed the sauteuse and dropped it at the center of the table, pulling my hand back with a loud "Ow, *scheisse*!"

Verbin took my hand.

"Oh no, your ring finger." She frowned and then kissed the burn and cooled it with her tongue. She then examined the area closely.

"This too shall pass," she announced.

"Ring finger? It's already passed," I said and held out my other hand. She laughed and kissed it too, then tackled the sauteuse with considerable success.

"Open wide," she giggled, "here comes the airplane."

I divided the rest of the wine between us and shoved my nose into my glass.

"Smell it," I said.

Verbin swirled her wine around and inhaled. The fumes rose through her nasal cavities and into her brain, pleasantly numbing. Sunflower and eucalyptus fields on the sides of dusty roads. A painfully bright sky. The scents of the small orchard during a heat wave, when her father turned on the sprinklers and filled the entire house with a cool, fragrant mist. The better Israel, the Israel taken from us through the schemes of rabbis. And her Gil, rotting away in Loewenstein.

"Come here, you fat man." She patted the seat next to her. I sat down and she placed her head in the crook of my neck. I kissed her hair and a few tears escaped her—I collected them with my tongue, then slid my hand down her jawline to tip her head toward me, scratching under her chin. She laughed and let out a small bark, before her eyes finally met mine.

"Have they found him?"

I shrugged. "If they had, I assume Kahanov would already be here with a scalp hanging from his belt."

"Are you afraid?"

"Those who are afraid die seven deaths—and those who die seven deaths fear only once," I said with an exaggerated Arab accent. "Don't worry. Kahanov's guys are good at their jobs. This is a cakewalk. And statistically, we should be fine."

"Statistically?"

"I've neutralized a lot more people who wanted to neutralize me than the other way around. Fact: there are zero neutralized Avners on the scoreboard."

"You are truly and thoroughly insane. No textbook could prepare me for this kind of crazy. I want to—scratch that, I'm *going* to force you to marry me," she declared.

I swirled my wineglass and sniffed. "Excellent wine. Just needs to breathe a bit…"

Verbin burst into laughter, and I followed.

"You're right, it needs to breathe… but not too much. Don't want it to—"

I tossed back the wine like it was a shot of vodka, deciding that I would drink deep from the poison cup—and like Socrates, I would do it with a smile.

"*Ave dotore, morituri te salutant*," I announced theatrically. Those who are about to die salute you. "Where's the ring?"

"Ring?"

"You're proposing without a ring? What sort of man do you take me for? Let's go. I'll sanctify you by consummation, like in the olden days[35]."

"Now?"

"Here and now. No time like the present."

I lifted her up onto the marble countertop.

"Music?"

Verbin batted her eyelashes like a stoned princess.

"Sting or Pavarotti?"

"Both."

Pavarotti started and Sting joined in. By the time "Panis Angelicus" came to an end, we were married.

"Listen closely, my little Mrs. Dr. Rosa Luxemburg-Verbin-Ehrlich-Ne'eman-et al., because I'm only going to say this once. I love you. And I will protect you. And I will clean the dust from your wrinkles, if and when you ever deign to finally grow old."

---

35 In old Hebrew custom, an official engagement (in which the bride is "sanctified" to the groom) can also result from intercourse. This was later prohibited by the Talmud.

She held out her hand. "Come with me."

"Where to?"

"Close your eyes until I say otherwise."

I followed her, my eyes closed, and suddenly a gushing torrent of water showered us from all directions. When I was permitted to look, I saw the biggest rain showerhead I'd ever seen. We cuddled on the tiled floor, surrounded by the wonderfully heavy rain. Verbin told me that she had a vision of me folded up inside her uterus, smoking a cigar. I tried to oblige, but the cigar refused to remain lit under the water, so I gave up.

She told me about the odd visit of the Bavarian TV crew, and the German director who had taken photos from the roof for her B-roll, and the platinum-blond cameraman. We eventually started to doze off beneath the water, and so we took off our wet clothes and went to bed.

Around four in the morning I woke with a start, drenched in cold sweat. Just who the fuck, I thought, were those Bavarians? I turned to wake Verbin, but she wasn't there. I frantically checked every room in the house. The guy who'd replaced Marciano told me no one had left the property. The dogs were also nowhere to be found. What in the unholy fuck was going on?

Eventually, I spotted her by the grave. Garibaldi and Adolf were lounging beside her. She was talking to Eran, telling him about the little brother cooking inside of her. I dared not intrude.

I quietly went back inside, got dressed and left to find out who those Germans were.

I left her a note on the pillow, under a daisy I'd picked from the yard. "Work. Went out. Will call."

82.

The photos of the bald director and the bleached-blond cameraman, pulled from the security cameras, stared back at me from Nora's computer screen. We were at her temporary desk at Kahanov's Jerusalem office. The Service's sketch artist placed a recent close-up of Imad by the screen, pulled by Albert from the cams at Gatwick, and worked the photo of the cameraman on the screen, removing the earring and sunglasses, then dyeing the hair black. My heart sank.

That motherfucker, Imad Akbariyeh al-Nabulsi, was in my house. He was a knife's throw away from Verbin.

I experienced a new, violent breed of petrifying terror. Nora gave me several worried glances and then disappeared into a series of phone calls informing Kahanov, Bella, Froyke and the DM of the new state of affairs.

After a while I came to my senses, reevaluated the situation and came to a decision—I was flying Verbin out of the country, and not letting her back in until I destroyed that schmuck once and for all. Bruno's summer home in Umbria and O'Driscoll's farm in Jonesboro, GA came to mind. If she wouldn't agree to a flight, there were VIP guest rooms at the Mossad facility.

I drove to the hospital, where I found Kahanov just finishing up Verbin's debriefing. As expected, she outright refused any solution involving what she considered to be abandonment. In the meanwhile, she received phone calls from Froyke and the DM, who also tried to convince her to leave the country. At least they doubled her security.

Now the little doctor had two broad, muscular guards at her side.

"Two?" she grumbled. "Is this really necessary? They're making my patients uncomfortable."

"Only one of them is for you. The other's securing my kid."

Imad's photo, both blond and dark-haired, was distributed to all patrol units and roadblocks around the Jerusalem area. The Shin Bet increased their pressure on their informants, and Unit 8200 perked up their ears. Everyone went to DEFCON 2. Two new members were added to the multiagency task force—the chief of the Combat Engineering Corps, and Professor Ben-Porat, an archaeologist who knew the ancient underworld of Jerusalem tunnels like the back of his hand. They employed a team of engineers to locate the likeliest destinations of an attack meant to demolish the mosque. The DM arrived at the operations room, along with the head of the Service, the police commissioner, the captain of the Jerusalem PD, the chief intelligence officer and the prime minister's bureau chief.

The chief combat engineer quickly reviewed the tunnel warfare capabilities of the Samur unit[36]. Someone from Electronic Warfare presented their Netline system, which uses PJPs—jamming grenades—to locate and sabotage electronic devices and communications.

Kahanov reported preventive arrests of Almoravid activists, as well as activists from the northern Sheikh Ra'ad Salah sect, who never missed an opportunity to incite trouble.

The seemingly endless meetings, crowded and verbose, made me feel useless. I was soon restless. I asked Froyke to take over for me and went underground, to Kahanov's operations room, from which I could keep an eye on Verbin and my little Eran. Much closer, and much more effective.

---

36 Samur (lit. "weasel") is a Combat Engineering Corps unit which specializes in finding and destroying smuggling tunnels and hidden weapon caches. -TK

83.

Imad left nothing to chance. After a brief conversation with a terrified young Haj Kahil, Imad ordered his engineers to wrap the charges around the eastern support pillar, 360 degrees, all the way up. That way, even if one of the charges failed to trigger, the chain reaction would go on. Haj Kahil was occupied with thoughts of his father's reaction upon finding out that his son had taken part in the destruction of his beloved mosque.

The charges had all been attached to the support pillar, which now held the appearance of a large, bandaged arm. Only then did Imad, now sporting a large silver beard, break the radio silence he'd imposed on the rest of them. He radioed Professor Barghouti and reported, "The uncle is ready for surgery and will arrive tomorrow morning, right after the prayer at the Temple Mount."

He then left for the mosque, to meet and brief the three shahids for the final time. Entering the Old City, they found security at the Damascus Gate stricter than usual. The queues were exceptionally loud. Imad spent the time visualizing tomorrow's events.

Phase 1—The shahids will arrive at the Mount, each entering through a different gate, and convene near the eastern column in the prayer hall.

Phase 2—They wear their kippahs and tallits and begin praying like Jews.

Phase 3—Imad raises his hand and Ibrahim cries out the Jewish *shahada*: "*Shema Yisrael, adonai eloheinu, adonai echad*." Anwar and

Latif will echo him, loudly and clearly.

The dozens of smartphones distributed among the Almoravids would capture the Jews defiling the holy mosque and transfer them to the main server of the Bir Zeit University's Science and Technology Department. Professor Barghouti will then relay them to his people at Al Jazeera and the social networks.

As the worshippers in the mosque swarmed the three "infidels" by the column, Imad would lower his hand, and Ibrahim would set off the charges stuffed inside them. There would be commotion, injuries, deaths. The eastern column would crack, and even if it didn't no matter. What mattered was the footage—live footage of the Jews defiling the mosque, trying to tear it down. The Israeli and Jordanian security cameras and the sound of explosions would alert the Israelis, who would charge into the mosque with full force, trampling everything in their path. Another fantastic photo op.

And then, the final phase, the *coup de grâce*. Once the professor confirmed that the material had been transmitted, he would signal Haj Kahil, who would be waiting at the butcher shop. The charges attached to the underground support pillar would activate, and the mosque would crumble on top of thousands of worshippers, in what would appear to be the natural conclusion of the first explosion. The Israeli forces below would undoubtedly open fire, adding to the chaos. The Muslim world would lose its mind. A new, raging intifada will ensue, and the Arab coalition would be forced to unite and prepare for their inevitable retaliation. And then Imad could finally move in to his own final phase—the phase that would avenge the greatest loss he had ever suffered. And if not, then perhaps there would at least be some comfort in it.

84.

Professor Barghouti had been declared a suspect, but not wanted, and so until this point he hadn't appeared in Unit 8200's list of dangerous wanted activists. The long phone call he made to the sultan, however, piqued the curiosity of the already-anxious duty officer.

Missiles. Explosion. Semtex. Nasrallah. Temple Mount. Muhammad. Al Jazeera. Imad. Each keyword listed in the search database raised the call higher on the urgency list—but the combination of all of them shot it to the very top. Within seconds, the information was passed on to the task force. Plans were put forth and strategies considered. Soon, Operation: Holiest of Holies was underway.

A general curfew was placed on the Yesha[37] territories. The civilian and border police and the Shin Bet were reinforced with every scrap of available personnel. Central command received approval to bring in reserve duty units. The Samur fighters from Combat Engineering, along with Professor Ben-Porat and an Electronic Warfare team, scoured the tunnels under the Old City. Inch by inch, bent over in the crammed tunnels, they made thorough, but excruciatingly slow progress.

While this was going on, three hundred inner-circle Almoravids were arrested during a beautifully coordinated operation by undercov-

---

37 A Hebrew acronym for "Judea, Samaria, Gaza"—a geographical area, roughly corresponding to the West Bank and Gaza Strip combined. -TK

er Unit 217, Sin Bet and police operatives. The questioning strategy dictated by Kahanov included a fast initial classification of threat, and a brief and aggressive interrogation for each suspect in custody, followed by either release, continued detention, or another round of more thorough interrogation.

This was how we found Ibrahim, one of the London stuffed shahids, who was detained in one of the roadblocks. Finally, our first break. And it could explode in our faces at any moment. Kahanov took charge and handled the whole thing with superhuman efficiency. Ibrahim was placed in a remote, isolated cell, in an abandoned basement. A wall of sandbags was erected around it, and in under an hour a team of technicians arrived with a Netline system and a portable X-ray machine. Diagnosis: Ibrahim's belly was jam-packed with gel-form PETN. The electronic activation system, however, hadn't been installed yet. They'd apparently decided to postpone that until the last possible moment, due to the substance's volatility.

We decided to proceed with the interrogation, but Ibrahim wouldn't stop puking, and he passed out during the second round of questioning. The interrogators had to take him to the battalion aid station, where they managed to revive him to a certain extent. According to the interrogator that escorted him there, the Almoravids had been recruited to take videos of some Jews that planned to go up the Mount and pray in the holy mosque. The offensive prayer, a flagrant act of defilement against the holiest of holies, would then be broadcast to the world and was meant to pressure the Israeli government into forbidding any Jews from approaching the Temple Mount.

I wasn't really buying it, though.

The battalion surgeon was telling me that, unless Ibrahim underwent surgery within the hour to clear the toxins spreading inside his abdomen, he could die.

"How much would that bother you?" I asked.

He twisted his knit kippah in his hands and replied with a heavy American accent, "The greater good is what matters now." I couldn't agree more. I sent him and Kahanov away and remained there with Ibrahim.

Kahanov was subject to a veritable slew of restrictions, like any Shin Bet interrogator. I, however, wasn't a professional interrogator. And with Imad threatening my family, I had no notion of restrictions. An odd vision flashed in my mind—Imad was walking toward Verbin and I fired, round after round into his forehead, and Verbin was telling me off: he's wounded, she's treating him, seeing to his injuries. She was taking a selfie with him, smiling. I shook the image from my mind, unnerved.

I remembered a story that used to be told around the intelligence community's proverbial watercoolers: after two interrogation teams had failed to extract from a suspect information critical to the prevention of a suicide bombing that was already underway, Agent Y took over the interrogation. He placed the suspect in a large sack, which he then hung from a hook in the ceiling and beat with a shovel as hard as he could. Two hours later, he had the information they needed. The suspect never spoke again after that.

I asked Kahanov to leave us. He hesitated for a moment, then left.

I regarded Ibrahim. His face was a bright, nearly luminescent green. I gently tilted his head back and poured some water down his throat. I asked him, as softly and nonthreateningly as I could, where the pain was worst. He indicated a large, oozing surgical scar on his lower abdomen. I tore the sheet that covered him, wrapped my right elbow, placed it on the scar and leaned my entire weight into the wound.

Ibrahim screamed, gurgled, foamed and eventually passed out.

I woke him with a sharp slap and gave him more water. He gagged and swallowed.

I explained to him that Imad was threatening my family, my wife and my child, and I would do whatever I deemed necessary to find him.

He remained silent, and I grabbed the chair, smashed it against the wall in a fit of rage, and brought the iron-plated tip of my boot to the wound in his gut. A perfect match.

"You choose," I said. "Who gets to operate on you, me or the doctor?

I'm cheaper, but there's no anesthesia, I'm afraid."

Ibrahim didn't know how to reach Imad and started mumbling incoherently about a second phase, activated from the imam's butcher shop, before he slipped back out of consciousness.

I poured water on him, shook him—no response. It was only when I applied pressure to the scar again that he woke up and started weeping.

"One last question," I said, "and then you're dismissed. Phase two, explosion at the butcher shop. What's phase one?"

Ibrahim opened his eyes and smiled. His speech was clear and fluent. This, I knew, would be his swan song—and he seemed happy to be relieved of the burden.

"Phase one begins Friday morning," he said. "Anwar, Latif and I will go up to the Mount, walk into the mosque, wear kippahs and tallits. The Almoravids will film the whole thing. The entire world will be watching."

He then proceeded to die.

I gave him back to the battalion surgeon and the medic, who transferred him to the field hospital for an autopsy.

I ran up to Kahanov's room and told him about the imam's butcher shop. But phase one, at the Temple Mount—that, I kept to myself, contrary to all directives, protocols and common sense.

To quote Kahanov—fuck protocol. Losing him once was more than enough.

85.

The Samur team, followed by the Electronic Warfare team and the archaeology professor, blasted through the entrance gate to the Western Wall Tunnel. After six minutes of bent, painful running, they stopped beneath Haj Kahil's butcher shop, near the wall blocking the entrance to the Temple Mount's underground. Across the wall stood the eastern support pillar. The Electronic Warfare team set up the Netline system and started their slow, nerve-wracking scan for the electronic components of the explosives.

Upstairs, Border Police and IDF secured the nearby perimeter, clearing away the shop owners and passersby. The strike team was prepared and awaiting the go-ahead. One of the Electronic Warfare team soldiers knelt down and activated the signal jammer. That was that—no electronic signals of any shape or form from this moment onward. The battery-operated drills came out and marked the path for the robotic drills, which began to chomp at the concrete wall.

***

When the robotic teeth encountered the steel rebars enforcing the concrete, the threatening crunching sounds became a blood-curdling screech. Imad was struggling to keep his emotions in check. The haj had just informed him of Ibrahim's arrest. The entire operation was hanging by a thread now. His instinct was to activate the main charge now—take out the support pillar, bring down the mosque, flee during the ensuing chaos. The two engineers, however, adamantly refused. Without the operation and broadcast from the mosque, they said, it would constitute a pointless, sinful injury to the holiest of holies. Imad aimed his weapon at them, but they just stood there, unmoving. He cocked his weapon.

The older engineer knelt in the dust and prayed. The other one soon joined him. Bits of plaster and concrete were crumbling from the wall, and they could hear the metal beasts on the other side, chewing through the wall, getting closer. A cacophony of electronic alerts sounded, and shouts in Hebrew: "Live charge, get back, charge positively identified!"

The engineers were still praying. Imad realized that he could only accomplish his goal by killing the two of them and attaching the detonator to the pillar himself. No time for that—the soldiers would break through in any moment. The screech of metal crunching stone came closer. Suddenly, he felt the cold muzzle of a gun, pressed against the back of his head. Young Haj Kahil was standing there, holding the gun, his hands shaking. The haj took a hurried step back and shoved a large cardboard box with his foot, sliding it in between Imad and the two engineers.

"This is your only way out," he said, still retreating, keeping a clear line of fire to Imad's head. The younger engineer opened the box and took out three IDF uniforms and three short-barreled M16s. Imad scrambled to don one of the uniforms, pulling it on like a life vest. The two engineers followed.

"Hurry," cried out the older one, heading toward the tunnels. "Hurry, or we die here like dogs!"

Imad and the younger engineer followed. Haj Kahil fell to his knees, muttered a prayer, pressed the gun against his own temple and pulled the trigger.

Kahanov and I arrived at the butcher shop just as the strike team was finishing up the scans and the forensic team from the Service was taking over the scene. The sheer volume of IDF-issued explosives attached to the support pillar was mind-boggling. Had it been detonated, it would've taken down the entire mosque—"along with at least half of Suq El Qatanin, along with its inhabitants," said the chief demolitions officer.

Kahanov reported the all clear, permitting his politician to alert the media, inform them with great pomp and circumstance that the threat had been neutralized, praise the government's impeccable security policy, and justify the absence of political progress with the same tired, well-worn bullshit about there being "no partner for peace."

The Almoravid activists who'd been interrogated seemed convinced this whole thing was some Jewish provocation. The old haj, who was also arrested, wouldn't stop praying for long enough to answer the questions presented to him. His son, the young haj, was found shot. The waqf blamed the IDF for shooting at the young haj mid-prayer and presented the 5.56 IDF bullet case as evidence. The minister of public security lifted the general quarantine on the Yesha territories, keeping it confined to the greater Jerusalem area.

The hunt for Imad and his shahids was now in the hands of the intelligence community; intensive reconnaissance activities were initiated out in the field, in homes and caves, at roadblocks and barricades, and in the various signal intelligence units. We had no idea where Imad was now, but I knew exactly where he would be tomorrow morning. I realized I had no choice but to share this intel.

"Are you fucking insane? If you ask me, you're fucking insane!" Kahanov yelled angrily after realizing I'd kept Ibrahim's intel about the mosque operation tomorrow to myself. I decided to keep quiet while he came to terms with it.

After driving silently for few moments, he said, "You were afraid that if we knew their plan to blow up the mosque, we'd close down the Temple Mount. No one goes in."

"Affirmative."

"And?"

"And then Imad and his stuffed shahids would disappear, and reappear who knows where, when it would be much less convenient. If I were him, I'd vanish for a month or so, let everything return to normal, and then..."

"And then Verbin?" Kahanov half-asked, half-stated. "But if you ask me, it's not like we're better off now, when we have no lead on him, his shahids and those engineers that set the charges in the tunnel."

"We're much better off," I insisted, "because if the Mount's still open, he'll be there tomorrow morning with his shahids. I guarantee it."

"So you thought you'd stroll on up there and take them out by your fucking lonesome?"

"Negative," I replied. "I need a team of undercover operatives and someone to paint a mustache on my face—"

"You're a goddamn maniac. Do you even realize what you've just signed up for?"

Of course I did. Imad being alive—that was my fault. The fact that this piece of garbage was now threatening Verbin and little Eran—that was on me, too. So it was my mission. I'd made this clusterfuck of a bed, and I'd be the one to destroy it, whether I could live with the necessary violations or not.

When we arrived at the hospital, I asked if he wanted to come visit Verbin and the little Ehrlich baking inside her over coffee. I'd just gotten her an espresso machine for her office—a small compensation for missing Bruno's summer home in Umbria, and the Sting concert she was supposed to see there with his wife, Julia.

"I have work to do," he grunted and joined Marciano and the other guard, Chayyim, out in the hall.

"Dr. Verbin! I was told there would be coffee," I declared in a deep voice as I entered, but I quickly fell silent when I noticed she was in a meeting with Professor Gorni, the hospital administrator. She still got up and hugged me.

"This is Professor Gorni, my boss. Boss, meet the Neanderthal—my doting husband, Avner."

"We've met," Gorni and I said in unison, and he patted me on the back and quickly left the room.

"Good guy," I said. "Went on a couple of ops with us." Verbin attempted to sink deeper into my chest.

"Hey, doc, you're wrinkling my kid's ears," I scolded her, then raised her shirt a bit to kiss our tiny offspring.

"You coming home tonight?" she asked.

Kahanov knocked lightly and entered the office.

"No. I'm with the bad guys tonight," I said, looking at Kahanov, who was already listening intently to Verbin's small bulge and seemed to be having a wonderful time.

"Tonight you'll sleep at our place, okay?" said Kahanov.

Verbin glanced at me questioningly. What she saw in my face made it clear that this time, it was necessary.

"Just for tonight," he said. "Just this one night, and tomorrow everything'll be over. When you're done here, go with Marciano and Chayyim. Bring whatever you need for tonight and tomorrow. They'll drive you to our safe house in Rehavia. It's a nice place, honestly. I'll leave you to it," he said and went back out to the hall.

"I'm glad you're not in Italy," I said.

"Oh, this is new," she said. "What happened?"

I stroked her belly. "It's not just that the kid needs its dad, you know. A dad needs his kid, too." I said. "And… I don't know, maybe its mom, too. A bit."

Verbin flipped me off, grinning.

I blew her a kiss and joined Kahanov outside.

86.

"Now shut up and listen," said Kahanov, back in the car. "I checked on Ibrahim. He's still at the battalion aid station, recuperating. We'll gently wake him and take him out of there at four hundred, four fifteen. Dr. 'Greater Good' will sign him over to us and mark the date and time. We'll interrogate Ibrahim, and by the time he gives us the intel, we'll have no time to report it, no time for anything other than getting up there as soon as possible. Gates to the Temple Mount open at five a.m. You got all that, Mr. RP?"

It was an elegant solution.

"I need a team of undercover operatives, with a Netline for jamming and for possible explosives."

"It's all ready," said Kahanov, snorting when he noticed my raised eyebrows. "Some of us don't just fuck around all day, PR," he added. "We can't all fly to Europe once a week in swanky-ass suits and thousand-dollar shoes, change our panties and passport at some connection and have a bunch of fancy lunches with our local service buddies. This is the Levant. Here we don't fuck around."

When Kahanov and I arrived at Ibrahim's, we found out that at 02:00, he'd finally managed to claw his way into the bosom of Allah.

"May Allah have mercy," I mumbled, pensive.

"You, go, now!" Kahanov ordered, "I'll handle the paperwork here and join you later. Micha from 217 is waiting at the Damascus Gate with your mustache. Get dressed and get up there… your bike's still here, right?"

Kahanov brought me the clothes I had worn for the tanker operation in Lebanon. They exuded a slightly sweet odor, gunpowder and rotten eggs. I couldn't afford to waste time, so I wore the sticky mess, taking comfort in the thought that they had served me loyally once before, and the fact that the doctor wasn't here to smell me. She would most likely get a restraining order… and possibly stick me in quarantine.

I took the Harley. I had to get up the Mount before Imad and his shahids got to the area, saw me there and bolted. I parked the bike in an abandoned yard surrounded by a rusted wire fence and went up to the gate. Micha and his team were waiting for me in full disguise, along with Roei, an officer from the Engineering Corps bomb squad. He was also provided with a disguise, and by the end of it he looked as local as one of the undercover Unit 217 boys. The jamming system, intended to disrupt wirelessly triggered charges, was hidden in the leg of his wide harem pants.

On our way up the Mount, we passed an angry mob of the Almoravid wives, swarming the gates and the road to the mosque, moaning and wailing at the top of their lungs. A good enough reason, as far as I was concerned, to get our asses out of there and let them do whatever they wanted with this holy fucking mountain. Holy sites and holy men have always made me uncomfortable.

***

Inside the mosque, we removed our shoes and scattered. Roei from the bomb squad went with me. We positioned ourselves about thirty yards from the eastern column and kneeled in prayer, me mimicking the movements of the worshippers in front of me, Roei mimicking me. Micha and his 217 operatives were spread in a loose arc around the mosque's entrance and prayed devoutly. The prayer continued in a sort of monotone murmur, occasionally breaking when one of the worshippers raised his voice in a fervent "*Allah hu akbar*." Roei and I joined in on the cries when others did. The rest of the time I muttered other prayers and waited.

The morning prayer ended and the targets were still nowhere to be seen. I looked back at Micha, who had a tiny earbud hidden under his keffiyeh. I tried to put myself in Imad's place and realized that it would make a lot of sense to wait for the noon prayer, when attendance would be at its peak.

I went to take a piss and Micha came with me. We agreed to wait for the noon prayer, which started at 11:00. We passed the time taking shifts going to the restrooms, praying to Allah and swapping hushed jokes. Of course, the slipped discs in my back chose the worst possible time to throw a tantrum—my right arm fell asleep, and all my attempts to wake it failed spectacularly. It was nearly 11:00. If Imad didn't show up soon, it probably meant he'd decided to postpone, even call the whole thing off. I wondered if he was aware of Ibrahim's predicament and estimated that he would come up there and try to execute the plan either way. If he succeeded, I would be in large part to blame.

The thought was horrifying. I envisioned the mosque crumbling to pieces—hundreds of thousands of Arab soldiers marching in from all sides. On foot, on oxcarts, on cars and tanks, up the Mount they'd go, burning and crushing. I'd call Froyke, beg him to get the prime minister to use our nuclear option. "It's our last resort!" I'd cry. The prime minister would refuse, claiming that it would be politically unwise. I am placed in the corner of Froyke's office. My hands are cuffed. "Never try, never fail," I say to Froyke, winking. Froyke is cold and distant. "As usual, you have exhibited a blatant disregard for the chain of command and your direct orders. Violations we can live with, huh?" he mocked me. "Never try, never fail—and when you fail, there's hell to pay. You've failed. Now pay!"

Eran and Ya'ara were standing there, with my mother and father, and Verbin. They were applauding Froyke's vicious rant. Fuck, it hurt.

I snapped out of it, just barely managing to scrape away the image.

***

Imad chose to ascend from the El-Hadid Gate. According to his instructions, the stuffed shahids were to come from separate gates, carrying no electronic devices save for Anwar's cell phone, programmed to set off all three charges simultaneously. Imad passed security and slowly walked up the path to the mosque, as was appropriate for any devout, well-bearded Muslim—but inside of him, under the beard, raged a tempest. He felt the surging adrenaline, his battle readiness kicking in, taking over. Years of combat had been needed to perfect the mechanism: his vision, hearing and smelling sharpened, suddenly aware of the smallest changes in his surroundings. His muscles tensed and an armor seemed to rise from inside of him, sealing away his consciousness. Now he feared no one, and pitied no one. Not even himself.

He moved slowly, trying to pick out his shahids from the massive crowd. At the entrance to the mosque, he finally spotted Anwar and ordered him to stay close. They entered the prayer hall together and scanned it intently. Still no sign of Latif. Imad decided that with or without him, he would order Anwar to detonate. Once they had failed to collapse the underground support pillar, the bombing in the mosque became the crux of the entire operation. His thoughts momentarily carried him to Agur, to Ehrlich's home—he managed to shove it to the back of his mind, but it wasn't easy. This had to succeed. And he had to find Latif, or the bombing would be lacking.

***

The morning turned to noon and the worshippers were changing shifts, allowing me a moment to sneak a glance to the side. I noticed with alarm that some of them were taking out cell phones and taking videos of the prayer. We were in business. I had no idea how to stop them from filming, but suddenly I spotted Latif entering the prayer room. I choked back the urge to charge and neutralize him. I needed Imad.

"Watch him," I whispered to Roei, our foreheads pressed against the floor in prostration.

The sharp smell of burning rubber filled the mosque. I inched toward Micha, who mumbled that a full-blown riot had broken out down by the gate. The younger Almoravids hadn't been allowed to enter the Mount, and the response had been burning dozens of tires, brought along for this purpose, and throwing stones at the security forces. We each returned to our place. Micha scanned the entrance and occasionally gave me questioning looks. I signaled him to be patient and kept praying.

I then spotted a tall, bearded man.

It was him. Wearing dark sunglasses and a large beard, but him nonetheless. I rose, painfully slowly. I had to somehow signal Micha to block Imad's escape route, but he was still searching the entrance with his back to me, and I failed to catch his eye. I started inching toward Imad. Step, pause. Step, pause. He could make me out at any second, and then all it would take was a small, easily created distraction, and he'd disappear among the thousands of worshippers.

I turned around to get out of his field of vision and flank him from behind. I was walking at a snail's pace, in a sort of half-crouch—my back was screaming, demanding to be straightened. I forced myself to continue the slow, excruciating progress, estimating that I'd reach him from behind in around three minutes. By then I hoped to capture Micha's attention and get him to block the exit. I couldn't lose Imad, not again.

Imad was praying now, and I could afford to move a bit quicker. About two minutes until I was on top of him.

Latif suddenly rose, standing with his back to the eastern column and wearing a large black kippah he'd taken from his pocket. Roei didn't wait for orders—he activated the Netline system, and a series of loud electronic alarms pierced the air. The worshippers around him stood up and started shouting, several of them closing in on him, moving quickly and threateningly. Roei, who had never been trained as an undercover operative, called out, "Live charge! Charge positively identified!" in loud, crystal-clear Hebrew.

"Exposure! Formation!" Micha yelled and sprinted toward the eastern column. The 217 team drew their weapons and converged into a star formation, back to back. They moved like scorpions, back and sideways, on their way to extract Roei. Chaos ensued. Yelling, shoving, cries of *Allah hu akbar* filled the mosque. Micha fired shots in the air, violently cutting through the wall of worshippers closing on Roei. Latif, still wearing his kippah, was swaying back and forth, his eyes closed. Micha fired a bullet to his center of mass and two more to confirm, then collected Roei and began retreating toward the exit. The star formation moved slowly, occasionally firing shots in the air. Anyone who dared approach them was rewarded with a rifle butt to the face. The crowd backed away from them, yelling and wailing.

The time was now. I drew my Glock and lunged at Imad. He took a step back, grabbing Anwar's throat and using him as a shield. The crowd of worshippers around us staggered back in terror, clearing the area.

I considered firing at Anwar, rolling to the right and firing at Imad. Then again, firing at Anwar might activate the charge stuffed in his gut, killing him along with Anwar, Imad and myself. I focused on Imad and continued moving toward him. He stared right back, slowly retreating, dragging Anwar with him.

"Activate!" Imad was yelling. "Activate!"

Anwar frantically tapped his phone, over and over again—nothing was happening. Imad snatched the phone away and roughly shoved Anwar toward me. I took half a step and lunged forward, my fist spinning into the center of his torso. There was a sharp *crunch* as his ribs cracked, followed by a hollow whistle of escaping air. Mass times acceleration—his sternum had just collided with about half a ton of force. I heard what sounded like a muffled explosion, and blood burst from his body. Anwar fell, unmoving. I rolled to the right. Someone threw a grenade and we were enveloped by yellow smoke. By the time I found my way out of the cloud, Imad was no longer there.

I carved my way through the rioting crown, but who was I kidding? He was gone. *Scheisse.*

Micha's team struggled to clear a path through the mob, firing and throwing stun grenades at their attackers. A Border Police squad came up the road to the mosque, shoving and hitting, knocking down anyone on their way. They formed a defensive ring around us. Below us, the Almoravid wives were shrieking and howling. The cops, who were already at the end of their ropes, were becoming increasingly agitated. A squad car was hit by a thrown Molotov cocktail—it caught fire and began to burn. Thick black smoke rose up and obscured the sun.

"The mosque is clear," Micha alerted headquarters. "Repeat, the mosque is clear of charges. Two dirties neutralized. One escaped. No injured among our forces."

"The Temple's safe," I told Kahanov, "but Muhammad's off the Mount again. Did you manage to get their phones?"

"Why on earth would I confiscate phones?" he said, feigning innocence.

I realized that he'd activated some sort of jamming signal to block all cellular frequency bands in the area. None of the videos would've been transmitted, and it would explain why Imad couldn't activate Anwar's stuffing.

"You're the best," I said.

Kahanov went by the book and had roadblocks and checkpoints set up throughout the area, but we both knew this was not the way this sneaky fuck would be found. For a pro, the fog of war provides excellent cover—and Imad was a true pro.

87.

After the debriefing I hurried to the hospital to pick up Verbin. She opted for dinner at Machneyuda, a fancy Jerusalem restaurant. On the way there, I did some reminiscing. For the fourth time now in a decade, that piece of shit had managed to slip away from me. This time it would be different. He'd gone and made it personal. I recalled one of Tarantino's gangsters saying that family isn't the most important thing—it's the only important thing.

I picked up Verbin, and Marciano and his partner Chayyim followed us in a separate car. On our way to the restaurant, Verbin decided she wasn't really up for all the fanciness, and what she really, truly wanted more than anything was falafel. We pulled over next to our favorite falafel place, and for the first time in my life, I examined the oil in the deep fryer and asked, "Why does the oil look so shitty?"

The falafel man shrugged. "Like you look so hot at the end of a workday." Verbin laughed her ass off and asked him to be more understanding, seeing as I was pregnant.

"*Mazal tov*," he said. We ate our falafel, with Marciano and Chayyim at the table next to us. It was absolutely repulsive, but Verbin seemed to enjoy every bite, and so I really couldn't ask for more.

When we were done, we wanted to return to Agur, but Kahanov wouldn't hear of it. We were directed to the apartment the Service kept at Rehavia.

Kahanov woke me at 05:00. "Balata!" he barked into the phone. "Get ready. I'm six mikes out."

"Keep the kid safe," I whispered, stroking Verbin's small belly.

She hummed in her sleep and rolled over.

Kahanov came in a gray Land Rover Defender, shielded and bursting with antennas, which looked like he'd just stolen it from a Mad Max set.

"Balata?"

"Affirmative. Good chance he's down there," he said. "Not the nicest fucking neighborhood, if you ask me."

I happened to agree. Balata had the narrowest, most twisting alleys in the whole narrow, twisted Middle East. This shithole of a camp was controlled by private gangs, contractors for Hamas and Jihad. The whole town was held hostage by masked armed hostiles, ages twelve and up. The Palestinian police forces dared not treat there. The IDF only operated in Balata as an absolute last resort and always entered in large numbers. Any movement of tanks, APC or other armored vehicles required the demolition of whole streets. The hostiles were perfectly aware of the political and logistical difficulties involved in any large-scale military operation. The military lost its tactical advantage and got pulled into low-intensity, symmetrical retaliations. This played into the hands of the terrorists, who had no qualms about dragging the fighting into civilian homes. This is what urban guerilla warfare has always looked like.

"Aren't you gonna ask how?" Kahanov snapped me out of my thoughts.

"How?"

"Excellent question. At oh two hundred, one Ayach el Azazma breaks into a bait car in Kfar-Saba and drives it all the way to Ramallah. Police auto crime team tracks it. Apparently this guy's a real prince. Child sex crimes. Smuggling. You name it. Then this fucker tells the blues that he was the one who got Imad the Semtex, and he's willing to give us everything on the Israeli buyer, in return for a dismissal of all charges against him. Maxim, the interrogator, got him to promise to give us Imad's safe house in Balata. He wanted cash for that, on top of the dropped charges."

"Did you take the deal?"

"I promised that if we found Imad, we'd give him everything he asked for. Then again, I had my fingers crossed."

"Can't this fucking thing go any faster?"

"Eighty-six miles per hour, top speed. This is a Land Rover, not a fucking Ferrari. By the way, you should know Imad also has two of his Shabwah engineers with him—"

"What happens now?" I interrupted.

"We get to work. The territorial brigade and the Haruv commandos are closing off a perimeter. Inside there's a paratrooper reconnaissance platoon and a Unit 217 force, including rooftop snipers and a shitload of my own men."

"And what—"

I was cut off by the sound of rolling thunder. Kahanov answered the phone and put it on speaker. "Hey, Mizrahi."

"Evening, Kahanov. You by yourself?"

"Evening, Colonel," I chimed in.

"Is that RP I hear?!"

"In the flesh."

"Two hundred and thirty pounds of rage and power! *Bdalak, ya ibni, Bdalak*, we are honored. Welcome to the Middle East. When are you getting here?"

"Four to five mikes."

"Okay, we'll talk when you get here. RP, come get a piece of the action, I'm giving them hell down here."

"What kind of hell?" I asked after he'd hung up.

"Trying to trigger retaliation," Kahanov explained, and I remembered the last time we'd seen Mizrahi, in the chopper after we'd blown up Victor's tanker, and the time before that, when he was coming up my driveway with the others to tell me about Eran.

Kahanov laughed. "He's been a brigadier general for three years, but you can't take the battalion commander out of the boy."

Brigadier General Yosef Mizrahi—"the Colonel," as we'd called him since he came back from a training course at Fort Bragg—had spent most of his long military career out in the field, whether he was required to or not. Mizrahi grew up in Iraq, and some claim that it was he who had originally coined the adage "A good Arab is a dead Arab"—if not, he had certainly done more to propagate it than any other man alive. The Colonel was considered the father of the IDF's low-intensity combat tactics. He was also the first to blast through the walls of houses in refugee camps, to move the forces off the streets and avoid side charges and sniper fire. I was one of the first junior officers to apply this tactic in the Jabalia camp.

More rolling thunder.

"Kahanov, you alone?"

"Yeah, Maxim. Just me and RP."

"He's on his way to you. Nothing more to be gained by interrogation. He's done."

"You didn't break him?"

"You know the Supreme Court's on my ass," said Maxim defensively.

"I've got no one on my ass," I cut in. "Not the Supreme Court, not the Heavenly Court of the almighty himself. Bring that fucker out to the field."

The Colonel suddenly barged in on the radio. "RP! Kahanov! Heat waves in the house, I'm starting a 'pressure cooker.'"

"With you in three," said Kahanov, pressing the gas pedal as far down as it would go. I called the office.

"Bella, get me Froyke."

"They're both at the prime minister's, with foreign guests."

"Let him know I'm with Kahanov on the way to Balata."

"You know you're not supposed to be down there," she gently scolded me.

"I know. I know I'm not. Be sure to tell him. Bye."

88.

The UAVs hovering over the camp sent their footage to the screens in Mizrahi's command post. One UAV surveilled the whole camp, providing the big picture, while the other lingered above the house. The Colonel was wearing a perfectly pressed dress uniform as he did during every combat op. He pointed at Yuval, the reconnaissance company commander, and brought two fingers to his eyes spread in a V shape—the signal for "give me eyes."

Yuval had recently collected on a debt owed to him by Sela from the Matkal intelligence team, borrowing a set of XAVER 100 radar imaging systems, for detection through walls—until now, only Flotilla 13 and Matkal teams had had access to it. But now, he was failing to calibrate the device. The division intelligence officer removed his helmet and tried to finish the calibration himself, and a rock thrown from one of the rooftops hit him in the head. As the medic tried to stop the bleeding, a single shot cracked through air. A 217 sniper, positioned on another rooftop, fired without waiting for approval. A boy of about fourteen tumbled to the street, a bullet in his forehead.

"Shit! Shit, shit! A kid? Why a kid?!" Mizrahi muttered furiously.

A mob of old, veiled wailing women appeared, seemingly out of thin air, and collected the body, all the while howling obscenities at the soldiers. The soldiers were firing into the air, trying in vain to scare the women away. Some masked adolescents drew courage from the group of women and began to throw rocks, wooden planks and garbage cans at the soldiers. Someone spilled a tub of boiling oil from a window onto a patrol jeep, burning the driver. A medic from the battalion aid station ran to his aid, slipped on the oil-covered cobblestones and sprained her ankle. The crowd around her cheered.

"Starling[38], get someone to evacuate the kid's body," said the Colonel, glancing at Kahanov. "They've got me dispersing demonstrations now in my old age. Didn't even give me a damn water hose. Seventeen, bring the teddy bears and clear everyone from the street, over."

"Crown, this is Starling. Body's not here. They must've taken it, over."

"Great, now we'll have a huge funeral… goddamnit. Where's the teddy bear?"

"Crown, this is Screwdriver. We can't go in with the teddy to evacuate people, only—"

"Shut up. Out." Mizrahi cut him off, furious.

A squad of paratroopers and a young lieutenant from Unit 504, the Human Intelligence Formation, had taken over the PA system of the nearby mosque. The officer ordered the crowd to clear the area around the house immediately and addressed Imad and the two engineers by name, ordering them to exit the house unarmed and with their hands in the air.

"This is your first and final warning," he said in perfect Palestinian Arabic. "You either exit the house within the next three minutes or you'll be killed. You're surrounded and out of options. Come out and live. The countdown begins now."

He then went back to warning the other residents of the camp to clear the area. The masked teenagers were still throwing rocks and planks at the soldiers, who retaliated with gas grenades. One of the boys came too close and was captured and handcuffed, as his friends continued to rain bricks and random debris at the soldiers. The soldiers fired high above their heads, trying to keep them away, but they

---

38 IDF call signs: Starling—company sergeant major; Crown—commander; Screwdriver—operations officer; Teddy Bear—Israeli armored Caterpillar D9R bulldozer. -TK

wouldn't stop. More rocks came. Two soldiers were mildly injured and taken away. The other soldiers lowered their rifles and fired at the ground. One of the boys was shot in the knee and the other in the face. Their friends dragged them back toward a waiting Red Crescent ambulance. Mizrahi ordered the soldiers to grab anyone filming with a smartphone or a camera.

"A kid with a smartphone had more power over the field of battle than a trained infantry brigade. If you see one, fire in the air and neutralize them, or their cameras," he said. "After that, do your jobs. Yuval, look alive!"

"Yuval team, this is Crown." The reconnaissance company commander gave a messy salute and started walking toward the house, speaking into his walkie at the squads perched around the house.

"One, here."

"Two, here."

"Three, four, five?"

"Three. Four. Five. Ready."

"One, two, three, four, five. Good luck. You are go."

A barrage of bullets ventilated the walls of the house from all directions.

Yuval looked up at the Colonel, who raised two fingers, like a basketball coach signaling a play. At the end of the street, I could just barely make out the tips of Corner Shot barrels peeking out from behind a wall and disappearing. Occasionally the snout or wagging tail of an Oketz dog peeked from the corner before it was hastily restrained by its handler.

"We need to wrap this up," grumbled the Colonel, "before the whole camp gets here along with the bleeding hearts and their damn film crews and media circus."

Another barrage rained on the house. No response.

The 504 officer gave the besieged another ninety seconds.

"Yossi," I addressed the Colonel, "I'm going in with the recon team. I need him alive."

"No one goes in there. Sorry, RP, not even you. He either comes out or he dies. There's no other option—charging in there can only end with our guys in the shit. Ain't happening. And you sure as hell aren't stepping foot in there. Sorry, really, I am. But you must know, a good Arab is—"

"Yeah, yeah," I spoke over him, "a good Arab is a dead Arab, sure, okay, but this one, he's a really bad Arab, and I need him alive."

"The one who's coming after you? Oh, I am definitely killing him. And his fucking mother."

The officer in the mosque again addressed Imad by name. "The clock is ticking. You have twenty seconds to get out of there alive."

Yuval decided to lend some weight to the countdown and ordered another barrage.

The commander of the antitank platoon requested permission to fire a missile at the house. Mizrahi denied it. "Too much collateral. And a hell of a photo op."

He ordered the two teddy bears to approach. The two armored bulldozers came forth and sank their metal claws into the walls of the house. A series of underground charges was activated from inside, exploding violently. At the same moment, Yuval dove to retrieve the XAVER system and was buried under the collapsing wall. My heart skipped a beat and I moved forward, but Kahanov held me back. Two of Yuval's troops sprung out of cover to charge forward and retrieve Yuval's limp form from the wreckage. They huddled around the medic who ran out to examine him. "He's alive!" the medic cried out. Yuval was still stubbornly clutching the XAVER system when they carried him to the rescue chopper.

The explosion left no chance of survival for anyone inside the house. Meanwhile, the bulldozers kept tearing away at the walls. The clouds of dust and the smoke from the explosions mingled with the yelling and commotion. The large teddy bears then began to clear away the wreckage—bricks, logs and pieces of mangled corpses were tossed to the other end of the street, and the soldiers began a gradual evacuation.

We left the dark and battered Balata behind us and headed for Jerusalem. Kahanov broke the heavy silence with, "So the schmuck is finally dead!"

"Last time he died, he came back alive," I said and hesitated. Something was troubling me. "Before I went up to the mosque, I asked you for a team of undercover operatives and a jamming system. It was already set up, though. Micha and his team, the guy from the bomb squad who didn't know his ass from his elbow—how did you get it all ready in time?"

Kahanov laughed. "Took you a while, Mr. analytical mastermind. Here, take a look." He handed me his phone. "Go to the gallery."

I found a video of me interrogating Ibrahim—he was telling me about the planned attack at the mosque. The intel I'd kept to myself, shared with no one—this bastard had known all along. He'd been watching my back. I lit two Cohibas and placed one in his mouth.

The sound of rolling thunder rose once again from his phone.

"Motherfuckers," rumbled the Colonel. "The kid… Yuval, he lost an eye."

My impression of Yuval was of a skilled, decisive young man—he was Eran's age. They might have even known each other. I'd give anything for Eran to have just lost an eye. Fucking hell…

"So now he can be a general," I said. Ami shot me a sideways glance. The Colonel asked that we stop by the hospital to visit Yuval, "cheer him up a bit."

"On it," said Ami and hung up.

"There's something wrong," I said eventually. "Something deeply wrong with all of this."

"How do you mean?"

"I don't know… this… asymmetrical war. Helicopters, UAVs, armored bulldozers, this insane order of battle, all this power just to catch one terrorist. This can't work. Like it or not, when it comes down to it, we have to live with these people. Those kids with the rocks… if you were a Palestinian child, wouldn't you be out there, throwing rocks? Sure you would. You'd be good at it, too. So would I."

"Same old spiel. One man's terrorists are another man's freedom fighters."

"Yeah. Well, at least now I can get rid of your security."

"Officially, I can only call them off tomorrow, after the debriefing."

He took a long drag and tried unsuccessfully to pop out some smoke rings before calling Marciano and relieving my security detail. "Both of you keep securing the First Lady, though," he added before hanging up.

I gave him a questioning look and he shrugged. "What kind of Uncle Ami do you take me for?"

I wanted to thank him but smacked him on the back instead. We enjoyed our cigars in silence.

89.

Imad moved slowly, just as he had taught his warriors in Shabwah. But the dunes of Shabwah were soft desert sand, and this one was a bed of small rocks, sharp as blades. He absorbed the pain and overcame the powerful urge to stop and shake the jagged rocks out of his boots. He instinctively wiped his lips of sand that wasn't there, rose carefully from the ground, and then broke into a hunched sprint, his hand never leaving the ground. He reached the small cave and dove inside. A bat flew by, which meant everything was clear. He then waited, for an hour or so, his ears perked.

The low, hushed howl of a jackal finally sounded, and Imad replied with a howl of his own. Three short howls were the response. Mahajna's "all clear." Under the cover of thick darkness, Imad crawled from the cave down to the family olive grove, at the outskirts of Nablus. The stumps of old olive trees looked like vanquished giants, left to die on some ancient battlefield. Whoever had felled them had left some unharmed, perhaps to bolster the sense of destruction.

"This was the tree your father planted when you were born." Mahajna pointed at one of the stumps and handed Imad a cup of coffee he'd poured from a large thermos. Imad gratefully drank.

They got in the minivan and drove to the cousin's house. Mahajna told Imad that although they had failed to bring down the mosque, heavy riots had broken out following the Jews' decision to prohibit entrance to the Temple Mount. Thousands of teenagers from all around the Western Bank had already joined the fight. They were calling it "the Temple Mount Intifada." Fourteen adolescents had already been shot and killed attempting to stab Israeli soldiers or police officers. Dozens had been injured. The actions of the enemy were constantly being broadcast over Arab television stations and social media. "This intifada of yours is going swimmingly. Good thing you didn't blow up the mosque. The old haj would've slaughtered you."

Mahajna then told Imad that he was in dire need of a shower, a change of clothes and some rest, because he wouldn't be getting into any hospitals looking like he did, or really into anywhere other than maybe a graveyard. The relative peace Mahajna enjoyed thanks to his position as a Shin Bet informant should provide Imad with a night of undisturbed sleep. Mahajna mentioned that he occasionally found some worthless worker he'd smuggled in illegally and handed him over "to the dogs," to maintain that peace.

After a shower and a dinner that Imad hungrily wolfed down, Mahajna briefed him on their findings: "Ehrlich and his woman, the doctor, spend most of their time in one of three primary locations—the Mossad compound at Ramat HaSharon, their house at Agur, and Hadasa Hospital in Jerusalem. His boss goes there often—cancer. We didn't manage to find his son, Eran—there's no sign of him. Probably smoking pot somewhere in India or Bolivia, like all Israelis do after the army. I suggest we let it go for now. Right now, we can either ambush them on the road with a large truck, run them over, or we can infiltrate the hospital. We have people in there, doctors, nurses, orderlies. We can capture the doctor and lure Ehrlich there. Sleep on it. Let me know tomorrow what you've decided, and I'll make arrangements."

90.

ZAKA teams worked alongside Kahanov's cleaners throughout the night at the scene of the event, well-lit and secured. The series of explosions and the teddy bears left very little that could be recognized as human parts. Anything that could be collected was quickly passed to the genetics lab, who was ordered to work on nothing else until they had results. When the lab found that the parts came from only two people, Kahanov panicked. If one of them got away, there was a thirty-three percent chance that it was Imad—except of course that this was Imad, and therefore it was a much, much higher chance than that.

"I need DNA, now!" Kahanov barked into the phone. "Now!"

"DNA fingerprinting takes time," replied Gottfried the lab tech in his musical Argentinian accent.

"There is! No! Time!" Kahanov yelled hoarsely. "I need an immediate ID, right fucking now!" He slammed the phone. A second later he yelled, "Get me Avner! ASAP!"

A short time later, Marciano arrived, his face ashen. He reported that they hadn't been able to find either Avner or Verbin. Calls were going to voicemail. No one at the hospital or the Mossad knew where they were.

"Unbelievable!" Kahanov shouted. "Is everyone here an impotent piece of shit? Blind? Deaf?! Have you seriously *lost* the Mossad's deputy chief of operations, a two-hundred-and-fifty-pound man? Gone, disappeared into thin air?! You bunch of useless, ass-fucking clowns!"

Marciano, who'd been under Kahanov's command for over a decade, had never seen him like this. He considered reminding Kahanov that he was the one who had withdrawn Avner's security, just yesterday, but thought it better to wait for him to finish.

The phone rang, with Froyke on the line.

"Have you found him?"

"Negative. No sign of him. His car's parked at home and so is the Harley. Neither of them is answering the phone."

"Ran is on his way. Set up a special investigation team. I'll be there at fourteen hundred. Inform me if anything comes up. Anything, you hear? Hang on." Froyke brought Bella on the line. She'd just received the DNA results, which confirmed that Imad was not among the dead. Kahanov's panic grew, multiplied.

"Bella," said Froyke, "any call that comes in about Avner, you let me know immediately."

"No problem," said Bella, "but why are you looking for Avner?"

"There's been no sign of him all day."

"Well, of course not. It's the twelfth."

"And?" Froyke urged, a slight hope flickering in his voice.

"It's Eran's Day."

"And?" Froyke and Kahanov spoke in unison.

"Oy, you two… never mind. On Eran's anniversary, Avner always disconnects. From everyone. Understandable, I think."

"Bella, I love you!" said Froyke, scrolling through his calendar. "He did take the day off… you keep up the search, just in case," he added. "I'll try to see where he goes when he… disconnects. Bella, get me Snir from operations."

Kahanov remained on the line to request emergency measures—roadblocks, patrols, reconnaissance teams. Everything was approved. He then ordered his men to apply heavy pressure on their main sources and the rest of the informants, and they did—but nothing relevant came up.

"Any informants we haven't brought in yet?" asked Kahanov.

Hanan, one of Kahanov's agents, raised his head from the lists, saying, "Nope, we've interrogated everyone. Except for Mahajana, the guy smuggling the illegals."

"And why was he left out?"

"Mahajna? Nah, he's one of ours. If he knew something, he would've said."

"Get him in here, now!" barked Kahanov.

After the initial investigation, Maxim was convinced that Mahajana possessed no relevant information.

"It's unlikely that Imad would share his intentions with him," he told Kahanov. "And if he'd left us anything, it would probably be misinformation," he added, using his new favorite word.

Kahanov still insisted that they keep leaning on Mahajana. Maxim argued that too much pressure would just result in him telling them whatever he thought they wanted to hear.

"Enough time together, and I can get a signed confession for anything. Any murders you want pinned? JFK? Jesus?"

"No need," said Kahanov. "Just ask him what he'd do in Imad's place."

Maxim shrugged, then went back inside the interrogation room and asked. Mahajna, who sat there wringing his hands, seemed surprised at the question. "In his place? I'd run. Get as far away from here as possible, as soon as I could."

"Run where?" Kahanov joined in.

"Jordan. No, Syria."

"He's probably working alone," Maxim said quietly in Kahanov's ear. "And if he is, it'll be a while before we find something."

Kahanov asked that he cut the bullshit. "There's no such thing as a terrorist working alone. It's an urban legend—doesn't exist. Lone-wolf terrorism was made up to protect Palestinian politicians from their responsibility for terrorism and protect our politicians from their responsibility for defense." Louder, so that Mahajna could hear, he added, "Put him back in his cell! If anyone knows about Imad, it's him. Let him stew, then question him again. I won't mind if he happens to slip on the way and break his jaw."

Mahajna grinned and spat, "All I know is that Imad is going to fuck you up. All of you!"

Maxim smacked him across the face, hard, and dragged him back to his cell.

91.

Before Verbin came into our lives, I used to spend Eran's Day near the grave, with a bottle of Macallan. Just Eran, the bottle and me. Garibaldi and Adolf would occasionally come to check on me, and before returning to their patrol, Garibaldi would sit by me, lick my nose and the salt of my tears. I'd also spent some Eran Days with O'Dri—the two of us along with John Jr., his own kid, Eran and two bottles of Kentucky straight bourbon.

Verbin suggested that we finish the western stretch of the Israel National Trail. Eran and I were supposed to finish it on his next R&R, the one he never got. It felt... right.

We drove down to Route 90 and, after Tzofar, arrived at the Incense Route. It was the middle of the week and we had the glory of the desert all to ourselves. Occasionally we encountered a wandering camel, with its Bedouin never too far away.

The ATV me and Eran bought, a CAN AM Maverick X3, was a ferocious machine with over two hundred horsepower. A monstrous suspension system and improved engine performance allowed us to fly over the rocks and pits at a terrifyingly high speed. We arrived in about twenty minutes, drove up the final ramp in a single lunge, and stopped there, the clouds of white power slowly settling on top of us. Verbin's face looked like a Japanese mask—chalk white, all but the shadow left by the dust goggles. I used a wet wipe to reveal her true face, behind the white.

"Just practicing for when I need to clean the dust from your wrinkles," I said. "Onward?"

Verbin stroked her belly, the bulge still barely noticeable, and addressed the question to it. "Onward?" She nodded. "Onward!"

We climbed up Mount Kipa, to Rotem's Lookout. I leaned my back against a large, smooth rock. Verbin folded inside of me. We breathed in the primordial landscape. Our Israel, mine and Eran's, and now hers as well. I told her, like I'd told Eran back then, how Rotem had been killed in this wadi, just beneath the lookout. Such a waste.

I took out the small gas stove and made coffee, letting it boil seven times before finally pouring. Verbin gently cleaned my face with a wet wipe. "I think… I'm sure Eran will love the baby. And so will Gil."

We'd recently been discussing our thought of their future relationship. We had no doubt that Eran would be overjoyed with his new sibling, though we still hadn't settled on a name for our new Ehrlich.

I jumped at the sudden, distant drone of an approaching helicopter. I looked around, seeking shelter. Nothing. The mountain was a large, smooth dome. I hurried to the ATV's side bag and pulled out the Glock that Kahanov had ordered me to carry as long as the threat persisted—but Imad was supposed to be dead, and where would he get a helicopter? Still, I loaded and cocked it and put my arms around Verbin.

An air force Black Hawk rose over the ridge and approached the center of the dome, preparing to land. I sheathed the Glock back in the bag. Verbin was staring at me. I smiled and said Froyke was probably missing us. The flight engineer came running, saluted lightly, as if he wasn't sure whether he was supposed to, and handed me a sealed envelope from Froyke.

> Avner, my friend.
>
> Next year, on this day, if you'd agree, I'll come to that mountain with you and we'll drink to Eran and Luigi.
>
> Today, it turns out, Imad is still alive. He has access to logistics and support, and he's looking for you and for Dr.

> Verbin. We have reason to believe he is also looking for Eran (he doesn't know). Come back with the helicopter. It has straps for your ATV.

After we landed at the compound's helipad, I let Kahanov unload his frustration on me while Bella and Verbin giggled and gossiped like teenagers.

Kahanov eventually calmed down. "Mahajna was probably the only one who knew something, but he slipped and broke his jaw, wouldn't talk after that. I let him go."

"Good call," I said. Tracking a released suspect in the hopes they'd lead you to the target, while being among the oldest tricks in the book, is rarely done. I suppose the weight of the responsibility scares people.

"Not really," said Kahanov. "The minute he got his phone back and got past the duty officer, he turned around, tapped his phone, yelled *Allah hu akbar* and blew up."

"Casualties?"

"Negative. Just him."

How could I draw Imad out? I considered my options. I was afraid that if I wouldn't be the bait, Verbin would. I mulled it over but couldn't seem to think of a single good idea.

"Marciano is securing her, along with Chayyim," said Ami, reading my mind as usual.

92.

The bearded orderly who arrived at the oncology wing proceeded down the hall toward room 269—Dr. Verbin's office. He passed by room 275 and 273, and then, near 271, the hallway curved to the right. The orderly stopped momentarily. About ten feet ahead, beside the door to room 269, near the reception chairs, a young, healthy man was comfortably slumped on a wheelchair, smiling amiably, his legs stretched forward across the hall. The seemingly casual blocking of the hallway, the tiny earbud barely visibly in his ear, the baggy shirt spilling over the waistline of his pants and the pair of Ray-Bans peeking from his pocket—all these, the orderly knew, meant trouble. Security personnel all around the world share these exact characteristics, but even more revealing is the vigilance in the eyes, the casual glances, the constricting pupils.

The orderly knew he must either keep moving, now, or address this Shin Bet shithead with a question. He walked by the room, and the man folded his legs to let him pass. When he shifted his pose, he placed his hand on his right hip to stop his shirt from hiking up and revealing his gun. The orderly noted that he was left-handed, and kept going, toward the restrooms.

Verbin came out of her office, and Marciano stood up and stretched.

"Mr. Marciano, I'm going on my rounds. You probably skipped breakfast—get to the cafeteria before the omelets go cold."

Marciano looked at his watch. "Okay. I'll wait for Chayyim to get here, though. What should I get you?"

"Thanks, I'm not hungry."

"You might not be, but the kid"—he patted his stomach—"kid need to eat. It's Avner's baby, probably waiting for its steak."

Verbin smiled. "The little Ehrlich can keep waiting. But some fruit might be a good idea. I'd like some orange juice and a banana, please, and for God's sake, lighten up a bit—you don't have to wait for Chayyim. Good things pass by those who wait," she added, smiling inwardly at her Avneresque turn of phrase.

"If you don't eat, you'll never get bigger," Marciano mumbled sadly and left toward the cafeteria.

The orderly glanced at his watch and entered the staff restrooms. The Arab doctor that had just exited the restrooms left quickly, his eyes lowered. The orderly waited for him to get out of sight and entered the second stall on the left, where a large stuffed doctor's bag was waiting for him. He quickly changed into the green doctor's scrubs, draped the stethoscope on his neck, cocked the loaded Mauser and shoved it into his waistband, under his shirt. He attached the scalpel to a strip of Velcro stuck to his leg and returned the electrical tape, the cable ties and the three IDF-issued frag grenades to the bag.

Just as he left the stall, Chayyim walked inside the restroom. Born and raised in Gush Katif in the southern Gaza Strip, Chayyim despised Arabs, and not for nothing. Musa, the loyal foreman that his father had raised and nurtured, had also been the one to murder Chayyim's father and set fire to their tomato greenhouses.

"Dr. el-Masri," Chayyim said, reading from Imad's name tag. "Papers, please."

Imad reached into the pocket of his scrubs and drew his hand back out in a swift, wide arc to the left, following up with the rest of his weight and raising his right foot in a high kick to meet Chayyim's face. Chayyim was caught off guard and crashed back into the wall behind him. Imad pressed his left palm to the side of Chayyim's face and wrapped his right arm around his neck. He broke his collarbone, then snapped his neck and hurriedly dragged his body back into one of the stalls, sat it down on the toilet, locked the door from the inside and climbed out, eyes scanning the room in preparation for another attack.

There was no one there. Imad knew that there was no going back—the situation had become strictly kill or be killed. He took several deep breaths. Ten. Nine. Eight. Seven. He raised his head and rocked it right and left, loosening the tension in his neck. Another deep breath. Time to go.

When he got back to the hall, he noticed Marciano approaching the office, holding a bottle of orange juice and two bananas. The hallway was empty. Imad estimated the shrinking distance between them. The attack should ideally take place as close as possible to the door of Verbin's office. He slowed his approach so that they would meet at the best spot. Marciano walked past him, smiling, and raised his hand to knock on Verbin's door. The time was now. Imad spun back and his open hand chopped down on the back of the Marciano's neck, delivering an accurate, powerful strike directly to the brainstem. Marciano lost his balance. The walls swam around him. He tried to stay upright, but his muscles wouldn't obey him and he swerved, slowly falling to the floor. Imad caught him, appropriated his heavy Jericho gun, eased him into his wheelchair, grabbed his head and, with a quick twist, broke his neck. He opened the door to the office and shoved the wheelchair inside.

"Mr. Marciano, join me for coffee?"

"I'd love some. Thank you," replied Imad.

"What..." Verbin turned from the espresso machine and her welcoming smile froze. "What... what is this?" The cup fell from her hand and shattered at Marciano's feet. He neither moved nor reacted in any way.

"Call him, now! Tell him to get over here. Anything extra and I blow your fucking head off."

Verbin stared at Marciano, his slack jaw and the lack of muscle tone in his neck, and realized he was dead.

"Call who?" she asked, her voice shaking.

"Your husband, you dumb bitch."

"I'm not married. I don't have a husband," she said, feeling her hands descending to protect her belly, as if of their own accord. She forced herself to raise them back up. He couldn't find out she was pregnant.

Imad grabbed her neck and shoved the gun's barrel into her mouth. She choked and gurgled, and when he loosened his grip a bit, she tried to knee him in the crotch but couldn't reach. He raised his hand and slapped her forcefully. It was a new kind of pain, one she'd never felt before. She felt the inside of her head smacking against her skull, tried to steady herself—but the vertigo was too powerful, and she ended up falling on her back.

Imad placed his foot on her neck, drew out the scalpel, grabbed Verbin by the hair and pulled her up with the scalpel shoved into her mouth. She clung with both hands to his wrist, trying to push out the knife. Imad just smiled and tightened his grip. The scalpel cut the inside of her mouth and she cried out in pain. When Imad let go and backed away a bit, she snatched the iPad from the table, raised it and slammed it down on the scalpel with all her strength. Imad blocked her easily and grabbed her throat again, smiling. For a moment, she reminded him of Anna. The same shocked insult on her face, quickly morphing into an uncompromising power, fueled by desperation. He knew there would be no surrender here, and if he'd had time, if he hadn't had to get Ehrlich and his son, he would have truly enjoyed this game.

Verbin raised her hand in surrender, as if to prove him wrong, and he released his grip around her throat. She wiped the blood from the corner of her mouth. There should be a letter opener and a pair of scissors, somewhere on the desk. Imad grabbed her by the hair and tilted her head back.

"Call your husband, or I blow your head off."

Marciano's body suddenly slipped from the wheelchair and his head smacked against the floor. A thin trail of blood mixed with saliva dribbled down his face. Verbin couldn't tear her eyes away from him.

"This is what I'll do to you. Unless you call Ehrlich, now."

Verbin was gagging, struggling to breathe, and once again caught her hands from dropping to protect her belly. "You don't scare me. When Ehrlich gets here he'll destroy you."

"Call him, now!" He held out the phone, lying on the floor.

She took it and smashed it on the floor. The parts scattered across the room. "Call him yourself!" she said, her eyes still scanning the room for the letter opener.

Imad bent her down toward the floor. "Pick it up." The hand around her throat squeezed harder.

When she managed to pull enough air into her lungs, she kicked at the phone battery. It slid under the screen obscuring the examination table. Imad pulled away slightly and raised his fist, aiming at her face. She raised her hands to protect her eyes, then instinctively lowered them to her belly. Imad realized that a change of strategy was in order. He slammed her into the chair, took out the electrical tape from his bag and wrapped it around her mouth.

"Breathe through the nose, Doctor. It's so much healthier," he said cheerfully, tying her arms together and her legs to the chair.

As he searched for the phone battery behind the screen, he noticed a hook attached to a long screw that fastened the screen to the wall. Perfect. He removed the hook and screwed it into the upper corner of the left door, all the way in. He then reassembled her phone and scrolled through the contact list. There was no "Avner" or "Ehrlich," but "Honey bear" gave him pause. He scrolled through her WhatsApp conversations. "Oh, look, a photo of honey bear," he said, grinning with satisfaction.

He put the phone down and pulled out four cable ties. "See? Big enough even for your big ol' honey bear." He pushed the chair under the door handle, blocking the entrance, and sent honey bear a text: "I need you. Come quick. I'm at the office."

He pulled a hand grenade out of his bag and used another cable tie to attach it to the air conditioner vent above the door. He checked to see it was secure and then slipped another cable tie into the safety pin's pull ring. Now he just needed to attach the other end of the cable wire to the hook he'd screwed into the door, but that would wait until Ehrlich and Eran were there.

Verbin breathed slowly, as deeply as she could, and gradually managed to put her mind in order. *This is obviously Imad, and he is obviously after Avner. I'm the bait. He won't kill me, at least until he has Avner—then he'll probably use me to pressure him. He wants to get something out of him. But what?*

It suddenly dawned on her that if she'd called Avner, like Imad had asked, she could've found a way to warn him. The unexpected cold touch of steel against her eyelids made her shiver. Imad was pressing a hand grenade to her face. "Do you know what this is?"

Verbin nodded.

Imad pulled out the safety pin and shoved the grenade between her tied hands. Verbin pressed against the strike lever as hard as she could.

"Let go, and you have four and a half seconds to live."

93.

"I need you. Come quick. I'm at the office."

A WhatsApp message, declared by the opening notes of *La Donna è Mobile*. She didn't pick up when I called her back. Strange, she'd just sent the text. I called again, and again made it to her voicemail. I decided to wait a bit before calling again and got back to the matter at hand.

Kahanov and I were going over the footage of Mahajna's interrogation, again, trying to find something we might've missed. Mahajna had enjoyed special privileges—the Service turned a blind eye to his business of moving illegals past the border. It did not look good for Kahanov that he turned out to be a double agent. I suggested that Mahajna might have been blackmailed and recruited only recently by Imad. Kahanov tended to agree, and then we were interrupted once again by *La Donna è Mobile*. The same text—"I need you. Come quick. I'm at the office."

I told Kahanov that "pregnancy brain" was taking effect sooner than I'd expected—far sooner—she was at her hospital, protected by two experienced Shin Bet bodyguards. What's so urgent?

"You should go see her," said Kahanov. "I'll be fine here."

"You sure?"

"Yeah, don't worry."

"On my way," I texted her, still feeling awkward about leaving Kahanov to sort through the shit by himself. Still, I got in the Harley and drove to the hospital.

At the entrance to the hospital, there was an anorexic-looking teen, probably a junkie, selling roses. I bought the whole bucket and told her to keep the change, then went up the stairs to Verbin's office.

***

"Dr. Verbiiiin," I called out when I reached her closed door, sniffing the red roses. They were disappointingly lacking in fragrance. I assumed she was busy with a patient and sat on one of the reception chairs outside. But something was bothering me.

Where was Marciano?

Realization hit me like a bolt of lightning. I should have called Kahanov but couldn't stop myself—I barged inside and found myself staring at a barrel aimed to my center of mass, and Verbin tied to a chair, a grenade between her hands, positioned between me and Imad's gun. She squirmed a bit, as if trying to tell me something.

"Shut the door, and sit down. Now!" Imad ordered, his right arm still aiming at me, the left pushing a scalpel against the back of Verbin's neck. She made a strange, strangled sound. I kicked the door closed, my eyes never leaving her. I placed the roses on the table and slowly sat down, considering my options. If I attacked, would he go for Verbin? Yes, of course he would. He had nothing to lose. He'd hurt her anyway, and where was Marciano?

"Go to the door," Imad said, gesturing with the gun. I approached the door and noticed the grenade attacked to the vent.

"Take the end of the cable tie connected to the pin. Connect it to the hook stuck in the door."

The kill range of the grenade would be around five yards. Fragments are effective up to fifteen yards. In other words, anyone who broke into the room, and anyone in the room, would be fatally injured if it went off. I could get control of the grenade, but he would just shoot Verbin, and the grenade would drop from her hands and finish the job. I slipped the end of the cable tie in wrong way up, so it didn't catch. As I'd hoped, Imad didn't notice. One trap neutralized.

"Where is your son, Eran?" he asked.

For a moment I wasn't sure I'd heard him.

"How should I know?" I eventually replied. "He's a big boy. He does what he wants."

Imad pressed on the scalpel, again tearing that strange sound out of Verbin. When he decided it was having the appropriate impact on me, he asked again, "Where is your son, Eran?"

"I can have Taissiri brought here. Let her go and I'll have it done."

"Where is he?"

I counted to ten and slowly said, "He's at a Shin Bet facility in Tel Aviv. If anything happens to her, you can forget about him."

Imad raised the gun toward me and with his left hand sliced her forehead with the scalpel. It bled generously. "Okay, okay. Stop it, let her go. What do you want?"

"I want you to get your boy over here!"

"What's he ever done to you?"

I was buying time. At some point, Marciano would get here, and hopefully Kahanov, and I needed to figure out how to warn them about the booby-trapped door. I hoped they had the sense to insert a fiber camera before charging in.

A thin, cruel smile stretched his lips.

"He's done nothing to me. But he's about to give me so much."

He seemed to realize that I was trying to plan my next move, and in response he pulled another grenade from his bag and pulled out the pin, holding down the strike lever. He now had total control of the room. A gun aimed at me, a grenade in his left hand, another one booby-trapping the entrance, a third in Verbin's hand. And where the fuck was Marciano?

"If you let her go, you survive this," I said again. "Hurt her and you end up like your daddy and your little brother Nasser, and Anna, and your cousin Mahajna. I personally killed every one of them."

He didn't seem affected. He kicked four thick cable ties toward me.

"Tie yourself to the chair," he ordered.

I slowly wrapped the cable tie around my left leg and the chair leg and again said, "Release her or you get nothing. And you'll be dead."

"Oh? Do you plan on killing me?" he sneered.

"Either me or someone else. They're already looking for me. My security detail, who by the way are here in the hospital. Shin Bet. Police. Mossad. Do you really think you have a chance?"

"Your security detail is already here." He nodded toward the screen obscuring the exam bed, and for the first time I noticed Marciano's body. I took a deep breath. I felt my blood boiling, searing my skin, pounding at the insides of my eyes.

"That's her guard, not mine." I spoke as indifferently as I could. "And that was only one of them. And there is only one of you."

"Tie it already!" he barked, pressing the gun into Verbin's ear and eliciting another strangled, painful cry.

I fastened the cable tie, knowing that whatever small window of opportunity I had here would close the moment I finished tying my other leg. I carefully felt for the pocket in my boots with the small knife Eran had given me, the one that had gotten us out of Lebanon.

"Wonderful," said Imad. "Now the other leg."

I kept feeling around for it but couldn't find the knife. Then it hit me. The knife was in my old Blundstones.

A roaring *Allah hu akbar!* rose from my pocket. Kahanov's ringtone.

"Take it out, slowly, and toss it over to me," he said, shoving the gun against Verbin's ear. She groaned.

I reached into my pocket and slowly drew out the phone. If only I'd taken a Glock, I could have killed him, right now. I caught a glance at Kahanov's smiling face on the screen and threw the phone to Imad. He crushed it with his heel.

He approached me slowly. Verbin was staring at me, and I tried to somehow transmit my thoughts to her. Sometimes it works. I wanted her to know that I wouldn't let anything happen to her or the baby. A sequence of orders suddenly surfaced—locate the primary threat. The grenade? No, Imad wouldn't use the grenade. He wants to live.

The primary threat is the gun. Divert! Strike! Control! That was my strategy—I'd practiced it dozens, hundreds of times.

Verbin's eyes were still on me, searching, probing for an answer. I gave a fraction of a nod, hoping that translated as "whatever you do, don't drop the grenade." To my surprise, she burst into laughter. Imad swerved around in response, and she pushed her chair back with all her strength. The chair tipped and fell back, Verbin along with it. Imad was staring at her, uncomprehending, confused. I leapt up from the chair, my right shoulder smashing into his face. I cracked his jaw, and he lost balance, tried to steady himself. I grabbed the barrel of the gun with both hands, tried to divert it. This maneuver should be performed quickly and continuously, but with one leg tied to the chair, I couldn't create momentum. I struggled to shift the gun away, and he was still resisting.

I was holding the barrel, but it was still aimed at me. Imad managed to pull the trigger and hit my shoulder. A split second of silence. I snapped out of it first. I lunged at the gun, pain screaming inside my shoulder. Imad stepped back, and I managed to grab the gun and move it away but couldn't follow up with a strike. Imad struck my ear with the grenade in his other hand. I took it and kept struggling, moving in a half-spin that brought my shoulder into his face, and leaned my entire body weight onto the hand with the gun. His wrist gave under the weight and he dropped the gun. I bent to pick it up, and he kicked me in the face, snapping my head back. Blood trickled into my eyes. The shoulder he'd shot was a burning orb of pain, the rest of the arm paralyzed. He realized this and kicked the bullet wound. I tried to fire, but my hand was limp and useless. He was panting, trying to prepare for his next attack. So was I. *Eran, my Eran, be here with me*, I thought, or maybe said out loud. It suddenly occurred to me that it wasn't just hard for me; it was hard for him, too. The survivor here would be the one who could move past his breaking point.

I filled my lungs as much as I could and let out a booming *kiai* that seemed to stun him for a fraction of a second. I then fired three bullets into his torso. Two of them hit the mark. He grabbed his stomach with both hands, and the grenade fell from his grip and rolled toward Verbin.

Four and a half seconds.

I dove after the grenade and grabbed it.

Three and a half seconds.

I grabbed Imad by the hair, slightly lifting him.

Two and a half seconds.

I shoved the grenade underneath him.

A second and a half.

I fell on top of him, pinning him to the floor.

Boom.

94.

Imad's body was torn in half. Blood was gushing from my throat. I tried to stop the bleeding, but my hand refused to move. Shrapnel must have hit my carotid artery. I was floating in a dark space, in a fetal position, spinning weightlessly, like an astronaut, faster and faster. A white beam of light pierced through the black. I was spinning faster, uncontrollably. I felt like my head would split down the middle, and I blacked out.

The next thing I remember was Kahanov's voice.

"RP! RP, can you hear me? Stay with me, RP. Avner! Medic! Stay with me." His voice faded and multiplied, rolling like distant waves, humming with a strange metallic echo.

I heard him but couldn't see anything. I felt weightless and immaterial, and I yelled at him to check on Verbin and the baby, but nothing came out.

Soon, I could hear nothing, too.

Epilogue

In a private hospital room, at the end of a secured hallway, stood the DM—who apparently used to be a lawyer—reading aloud the marriage agreement between Dr. Rosa Luxemburg-Verbin (hereinafter referred to as "The Bride") and Avner Ehrlich Ne'eman (hereinafter referred to as "The Groom").

"A. The bride and groom will love each other forever and behave accordingly: with love, patience, honor and friendship. B. This contract shall remain in effect for as long as the bride and groom love each other. C. Witnessing this union are Mrs. Bella Kaufman and Misters Ami Kahanov, Efrayim "Froyke" Dashevski, Professor Ram Gorni and Moshe Halevi. I, Moshe Halevi, Esq., by the power apparently invested in me, hereby declare these two wed. They have sworn in front of these witnesses to honor the contract, as it is written, in its entirety. The groom will now provide the ring." He paused, and a brief, mischievous smile appeared on his face. "RP! The ring!"

He had never called me that before.

Verbin scrambled to retrieve a small leather pouch from her bag and handed it to me. "This is the ring you bought me," she grinned and kissed me on the cheek.

"I haven't authorized any kissing yet," said the director, who began filling some wineglasses.

"Wait a minute," said Kahanov, grabbing the microphone from the portable stereo system. "This is your DJ, Amiiii.... Kahanov! Now dance, you bastards! Dance!" He pushed play on the wedding march.

Bella wiped away a tear and hid behind Froyke, who also seemed somewhat tearful.

The director raised his glass. "All right, friends, we're done here. Some of us lounge in bed all day"—he nodded toward me—"and some have to work for a living."

He set down his wineglass, opened the door for Bella and left.

"Where are you going?" I asked from my bed, but he didn't reply.

Glossary

AISI—Agenzia

Informazioni e Sicurezza Interna – The domestic intelligence agency of Italy.
CornerShot—a weapon accessory allowing the operator to aim and fire around a corner, without leaving cover.

DM—The director of the Mossad. Equivalent to the IDF's chief of staff.

EEI—essential elements of information. The top priority items of intelligence information that are vital for timely and accurate decision making.

Flotilla 13—An elite commando unit of the Israeli Navy (the Israeli equivalent of the US Navy SEALs). Specializes in sea-to-land incursions, counterterrorism, sabotage, maritime intelligence gathering, hostage rescue etc. The unit is trained for sea, air and land actions.

GRU—The military intelligence service of the Russian Federation.

IDF—Israel Defense Forces. The military forces of the State of Israel. It is the sole military wing of the Israeli security forces and has no civilian jurisdiction within Israel. Headed by its chief of staff, who is subordinate to the defense minister.

KGB—The main security agency for the Soviet Union before its collapse.

Kidon—(lit. "Spear")—The Mossad counterterrorist unit.

Matkal (nicknamed "The Unit")—An elite special mission unit, subordinate to the Military Intelligence Directorate of Israel. Primarily a field intelligence-gathering unit, conducting deep reconnaissance behind enemy lines, Matkal is also tasked with counterterrorism and hostage rescue beyond Israel's borders (the Israeli equivalent of Delta Force in the United States).

MI5—The domestic security service of the United Kingdom.

MI6—Foreign intelligence service of the United Kingdom government.

Mossad—(lit. "The Institution") Israel's foreign intelligence agency (Israeli equivalent of the CIA). It is responsible for intelligence collection, covert operations, and counterterrorism. Unlike the government and military, the goals, structure and powers of the Mossad are exempt from the Basic Laws of Israel. The director answers directly to the prime minister.

PJP Grenade—Portable Jammer Pack made by Netline, in the shape of a hand grenade. Designed for blocking the signals of radio-proximity fuses, for radio-detonated bombs and improvised explosive devices (IEDs).

Oketz—(lit. "Sting") The independent Canine Special Forces unit of the IDF. The unit specializes in training and handling dogs for military applications, such as sniffing out explosives.

Shin Bet—The Israel Security Agency (often nicknamed "the Service") is Israel's internal security service (Israeli equivalent of the FBI). One of three principal organizations of the Israeli intelligence community, alongside IDF intelligence and the Mossad. Responsible for safeguarding state security, exposing terrorist rings, interrogating terror suspects, providing intelligence for counterterrorism operations in the West Bank and the Gaza Strip, etc.

Spetsnaz—A Russian umbrella term for Special Forces. Historically, Spetsnaz referred to special military units controlled by the GRU. It also describes special purpose units, or task forces.

The Pit—the IDF's command center bunker, located under the government central facility in Tel Aviv.

UAV—Unmanned Aerial Vehicle, commonly known as a drone.

Unit 504—The Human Intelligence Division, one of the IDF's most classified units. It deals in the recruitment and activation of secret agents around the borders of Israel, operating in the gap between the Mossad and the Shin Bet.

Unit 8200—Israeli Intelligence Corps unit responsible for signal intelligence collecting and code decryption.

Unit 9900—Israeli Intelligence Corps Visual Intelligence Unit, responsible among other things for satellite intelligence and airborne reconnaissance.

Made in the USA
Coppell, TX
07 June 2021